BEYOND THE DOOR

"We're going upstairs," Lina said, taking me by the hand.

But we didn't go into the bedroom. We went on up to the top floor. I hadn't seen it, nor had it interested me until now. There had always been more than enough to occupy me on the two floors below, and I had assumed this was just an attic. It wasn't. We came to a small landing. There was one door, locked. Lina had a key in her other hand.

"Another playground," I said.

"When we go in," she said, "you can't turn back. And not a word, not one. Now, listen carefully, Tom. Once we're inside, you're going to forget about me. I won't be there for you, do you understand? I said I had a present for you, and it's in that room. You're going to do whatever you want, whatever comes to you. And we're not coming out until it's over. *Whatever.*"

There was an edge in Lina's voice I hadn't heard before. Barely contained excitement edged unmistakably with fear. Her expression, her entire body language, seemed to say that something was about to happen that even she might not be able to control once it started.

FINISHING TOUCHES

THOMAS TESSIER

LEISURE BOOKS NEW YORK CITY

For Peter Straub

A LEISURE BOOK®

August 2005

Published by

Dorchester Publishing Co., Inc.
200 Madison Avenue
New York, NY 10016

Finishing Touches copyright © 1986 by Thomas Tessier

Father Panic's Opera Macabre copyright © 2001 by Thomas Tessier

This novel is a work of fiction. Names, characters, places and incidents are either the product of the author's imagination or are used fictitiously. Any resemblance to actual events or locales or persons, living or dead, is entirely coincidental.

ISBN 0-8439-5559-7

The name "Leisure Books" and the stylized "L" with design are trademarks of Dorchester Publishing Co., Inc.

Printed in the United States of America.

Visit us on the web at www.dorchesterpub.com.

FINISHING TOUCHES

TABLE OF CONTENTS

I

FANTASIES

In every man's life there has been a "minute too much" which he longs to buy back from reality, no matter what the cost. And so this "surplus" of the real becomes a nightmare.

—PAUL VALÉRY, *ANALECTS*

ONE

The first time I met Roger Nordhagen I was nursing a pint of lager in the Carlisle. It was a few minutes past seven on a rainy evening. The after-work crowd had drifted away and the place was fairly quiet. I didn't feel like sitting, so I stood, leaning against the bar. It was a Thursday in October. And it was London, still new to me. I was on my own. I was doing nothing, going nowhere. It had taken me more than twenty-eight years to arrive at that point.

Nordhagen started talking to me, I forget about what. Idle pub chat between strangers, most likely. I answered him, responding minimally, as you do when you don't want to be rude but are otherwise uninterested. Gradually, however, I came to pay more attention to him. He was not immediately impressive, but there was something vaguely distinguished about his appearance. He might have been a once-successful businessman who had fallen on leaner times. He had the dignified but slightly lost look of a man whose career was drawing to a close. He had to be in his sixties, I thought. The face was old and tired, but the eyes were still sharp—and they drew me out.

He was drinking red wine, and when ordering a refill he bought me another lager. So I was stuck with him, for one round at least. Like me, Nordhagen was a foreigner in London, but he lived there and had done so for many years. He had long since attained permanent-resident status, he told me proudly. We talked a bit about America, my background, and then he gave me some tips on London—where to eat, where else to drink, what to see, and what not to bother with. I took in some of it, but I liked to find my own way.

The awkward moment came when he asked me what I did back in the United States and I told him I was a physician. Nordhagen's eyes lit up at that and he clapped me on the arm.

"But so am I," he said.

I almost didn't believe him, or perhaps I just didn't want to believe him. One of the most unpleasant thoughts a person can have is: That's me thirty years from now.

"What are you in?"

"General practice," I replied. "And you?"

"Cosmetic surgery."

"Is that right? It's a pretty lucrative field in America. How is it here?"

"Oh, comfortable." He made a little ceremony of shaking hands with me. "So, we are colleagues, are we not?"

I nodded, then tried to flag down the bartender so I could buy Nordhagen another glass of wine, thus ending my social obligation. But at that moment the old man squeezed my arm and fixed me with a peculiarly intense look.

" 'If I had not known you, I would not have found you,' " he said, smiling earnestly.

I didn't much care for that.

4

"I'm not gay," I told him quietly and politely, but firmly. Then I carefully removed my arm from his grasp.

For a moment his face went blank, but then Nordhagen laughed. He was definitely more amused than embarrassed.

"Oh, my dear fellow—oh, I am sorry. No, no, nothing of the sort. I was merely quoting Pascal," he explained, as if it made perfect sense. "No, I do assure you my inclinations are not at all along those lines. You see, you are a physician, and I am also a physician, and by fate or coincidence we meet in this pub. So it just occurred to me that those words of Pascal are really quite appropriate. Don't you agree?"

"I guess so."

But I didn't know whether I did or not. I'd heard of Pascal; the name rang a distant bell; so I'd probably been taught something about him in college. But now he was just a name that meant nothing to me, and I couldn't have said whether he was a Roman statesman or the inventor of the automatic transmission.

If I had not known you, I would not have found you.

That was where it all started. A few words from Pascal, quoted by a strange little man, a cosmetic surgeon, in a pub in Soho. I was there for no other reason than that I had time to kill. I had come to this city free and clear. I had already placed myself on leave from everyday life. Nordhagen found me at the right time.

I had invested years of study and hard work to reach that point at which one supposedly has freedom, means, and opportunity. Medical school was behind me, and I was employed at a hospital. I could simply stay on where I was—New Haven—putting in my time. I could pursue further studies in one specialty or another. Or I could look around for a ripe old practice out in the eternal suburbs and hope to buy in. But medicine in America is changing, and there were other possibilities for me to consider. New clinics and drive-in facilities are opening everywhere, like fast-food franchises; I could form a partnership with some colleagues and establish such a business. Or a laboratory, to provide an analysis service. Of course it isn't as simple and easy as it sounds, but the fact remains: doctors don't suffer unemployment in America. On the contrary, they usually write their own tickets.

I had money, and money, as we all know, does strange things to people. An aunt had died conveniently, settling a happy sum on me—not delirious, but happy. It was enough to enable me to move in any direction I chose. The matter required a good deal of thought, and I mulled it over for several weeks. There was no urgency about it, and yet I felt I had reached a turning point in my life—and I didn't want to mess it up.

What I was experiencing may have been nothing more than the typical feeling a person has on finally leaving school, the feeling that you are facing the world and now you have to get on with the job of making your life. If so, I was a few years late in reaching this threshold.

Whatever, I decided to take some time off and travel. The idea seemed outrageous, certainly frivolous, but in the end it proved irresistible. I had spent so long in the cocoon of the educational system, only to emerge into the slightly larger cocoon of hospital life and work, that it was as if I had had no other life for as long as I could remember. Something in me pushed to break out, if only for a short while, to smash a hole in the wall and see if I could make it a window. They say a change is as good as a rest, and I knew that if I didn't get away at that point I'd probably never manage it. The fear of lifelong regret is not to be taken lightly; once I had satisfied my wanderlust, I could return and carry on my medical career.

The reactions of my parents were about what I expected. My mother could see the wisdom of taking a week off, two at most. A nice, relaxing trip to the Caribbean, she suggested. And then back to work. After all, I had studied so long for the express purpose of practicing medicine, why, now that I was fully qualified, postpone it just to bum around? I fought this line of attack as best I could, and I had some help from my father. He thought a month or two off would be good for me and he believed, as I surely did, that I deserved it. My father has never ventured far from his little plot in Ohio. He has hoed his row well all his life but scarcely seen beyond it, and thus he has rather vivid ideas of "what's out there." Television, no doubt, nourishes the dream. Anyhow, I'm sure my kicking around the landscape for a month or two would be the fulfillment of one of my father's own special fantasies, and that's why I had his support.

Not that I needed it; it just made things easier. I intended to take off for three or four months, perhaps even longer. My first thought was to head for California. I had never been there, and I knew some people who lived in the Bay area. If I liked the place I might even decide to stay on permanently. Or I could journey south to Los Angeles, and Mexico, and keep on going from there until I had seen and done enough. If nothing else, the climate would be a welcome change from chilly New England.

However, I had entered my name with an agency that arranged international house swaps. One of their people, a Mr. Curtis, had come along to inspect my place, and he was frankly not very encouraging. I could see his point. I lived in one of the smallest, least impressive condominiums on the coast of Connecticut, and nearly all of the agency's clients were families in need of larger accommodations—proper houses. And if that were not enough, most of their swaps took place during the "good months," between April and September. I was proposing to set out in October. Mr. Curtis said he would put me in his data bank but he advised me not to hold out much

7

hope for a suitable swap. I didn't, and so I was pleasantly surprised when he telephoned me one evening a couple of weeks later.

"I have something that may be of interest to you."

"Good. What is it?"

"We have an English client. He teaches at a university there and has to do some research in New York, at Harvard, and at Yale, so a place in New Haven would suit him just fine."

"And will my place do?"

"I think so," Mr. Curtis said. "I'm still waiting to hear from him about it, but he'll be coming alone, so he won't need anything large. Now, in exchange he is offering a second-floor four-room flat in London. I'm told it's in a nice neighborhood. How does that sound to you so far?"

"Pretty good," I admitted.

"Okay, now the big one. He needs the place for six months, first of October to the end of March. Is that too long for you?"

"Six months . . ."

"Yes, I'm afraid so." Mr. Curtis paused to let me think about this. Then he continued. "I see from our printout that you were hoping for a swap of three or four months."

"That's right."

"Well, think it over," he said. "I'll call you Friday, if that's all right. I should have heard from London by then. Okay?"

"Fine. I'll give you a decision then."

"It all depends on where you want to go, and for how long, but I do think we were lucky to have this one come our way, and I wouldn't hold my breath for something better."

"I understand."

Was I interested? Sure. It was not what I had been

thinking of. London, to me, meant fog, cold, and damp, whereas California and Mexico meant warmth and sunshine. And six months was rather longer than I had planned for this adventure in self-indulgence. But it was the time of year I'd hoped to leave, and there was no question London was an attractive alternative all by itself. Moreover, it would be a great base from which to explore the rest of Europe. Amsterdam, Paris, Rome, Munich, Copenhagen, and many other cities beckoned just across the English Channel. South of the border began to seem one dimensional by comparison. Another important point was the fact that a swap like this would save a small fortune that I would otherwise have to shell out for hotels, motels, and inns along the way. It would mean that much more money for good food and drink, and it also would make six months seem a little less extravagant. I called the agency a day early and told Mr. Curtis I was agreeable. Happily, he had just received a fax from London saying yes.

Later I realized that the best part of the London swap was that—unlike California—it was a place where I had no friends or even casual acquaintances. I knew no one in the whole of Britain, period, and that enhanced the sense of freedom and anonymity I was seeking. I think I needed to go somewhere and do something that, if the rest of my life were humdrum and uneventful, I would be able to look back on with a certain measure of wonder.

My father thought London was an excellent choice, and on my last visit home I could see by the sparkle in his eyes that he too was thinking of all the places to visit in Europe—the sights, the wine, and the women. My mother regarded six months as insanity. The only positive aspect she could find was that I would have plenty of time to see how appalling the British nationalized health system was, and that undoubtedly would send me home with a renewed appreciation of an American medical career.

Mr. Curtis came around with the documents a short time later. I signed them, and thus was fully committed to my great escape. There would be no backing down at the last moment.

When the time came, I gave the required notice at the hospital. All the people I worked with were surprised, and some were utterly bewildered by my decision. America was where it all happened—*it* being everything, I guess. A short vacation was one thing, but six months? These people, like my mother, obviously thought I'd slipped a gear.

Others, however, were openly envious. They wished me the best and said they'd do the same thing if they had the money and the nerve. Of that I had no doubt. What's more, I'm convinced that nerve is by far the greater problem of the two.

I saw to all the necessary preparations: passport, airplane ticket, clothes, luggage, settling accounts, and so on. I did have doubts, plenty of them, but they were always overcome by the building sense of adventure and excitement. If it was un-American to throw aside a good job and forget about making money, then I was ready to be a traitor for six months.

I was given a couple of pages of names, addresses, and telephone numbers of people in London and other places I might get to in my travels—friends of friends. I promised to get in touch with all of them, but then I left the list of contacts behind, in a litter basket in the departure lounge at Kennedy Airport. I was off on my own and that's the way I wanted it. I had no desire to spend valuable time overseas getting to know people who knew people I knew too back in America. It would make no sense. I was leaving my past behind. The last thing I wanted was any link, however indirect, back to it. The next six months were a blank sheet. I was going to learn not only about London and parts of Europe, but also about myself—perhaps most of all about myself. This was more than a vacation, more than a long adventure. It was like starting out as a new person.

Finally the day came. I phoned home to say good-bye to my parents. I checked my luggage several times to make sure I had everything, and I inspected each room in my condo until I was convinced the place was as ship-shape as it was ever going to be. Late in the afternoon Mr. Curtis stopped by to pick up a set of keys and to drive me to downtown New Haven. At the Park Plaza Hotel I would be able to get a limousine to the airport.

"It seems odd," I told Mr. Curtis.

"What does?"

"Well, the whole thing. I mean, someone is coming to live in my home for six months while I go to live in his. We don't know each other and we'll probably never even meet once."

"That's the beauty part," Mr. Curtis said. "Take my word for it."

The sweetest moment I had known since childhood came later, when my jet roared away into the black, black night over the north Atlantic.

Good-bye, good-bye.

Here I come.

I was met at Heathrow by Mr. Curtis's opposite number, a certain Owen Flaherty. To be precise, *I* found *him*. He was in a crowd in the main lobby, holding up a placard with my name on it. We shook hands and he quickly took the smaller of my two suitcases. He led me to the underground train, and after a short wait we were rolling gently into London. The long night was catching up with me fast. I was nodding off and didn't pay much attention to Mr. Flaherty, but that didn't seem to bother him. He talked almost all the way, and I'm sure he told me some useful things. Unfortunately, I didn't retain any of them.

We got off the train at Earls Court and took a taxi the rest of the way to my new home, which was on Matheson Road. The so-called second floor turned out to be the third floor, and of course there was no elevator. My building was a plain brick structure identical to every other one on the street, but the flat itself was clean and comfortable. I had a bedroom, sitting room, and study, along with a bathroom and a galley kitchen that offered a view of several back gardens. Property here was carved up and walled off in narrow strips, I could see.

Mr. Flaherty showed me around, explaining about the stove, the heating system, and the fuses. All in all, the tour and lecture lasted a good ninety seconds. Then he gave me a set of keys and his card, and told me to ring him any time I had any problems or needed information. Before he reached the street I was asleep in my new bed.

My first week in London was a fantastic rush of bright new images. I wandered everywhere. I ignored all the usual tourist attractions except for those that happened to be where I was walking. I found my own way. Slowly, I began to get a feel of the city, and I liked it. I think the most agreeable surprise to me was that London was not purely, exclusively English. It's thoroughly English, of course, but that's all I had expected it to be—and it is much more. London is also Irish, Chinese, Indian, Arabic, Persian, African, and Jamaican. It was far more international than New York or any other place in America that I knew. I loved the mix; it felt right to me from the very first day. I was just another alien in a city full of aliens.

Mr. Flaherty phoned a couple of times to make sure I was settling in well and to offer his tips on dealing with banks and utility bills. I had no problems and didn't need his help, which I'm sure was a relief to him.

Every day, I walked and looked, took a bus, looked, rested, walked some more. I drank a different beer in each pub I went into—the choice of brews seemed endless. I ate foods I'd never seen or heard of before. It didn't take me long to realize how narrowly drawn my world had been back in New Haven. I was no butterfly, but I surely had broken out of a cocoon.

I met one of my neighbors early on. Eileen Fothergill was single, post-forty, and she lived in the other flat on my floor. She was pale, as the English so often are, and she was very polite. Her speech was so correct she made me feel I spoke some other language. Fortunately, I didn't see much of her. Not that there was anything so terribly wrong with her, but I soon had the feeling it would always be something of a strain to make conversation with her. She worked in an office in the City and undoubtedly she was quite efficient at whatever it was she did there. Her employers, she once told me in a whisper, as if it were a state secret, were the largest veneer dealers in the United Kingdom. I wouldn't have been surprised to learn that Eileen ran the place without their knowing it.

She was up and out most mornings before me, and her lights were off when I got back most evenings, so we tended to exchange our few words on weekends. Occasionally we ran into each other at the Lyons supermarket next to the Olympia, and then we'd walk down the North End Road together. To her credit, Eileen didn't pry or ask too many questions. I told her I had come to London for six months to see what it was like, and that was good enough for her.

It must have been the last Thursday of October when I went into the Carlisle for a drink. I had been in London for almost four weeks by then and I was developing a routine. I had explored enough to know my way around without getting lost; I no longer needed the map in my coat pocket. I felt comfortable with the city. I slept late mornings, almost until noon, but that was simply the result of staying up most of the night.

Somehow I stumbled into the habit of having my main meal of the day at ten or eleven at night, when I could linger at the table over wine and brandy until the restaurant closed. If I wasn't dining, I'd be at a night club or a strip joint or a late film. Although London appears to close at eleven, when the pubs start chucking out the drinkers, I soon learned that the city stayed awake and lively in plenty of other places—some that didn't even open until ten or eleven at night. My days ended when I could no longer keep my eyes open. Then I would find a taxi to haul me back to West Kensington. In only a month I was well on the way to being a total night person, a regular in London's peculiar night world.

It seemed so natural, as well as enjoyable, that it could only be right, and so I was neither surprised nor alarmed. If my hours had changed from day to night, well, so what? If anything, it seemed to prove how right I'd been to choose these six months in London. It was as if there were another part of me that had been waiting all those years to be aired out.

What *was* worrying, though, if I allowed myself to think about it, was how quickly and completely my life in America was falling away from me. Each day it receded a little more. I was managing to leave it behind all too well. The American me was becoming a stranger to the new me, the London me. And when I did think about it, I felt almost giddy with power, or that spurious sense of power offered by anything new. It was as if I owned London. I could go anywhere, do anything. The city existed for me, and I was just getting to know it. Having money helped, and to a certain extent I was finding what I wanted to find, but my relationship with London that October was like a torrid, all-consuming love affair. Only later, when it was too late, would I begin to realize how dangerous I had become to myself—and how disastrous I was for others.

When I went into the Carlisle and was conversationally shanghaied by Doctor Roger Nordhagen, the day was just getting under way for me. I had slept until three that afternoon. I had taken a long hot bath. After dressing, I made some toast and warmed up a can of Frank Cooper's game soup. Call it a late brunch. It was nearly five when I boarded a number 9 bus for Picadilly.

I had a drink at the Tom Cribb, a couple more at the Blue Post, and a short at the French pub. Early evening can be a terrible time. You're waiting for the night to take hold. Nothing's really happening yet. You've had something to eat but there's still an empty feeling in you. The first few drinks go down roughly. So it was with me that evening. By the time I got to the Carlisle I had read all there was to read in that day's *International Herald Tribune* and I had set it down on the bar when the old man started talking to me. From the sports page a photograph of Tiger Woods looked up, witnessing the occasion.

After the introductions, and that Pascal business, and ten minutes of chat about London, Nordhagen put the question to me.

"So, what is a young American doctor doing in London? Why are you here and how long are you staying?"

I told him my situation. I kept it short, and he accepted it at once, nodding before I had finished my explanation, almost as if he already knew. I had done the right thing, he assured me.

"No matter what your friends and relatives may say, you did what you had to do," he insisted.

"I'm glad you think so."

He was so emphatic you'd think he was discussing a matter of life or death. I couldn't help smiling, but at the same time I was intrigued. When someone, especially a stranger, talks knowingly about you, there is a strong temptation to shut him up, put him down, or write him off as presumptuous at the very least. I don't know why I didn't feel that way about Nordhagen. He had the ball, let him run with it. He was amusing, but with a hook that pulled me along. There was something oddly familiar about him, and you could tell there was a sharp mind on the other side of those sharp eyes. He may have been a barfly but his brain still worked. "It was your youth."

"What was?"

"What you grabbed. Your youth," he said, continuing his amateur analysis. "Even as it was slipping away from you, disappearing day by day, you grabbed it. Most people let it happen; indeed, they hardly notice. But something inside you, Doctor Sutherland, something basic protested. That is why you stopped and said, Wait a minute. That is why you are here. You have created a pocket of space and time in your youth that otherwise would not have existed."

"You could be right," I admitted. It was hardly something to argue about with a stranger. Besides, I really did think he was on to something.

"But you have made one slight miscalculation," he went on. "Nothing serious, I'm happy to say. Nothing that won't become perfectly clear in due course."

"Oh, yeah? And what's that?"

Nordhagen paused. Obviously he was enjoying the moment. He sipped his wine and smiled—to himself, it seemed, as much as at me. Then he resumed.

"You apparently think that you will return to the United States when your six months here are up, and that you will take up your work there and carry on as if nothing had happened."

I took a gulp of lager before responding to that. British pints are larger than American ones, and I was still in the process of getting used to them.

"Sure I'll return home," I said. "No question of that. I have to. But—well, I will go back to practicing medicine, because that's the only thing I'm qualified to do. But it won't be as if nothing had happened. The reason I've taken these six months off is just so my life won't ever be the same again."

"But you won't."

"Won't what?"

"You won't leave London."

"Why not?"

"Because you won't be able to."

The cheerful smile and persistent, too-confident manner were beginning to wear on me just a little. This fellow was a bit too convincing in his chosen role of clairvoyant.

"Why not?" I asked again.

"Because your work—your life—will be here."

Oh, yeah, sure. Of course. Why hadn't I thought of that? Now it was my turn to laugh.

"And how do you know all this?"

Nordhagen shrugged. "I have a feeling about these things," he replied. "I can't explain it, but I have an ability to look at people, to listen to them, and to see and hear more about them than they imagine they are revealing. No, no, not in a bad sense, dear boy. I would call it an intimation, more than anything else. I would just say I am good with people that way."

"Is that right. And your intimation about me is that I've come to London to stay?"

"That is correct."

"Well, Doctor, I—"

"Please. My name is Roger."

No doubt about it, the guy was determined to be my friend.

"Well, Roger, I'm afraid you're way off base this time."

"How is that?"

"When my six months are up, I'll have to move back to the States. It's that simple. I won't have a flat or a place to stay, and I'm damn sure I'll be out of money by then. I can't practice medicine in this country, so I'll be heading back to the good old U.S.A. To earn my living."

Even as I was laying it all out for Nordhagen, I was aware that this was the real anchor I had been relying on: money. It all came down to money. Mine would be gone in six months. It didn't matter how much I loved London and my night life; money, or the lack of it, would put me back in the daytime world. Yes, I'd be back home, working and paying my way like any other citizen. London was a spree, an extravaganza. Nothing more.

But there was Doctor Nordhagen—Roger, my sudden new chum—perched on the barstool like some strange bird, smiling and shaking his head as if I were a thick schoolboy who couldn't see the obvious.

"A flat, a place to stay, money," he scoffed. "These things are details, trivialities." He seemed genuinely offended that I would stoop to so low an argument as mere practicality.

"You'd be surprised how many people have to pay attention to those things," I said. Then I added, "Most people have no choice in the matter. Those trivialities, as you call them, rule their lives."

"That is correct!" Nordhagen exclaimed, as if I had just proved his point. "And do you know why I call them details and trivialities?"

"I really don't have the slightest idea," I said.

"Because they are the easiest things to get. I am serious. Listen, Doctor Sutherland—"

"Call me Tom." What the hell!

"Listen—thank you, Tom—listen, Tom, six months from now, when you—"

"Just about five months, now," I corrected.

"Whatever it is, it doesn't matter," Nordhagen went on doggedly. "By then you will have whatever you want, if you want it badly enough. Money, a better place to live—these can be very easily gotten, if you know how."

I couldn't tell whether, in his peculiar way of talking, he was trying to set me up for some sort of scam, was spinning his own dreams on my youth, or simply blathering away on the strength of wine consumed. Most likely the last, I thought.

"Yeah, well . . ." I waved a hand dismissively.

"I am serious," he insisted, clutching my arm. Nordhagen was a scrawny old bird, but he surprised me. There was no mistaking the power of a surgeon's hand in that grip. "Tell me now," he went on, "when you were first coming here, didn't you think to yourself, London, all London, is at my feet; I can do anything here. Didn't you have such thoughts?"

"Sure, but that's just a feeling of freedom. Everybody gets that feeling when they leave work to go on vacation. Holidays."

"Yes, yes," Nordhagen agreed quickly. "But the difference is this: people never pursue the point. You can. You have a special opportunity. You have given yourself six months. Don't you know, dear boy, that worlds can be won and lost in less time than that? Much less time."

"Oh, I know," I said inanely. I was getting a little tired of this line of conversation. "Thing is, all I want to do while I'm in London is have a good time. You know?"

"Of course, of course," Nordhagen said, nodding. "That is what it all comes down to, isn't it?"

"Damn right."

"A good time," he echoed, frowning.

I noticed, gratefully, that our drinks were nearly gone. I had already bought one for him, so we were quits. It was a good time to leave. I get tired when I sit in one place too long, especially so early in the evening. Were my gestures and expression that easy to read? Nordhagen spoke as if he knew what I was thinking.

"Tell me," he said, "have you been to Terry's? No, of course you haven't. It's a private club, and you're new to the city. It's just around the corner from here. Would you care to adjourn there for another drink?"

"Uh, well . . ."

I wasn't enthusiastic, but Nordhagen had used the right word to entice me. *Private*. I'd probably never get to see the members-only world of London on my own. The old man could prove to be a pest, but if he did, I could always leave whenever I wanted. In the meantime, it was something to do. And I would get to see a little of private London. We left the Carlisle.

"You certainly are going about this the right way," Nordhagen remarked as he led me through Soho.

"What do you mean?"

"The best way to see a place, to see it as it really and truly is, is from the bottom up." He smiled again. "Here we are, come along."

TWO

We went to Terry's that night, and a few other places as well. Nordhagen seemed to know every unmarked hole-in-the-wall drinking joint in the West End. And they all knew him well. The little doctor—as I heard someone refer to him when we came into one club—drew smiles and nods and waves wherever we went. He became quite jovial as the evening wore on and the drink flowed, but he didn't get roaring drunk. His speech remained unimpaired, and he had no trouble walking to the loo or the next bar. He simply became—well, jollier.

It wasn't long before I concluded that Nordhagen really was what he said he was, a cosmetic surgeon, and that he was interested in me only as a potential drinking companion. He lived alone, or so he said, and had no one he would call a close friend. Only the many familiar faces in clubs and pubs around London. I put a few questions to him, not very subtly, I'm afraid. Drink overcame tact, but at least my doubts were cleared up.

"How often do you actually perform—surgery?" I was sure age and alcohol affected his work.

"Why, every week, of course," he replied. "I have to earn my keep too, you know."

"What sort of—I mean, nose jobs and like that, right?"

"Oh, I bob noses, yes indeed. I couldn't begin to guess how many noses I've put right." Nordhagen hesitated, as if the thought was staggering even to him. "And everything else. Skin grafts, chins tucked, faces lifted, breasts inflated, thighs tightened, ears flattened back—that's a popular item here, I can tell you. When it comes to looking like a member of the royal family, that's where a lot of people draw the line."

"It's an area of medicine I never gave any thought to," I admitted. "It always seemed sort of Hollywood stuff to me. I'm sure it's not, but—"

"Well, it is, actually," Nordhagen said. "But it was all I was ever interested in doing. Making people over. Making them feel better about themselves—and look better." Then, perhaps fearing that he was beginning to sound pompous, Nordhagen laughed and said, "I've even devised a technique for giving people ear lobes."

"Giving them ear lobes?"

"Yes. People who aren't born with them, naturally. It's not all that difficult, either. You can't imagine how many people think the absence of ear lobes is the sign of a mass murderer. Complete rubbish, of course."

"You like what you're doing," I said. It was no small point. I'd already given a chunk of my life to medicine without finding one special area that grabbed me and excited me. I was in general practice by default more than anything else.

"Oh, yes, absolutely. In fact, you mentioned noses, and I think I would have to say I like working on noses best of all. Yes, noses are the best part of the job."

"You're kidding."

"No, I'm quite serious," Nordhagen insisted. "Noses on the faces of pretty young girls. Ah, there's nothing nicer than to take a pretty young girl of sixteen and make her dazzlingly beautiful by fixing her nose. It's wonderful, it really is—there's no other way to describe it. You know what it's like? Shall I tell you? But it will sound—"

"No, go ahead. Tell me. What?"

He had a dreamy look on his face, a look that was probably close to downright sappy. I guess it was kind of comic at that, an old man in a rhapsody on the subject of noses. I could have shut him off, but I didn't, since it obviously meant something to him.

"Well, when I see a young girl," he continued, "beautiful eyes, beautiful hair and teeth, lovely in every way except for her nose, it makes me think that God knocked off work early the day He made her, that He quit before He was done and that it's up to me to add the finishing touches. That's what I do; I add the finishing touches. A rare privilege, don't you think?"

I don't know how many places we hit that night. They were all either up a flight of stairs or down one, rarely at street level. None of them were jazzy, they were essentially places for drinking, and anything else, such as decor, was strictly incidental. I noticed that we never stayed long in any one club. Just as a place began to seem dreary we were off to the next. Nordhagen would always signal his departure by a glance at his watch, as if he had worked out a timetable for the night in advance.

He was not at all a Mr. Hyde on the loose, but he certainly did enjoy getting out on the town at night. Doing his rounds—that was his way of putting it. Nordhagen struck me as a rather lonely old man, one who needed the superficial warmth that drinking clubs offer. He was a regular at them and he knew most of the other regulars, but they were still strangers to each other. They came together to drink in each other's sight, and that was all. And in spite of his talk of performing surgery every week, I suspected all was not well with Nordhagen's practice. During the occasional silences that punctuated our talk that night his eyes would take on a distant look, the look of a sentry on the watch for some threat along the horizon. Perhaps this club-crawling was a way Nordhagen could escape for a while from a major problem that stalked him. For all I knew, he might have terminal cancer.

At some point I reached my alcohol threshold and my body went onto automatic pilot. Drink doesn't make me sick, and I don't pass out—at least not until I get home. I become a kind of homing robot. I stood up suddenly, abandoning an unfinished pint, and marched myself out of the club. On Old Compton Street I found a taxi willing to take me back to Matheson Road. I spent the entire journey wondering whether I had even said good night to Nordhagen; I feared not. I didn't like having been rude, but he would surely know I was drunk, and besides, I didn't expect he and I would see each other again.

The next day I paid for my excesses. It took two doses of Panadol to quell my headache, and although I had slept until late afternoon I was too tired and weak to go anywhere or do anything. I couldn't even drag myself out to get a newspaper. After a while I almost persuaded myself to struggle to the nearest pub and investigate that hair-of-the-dog business, but it seemed too risky and, anyhow, my body was in no hurry to move. Lying stupidly on the couch was about all I could manage. The telephone rang cruelly.

"Hello."

"Tom? Is that Tom Sutherland?"

"Roger?" Wearily. I couldn't believe I'd actually given him the telephone number of the flat.

"How are you?" He sounded cheery.

"Not too good."

"Oh, dear. You did leave in a bit of a rush last night."

"Sorry if I was rude."

"Oh, no, not at all. I was a little concerned that you were all right and I just wanted to ring to make sure."

"I'm okay, really."

"Are you sure?"

"Just the usual headache. I'll live."

"You don't sound at all well. Would you like me to prescribe something for you—a restorative tonic."

"No. That's not necessary, thanks."

"Well . . . Do you have any B vitamins? Brewer's yeast, anything like that? If so, give yourself a hefty dose of it."

"I hadn't thought of that," I said truthfully. Oh, what a smart doctor am I!

"Now listen, Tom," Nordhagen went on briskly. "The other reason I'm ringing is to find out if you're free tomorrow evening."

"Tomorrow?" It was still a big concept to me.

"Around eight or nine."

"I'm not sure. Why?"

"I was thinking how nice it would be to go out and have a good meal in town—if you'd care to join me. And then, after, we could stop by a rather special place I know."

"You mean Terry's, or Toby's?"

"Good Lord, no, nothing like that." Was he smirking? He'd taken me to those places, after all. "Somewhere quite different."

"What is it?" I was stubborn, befogged.

"Come and see, why don't you. If you don't like it, you can leave, and at the very least you will have had a pleasant meal beforehand. Fair enough?"

"Well . . ."

"Shall we meet at the Carlisle at eight? We'll have a drink and then adjourn from there."

"All right."

There was no way to get out of it. If half the people in the world count on the other half being unable to say no, I knew which half I was in. Of course, I had twenty-four hours in which to come up with a good excuse to cancel, but I couldn't kid myself. I would go, because, regardless of any misgivings I might have, I wanted to go.

There was something odd about it, perhaps even something vaguely nasty—running around with a guy who had to be thirty or forty years my senior. It seemed like just the kind of thing I'd worry about if I gave it any serious thought—which I tried not to do. Nordhagen was a colleague, after all, a fellow medicine man. And he had already taken me to a few places I wouldn't otherwise have seen. It didn't matter that they were only dingy drinking clubs; they were still part of what I'd come to London to experience. Undoubtedly there was more to see, so let him lead on. The little doctor would be my guide to the secrets of the city for at least one more evening.

Later, when I got around to picking up my clothes, which I'd strewn drunkenly on the floor very early that morning, I found a crumpled white card in one pocket.

Roger Nordhagen
109 Millington Lane
Mount Street, W1

The card also had a telephone number on it. I checked in the L-R volume of the London directory, and, sure enough, he was listed there: same address, same number. Furthermore, his name carried the notation M.D. That seemed to settle the matter. But then—I don't know why—I picked up the phone and dialed his number. What did I expect? What I got was the voice of a young

woman who sounded bright and even breathy. A class receptionist, I guessed. She answered on the second ring.

"Doctor Nordhagen's office."

I hung up the phone, pleased. You have to be a little
wary of someone you meet in a bar, a complete stranger.
It was hard to imagine jolly old Roger a liar, so I was glad
to find he really was who he claimed to be. The little doctor, Roger Nordhagen, M.D. Jolly Roger.

Still, he was something of a puzzle. I hadn't been in
London long, but I had walked around enough to know
that Mount Street was in Mayfair, and that Mayfair was
not easily confused with Cheapside. Nordhagen was in
one of the most financially rewarding fields of medicine,
and his practice was located in one of London's poshest
neighborhoods. That much made sense. But then there
was Nordhagen himself—humbly dressed, doing his
rounds of the shabby depths. He had a secret, I was sure
of it—and that, as much as anything else, was why I
wanted to see more of him.

I had finally washed, shaved, and dressed, when there
was a timid knock at the door. It was Eileen Fothergill,
my neighbor and toiler in the veneer trade. She was smiling shyly, as if she had something silly to say. She did.

"There was a tombola at the office, and I've won a
tinned ham from Denmark," she explained. "I'm cooking it this evening, and there's far too much for me.
Would you like some?"

"Oh—uh, well—uh, thank you, but I wouldn't want to
take it away from you. Ham will keep, won't it? What's a
tombola, anyway?" I managed to shut up at that point.

"It's sort of a raffle thing. You know. And ham will
keep, but there'll still be plenty left over for me. It's a five-
pound ham, I think. It's huge, too much for one person.
Why don't you have a plate—or have you eaten already?"

"No, I haven't. . . ."

"Good. Come along in half an hour. All right? Or come sooner, if you like."

"Oh." Stupidly, I had thought she'd just pile up a load of ham on a plate and leave it at my door. I wasn't in the mood for a social evening, and my system was definitely in no mood for a lot of heavy food. But I'd landed myself in it now. "Fine," I said, striving for courtesy as Eileen backed out the door. "I'll be there in a few minutes."

As soon as she was gone I went to the bathroom, knelt down over the bowl, and jabbed a finger down my throat. If there was going to be any puking, I wanted to get it done in my flat, not hers. I barfed up the thin residue of my early-morning revels. I made sure there was nothing left to come, then I brushed my teeth again, gargled with mouthwash, and forced down a little milk to prepare my stomach for the coming onslaught.

I thought it would be a pretty slow and dull time, since Eileen and I never had all that much to say to each other, but it turned out to be much more interesting than I had expected. In her refined, genteel way, she was in something of a tizzy—or as close to one as she was ever likely to be. It took me a while to figure it out. Eileen was probably very cool and efficient in dealing with the men at work, but a man alone, here, in her flat—that was a different matter. I guessed that male visitors were rare in her life. The mere fact of my physical presence had an obvious effect on her. I'm not handsome or suave or muscular; I'm thin, reedy, and utterly ordinary in appearance. But I wasn't imagining Eileen's state; I was male and I was there, and that was apparently enough.

I began to enjoy the situation. I'd never been in one anything like it. Eileen was middle-aged and not especially attractive. She had the kind of ash-blonde hair that drifts into white over the years without anyone noticing. Her figure was slight. She might even still be a virgin, for all I knew. I discovered that it took only a brief intense stare to set her trembling and to bring the color to her cheeks in a rush, so I doled out such looks at regular intervals. But to my disappointment, it didn't take long for Eileen to regain her composure, and the game soon lost its novelty. During the meal she did her best to keep the talk on a chatty level.

At some point, having nothing better to offer, I told her, "I was out drinking with a plastic surgeon last night."

"Not that chap Nordhagen," she said, casual as could be.

"You know him?" I was stunned.

"It *was* Nordhagen? Fancy that. No, I don't know him, but I have heard of him. He's very well known."

"Oh, yeah? How? I mean, what exactly have you heard about him, and where?"

"Well, not much, really. You see his name in the papers every so often. Society pages, gossip pages, that sort of thing. Usually it's about his doing some work on a distant member of the royal family or the minor nobility. Or fixing up debutantes. Nothing at all scandalous, just the sort of tidbits some people would prefer to keep private."

"Society girls aren't supposed to have crooked noses, and so they shouldn't need to have them straightened—is that what you mean?"

"Something like that, yes." Then Eileen asked, "So what's the distinguished Doctor Nordhagen like in person? How did you happen to meet him?"

"I met him in a pub," I said. "He's a funny character, hard to figure out. That's what I was thinking about when you knocked on my door. It was like he was slumming last night, but at the same time he seemed to fit right in, as if he belonged."

"Where?"

"Oh, some drinking joints in Soho. The kinds of places in which you would least expect to find a prominent surgeon."

"I wouldn't call him prominent," Eileen said. "Not like some doctors who are always having their pictures taken at grand social functions, charity balls, and so on. He doesn't have that kind of image, but he is known as the best cosmetic surgeon in London, and there's something distinguished about that."

"I guess so."

"Oh, yes. He is *the* man to go to, they say. If you can afford him, of course. Lots of Arabs and other foreigners come here to be treated by him too."

"A gold mine," I said, picturing a line of Arab noses stretching to the horizon and beyond. "What a funny little guy he is. I'm having dinner with him tomorrow night."

"I must say, it hasn't taken you long to move up in London society," Eileen said. She was kidding me, but she was also impressed, just a bit, which made me smile.

After the meal we had coffee and brandy, but I was poor company. The information about Nordhagen distracted me. Another small piece of the puzzle.

Fortified by food and drink, Eileen was considerably more sure of herself. She even contrived to linger close to me a couple of times. Christ, did she hope I'd grab her slim hips in a fit of Yankee bluntness? My mind was elsewhere, and I'm afraid that if she had any romantic notions for the rest of the evening I left them unfulfilled.

I went back to my flat early and straight to bed. My body was still recovering, recharging itself. The meal helped, actually. I slept until just before noon, woke feeling hungry again, but full of energy, ready to go.

I put on my only suit for dinner with Nordhagen that evening. I guess I expected him to be in the same worn duds he'd had on the previous night, because I was surprised to find that he had on a suit too—and his was obviously much more expensive than my off-the-peg number. Now he looked his part.

"So we've both dressed up for the occasion," the old

fox said by way of greeting me. "Our minds must be at-tuned."

It was a typical Nordhagen remark: perfectly innocent, if weak, humor, but, somehow, delivered with an edge, as if we shared a dark secret. The bartender leered, as if he were in on it too. I was less than pleased.

I was a little nervous at first. Residual fears that this was all a big mistake, I guess. But after a couple of rounds Nordhagen and I were once again the same happy pair of jovial boozers out for a night on the town.

We strolled down to Gerrard Street, where we had a leisurely, light, but delicious Chinese meal. It was a good choice—the food was excellent and the restaurant comfortable, not in the least stuffy. Nordhagen delivered a running commentary on what we were eating, and on Chinese cuisine in general. He was witty and informative without ever sounding pompous or condescending. We also played guessing games with each other.

"I'd say you had a firm religious upbringing," he speculated.

"Right."

"Christian, of course."

"Right."

"Protestant."

"Yep."

"I thought as much. You don't have that haunted, furtive, guilty look Catholics have. Even lapsed Catholics have a hard time shaking it."

"No Catholics in our crowd," I confirmed.

"No. And you have Scottish blood in you somewhere, if your name is any indication. So, you must be—what? Presbyterian?"

"Of a sort," I admitted. "Watered down through several American generations. I haven't had anything to do with it since I was—oh, fifteen, or so."

He nodded and smiled.

"Yes, well, you know," he said, "all the little twists and kinks are put in place at a much earlier age."

Nordhagen put this to me with such a merry, mischievous smile it was impossible for me to take offense. But I knew I would like it less and less the next day.

"But, tell me—you're not British," I said. A sudden inspiration, turning the tables. "You told me you're a foreigner, like me. What is Nordhagen, a German name?"

"Scandinavian."

"Where? Norway, or—"

"Up there, somewhere, yes," the little doctor said quickly. "It's all pretty much the same to me. I've been away from there so long the place means nothing to me anymore. I have no roots there, and I've been here long enough to feel British."

"Are you—"

"Are we ready? I think it's time we were moving along," Nordhagen said smoothly.

Had I come close to a nerve? The old boy wasn't happy talking about his background, or so it seemed. I didn't pursue the subject; I had no desire to aggravate my host, especially since there was something I liked about him. But I tucked the matter away in the back of my mind—I'd think about it again, later. It was, surely, an important part of the secret I was hoping to learn. Was he an ex-Nazi? A war criminal? Or a collaborator? Maybe that was why he wasn't back in Denmark or Sweden or wherever he came from. Whatever the secret was, it must be something worth burying.

But no—if there was something terrible in his past, something he wanted to keep hidden, Nordhagen would hardly set up a medical practice in the middle of London. According to Eileen, his name and picture appeared in the press from time to time—not the kind of thing a fugitive Eichmann would ever allow.

More likely, he was a victim, a refugee who had escaped with his life. Perhaps he had lost friends, loved ones, or perhaps he had always been pretty much of a loner. I really had no idea whatsoever, but part of what made Nordhagen so fascinating was that there was something about him that set you to wonder.

We came out of the restaurant and walked back up to busy Shaftesbury Avenue.

"Do you mind if we stroll on a bit?" he asked.

"Fine by me."

"A very moderate pace helps settle the stomach and it facilitates digestion," he explained.

It was, I would learn, another one of Nordhagen's little rituals. I didn't mind, although I prefer to settle my stomach after a meal in the traditional manner: by collapsing in an easy chair. We wandered on up through Soho Square to Oxford Street, where Nordhagen flagged down a taxi.

"Park Street," he told the driver.

"Where are we going?" I asked as soon as we were under way. "Another one of your clubs?"

I heard him laugh softly to himself.

"In a manner of speaking."

"London seems to be full of clubs."

"That is precisely right," Nordhagen said emphatically. "London is *all about* clubs, clubs of one kind or another."

"How many do you belong to?"

The little doctor waved a hand as if to say it didn't matter. "There are—well, I have no idea, to tell you the truth," he answered. "Membership is a funny thing in some of these places."

"Don't you have to know someone?"

"Or someone who knows someone else, yes. It helps at times. But, I was about to say, there are clubs and clubs. Those places we visited the other night are basically legal entities designed to get around the vagaries of our licensing laws. Some are rather pedestrian middle-class places, social clubs for quiet drinking and gossip. Others cater to the lowest of lowlife. Oh, I could take you to some frightening places, my boy."

"Great."

"No, not really. You only think so." Nordhagen cleared his throat before continuing. "Then you have the proper clubs—the Carlton, the Reform, Boodles, places like that. Great institutions, but slowly dying off, I fear."

The taxi turned a corner, then another. A few moments later I spotted the American Embassy looming up ahead on the right. The giant eagle looked like a night bird of prey, poised to fly. We passed on, then swung into Park Street.

"Ah, here we are," Nordhagen announced.

While he paid the fare, I walked up and down in front of the place, looking it over. It was a brown brick building, elegant but very narrow—it couldn't have been more than twenty feet wide. The windows revealed nothing but glimmers of light here and there, as if they were shuttered on the inside. I counted five floors.

"Rather deceptive," Nordhagen said. "Looks a small place but it's actually quite deep. Probably built by a Dutchman."

We went up a few steps to a heavy wooden door, illuminated by an electric lantern. Nordhagen rang the bell, which was mounted inconspicuously on the side of the door frame, a few inches from the discreet bronze plaque that told us we had come to the Feathers.

Gay baths? A high-class brothel? I almost hesitated, because this didn't look like the kind of place it would be easy to walk out of should I suddenly find myself in an awkward situation. Now was the time to demur.

But then the door opened, and I followed Nordhagen into an anteroom. The floors, walls, and ceiling seemed to be covered with dark green velvet. Not so the two sturdy fellows in evening dress who obviously served as the screening committee. They knew my host, and we were smoothly ushered through to a foyer. Stairs went up into the building as well as down below street level. A fine old cage elevator had been installed in the central stairwell. In addition to a coatroom, there were a couple of unmarked doors off the foyer. The building seemed completely quiet. Nordhagen paused, considering where to go.

"The Feathers," I said. "What is this place?"

"Why, Tom, you look positively nervous," he said, his face breaking out in a wide smile. "No need to be, dear boy. Come along. Let's have a drink in the piano bar and settle you down straight away."

The piano bar was up one flight. It was very dark, a cavernous room lit only by candles in red jars on a scattering of tables. Each table was screened off to provide extra privacy. Somewhere in the room, a piano was being played. The carpeting was so deep it felt as if we were walking on pillows, and the seats were equally luxurious. I spotted the bar, but it seemed to be unmanned; in fact, it was, literally. A young woman came and took our orders. I was unprepared for the sight of her and, I suppose, I was startled, but I was ready when she returned a few minutes later with our drinks. She was tall, slender, very pretty, and her entire outfit consisted of two or three silk scarves tied around her waist.

"What is this, a Playboy Club for grownups?" I asked when the girl had left.

Nordhagen laughed quietly. "Not at all," he said. "It *is* a kind of club—I guess you could say that—but then again, it is unlike any other club in London. Cheers."

We sipped our drinks. I had ordered bourbon, since beer didn't seem right for this place. Now I noticed that I had been served a large crystal tumbler full of extremely

35

good sour mash on ice—an amount of liquor far in excess of any normal bar measure. A few of these and it would be a rough night.

"This is very much a private enterprise," Nordhagen elaborated. "A club, yes; we can call it that. But membership is strictly limited to—well, let's just say it's under a thousand. And, as you saw, the name is on the front door. It's not hush-hush, like some places I know, but it is most decidedly discreet. No new member may join unless one dies."

The little doctor gave me a long look when he said that, as if to underline the point.

"A thousand members? But surely this place isn't big enough to handle a crowd—"

"Under a thousand," Nordhagen said, cutting me off. "And that's worldwide, Tom. Some members only get here once or twice a year. Of course, those of us who live in the neighborhood can enjoy it any time we like. As can our guests."

"Very nice."

"Oh, it is, it is."

"When is it open? I mean what hours?"

"Forever."

"It's always open."

"Oh, yes." Nordhagen smiled fondly. "Someone once said, in this bar, in fact, that the Feathers is a fantasy. Well, perhaps it is that, but what's the point of having a fantasy if it isn't there all the time? Even if you're busy, or elsewhere, it is still here, available, unending, and you know it. Isn't that what a fantasy has to be, after all?"

"Definitely." I was impressed. I knew now I was sitting in the midst of a lot of money. Money and power.

"On the ground floor we have a gymnasium," Nordhagen told me. "Excellent equipment, a steam room, a sauna, the works. And we also have, on this floor, a dining room—or, rather, a series of private dining rooms. As with everything else, the kitchen is in operation all the time. What else? Let's see. Upstairs we have another bar, quite unlike this one. And there are rooms for members' use. A games room, a conference room, and a goodly number of bedrooms and suites for those who are staying overnight. Oh, I almost forgot—we also have a cinema. Rather teeny, I'm afraid, but the film library is extensive."

I was still on the word *teeny;* he made even that sound like a virtue. "Why would anyone ever leave?" I asked.

"Why indeed?"

Nordhagen was smiling to himself, pleased, I thought, with his club and pleased that he could show it off to me. Fair enough. It made me take him a little more seriously.

"Let's go downstairs," he said a few minutes later. "We can get another drink there, and I want to show you something."

"All right."

By the time we reached the foyer I felt dizzy. The tumbler of bourbon, on top of the Chinese meal, the drinks before that, and my generally indulgent London lifestyle were all having an effect on me. Nordhagen steered me down more stairs. We were going into the cellar, or whatever it was.

"The grotto," he said. "The steam room's down here too. Good idea? What do you say?"

"Okay." I couldn't argue, even if I had wanted to.

"Yes, let's shed a few toxins," Nordhagen said.

And, for the next hour or so, that's what we did. We sat in the steam room for as long as we could take it, sweating like pigs. Then we showered and went back in to sweat some more. After a final shower, we climbed up on tables, and a couple of masseuses went to work on us. Mine sat on my back, walked on it, and pounded me up and down. But at the end of it, I felt terrific—light, limber, strong. She knew what she was doing.

Nordhagen handed me a robe. "Silk," he said. "It's all you'll need in the grotto."

The grotto was beautiful. Instead of putting in an ordinary swimming pool, they had built a vast underground cavern, a real rock-lined pool, complete with cascading waterfall at the far end. Nordhagen and I swam for a while, then dried ourselves off and lounged in our silk robes at the water's edge on mounds of fluffy pillows. There had been a couple of other men in the steam room, but we had the grotto to ourselves.

If Nordhagen signaled, I didn't see it, but fresh drinks arrived, delivered by another beautiful young woman, naked but for the string of scarves.

"Don't leave us, darling," the little doctor told her. She remained standing there. "Isn't she gorgeous, Tom?"

"Yes, she certainly is."

"Eurasian, of course. The most beautiful women in the world are Eurasian. What shall we do with her?"

No answer seemed called for, so I just smiled. Nordhagen rose and whispered to the girl for a few moments.

As for me, I was lost. Never mind London; I was no longer sure I was anywhere on the planet Earth. The Feathers was a secret side of London I'd hardly dreamed I might see.

The girl disappeared, then came back a minute later with two plain bottles. I had no idea what was in them. She set one down and began to splash liquid from the other all over her long, beautiful body.

"She's doing this for you," Nordhagen said. His voice was distant, as if coming from some other place, or in a dream.

The girl was close to me, kneeling, and she rubbed the liquid on her skin slowly. Her eyes told me she was enjoying it and that she wanted me to enjoy the sight of it. She was using suntan lotion or baby oil, something like that. I didn't care.

She took special care slicking down her pubic hair, reaching deep between her legs, and behind. Then the long black mane that flowed from her head. She covered her face, and then rubbed her nipples until they were alert. It all took time, but we had forever. Her performance was truly hypnotic.

When she was finished, she was some strange, erotic, shiny creature whose eyes paralyzed me. Dimly the realization came that I had never been so close to so beautiful a woman at any time in my life.

Now she sat back a step, regarding me. She picked up the other bottle, stood, and poured that liquid on herself. She didn't rub it into the oiled skin, just sprinkled it generously all over her body. It had a strong, vaguely familiar scent. But I was watching, not thinking.

Finally she put down the second bottle and stood there, as if waiting for me to do something. Hands on hips, she leaned toward me slightly, smiling.

"Touch her," Nordhagen whispered. I wasn't looking at him but I could feel the force of his interest now. "Touch her, Tom." It was a command.

Slowly, I moved forward. My arm reached out to the girl. The long silk sleeve of my robe rustled, charged. When my hand was close enough, the static spark jumped to her—and she was covered with flames. She was burning up in front of me. I jumped back, then reached out to help her, but Nordhagen's hand held me back. I was terrified, but frozen.

"Look," he hissed.

From her feet all the way up to the top of her head, the girl seemed to be clothed in blue fire. It sizzled and spat. But she stood there, writhing, arms raised like a dancer. Her eyes were closed, and she was smiling through the flames.

It began to get to her. The fire was either burning through the oil or it was heating it up. The pain showed

on her face, but she refused to move. Then we could hear
tiny cries welling up in her throat, and her face became a
mask of agony. She stretched her burning arms back,
arched herself, and dove backward into the pool.

I felt the breath rush out of me. She swam in the cool
water for a few minutes. I could see her smile. She was
pleased with herself, and maybe also with what she saw
on my face.

"Would you like her?" Nordhagen asked me.

I felt weak. "You mean—do I want to fuck her?" Part
of my brain was trying to tell me to get out of this place.

"No, no, dear boy." Nordhagen smiled to himself
again.

The girl came out of the pool and sat down next to me.
She was like a cat, stretching, rubbing against me. The
air held the scent of smoke and perfume.

"It's an interesting question," Nordhagen said. "What
would anyone do if they were given another person.
Given, I say. Have you ever considered it? Probably not.
After all, the possibility never arises. Well, almost never."

I found it hard to think, especially with the girl lying
there against me. I was already stroking her breasts,
teasing her nipples.

"You make it sound like you mean—really—giving
someone another person. Like, well, slavery."

"Yes."

"To do whatever you want with—keep, throw away."

"Use, destroy."

"Yeah," I said. "Sure. Ha ha."

"Ah, but, you see, I do mean it," Nordhagen went on,
his eyebrows rising. "That is just the question I am asking you, dear boy. Would you like to have her?"

THREE

I found myself in cold, thin daylight when I left the Feathers. The sky was clear, and the sun was visible; distant and washed out, but there. Which was more or less how I felt. I'd seen the night through and bottomed out in the next day—it was probably some kind of first in my life.

I crossed Park Lane and walked through Hyde Park toward Kensington at an unhurried pace, partly because I was plain tired but also because my mind needed time and fresh air to sort itself out. I had a lot to think over—such as, what the hell was the previous night all about?

The Feathers. Reality stopped at the front door of that place—which I guess was the point of it. I'd been in some other world, or so it seemed. But I couldn't tell yet whether I'd been given a glimpse of rare, high privilege or simply been snowed at an expensive whorehouse. A little of both, maybe.

But why? Roger Nordhagen had covered everything. The last thing I'd paid for was his glass of red wine at the

Carlisle. Perhaps he had nothing better to do with his money, but it bothered me when I thought about it. Not that I could afford the kind of treatment available at the Feathers. But as I made my way along the Carriage Road I realized that I'd let another man spend a lot of money on me, and that left me with an uncomfortable feeling.

The Feathers. I guess I'd known such places exist, though I'd never given it much thought. It made sense. People with money had to frolic somewhere, and the Feathers was just one of their playgrounds. It wasn't even outrageous, just very impressive. By telling me it was run for fewer than a thousand people world-wide, Nordhagen seemed to be suggesting it was more a secret society than a mere private club. I took that to be Nordhagen's way of inflating his own importance, and I suspected the truth was more down to earth. There are clubs and there are clubs, as he had told me. No doubt about it, the little doctor wanted to impress me, and show me he was not only a swell guy but important as well.

Why? That question came back to me whenever I forgot about the pleasures of the Feathers. He hadn't come on to me like an old fairy, when he might have, and I had an instinctive feeling that he really wasn't that way inclined. I had a vague recollection of warning Nordhagen off in that regard when we first met. So perhaps he was exactly what he appeared to be, a lonely, more or less friendless old geezer. Well off, yes, but on his own. For all I knew, it might be a habit of his, picking up strangers and milking them of company and conversation, treating them handsomely in the process. If that were the case, he'd probably tire of me soon enough. Already had, more likely.

Drink is the assembly line of guilt, and once again I was sure I'd finished an evening with Nordhagen badly. I must have struck a pretty inane pose when I grandly pronounced, "You have your freedom, then," to that girl in the grotto. She looked disappointed, and Nordhagen managed only a sad smile. The girl dove back into the pool and swam away. Okay, it was not a great response to their joke, but they took it so seriously. What did they expect? Did they really think I'd swallow that nonsense about having the girl, actually owning her, to do anything with I wanted? The old man had carried it off rather well at the time, I had to admit, but now, in the chill morning, it all seemed merely silly. But I had failed to play along with their game, and that in itself might cost me further entertainment with Nordhagen.

I wasn't sure I'd mind. I remembered the strange sound in his voice when the girl caught fire: a manic hiss. And, when I'd glanced at him a few seconds later, the expression on his face: eyes too wide open, the look of someone slightly crazy. I thought I'd had just about enough of him. After the girl left us, our talk slackened, became sporadic and tired, inconsequential. We drank more, but seemed to occupy separate silences in that stunning grotto. Finally I hauled myself up and thanked Nordhagen for a fine time, got my clothes on, and stumbled outside. No talk of seeing each other again soon, or anything like that.

By the time I reached the Albert Memorial I was convinced I had fallen far short of being the amusing guest someone like Nordhagen would want. Maybe I'd even been monumentally blind; maybe he had hoped to be treated to a front-row seat at a wild sexual performance by the Eurasian girl and me. We'd almost gotten down to it, at that, and now it seemed more and more amazing that we hadn't. I'd declined the offer, but why?

I took a taxi the rest of the way home. I could hear Eileen Fothergill moving around behind the door of her flat when I reached the top of the stairs. I hurried to my own apartment, eager to avoid any encounter at that time of day. The expression on the cab driver's face had told me more than I cared to know about the way I looked.

Safely inside, I locked the door, stripped my clothes off, and flopped down on the bed. Now that I was lying still, my head began to spin, slowly but inescapably. It would be a long day, and my best hope was that I'd pass through it in a state of unconsciousness. I'd had enough of Roger Nordhagen, nose bobber of Mayfair. Something bothered me about him. I couldn't say exactly what, but my impression of the man was clouded. Perhaps he was simply too eccentric for me.

I didn't want to think about the Feathers, playpen for the pampered few. I was ready to sink back into my own life.

I came to my senses three or four days later. I'd gone back to my old routine of dining out, seeing a film or a play, visiting new pubs, and otherwise continuing my exploration of London. My hours didn't change; I was still a night owl at large in the West End. But something was wrong, something at the back of my mind was calling for attention. I was sitting in the bar in Ronnie Scott's, waiting for Scott Hamilton to return for a second set, when I began to think consciously about it.

I actually did miss the little guy. Maybe *miss* wasn't the right word, but I did regret, somewhat, that contact had been broken off between us. He was the only person I knew in London, not counting my spinsterish neighbor. I tried to describe Nordhagen to myself, to remind myself what he was like—for, although only a few days had passed, he was elusive in my mind. He was friendly, generous, jolly. But not really warm. He was intelligent and perceptive, and he didn't mind telling you things about yourself. But not about himself. That's it, I realized: I still had a puzzle to solve, and that puzzle was Roger Nordhagen. It wasn't the little doctor, my chum and colleague, I missed; it was Nordhagen the riddle, the strange, eccentric, hidden individual behind the charming exterior.

Now I wondered if it was the right thing to do, to let it go and forget about it. Could I do that? There had been something empty and incomplete about my wanderings through London since the night at the Feathers. Something was not right, and it seemed to me that I had, after all, been too hasty in writing off my acquaintance with Roger Nordhagen.

There were lots of different ways of looking at it, not least of which was the one that said I owed him, out of simple courtesy, a dinner in return. I had no intention of continuing to enjoy his largesse without paying him back in kind, at least to the extent that I was able to. The element of self-interest in this was clear to me. Nordhagen was still my only entrée to places in London I couldn't otherwise approach. Being towed around by the little doctor was, I concluded as Scott re-emerged from the back room, preferable to sitting in restaurants and bars alone. Especially since I had already been through a good many of the public places in the West End.

That "private" side of London nightlife still appealed, and it was hard to resist. I'd had only a brief glimpse of it with Nordhagen. There had to be more, much more. It wasn't just the Feathers—although I wouldn't turn down a return visit, nor would I necessarily dismiss that beautiful Eurasian girl if she were ever presented to me again—but the thought of missing a great deal of London. The more I considered it, the more it worried me. I was there for a limited period of time, and I wanted to make the most of it. Perhaps Nordhagen was one of those little quirks of fate. Perhaps I'd met him because I was meant to meet him, and he was my key to the city. Surely it would be a mistake to squander that resource— all the more so since I had no other person or thing with which to replace him. It was London, more than Nordhagen, I was after.

I made up my mind to get in touch with the little doctor, although it took me another few days to work myself up to the task. I don't know why. A strange kind of paralysis came over me as soon as the notion was clear in my mind. I couldn't pick up the telephone and call him. I wanted to, but every time I reached for the receiver I hesitated, feeling awkward, nervous. I was convinced I'd sound foolish, or opportunistic, or in some other way false.

One day I walked past the Feathers on Park Street, then along Mount Street to the entrance of Millington Lane. I couldn't tell, but I guessed that Nordhagen's offices were through the shiny black door at the far end. A massive Daimler was parked in front. A few moments later a middle-aged man came out through the black door, got into the car, and was driven away past me. Whoever he was, he could do with one or two fewer chins, which made me think he had indeed come from Nordhagen's place. Then it occurred to me that I'd been standing there at the mouth of the lane, loitering like some crazed adolescent. I felt extremely silly, ashamed of myself, and confused. I hurried away and walked until I was sure I'd put at least a mile between myself and Mount Street, and then I went into a quiet pub to chase away all thought with a line of pints.

Later, of course, I did think about it. Nordhagen had put no spell on me, I told myself, but he was an intriguing figure. More to the point, I'd been in London long enough to become a little lonely. That was probably what it all came down to—the accumulating emotional wear and tear of being on my own. I had no desire to call up Owen Flaherty and invite him out for a drink. Nor did I want to expand my acquaintance with Eileen Fothergill any more than was necessary. I could go along to a disco any night of the week and try to pick up a girl, but I hadn't played that game in a few years, since college, in fact, and I was reluctant to push myself in that direction. I'd always hated the ritual of picking up women, conning them even as they are deciding whether or not to do the same to you—and later, almost always, both of you finding out how uninterested you are in each other.

That left Nordhagen as the prime focus of socializing for me in London. It might not say much for me, but it was nothing to get spooked about, I reasoned. He's a lonely old man who enjoys company, and that's what I can offer. In return, he introduces me to what would otherwise be invisible London.

All this dithering, I would come to understand much later, was actually an elaborate defense mechanism that I was trying to employ against myself. It almost worked.

"I'm sorry I haven't called you sooner to thank you for that marvelous time the other night," I said when I finally got him on the telephone.

"Not at all," Nordhagen replied. "Glad you enjoyed it."

"The meal was great. And the visit to the Feathers," I added quickly. "That's quite a place."

"Isn't it?"

He was friendly enough, but he was letting me make the first move. I suggested we get together for a drink. I had already decided to see how that was received before proffering a dinner invitation.

"Why don't you come round here," he responded. "We can have a drink and I can show you my offices and home and all that sort of thing."

"Fine," I said. "I'd like that very much."

"We can always adjourn somewhere else later, if that's what we want to do."

"Yes, whatever."

"Good. But not tomorrow, I'm afraid. How about the day after, Friday. Is Friday all right with you?"

"Sure, no problem."

"Come about five, then. Do you know where I am?"

"I have your card."

"Excellent. See you Friday at five."

It wasn't long after I'd hung up the telephone that something came echoing back to me. The words *if that's what we want to do*. It was another typical Nordhagen turn of phrase. Innocent, trivial, but lingeringly unpleasant. It's just the way the man talks, I tried to tell myself. Of course we might just sit around his place and get happily sozzled there, without ever thinking of going out somewhere else, lest we lose the thread of our conversation in the process. But I was learning how you could hear different things in Nordhagen's simplest remarks. It didn't really bother me, but I was determined to stay alert for them, not to miss one overtone or veiled suggestion. I didn't want to come away from another meeting with him feeling stupid or naive, or buffaloed.

The next day I got an agony letter from my mother, with an equally worried, if briefer, note from my father enclosed. They had my telephone number, they could call up anytime, but no, instead they poured it all out on pages of transparent stationery. The problem was, they had heard from me only once since I had arrived in London, and that shortly after I had landed. Where was I, what had happened, what was I doing? And so on. Whatever they had was contagious, because I spent more than an hour trying to compose a suitable reply, explaining that I was still in London, hadn't got to the Continent yet, was having a smashing time, as they say here, missed them very much, and blah blah blah.

But as soon as I read it over, I tore it up and threw it in the wastebasket. Why was I so apologetic? They knew where I was. They knew I was on vacation, not in prison, where I could write letters all day, every day. I worked myself up into a properly aggressive state of mind, and then I called them. It worked. My mother was shocked to be talking to someone thousands of miles away. The thought of how much it must be costing was sufficient to reduce her to a rapid unintelligible stammer. My father took over, and I got the basic message through to him: I was fine, I was enjoying myself, and I would make an effort to send a few postcards, but they shouldn't worry about me. As I have had to do more than once, I reminded them I was a doctor and could take care of myself.

That night, sitting in a topless bar in Soho, half watching a woman in a schoolgirl costume strip and play with a vibrator, I began to grasp what the letter and telephone conversation really meant. And I was shocked. They missed me, worried about me, even more than I would have thought they could. But at the same time, I didn't miss them. I didn't miss New Haven, the hospital, my imitation Swiss-chalet condominium out on interstate 95. The people I knew and worked with, my family, the whole of my life back in the U.S.A.—I didn't miss any of it.

Nobody is invisible, but I felt close to it in London, and I liked that very much. I was leaving no footprints. Yesterday didn't matter. I took it one day at a time—as so many people claim but so few actually manage to do. The present was something I was truly making up as I went along. That, in itself, is enough to make a grown man shiver with fear and excitement. For the first time in my life I had an idea of what money could do: not so much free you as throw you, hurl you into yourself. I was getting a small taste of it, and for only a limited period of time, but I could see how it destroyed people. How many, condemned to the freedom of being themselves, find nothing there? Even now, in a small way, I was edging around that fire. Already London was teaching me things about myself. Was I a voyeur? I was sitting there watching the show, but what I saw was a previous life drifting away like a continental plate. London was my peep show, and I was in it.

But it was a phony thrill. I knew that when the time and the money ran out, I'd be back there in the real world, earning my way once again. But a taste, just one brief taste, can be enough to take with you to the grave, and this was it for me. I wasn't at all sure I could live this free for the rest of my life, that I could handle it. This vacation would be enough, maybe more than enough.

The schoolgirl was followed by a nurse, who in turn was succeeded by a pair of horny nuns, and a lingerie saleswoman. Each act was greeted enthusiastically by the audience, and afterward the performers allowed certain customers to buy them drinks. A table of Middle Easterners, reprieved from the strictures of Islam, got the two nuns and the schoolgirl, a thematically appropriate combination, somehow. A businessman with a German accent fell into serious conversation with the nurse; maybe they were discussing colonic irrigation. I couldn't be a poor sport, so when the lingerie saleswoman approached me, I sprang for one drink. She kept glancing at herself in the mirror behind the bar, as if her appearance were subject to transformation without prior warning.

"Do all men really have the same few fantasies?"

I was just trying to be polite, and get an expert's opinion at the same time. It seemed the best way to avoid the phony romantic talk that goes on in these places.

"Why, didn't you like the show?" My companion downed half of her tiny champagne cocktail (£10) in one gulp. "They're very popular acts. What would you like, something a little stronger? A little kinkier?" She gave me an encouraging smile.

"How's this for a fantasy?" I said. "Someone gives you another person, a gift, yours to use in any way or do whatever you want with, a gorgeous young girl—or, if it were you, a young boy, I suppose. Anyhow, the point is—"

"I know," she cut me off. "You're talking about the old slave fantasy. Collar around the neck, ankle chain, do this, do that. I know just what you mean, love. It's not unusual, you know."

"I suppose it isn't," I conceded.

"There aren't any good unusual fantasies left these days," she lamented. She looked sad, like a poet who'd run out of inspiration. "But yours is quite good; don't get me wrong, love. Lends itself to lots of interesting variations . . ."

It cost me another drink and some fanciful talk of various "scenarios of enactment" before I could get away gracefully. But I felt it had been worth it, somehow. I was still thinking of the Feathers, and wondering if what went on there was enactment or the real thing. Or was there any difference at all? As long as you could pay, you could keep the fantasy real.

I intended to ask Nordhagen more about the Feathers, and to tell him I hoped he would take me back for a second visit. I had made up my mind not to waste any more time on niceties, or to be shy about going for what I wanted or what interested me. I had only so much time in London, and the days were dwindling down. I still had more than four months left, it's true, and that might seem a long time to someone in jail. But I was in the opposite situation. I was enjoying total freedom and I had to make the most of it while I had the chance.

When I arrived at Nordhagen's offices at the appointed time on Friday afternoon, he was not there. The only person in the waiting room when I opened the shiny black door was his receptionist—but she didn't look like any ordinary receptionist.

"Ah, good evening," she said, rising from her chair behind the desk. "You must be Tom Sutherland, Doctor Sutherland."

"Yes, I am."

"I'm Lina Ravachol, Doctor Nordhagen's assistant."

"Pleased to meet you."

I was too. Lina Ravachol was a strikingly beautiful woman. And *woman* is the right word, since there was nothing of the pretty girl about her. I would say she was thirty, give or take a year or two. She had dark, lustrous hair that was long and thick. It set off her pale skin and electric blue eyes. She was tall but well proportioned. Her face and hands were exquisite. The strong impression created by her physical presence was immediate. She had the fine features of a China doll, and yet there was a larger-than-life quality about her. She almost looked too good to be only human. Not a Playboy blowup. Maybe a goddess.

The clothes went with the woman. She came around to the front of the desk, and the slit in her black skirt showed a length of silvery-stockinged leg. She wore a white blouse beneath an open vest. I don't know materials by sight, but I would have guessed that almost everything she had on was silk. It seemed a safe bet. The only jewelry she wore was a fiery blue opal on a silver chain around her neck.

Lina Ravachol was the kind of woman you wouldn't be surprised to find in the pages of *Vogue*. She looked out of place in the role of Doctor Nordhagen's assistant, but that didn't bother me at the time. Later, I realized that she was actually the ideal front person to deal with his clients (in cosmetic surgery you didn't have patients, you had clients). Upper-class folk wouldn't intimidate this woman.

"I'm so sorry Doctor Nordhagen won't be able to keep

his engagement with you this evening," she said. "He was called away unexpectedly on an urgent matter about an hour ago, and he was unable to reach you by telephone."

"Oh. That's too bad."

"The Doctor will ring you to arrange another date and time, if that's all right with you."

"Sure, no problem."

"Good." Lina Ravachol breathed the word, more than said it. "In the meantime, the Doctor asked if I would sit in for him at dinner with you this evening, and I said of course, I'd be glad to do so."

I hoped she'd told him no such thing. I hoped she'd waited until I arrived, so she could get a look at me before making up her mind.

"I don't want to inconvenience you," I said.

"You won't. Not at all."

"Are you sure? I mean, you don't have anything else to do this evening?"

"No, really."

"Well, fine. Uh, I don't know if Roger told you, but I'm new to London and I don't know many places yet. Is there anywhere special you'd like to go?"

"You're the guest," she told me brightly. "It's all been taken care of. We have a private dining room at the Feathers. Is that all right with you?"

"Definitely."

"Good. I'll just be a minute."

She disappeared into another room. Nordhagen had pulled a pretty neat surprise on me, but I didn't mind at all. As I waited, somewhat nervously, I was grateful to have a dinner date with such a gorgeous woman, and that was all I cared to think about.

Nordhagen's reception room was more than ordinary too, I noticed for the first time. The chairs were fine leather, the carpet deep, and the paintings on the walls looked like real art. Lina Ravachol's desk might have been a piece out of French history. The only things on it were a telephone and a huge crystal vase overflowing with fresh flowers. The magazines scattered about for the clients were French, Italian, and British *Vogue, Vanity Fair, The New Yorker,* and others of that sort.

"Ready?"

Lina Ravachol was back, in a silvery fur coat.

"Ready."

I felt a little like a vagrant next to this dazzling creature, but if she could stand it, so could I. We walked to the Feathers and were passed through by the same two men without question. Lina left her coat in the small coatroom.

"Let's have a drink in the piano bar," I suggested. "That is, if we have time. Or are we supposed to eat right away?"

"Whatever you want," she said. "We can eat whenever we're ready. It's early yet. Drinks would be very nice."

"Right, good."

I was like a kid who had bungled a golden opportunity and who suddenly, miraculously, has been given a second, even better, chance. Lina led me to a table in what might have been the darkest, most remote corner of the piano bar. The familiar nymph clad only in scarves took our orders—Lina asked for Stoli on the rocks, and when I heard that, I felt weak requesting a white wine spritzer. Getting blitzed on alcohol seemed half the point, or more, when in Nordhagen's company. But with this woman I wanted to make an attempt, at least, to stay reasonably sober. It was, as they say, a completely different situation.

One of the reasons I wanted to have a drink in the piano bar was to see how Lina reacted to the naked beauty who saw to the drinks. It was a cheap, schoolboy kind of move on my part, and of course Lina took no notice whatsoever—we might just as well have been served by someone in knight's armor.

The drinks, as on my previous visit, were mammoth, and by the time we'd gotten through one round, Lina and I had overcome the difficult small talk and felt more relaxed in each other's company. Into the second round, we were talking about Nordhagen and the Feathers. I sensed that Lina was being careful in what she said, but at the same time I didn't get the feeling she was actually keeping anything from me.

"Roger described this place as a fantasy," I said. "And that strikes me as just about the right word for it. But I wonder, how does it seem to a woman?"

"Like a fantasy," she agreed.

"Silly? It's so male—piggish, some might say."

"Oh, no, not at all. I don't think any fantasy is silly. I think everything should be a fantasy. Don't you? If you step outside and look around, at any street in the world, at any newspaper—well, you can see what the alternative is."

"Yeah, but—"

"Everything should be a fantasy," Lina repeated. "People have been trying to make a go of what they call 'the real world' for thousands of years now, and it hasn't really worked. I think reality should be outlawed."

I smiled at this—condescendingly, I'm afraid. "And how would you go about doing that?"

"By making everyone share my fantasy," Lina said simply, with a casual shrug. "By making mine theirs. That's all it takes."

"It can't be done, not with a lot of people."

"Politicians do it all the time."

"You mean that they sell visions in exchange for votes? I guess that's true to a certain extent, but doesn't it usually turn into bad dreams?"

I was smiling, as if I were clever, but Lina ignored this. "You said *fantasy* was the right word for this place," she went on. "I agree, I think it's a very good word. Doesn't it all seem a little unreal to you?"

"Yes, very."

"But don't you feel a little more comfortable here than you did the first time you came?"

"Yes, I do."

"And the more you come here, the more you'll accept it and fit in with it. The more the fantasy becomes real to you, so also will the outside become unreal."

"Yes, but you always go back outside, to your home, to work. This is all very well, but you don't live like this."

"Don't be so sure. Every time you go outside you take a little more of this with you."

"This whole London trip is one big fantasy for me."

"You see?"

"I'm not sure I see anything," I said. "I'm sorry if I keep smiling, but this all seems kind of strange. I'm thinking I should be asking you where you were born, where you went to school, do you have any brothers and sisters, how you got your job with Nordhagen—things like that."

"Do you want to know? Does it matter?"

"Well, no, not really."

I wasn't so big an idiot that I'd seriously argue with her. The Feathers and this remarkable stranger could do whatever they wanted with me. If Lina Ravachol wanted to talk about fantasy, no problem.

"So, is this place your fantasy too?" I asked. "Your deep, dark, secret fantasy?"

"No, not mine. It's a fantasy I can enjoy, being here, but it's not my special one."

"And what is?"

"I can't tell you, but I could show you."

"All right."

"Not now, not yet. Let's work on yours for now."

I laughed. I was enjoying this. I was dizzy.

"Do you think all fantasies are sexual?"

"The first wave, yes," Lina answered. "And most people never get beyond the first wave."

"But . . . ?"

Lina sat back and smiled before saying, "Beyond that are the *real* fantasies."

"And what are they about?"

"Don't you know?"

"I could guess," I said. "But I'd much rather have you tell me about them."

"I can't. Not yet."

That again. It made me wonder what the rest of the evening had in store. With someone like Lina sitting next to me, it was pleasant to think about.

"Fantasies are just fantasies," I said fatuously.

"We're in the fantasy business," Lina said smoothly. "People want their breasts enlarged or reduced. They want their thighs contoured. They want one youthful chin. It's all fantasy, isn't it?"

"You're just helping them feel better about their bodies," I pointed out. "And that in turn helps them get along a little bit better in the outside world."

"By taking a little more of the fantasy out with them. By making *them* more of the fantasy."

"Well, yes," I admitted. "You could say that."

FOUR

Lina Ravachol had me in the palm of her hand. If Nordhagen was constantly surprising, he at least had a familiar human appearance, down to earth, eccentric but recognizable. I could think of him as the odd kind of person everybody meets at one time or another in their lives. But Lina was something else. Lina was overwhelming. The word that keeps coming to mind is charismatic, and in her own way that's exactly what she was. She was not just beautiful. She was enormously sexy and she radiated that quality.

The conversation had no chance but to go the way she wanted it to go. Fantasy, fantasy, fantasy. It was a word I'd hardly ever used or thought about in all my previous life, but now it had come to dominate these few weeks in London. I was in a strange place. I wouldn't say I was vulnerable so much as exposed, and receptive. And lonely? Oh, yes. It was catching up with me at last. My sex life in America had been erratic and uninteresting. By now some considerable time had passed since I'd been with a woman I wanted, really and desperately wanted. Tonight was going to be either very good indeed or else terribly unsatisfactory.

The private dining room at the Feathers was a little fantasy in itself. Small and cocoonlike, it had cushions piled on cushions all around a low table. We left our shoes outside the door. The walls were draped with billowy rose satin from ceiling to floor, adding to the illusion of being in a desert tent. A wooden chest was packed with ice and bottles of wine and champagne. There were trays of fresh fruit, shrimp, meats, and other delicacies to nibble on. I shook my head, smiling. The more outrageous the evening became, the easier I found it to go along.

"Did you know that some of the most famous affairs of Victorian times were conducted in the private dining rooms of London?"

Lina stretched out on the cushions as she asked this, raising one leg slightly so that her skirt fell back pleasingly.

"Uh, love affairs?"

"Yes. Love affairs."

"No. I didn't know that."

I didn't mind a little history. I dipped a large shrimp in a likely looking sauce and held it to her lips. Lina smiled at me, then licked a bit of the sauce with the tip of her tongue before taking the shrimp in her teeth.

"Mmm."

I stretched out on the cushions too, near her. The room was arranged so that it was easy to be at table without the table coming between two people. In the back of my mind I was still laughing at myself, at this whole business, thinking I had been dragged into some grotesque reenactment of a Valentino movie. But the rest of my mind said, *Play on!*

"Do we really have to order a whole big meal now?" I asked. "I'm not even hungry."

"Whatever you want," Lina said. "We can just pick at these things and drink, if you prefer."

"That'd be fine, at least for now."

I filled a couple of crystal goblets with wine, and we drank and took turns feeding each other bits of food. The sauces were delightfully spicy and aromatic. They counteracted the effects of the alcohol, leaving the mouth tingling clean.

"Something's bothering you," Lina said after a while. "You've gone all quiet."

"Sorry. I was just wondering."

"Yes?"

"Well, I don't mean this in any negative way, but I was wondering about you. The Feathers is Nordhagen's playground, but I haven't quite figured out why you're here. Why do you go along with it? Why do you give up an evening to wine and dine someone who's a complete stranger to you? Surely it's not part of your job."

"Oh, but I'm glad to be here. It's an evening out for me too, and I'm enjoying myself. Does there have to be any other reason?"

"No. That's good enough, I guess."

"Thomas, Tom—by the way, what do people call you?"

"Most people back in the States call me Doctor." I meant it as a quick quip, and we both laughed at it, but as soon as I said it I realized it was a true comment on my life in New Haven. "But call me Tom," I added hastily.

"What else are you wondering, Tom? You're supposed to be having a good time, but there's a sad smile in your eyes and you can't get rid of it. You've been trying, but it's still there."

"Really? I don't know. I guess I was thinking how easy it would be to get used to living like this."

"Mm-hmm."

"I haven't been here all that long, but already home, back there, is like a distant star on the other side of the galaxy. A few more weeks of this and I wonder if I'll even know who I am anymore."

"Maybe this *is* who you are."

"It'll be hard to go back."

"Who says you have to?"

"Oh, I'll go back. I have to, for a lot of reasons."

Lina gave a small, dismissive shrug, as if she thought I didn't know what I was talking about. I was beginning to wonder about that too. I reached out and touched her face, tracing the line of her jaw, her lips. I was looking for something she could tell me in her expression or the feel of her skin. I had no idea what it was.

"I think I'm a little lost in all this," I said. My voice sounded like a strangled whisper.

"There's a great deal in front of you."

"What am I supposed to do about it?"

"Maybe all you have to do is close your hand around it."

"Maybe I can't."

"Why not?"

"Maybe I don't believe it."

"Maybe you're trying too hard to understand. Analysis can be a very negative, debilitating thing. Do you have to know all the contents of a room before you step into it?"

"No. But I like to know there's water in the pool before I go off the diving board."

At that, we both started laughing, and all the tension in the air disappeared.

"I want you to try something," Lina said, sitting up. "Now, just lie back and relax." She produced a small silver box, about an inch square, and she took a tiny white pill from it.

"I don't approve of multidrug experiences," I told her. "I can just about get by with drink."

"It won't clash with alcohol, and you don't have to

61

worry about bad results. It's nonaddictive and nonhallucinogenic."

"What is it, then? You can tell me—I'm a doctor."

I wasn't resisting, though. Lina was lying beside me, her breasts pressed against me, her face inches away and filling my sight. I didn't want this to end.

"It goes under the tongue," she explained.

"You first."

She put the pill in her mouth without hesitation, then got another one and popped it under my tongue.

"Close your eyes and let your mind stop," she whispered in my ear.

I reached to get one arm around her, then I shut my eyes and tried to be a good passive receptor. It was difficult, however, not to concentrate on her lovely long warm body, which seemed to glow next to me.

The drug, whatever it was, didn't make me sleepy or dreamy, and, as she had said, there were no hallucinations. But after a few minutes my mind really did appear to stop. Normal thought became a lost faculty, but I didn't miss it—in fact, I hardly even knew it was gone. I may have opened my eyes at some point, or maybe I didn't—I had no visual focus. My whole body had become transformed into a vague, amorphous presence. There was a sensation of being adrift in a warm sea, or of floating in clouds, but at the same time it was as if I were a part of that sea or those clouds. I wasn't a person, a separate entity; I was blurring, merging, becoming one with whatever it was that was all around me.

And that was only the smallest part of it. The real power of the drug was the overwhelming sense of relief it brought. A sense of total joy and peace washed through me in gentle waves. It was as if a billion tiny knots within me were unraveling, and every pain, however slight, from the first day of my life, was being erased. At one point I felt so happy, so *new*, that I was crying like a baby, and that too was a great release. Finally I became the waves, completely, and I was aware of nothing but the most vivid, ecstatic sense of well-being I have ever felt. And like the waves in an infinite sea, I went on and on. . . .

Inevitably, it began to wear off, and the surroundings asserted themselves once more. I was annoyed at this; I didn't want to be back where I was so soon—although I had no idea how much time had passed. But my body felt new, alive, as if all the alcohol and other poisons in my system had been purged and I had just awakened from a long, restorative sleep. Then Lina and I were smiling at each other, kissing, hugging, nuzzling like sleepy young animals.

"Come," she said softly. "Time to go."

"Where?"

"I want you to take me home now."

The next few minutes were a jumble of disoriented images, because I was still trying to get my bearings. But soon we were in the backseat of a cab, riding through the empty streets of London in the middle of the night.

"What was that stuff?"

"A special blend—I call it Special."

I could see her smiling in the dark, and then she kissed me again and I held her close the rest of the way, one hand buried beneath her fur coat. It seemed a fair drive before we were let off at a park.

"Where do you live?" I asked as the cab pulled away.

"The other side of the wood."

"The princess beyond the forest."

She led me into the park, and we made our way slowly along a rough path through trees and bushes. We were like hot teenagers, stopping every few yards, making out furiously. It was another bizarre shift. After hours spent in the rich luxury of a private room at the Feathers, here we were, poor lovers, groping wildly in the woods. But that made it seem even better, or maybe it was just that we could no longer stop ourselves, or even wanted to. . . . Then we were in a small grassy clearing, hemmed in on all sides by thick bushes and towering trees, and we could go no further toward her house. Not yet.

"Here, please, here, now, now . . ."

Her voice hoarse, urgent, at once a cry, a plea, a demand. We rolled together in the grass. My hands found the slit in her skirt, rode the silk to the stocking tops and the brilliant shock of her thighs, and I drove on, surging, burying myself in the deep enveloping warmth of her.

We did not lie there like spent lovers. Lina was on her feet again soon, moving like a playful spirit, and I was stumbling, chasing after her. I would catch her, only to have her break away from me.

At last we emerged together, in each other's arms, on a silent street on the other side of the wood. She clung to me like a tired child now, and we crossed to a respectable middle-class brick house with a small front garden. Every house on the street was identical. When Lina put the key in the lock, she turned to look up at me with a coy, teasing smile. She might have been a schoolgirl about to do something bold and daring, such as invite her boyfriend in when her parents were away for the weekend.

"Want to come in?" she asked sweetly.

Inside, the house was probably unlike any other on the street, or in the entire city. I didn't actually see most of the place until morning, since Lina insisted on leaving the lights off, but I saw enough. Plenty. She told me to remove my jacket, shoes, and socks. Then we went into the front room. The carpet was deep but springy, the closest thing to real grass I'd ever walked on. It wasn't grass, of course, but neither did it feel artificial. It felt natural, good. The room seemed to be almost without furniture. I was aware of a dark mass in one corner, which I assumed was an array of cushions, as in the private room at the Feathers.

But the focal point was on the far side of the room. It was the largest aquarium I'd seen outside a zoo. It was semicircular in shape and it stood on a raised base of rough stone. Even in the dark it was obvious that a lot of careful work had gone into the construction of it. The aquarium was about eighteen inches deep and six feet across at its widest point. It was dimly lit from underneath, and the effect was dramatic. Dozens of beautiful, multicolored fish swam through the gently waving plants. I knew several of them from the time in my childhood when I had a little five-gallon tank—neon tetras, zebra danios, various swordtails, a chocolate gourami, a headstander—and many more that were new to me.

"It's beautiful," I said at last.

"I can spend hours looking at it," Lina told me. "And sometimes I sit by it with my bare feet inside. It scares the fish at first, but then they become curious and they take turns coming round to see what those strange objects are. I love to feel them bumping ever so lightly against my toes."

And then:

"Sometimes I wish I could lie down in there with them and feel them all around me, all over my body. It's how I imagine the color silver would feel, if you could feel a color."

I couldn't think of anything to say to that. We were both quiet in the darkness for a few minutes, the only sound being the soft burble of the air pump in the aquarium. Then I sensed that I was alone in the room.

I went through the archway into the adjoining room, which was much larger and faintly illuminated by a window at the back. The same carpeting covered the floor here, except for the center of the room, where a huge black stain contrasted sharply. I realized it was a circular pit, some six feet deep and ten feet in diameter. I could just make out Lina, or her silvery fur coat, down in there.

"Hey."

"Come on."

I climbed down into the pit with her. The bottom was a waterbed, filled to a moderate ripple.

"This is terrific."

We sat back against some pillows, facing the rear wall of the room above us. Lina started pushing buttons, and I saw that the wall of the pit had a range of electronic equipment built into it. A television, stereo components, and I could only guess what else it might contain. Your basic modern toy box.

"Look," she told me.

Shades, or screens, which I hadn't known were there, went up on the back wall of the room, revealing a broad expanse of glass—not just the small window I'd first seen. Lina hit another button and all the shades went back down. This put us in total darkness again, but only for a brief moment.

"Now, lie back and look straight up at the ceiling."

I did so, half expecting to see a light come on and show us reflected in one of those bed-sized mirrors, but something very different happened instead. Lights did come on overhead, but they were tiny pinpricks, some white, some blue-white, some yellow, and others a dull red. Patterns formed, and then the depth of it really hit me. I was stunned. Lina had a small planetarium installed in the ceiling of her home. It was breathtaking, and I felt as if I'd suddenly been shot into deep space. I have no idea how such a startling three-dimensional effect was achieved, but it was utterly convincing.

"Jesus Christ," I exclaimed. "This is some kind of house you have here, lady."

"Thank you," she said proudly. "They're just toys, of course, but I love them."

"I don't blame you. Not one bit."

Lina turned off the stellar light show, and a couple of seconds later the pit was bathed in a misty green glow, so diffuse it was impossible to tell where it was coming from. But now we could see each other. The light was confined to the pit, and it occurred to me that to someone standing in the room above us this pit might almost look like a huge aquarium itself.

"Come here," Lina said, and we moved out into the center of the waterbed.

She touched more buttons on the unit in her hand, and before long we were surrounded by the dancing figures of tiny men, women, elves, animals, and other strange creatures of light, a miniature parade forming a panorama around us. I must have looked as if I were about to go into shock, because I could hear Lina suppressing laughter.

"Holograms," she explained.

"Right, right."

"Shall I tell you a little secret?"

"Please do."

"When I was a child I used to have a bedside lamp I just loved. The lampshade had all sorts of animals and gnomes on it, fairies, dwarfs, goblins. It was fantastic. And it gave off the most wonderful warm, golden light. Sometimes I couldn't even read, it gave me such pleasure to lie there in bed staring at the shade with the lamp on. And I always wished so hard, that all the little figures would come to life for me, and become my friends and play with me. I wanted them to take me back with them into their world, which I knew had to be the best, best place to live. I tried everything, I tried magic, spells, mind power—to make them come alive. But of course they never did."

There wasn't a hint of sadness in her voice, but it was the most personal, private thing she had said all evening, and I felt a rush of affection for her. Lina turned off the holograms and the green light was replaced by a rosy emanation that again seemed to come from no one fixed point.

"Now, this color is good old whorehouse red," she said with a broad smile. "Would you like a drink?"

"How about some more of that Special?"

She shook her head. "No. That requires a degree of moderation, I'm sorry to say."

"All right, a drink then. Whatever you're having."

Lina slid a panel aside in the wall, and a light came on automatically in a bar compartment, complete with a sink and a small freezer. I didn't even bother to comment on it. A moment later she closed the bar and we were back in the rosy light, drinking Chartreuse and soda on ice. Lina put on a tape that alternated between bluesy jazz and instrumental reggae. The drinks were large, and we must have lounged there, sipping and staring at each other, for more than half an hour without speaking a word. We had reached a point where we were comfortable with each other, and had no need for talk to fill the space.

I tried to think. All that came to me was the mildly comic realization that I had started out this evening, long hours ago, hoping to clear up a little more of the puzzle that was Roger Nordhagen. Instead, I'd found an even more remarkable mystery: Lina Ravachol. Beyond that my mind lost focus, so easy and so pleasurable was it to lie back and gaze at the woman herself. Lina, Lina, Lina—she filled my mind.

Eventually, she put her glass aside and climbed the built-in steps out of the pit. I wasn't sure where she was going or if she would return right away, so I held back.

She came along the edge of the pit and stood there, six feet above me. She was letting me look up her skirt, which hung open. It was a transfixing moment, an erotic image out of long-forgotten childhood. Then her skirt swirled, and she disappeared.

I followed her through the kitchen and back into the front hallway, then up the stairs to the next floor. We went into the front room. A king-size bed with no headboard was pushed right up to the window overlooking the street, with pillows banked against the sill.

I went to her and we embraced. Her eyes were closed, her arms snaked around me, and her breath was fast, hissing through her teeth. We tumbled onto the bed and covered every inch of its considerable area many times. Lina struggled and writhed and tossed her body, more and more frantically. We shed our clothes like snakes escaping unwanted skin, until I was naked and she wore only those two silvery stockings. Then my snake-woman coiled and twined about me in a fury. Her strength amazed and excited me—I was a man trying to rape a python. Suddenly I pinned her face down and slid into her from behind, and she accepted at once, and at last we moved as one. We roared into each other like two storms on an open sea, becoming a single cataclysmic explosion. And finally we surfaced in some new place of perfect stillness.

We drifted in and out of sleep together—it may have been three hours or only one, but it seemed a long, delicious spell, and I felt a great sadness when the grey light of morning would not be denied. A milk cart hummed by on the street outside. A few early birds were on their way somewhere.

"Where are we?" I had no idea.

"Where do you think you are?"

"Nowhere on earth."

Lina smiled approvingly. "My house is like nowhere on earth, so you see, you're right." Then she pointed to the park across the road. "That's Queens Wood. I love that place. I'll never leave here."

"I don't know how you can even leave this place to go to work every day."

"It's a remnant of the great primeval forest of Britain," Lina continued. "It's rather sad now, but not to me. I still love it. It's beautiful. It used to be called Church-yard Bottom Wood, and it's as haunted a piece of ground as you can find anywhere. During the time of the plague they dug a huge pit and threw the bodies in. Now it's a park. Mothers push babies in prams, kids run and play games, teenage boys and girls grope each other nervously, and tramps drink cheap spirits there. But just a few feet away, beneath all of them, hundreds, maybe thousands of bodies are buried. It's a huge, forgotten cemetery."

I wasn't surprised. It seemed appropriate. For, after all I had experienced in the past twelve hours—those moments of sexual union far more intense than any I'd ever known, and most of all this woman—I felt as if I'd somehow reached the end of my life. And I didn't mind.

FIVE

But it wasn't over yet. I fell back to sleep thinking Lina would wake me in an hour or so, she'd go to work, I'd go back to West Kensington, and that would be the end of it. As if it had all been a glorious dream that vanishes at sunrise. I couldn't believe that Lina, a woman like Lina, would long be entertained by the likes of me.

But when Lina woke me, it was nearly noon. She wore purple gym shorts and a matching basketball shirt that said Lakers across the front. The outfit went well with her dark hair and pale skin. Oh, yes, I thought, I can take it. Keep the dream going a little while longer, please.

I'd forgotten that my appointment with Nordhagen had been for Friday evening. That made this Saturday morning. Lina didn't have to go to work. Neither of us had to go anywhere. We had the whole weekend to ourselves. Thanks again, Roger. I wondered briefly if he had planned it this way all along, but I didn't care. I was more than willing to see this out.

We went downstairs—Lina gave me an oversized gym robe to wear—and had brunch on the sunken waterbed.

She didn't spend much time cooking, just sizzled a couple of fat Wiltshire steaks and served them with three bottles of champagne and a jug of orange juice. We watched an old film called *Dark Eyes of London* on the VCR. Bela Lugosi did a lot of lurking about in it but I couldn't keep my attention on the movie.

"I'm beginning to think this place is a local branch of the Feathers," I said.

"Sssh."

I put my head in her lap and started kissing and licking her thighs, getting my tongue up under her shorts. It became a game, in which I tried to draw her away from the movie and she resisted my ministrations. It was a good game, and a short film.

And a long weekend. We never left the house. We played games, lots of them, all different and all wonderful. We drank, though it never seemed to slow us down, and we even ate a little more food. Lina kept all the windows curtained shut, except for the upstairs front, overlooking Queens Wood.

Sometime, late Saturday night, I think, we took another dose of Special. This time Lina put us apart from each other, on either side of the aquarium. There were deep soft cushions arranged so you could lie there with your face resting inches from the glass. I saw her on the other side, through the swaying plants and the bright, darting fish, but then the drug took hold and I lost sight of everything. It was even better than the first time, but later, when it was over, I felt unhappy and a little worried. It made me feel *too good*, as if everything else in the universe were obsolete and unnecessary—including Lina. I didn't want that. I wanted to keep on wanting her, and having her. When I explained this to her, the warmest, sweetest, most natural smile lit up her face and she kissed me.

"You're lovely," she said. "We won't take it again."

"What's in it, by the way?"

"I can't tell you that."

If I had to guess, I might say it was heroin, but I'd never heard of it being taken in pill form, under the tongue. And besides, I really didn't want to think about it. One enthralling seduction was all I could deal with, and that was Lina.

How else could I describe what had happened? She had wined and dined me, dazzled me with her toys and her beauty, and she had seduced me. It was like an exaggerated reversal of the stereotypical playboy methodology, and when I thought about it, I almost laughed. Not that it bothered me; on the contrary, I'd loved every minute of it, and I wanted only more and more of the same. But there was still something relentless about it.

These thoughts occupied me Monday morning as the taxi took me back to Matheson Road. I felt like the residue of a human being—all that was left after a long weekend of sexual athletics, drink, drugs, and lack of sleep. Lina had said, yes, of course, when I asked her if I would see her again, but as soon as the cab let her out in Mount Street and I lost her sustaining presence, doubts and questions sprang up in my mind. Something seemed wrong, and I was afraid I knew what it was.

I bought a newspaper in North End Road, but I couldn't read it. I couldn't do anything but lie around the flat all day. I did sleep for a while, but woke feeling sweaty and cramped. The spider lady—that's how I was thinking of Lina then. But if I was the willing suicidal fly, why did I feel as if I'd been gently disentangled? No, it wasn't that. What was wrong was spontaneity, or the lack of it. I'm not talking about love at first sight, but simply of two people meeting, hitting it off quickly, and shifting directly into overdrive. But that wasn't how it had happened; not quite. Lina had moved on me from the moment we met in Nordhagen's office. That process may be all right when you're undergoing it, but later it is somewhat disquieting. It all seemed too good to be true, even though I wanted it to be true.

Late in the afternoon I went out for a walk. The weak English sun was making another brief appearance. It felt cold and harsh, and even the air bothered me. For the first time, my neighborhood looked dreary and depressed. There was something clammy about it, as if the houses and buildings were dead, vacant shells left by a receding ocean. I felt uncomfortable, and my mood wasn't improved when I went into a pub. The place was dank and dark—it was just a few minutes past opening time—and the beer tasted sour. Lina was right. I had taken a lot of the fantasy out with me, and back here reality was no fun.

In my flat that night I hung around restlessly. I thought about going into the West End for diversion, but I couldn't muster the energy or the enthusiasm. I hadn't phoned Lina during the course of the day. I might have imagined it, but it seemed we had a tacit agreement that we needed a day or two to recover from the weekend. Now I was sorry I hadn't called anyhow, and I was even unhappier that I'd somehow neglected to get her home number. It wasn't in the directory, and the exchange couldn't give it to me.

I wondered about Lina and Nordhagen. What sort of relationship did they have? It was painful to think about. All kinds of dark suspicions entered my mind. One weekend was all it had taken—I was breaking out in rampant paranoia. Had Nordhagen set me up with Lina? Why? And why had she gone along so willingly? What was it all about?

This absurd exercise ended mercifully with a knock on

my door. A familiar tap-tap. It was Eileen Fothergill. Neighbor. The veneer trade. Five-pound Danish ham. It was all coming back to me, like debris washed up from some other life.

"Hello," she said with alarming cheerfulness. "I was just wondering if you'd like to have a glass of sherry . . . ?"

At last, the sherry.

"Uh, oh, gee, that'd be nice," I said. "But not tonight, I'm afraid. I'm going out in a few minutes."

"Oh, well."

"Ronnie Scott's," I explained further. "I'm meeting someone there. First show starts just after ten."

It was a plausible lie, and Eileen accepted it.

"Another time, then," she said. "I noticed you were away for the weekend."

"Uh, yes."

"That's nice. Did you see some of our countryside?"

This just about paralyzed me. I had no desire to tell her anything, but it would be tricky to lie about some place in the country I had never seen—she might know it well.

"Well, not really. I was with some friends in North London. Distant friends of my family back home." Now I had it. "I'd been putting off seeing them, kind of an obligation, you know. But now it's taken care of, and it was nice."

It wasn't a great story. In fact, it didn't make much sense at all, but Eileen was too polite to take it any further. After extracting a promise that I would have sherry with her soon, she went away. Ugly, I thought, she really is kind of ugly, with that incipient white mustache. And sad. I hadn't noticed or thought about it before, but Eileen was a sad woman. Sherry—hell!

My ad-lib excuses made it necessary to go out after all, so I drank in a nightclub off Oxford Street. It was an expensive place, and the atmosphere was oppressive. It was full of the usual crowd of Arabs, Eurocrats, and marketing executives eager to sell Britain, even on a Monday night. The floor show was glitzy, and I didn't look twice at any of the wandering hostesses. Still, I stuck it out until three in the morning. Inertia maintained by alcohol.

The next day was passed in a kind of masochistic experiment. I stayed in, moped about the flat, did nothing but listen to music on the radio. I deliberately did not call Lina. I wanted to, and I almost did a couple of times, but I held out. What did this exercise teach me about myself? By evening I was in a state of acute distress. She really had me. That Special had been great stuff, but Lina Ravachol was my drug and I was exhibiting sharp withdrawal symptoms. I had a hard time sleeping that night. The following morning I called Nordhagen's offices early. Lina answered, and I felt better at once.

"I can't talk now," she said.

"When?"

"Ring tomorrow."

"Tomorrow? Why not later today, or tonight?"

"I can't help it."

That line kept me thinking all day and half the night. And the next morning we had virtually the same conversation. I hung up feeling sure a message was being delivered to me. Good-bye. Nice to have met you, Tom; so long now. I put another dent in the West End's liquor stock that night. But another startling turn lay just ahead.

A couple of nights later I was aimless in Soho, and, for no other reason than a pint of beer, I went into the Carlisle. Nordhagen sat at the bar. It was still early but he was already half in the bag. His eyes were watery, and he spoke with plodding care. But he did recognize me at once.

"Tom. Good to see you. Have a seat, dear boy."

I had a drink with him, then we had several more.

Nordhagen put on a we-should-see-more-of-each-other attitude, as if I had been avoiding him. I was going to mention that he was supposed to ring me to arrange a new dinner date, but considering his present condition there didn't seem much point.

We left the cozy confines of the Carlisle and headed down the now-familiar low road of drinking clubs. It was Seedy Dives Night, not High Times at the Feathers. But I went along, glad to have made contact with the little doctor again. Not that he was my main interest anymore. At Terry's or Toby's or some other such den, I began to question him about Lina.

"Ah, there's a beautiful child," he said thickly.

Then he gave me a long, very sly, cagey look, and I thought he was daring me to try to get more information out of him. We danced all around the subject of Lina Ravachol for some time, and I can't say I learned much. What discretion and secrecy didn't muffle, drink did. Finally I decided to stop being cautious, and to try bluntness. I had already resigned myself, at least partly, to having no future with Lina, since that's the way I read the signals. I figured I had nothing to lose.

"Does she have a boyfriend, or anything like that?"

Nordhagen smiled into his wine. "No, no," he said. "Not at all, nothing of the sort."

"Oh, well. Uh, I'd like to go out with her again. Do you think that's a good idea, Roger?"

"Smashing. Why not? She's there."

He made her sound like Mount Everest. But then Nordhagen arrived at one of those temporary interludes of calm and clarity that sometimes bedevil an intoxicated person. He became serious and earnest.

"Tom, I've been meaning to talk to you. I want you to work with me. Your future is here, you know."

It was clear to him, no doubt, but it made no sense to me. I knew next to nothing about his line of medicine, even if I could somehow qualify to practice in Britain—which in itself seemed most unlikely. Nordhagen paused, waiting for me to say something, but I passed. He could carry this ball.

"She needs help," he said, more to himself than to me. "I can't do it anymore. Too old. Too much, it's too much."

I wrote it off as alcoholic rambling, along with most of what he said that night. But the drinking expedition was far from a total loss. I already had what I wanted from him: confirmation that I needn't give up my pursuit of Lina. If she wanted to put me off, I would make her do so explicitly, in simple words. There was no boyfriend, incredibly; there was no existing relationship I might threaten. Not at all. She was there. Okay, good, I'd try again. I would have anyhow, but now I had a little more hope.

Nordhagen's words came back to me the following afternoon. He always seemed to manage at least one verbal time bomb that took a day or so to detonate. "There's a beautiful child," he had said of Lina. Now I wondered, could she actually be his daughter? She held a job, but no medical assistant is paid enough to kit out a house the way she had. And she . . . But if she already had money of her own, why bother to work at all? On the other hand, if she was working for her father, who had loads of vanity money—well, that might explain a lot. The different surnames could be easily explained. Roger Nordhagen and Lina Ravachol. Two puzzles, or the same one? The more I learned, the less I understood.

When I got her on the telephone the next time, she didn't attempt to put me off, but she became terribly vague and uncertain. She stayed on the line, but there were long pauses during which she said nothing.

"Do you want to see me?" I asked.

"Yes."

"Okay, when?"

"I don't know. Soon. Maybe."

"Lina, what's the matter?"

"I don't . . . Nothing."

"Just tell me."

(. . .)

"Lina."

"I'm—sorry."

"You don't want to see me."

"Yes, yes, I do, but—oh . . . Another part of me doesn't want to do this to you, Tom."

"What? Do what?"

(. . .)

"I'm coming to see you, at the office or at your house."

"No, no, don't do that. I won't be there. Listen, I'll ring you, I promise. Please wait until I ring back."

I waited three days. My visit to London had veered off into a strange, dizzying spin, but there had been no other woman remotely like Lina in my life. I felt like I was being whipsawed. She was engaged in a reversal of old-fashioned coquettishness, apparently. In the traditional chase the woman promises much but withholds delivery as long as possible. With Lina, everything had been delivered up front, the first time—after which there was nothing. Oddly, the results were the same for the hapless male. She had my nerves and emotions strung out like a frayed clothesline. And all this air of heightened tension and mystery—it was beginning to look like a warped melodrama. I didn't like it, but I would put up with it as long as there was the slightest chance of getting back into the playground with Lina.

Saturday night she called. It was just past eight and I was lying on the couch in a state of mental mummification.

"Can you meet me in an hour?"

"Sure," I said eagerly.

"The Edgar Wallace Pub."

She gave me directions, and I got there in half an hour. I sat nervously with a pint of lager I really didn't want. Too many things were rushing through my head. Lina came in at nine precisely. She was in her fur coat and leather boots. I didn't give her a chance to speak. As soon as I had brought her a double Stoli on the rocks I started talking.

"There are some things I have to tell you," I said. "I want to see you. Every day will do, but if not every day, how about every night? Weeks on end, nothing less. Of course, we'll have to give each other a break now and then, time off for good behavior, and I was thinking of one day a month. But if that's too much, we could cut it down to an afternoon, or an hour or so. I guess you must think I like you, but that's not it. I mean, it is true, but it's like saying rain is wet—it doesn't give you any idea of what a thunderstorm is like. You see? Lina, last weekend I took a step off the deep end and I haven't found my footing since. I hope it's a beginning, I really hope it is. But if it's an end, I have to know that too. I don't know what this past week has been all about, but I can't go through another one like it."

She put a hand on mine and squeezed, long and hard. When she spoke her voice was very quiet.

"If you get into my life, you might never be able to get out of it again."

I thought about that, then said, "It sounds like you're trying to frighten me."

"I am."

I thought about that even more. "Well, I'm still here."

We sat there looking at each other for some time, my hand tightly in her grip. The drinks were dying of neglect.

"Come on," she said at last, rising from her seat.

A few minutes later we were walking across Waterloo Bridge. It was cool and drizzly, but it was also Saturday night, and the West End was full of people. We stopped halfway across the bridge. Lina hugged me to her against the railing. Over her shoulder I could see the dark oily water of the Thames swirling far below. Lina was kissing my neck, and then she had my overcoat unbuttoned.

"Come on," she whispered urgently. "Come on."

I was leaning on her, one arm wrapped around the back of her neck, the other hand thrust up inside her fur coat. I could feel the excitement escalating in her—and in me. She had my pants unzipped, and I was quickly in a state of aroused erotic terror.

"Fuck me," she moaned softly.

"Lina—"

"Fuck me—now—here—now—pleasepleaseplease—"

Under the miniskirt was only Lina, drawing me in, and again, again. . . .

"Oh, yes, oh, yes, yes, fuck me." Her voice tiny, brief as vapor in the night.

I made long slow movements that prolonged the event, but also enhanced it to an almost unbearable degree. People were passing by, walking within a few paces of us. Nobody seemed to take any special notice, and I could only hope we looked like any other smooching couple out on the town. We didn't stop for some time.

"Oh, God . . . I don't believe you," I told her when we finished. "I honest to God don't believe you." And I was thinking: Talk about getting your fantasies out on the street! Talk about scenarios of enactment!

But now I was glad, even proud we had done it. And that smile on her face—I knew right away I'd do anything to keep seeing that smile. It unlocked new parts of me. For the first time Lina looked as if she really did believe in me. I felt I had crossed a line, passed an important test, and I was glad, very glad.

Later, in the back of a taxi, I said, "All I have to do now is persuade you to come back to the States with me."

Lina gave a short, high-pitched laugh, as if I'd said the silliest thing.

Six

Life became not easier but ever stranger. I spent the rest of the weekend at Lina's house. Thirty-six hours of almost nonstop sex, drinking, and more sex. We were like whipped kittens early Monday morning when a hit of Special revived us both, but before that our relationship had veered into what were for me dark and uncharted waters.

We seemed to feed off each other, Lina leading, driving me on, my willingness and enthusiasm fueling her hunger. I was learning about myself, as well as about her. What a dull, blinkered, uneventful life I had lived on the other side of the ocean. I had been some other person, less and less recognizable to me now. A sleepwalker, one of the ambulatory functional dead. It was not that Lina was showing me the good life, as it is commonly thought of and portrayed in advertisements, but, rather, that she was leading me in a dance that drew us ever closer to the searing, terrifying inferno at the very heart of life. It might not seem that. It might appear that we were exploring the farthest, most decadent fringes of behavior, but later I came to see that was the only route to the blinding center of things.

Sometime Sunday evening Lina came downstairs. She had a brush and a small mirror mounted on a stand. She was wearing a virginal white chemisette, which, with her pale skin, made her look more like a ghost girl, an apparition, than a real person. She sat on the far side of the pit from me, as if I weren't there. She was braiding her long hair. I watched for a few minutes, astonished by the seeming endlessness of this woman's beauty.

I crawled across the waterbed, and Lina looked up at me, startled, as if she had never seen me before. When I reached for her she hit out at me, slapping my face so hard I was dazed, my ear burning. I thought she hadn't meant to be so forceful, that she was resisting playfully, but she didn't give me a chance to recover. She pushed me back, slapping, kicking, fighting as fiercely as any cornered animal. I tried to pin her down and smother her hands beneath me, but she could barely be contained. Her fingers drew blood on my shoulders and chest, and then her hands locked in an incredibly tight grip around my throat. I couldn't get a word out, and suddenly I was frightened, and angry, and I responded furiously. I slapped her, again and again. Her cheeks turned crimson, and blood came out of her nose, but that only increased her frenzy. It was as if, knowing that I was ultimately stronger, physically, than she was, Lina was nonetheless determined to fight, to make me use every ounce of that advantage. The rhythm of the action took over, pushing us both to the maximum, and for the first time in my life I learned what it is to be enflamed by the sight of blood, to answer force instinctively with even greater force. I realized she really did want to hurt me, *was* hurting me, and so I wanted to hurt her back. More than that, I wanted to punish her for starting this. The fight became something other than sex play. It became a turn in our relationship. From the moment we'd met, Lina had led the way, but now I sensed the time had come to take a new hand in it. I wanted to beat her at her own game, mentally as well as physically. The longer you play a game, the harder it is to think of it as a game at all.

I did hurt her, forced her, humiliated her sexually, and then raped her—that is the only word for it. When it was over, I moved a little away from her and sat back against a pillow, letting my breath slow down. We had a lot of each other's blood spattered on our bodies. I was shocked, as much by my own behavior as hers, but I didn't regret it. Okay, my mind said, here we are, now let's see what this place is. I felt as though I'd pulled even with her somehow.

In that aftermath of silence I could have said something like, "Hey, let's take it easy, huh?" or "What the hell was that all about?" or a million other foolish things. But I said nothing. I was on course with her, and I had no interest in getting off. You want to screw on Waterloo Bridge with pedestrians passing by, okay. You want to try to tear out my throat, okay, try. There is as much to me as there is to you. Let's keep on seeing what it is and where it takes us.

And I was rewarded. As Lina lay there in her tattered white chemisette, her face smeared with blood and semen, that smile came back, a subtle transformation at the corners of her mouth and in her eyes. What did I see in that smile? That she was proud of me? That she felt she hadn't made a mistake? Perhaps even a sense of wonder that she had, after all, found someone equal to her? I wondered if I was imagining all this, if it was just something my ego had conjured up in the wake of sexual violence. But I didn't think so, because I had never seen that look on anyone's face before. And if a man needs to see anything else in a woman, I don't know what it is.

Later that night Lina and I made love again, as sweetly and gently as lovers in a daydream romance.

The days that followed were lost in withdrawal pains. West Kensington was beginning to seem as far away from where I wanted to be as America. I resented— hated—my time away from Lina. I had one nightmare, the constant fear that I would be restricted to seeing her only on weekends—and I had only a limited number of them left in my London visit. It was infuriatingly diffi- cult to see her, even in a pub, during the week. Nothing I could do or say worked. When the next weekend finally came, I did manage to get her talking about it.

"Is Nordhagen your father?"

"God, no." She laughed.

"He seems to own you during the week."

"I can't help it."

"What is it between the two of you? It isn't just an or- dinary employer-employee relationship, is it?"

"I can't tell you that," Lina said.

I'd heard that before, and I did consider the possibility that it was her way of confirming my worst suspicions.

"What is he like, really?" I pushed on. "I mean, I know he is one of the best cosmetic surgeons in Britain, and he has a thriving practice in Mayfair. The rich and super- rich follow their noses to his door, so it's not surprising he's involved in a place like the Feathers—which fits that wisecrack about a place God would own if only He could afford it. But then, other times I see him and he's juiced to the eyeballs, stumbling around from one Soho dump to another."

"It's complicated."

"Tell me."

"Roger was a brilliant surgeon," Lina said. "And he still is, no question about that. But there are problems. Not just the drink—he has that well in control, confined to regular, carefully planned and scheduled . . . binges. But there's something else."

"Is he ill?"

"I don't know, but I do know for sure that his age is wearing on him more. This last year it seems he's begun to die slowly inside."

"Why doesn't he retire and take it easy? He's loaded. He could relax and enjoy his old age on the Costa del Something-or-other."

"That wouldn't help; he's not that way inclined. Besides, the practice is the smallest part of his involvements. You might say it's only the tip of the iceberg, actually. There are other things he can't just walk away from."

"Such as?"

"I can't tell you that."

Back to Go, but do not collect £200. I had been thinking he kept a busy social calendar, or something like that, but Lina's last response seemed to blow that notion right out of the water. No matter what I heard, no matter how much more I was told, no questions were answered—only new ones raised.

"I still don't understand why I can't see you weeknights."

Lina nodded her head sympathetically. "I don't like it either, but that's the way it has to be, for now. But soon, I promise. Soon." And the word seemed to linger in the air, resonating with unspoken possibilities.

We talked every day. I worked hard to keep her on the phone a minute or two longer each time. It was desperately unsatisfactory, but it kept me going. I didn't completely understand it at first, but those five-day interludes also served to put the initiative back on her side. By the time the weekend arrived, I was a panting pup, hot and ready to please. When calm and equilibrium were regained, it was Monday again.

But one Wednesday night Lina surprised me. It was early, I wasn't thinking of going into town, but I didn't know what to do. Sitting around and moping was awful, and I'd probably end up in some dire nightclub in spite of myself. I heard the sound of fingernails scratching at my door. It must be Eileen Fothergill, I thought; the woman had finally gone over the edge. But no, it was Lina. Before I could overcome my surprise and say something, she had gently but firmly pushed me back into the darkened bedroom, pushed me down on the bed, and made love to me.

"A little present for you," she said softly. "I'll have another, much better, one for you. Very soon."

Then she slipped out and was gone. I couldn't move. I was sprawled across the bed, thinking: Don't let this end I don't know what it is love or madness but don't let it end not yet not yet. . . .

When Friday came and I turned up at Nordhagen's offices to pick up Lina, he was there to greet me in the waiting room. He was impeccably dressed, clear-eyed and genial.

"Lina will be out shortly, Tom," he told me. "Have a seat, why don't you. Would you care for a drink?"

We had whiskey and sat facing each other in the fat leather chairs. I was in a good mood because I was about to see Lina, and the waiting room had a comfortable, clubby feeling.

"You're a fortunate young man," Nordhagen said. "Normally I don't put much stock in luck, but sometimes it happens that the right person appears in the right place at the right time. Is that luck, or destiny? An irreversible process, in any event. Let's just call it good fortune, for it surely is that. Cheers."

Maybe I was being deliberately obtuse, but I had no idea what the little doctor was talking about. Did he think I was going to marry Lina? The notion was quaint. Not that I have anything against marriage, but my relationship with Lina seemed to have passed marriage by. It was on some higher, more intense level, and was still on the way up as far as I was concerned. Marriage suggested a certain plateau, a quietus even—the last thing likely with Lina and me. Why try to dam up a mighty river when the best thing you can do is enjoy it for all it is? Our relationship worked because it was open and undefined; it was a dynamic, a force, not a static thing or a mere fact.

Nordhagen was talking about London now, how was I liking it and so on. I was only half in the conversation, going through the motions. I was too close to Lina, my drug, to concentrate on small talk. But then Nordhagen got through to me.

"So, are you thinking of staying on here?"

The end of my time in London. Possibly the end of my time with Lina. The return to work in America. All this made up a sharp facet of reality I wasn't prepared to deal with yet. It loomed in the near distance like a thundercloud. I could try to ignore it for the time being, but I knew it would catch up with me eventually.

"I really don't know," I answered. "I haven't given it much thought. I'd love to stay, but I really don't see how that would be possible."

"One must go where one belongs," Nordhagen declared rather pompously. "Or stay where one belongs. Whichever the case may be."

He was in that kind of mood, but it did me no good to laugh silently at him. I felt like a small bettor on the verge of being forced out of a big poker game for lack of funds. But Lina appeared just then, to rescue me before depression could take hold.

On Mount Street I started looking for a cab, but Lina

took my arm. "Let's go to the Feathers first," she said. "Or somewhere else, if you like. We have to have a talk."

I was a little worried, since I couldn't imagine why we had to go anywhere other than her house by Queens Wood to do our talking. By the time we reached the Feathers I was convinced she had bad news to break to me, but when we were seated in the piano bar Lina was cheerful, even excited. She could hardly wait for the girl to bring our drinks and go away so that she could begin.

"Remember when we were talking about fantasy, and you asked me what my special fantasy was?"

"Sure."

"And I wouldn't tell you. Have you wondered since then what it might be?"

"Well, yes. But I can't imagine. Everything about you and the way you live seems to me to be one gigantic fantasy. That's what I like about it. Among other things."

"But one specific thing," she urged me on.

"When I first saw the inside of your house, I thought, This is it. This is her special fantasy, her house."

"But . . ."

"But it isn't, I guess."

"No."

"Then, when we fucked on Waterloo Bridge, I thought that really had to be your big sexual fantasy. But I guess it isn't what you're talking about either. They're minor fantasies, among many other minor fantasies. But still not the main one. Am I right?"

"Yes. Now go on from there."

"I don't know. As I said, I can't imagine what it might be. Anything would be fine with me."

We were sitting close together, but Lina moved even closer when I said that. She had on another slit skirt, and she held my hand tightly between her legs in a press of warm, silky thigh. Even in the dim light her eyes were bright with fire.

"Do you really mean that?" she asked. "Is it fine with you? Anything? Anything at all?"

I had already learned not to take anything Lina said as a joke. "Absolutely," I told her. I felt a nervous thrill, but I wasn't turning back. "Do you know that Dylan line: 'I'll let you be in my dream if I can be in yours.'"

"All right," Lina said. "That's it exactly. And you're in mine, and tonight we'll make it happen."

I was right where I wanted to be.

"Now, remember," Lina continued, "I told you I'd have another present for you? That's part of it too. You have to accept this gift I'm going to give you. You *have* to, otherwise the whole thing falls apart."

"No problem."

"Once we start, there's no turning back."

"I'm with you, I really am."

"All right. Good."

Lina would say no more. She rested her head on my shoulder in the taxi. It was windy and raining, and traffic was slow. There was nothing to be seen but blurred lights through the water-streaked windows of the car. I was glad we were headed for her house in North London—it seemed we wouldn't have to do this number out in public, which suited me fine.

But another one of Nordhagen's verbal time bombs went off in my head during the drive. "An irreversible process," he had said earlier, and now those three words seemed to take on an added significance. I was caught up in something I couldn't claim fully to understand. But I didn't want out. What if Lina wanted me to help her steal the crown jewels? Would I balk at such folly? I didn't know. I wasn't sure there was anything that could make me back away from Lina.

Once we were inside the house, we left our coats and shoes in the front hallway.

"We're going upstairs," Lina said, taking me by the hand.

But we didn't go into the bedroom. We went on up to the top floor. I hadn't seen it, nor had it interested me until now. There had always been more than enough to occupy me on the two floors below, and I had assumed this was just an attic. It wasn't. We came to a small landing. There was one door, locked. Lina had a key in her other hand.

"Another playground," I said.

"Yes, that's right. Another playground. A very special one. Now, out of your clothes."

She was helping me, unbuttoning my shirt, unbuckling my belt. It was easy to go along with this. I returned the favor, getting her skirt and blouse off, but she stopped me at that point.

"When we go in," she said, "you can't turn back. And not a word, not one. Now, listen carefully, Tom. Once we're inside, you're going to forget about me. I won't be there for you, do you understand? I said I had a present for you, and it's in that room. You're going to do whatever you want, whatever comes to you. And we're not coming out until it's over. *Whatever.*"

There was an edge in Lina's voice I hadn't heard before. Barely contained excitement edged unmistakably with fear. Her expression, her entire body language, seemed to say that something was about to happen that even she might not be able to control once it started. And that aroused my own sense of fear. I had the queasy intimation that the rest of my life, my past, America, my medical career, could all still be retrieved if I turned away from this door now—and that they might be lost if I didn't. I looked at Lina, and the hesitation dissolved within me.

"I thought this was your fantasy."

"Seeing yours is mine."

"Hey, I don't even know mine."

Lina had the look of someone dealing with a stubborn child. "I found yours for you," she said. "See if I'm wrong."

"Lina." Her eyes met mine. "I have this weird feeling, like I'm putting my life in your hands. Literally." That brought out the smile I wanted, needed, and then she kissed me. "All right," I said. "Let's go." I was excited, nervous, scared. An image came into my mind, familiar from a travel film or television clip out of the past. Where was it? Acapulco? A skinny teenager poised on the edge of a high cliff. Below: the rocks, the ebb and flow of the surf. He times it right and dives. He always makes it. That kid could be my brother now, I thought, because, although timing might not have so much to do with it, I felt that I too was diving into the unknown, hoping I would land safely. Somewhere.

We went into the room. It was all inky blackness, and I couldn't make anything out. I heard the lock click on the inside. I groped around, got the door, a wall, but Lina was somewhere out of reach. I was on my own, and it wasn't a comfortable feeling in these circumstances. It's hard to exaggerate your vulnerability when you're naked in total darkness in a place you've never been and where you have no idea what to expect. I was waiting, hoping my eyes would adjust somehow. If I stepped forward would I plunge my foot into razor blades or an attic beehive? I edged into the room a little more. The floor was covered with what felt like canvas or tarp, and I wondered about that. Meanwhile, my eyes didn't seem to be adjusting at all. There was just no light to pick up.

Suddenly a strobe blinked once, dazzling me, blinding me, then immediately leaving me in darkness again. But I thought I'd caught a glimpse of something ahead. The strobe flashed again. It was mounted in the ceiling over the center of the room, and the shape I'd seen was directly under it. I went that way. When I got there, the strobe began emitting short, staccato bursts. I was going on the most fleeting of half-images, blindly groping for something to grab onto.

The shape I'd seen was a large wooden T-bar, solid as a tree. As soon as I touched it I heard what could only be a chain clanking very close by, and it terrified me. I thought some animal was about to leap on me. But the next explosion of white light revealed a human figure, short, slight, female. In the ensuing blackness I thought it must be Lina—but no, Lina was taller. The strobe came again, quicker this time, as if it were tied to my progress, and I saw the face of an Oriental girl. Her arms were handcuffed behind her back, the cuffs linked to a length of chain, which was bolted to the T-bar. In the last flash of light before another temporary blackout, I saw the girl's fear of me.

I stood paralyzed through one or two more bursts of strobe, unsure what to do. Many things entered my mind. First, this was Lina's fantasy, and I was expected to do something. I had already refused the offer of one girl at the Feathers. Now Lina was giving me another one, to do with whatever I desired. *Whatever*, she had said. It reminded me of the slave fantasy I'd talked about with the stripper in Soho, although this was on a grander scale. Scenarios of enactment. If the girl resisted, well, I had already rehearsed rape and violence. But it all seemed too contrived and artificial. Still, I had to act. Why was I even thinking at all?

And then the simplest, most obvious explanation occurred to me. This girl had to be here voluntarily. Lina couldn't really have someone imprisoned in her attic. The girl, however frightened she looked, was not here against her will. She had been hired by Lina, and she would be compensated for her services. She was a performer, she would play her part in the game. And what was the game? Sex, surely, embellished with bondage. A little sadomasochism. As fantasies go, this one was hardly new. It seemed almost quaintly Victorian, and that reassured me. I'd expected something else, something more, from Lina. This, I could handle easily enough.

I went up behind the girl. She stood, frozen. She wore only a thin slip. I took her hair in my hand and pulled her head back onto my chest. The strobe didn't let up now, and abruptly the girl and I were hit by green rays of light, thin pencil beams that shot out from six or eight different places in the surrounding darkness. It shook me for a moment when I realized they were lasers. But they didn't hurt—theatrical-show lasers, dramatic but not strong enough to burn. It must have been a sight, the two of us in a crude sexual stance in a canopy of strobe light, bisected by a jangle of green laser lines. I hoped Lina liked the show. Then we were ringed by wispy, dancing holograms, ghosts that made up a menagerie of strange beasts close around us, dissolving in and out of the other light displays. Everything was in place, I guessed.

And I was ready too, a little surprised at how easily I had been aroused. I took the Oriental girl standing, quickly, clinically, efficiently. Then I spun her around and put her to work in other ways. I was getting into this weird show. The girl required a certain amount of force, but was compliant when prodded.

When I began to lose interest, I noticed a key taped to the upper edge of the T-bar. It was too high for the girl to reach even if she jumped, but I could get it without difficulty. As I thought, the key unlocked her handcuffs, freeing her. I figured that would give the game an extra dimension. I was right.

The girl responded instantly, scurrying out of sight. The strobe had slowed to random bursts. Where was she? This was the best part of the game. The chase. I moved cautiously, peering through the geometry of lasers and the ghost circus, using the brief flashes of strobe to search for the girl.

I heard the metal sound of the chain, and before I knew what was happening it hit me, the full length of chain wrapping around my legs, battering my knees, coiling tight and yanking me off my feet. I fell to the floor hard, hurt and stunned. The chain was ripped away, and I knew my legs were torn. I wasn't sure I could even stand up, but before I had a chance to try, the chain flew at me a second time, smacking across my back and banging the side of my head. I was crawling, rolling, trying to find escape in the darkness. My body wasn't working much better than my brain, which rang with alarm and fear. I knew now I was in real danger. If that chain hit me cleanly on the head I'd be in very serious trouble. I kept moving in what I hoped was the right direction—back and away from the T-bar, out of range.

I caught sight of it in a spasm of light, and I knew I was safe for the moment. The chain hung by itself. But where was the girl? I was like a stunned boxer trying to recover. I was angry, eager to strike back and regain control of the situation. I was embarrassed more than shocked—I should have anticipated violence in the game. I was still thinking of it in this easy way, as a game. My mind was not yet ready to accept what should have been obvious. I was in free fall, flying through clear air, the landing still out of sight.

I used the light to look around, then went where it had been clear as soon as the blackness returned. In this way I thought I was searching for the girl and keeping myself safe at the same time. The strobe picked up, like a nervous pulse, and that seemed to tell me I was getting closer. I felt really shaky but I thought I would be all right as long as I stayed out of reach of the chain. I intended to reconnect the girl to that chain, whatever it took to do so, and then I would see what I could devise as punishment.

But in an eruption of strobe light the girl was suddenly flying through the air at me, and in her hand was a big shiny knife, zooming out of the mouth of a hologram monster. I cried out, scared as I'd never been in my life. I fell to the side, trying to dodge the attack, but the knife scraped my ribs, and I could feel fresh warm wetness all over that part of my body. I was shocked by what was happening now. The silver blade had seemed unreal flashing out of the dark at me. But here was real blood, my blood, hot and too real, washing out of my body. The game had changed, and I was dimly beginning to think that it wasn't a game at all.

I didn't know how badly I was cut, but I wrestled frantically with the girl, trying to lock on the hand with the knife. I was sure now that she would stick me with it again and again, until I was gone. I dimly recalled what Lina had said to me: I won't be there for you. I was on my own. I had no choice. I knew that running would keep me on the defensive, hunted and exposed. I had to stop it right now.

I saw the blade and grabbed at it. The touch of steel turned my hand into an open wound, slick and sticky-hot. One by one, parts of me were turning into local conflagrations. But I didn't dare let go of the knife to try for a better hold. I used my other hand to punch the girl's face, then I went for the knife handle. Even as I did, her slender legs clamped around my throat, tightening like a hydraulic press. In no time my air was cut off, and lights flared and popped like balloons breaking in my head. Insanely, a wee voice at the back of my brain told me this girl was probably quite good at martial arts. Most of my body was useless because of the position she had me in, but I still had a bleeding hand on the knife and I continued to punch wildly at her body. I kicked off the floor with my aching legs, using my weight advantage, and that pushed us over. I rocked my whole body on her, crushing her under me. I had the knife suddenly free in my hand. It should have been over then, I told myself later. A game would have ended at that point. But there was one more movement to be played out. Lina's fantasy.

I sat up, the girl pinned beneath me. But she didn't lie still for a moment. She lunged forward, her hands grabbing at my balls. As soon as I felt her sharp nails clawing, the whole lower part of my body jumped back instinctively. I fell forward on the girl and put one hand on the floor to hold myself up. Now her hands were on my face in a flurry of scratching and digging, tearing my skin. I screamed in rage and fear and shook my head violently as I felt her fingernails at my eyes.

And the last pretense vanished in me. Wordlessly, at some level below thought, the realization finally took hold that the girl had no intention of stopping. She hadn't been hired for this; it was a life-or-death struggle to her. She wanted to scar me, mutilate me, kill me. She had become a frenzied animal, and she would literally tear me to pieces if I let her. I was caught in a killing dream with her, and like the slow-moving figure at the center of every dream, I was only beginning to understand what was happening.

Even then, I believe, I didn't want to hurt that girl permanently. I wanted to punch her into unconsciousness and put the chains back on her. It could have ended that way, bloody and brutal, but with no lasting damage done.

It didn't, because by then I was as much an animal as the girl was. I reacted furiously, seized with fear and anger as she tried to put my eyes out. I swung wildly at her with both hands, slapping, punching—not noticing I was pounding the knife into her body until the girl's hands fell to the floor and the life began to rattle out of her in a fine spray, like some dying sea storm. And then I became aware of the blood, jetting and spurting up out of half a dozen or more wounds I'd inflicted.

I was hunched over the girl. Somewhere, distantly, I felt relieved that I had survived the savage assault. But I was sobbing now, crying loudly at what had taken place. At what I had done. I couldn't believe it. I had never hurt anyone. How could I have let this come to pass?

"No-o-o-o," I shrieked.

The mad room swallowed it effortlessly. I felt alone, so alone, as the silence closed around me like the cloak of death. The strobe, the lasers, and the ghostly holograms continued to play the darkness, but I felt as if I were hardly there at all anymore. I was like a sun that had suddenly reversed its history, exploding back into its primordial cloud of swirling, scattered gases. I felt like I was disappearing. I seemed to have no center anymore.

Lina appeared, and I flung myself on her, grateful to have a new point of focus. We were at each other in a fury, as if through sheer driving force we could merge our two bodies and minds into one complete being. And so we made love there, in the blood spill, as if for the first and last time. We made love out of despair. We had burned and blasted out the deepest, most hidden pockets of ourselves, and now we had to see who we were that remained.

Later Lina led me out of the darkness. She cleaned my body and dressed my wounds, then washed herself. My mind was sluggish. I could have argued that I'd been tricked, misled, seduced into something I'd never wanted to happen. She had put my life in jeopardy, and that had brought about the death of another person. I could have insisted we clear this up properly, legally, whatever the consequences. But at the same time I rejected all this as stupid and pointless. I hadn't really been tricked. I'd been given every chance to back off, but I'd been where I wanted to be every step of the way. It was that simple. I couldn't fool myself. I wasn't a victim in this. I was a man in love with a fantasy, and that had turned me into a killer. A victim only of myself. But Lina was more than a fantasy—she was still real, she was there with me, and I still loved her. More now, I thought, since this new blood reality had surely bonded us yet more intimately to each other.

The love Lina and I shared was like an exotic plant that had to grow its own way, become whatever it was destined to be. It couldn't be cultivated or curtailed, or in any way directed. It had to follow its own sweet anarchy or die, and I surely didn't want it to die. I felt closer to Lina than ever. This new plane of existence was fearful, but also exhilarating.

Lina touched my face, as if she knew my thoughts.

"Now you know," she said quietly. "The ultimate fantasy is also the only reality. The two are one and the same. And you know what it is, don't you?"

"Power."

Lina smiled.

"Yes," she said. "Yes. Power." Her eyes held mine. "You are here because you believe. You understand now what you didn't before. That this is what drove you to leave the emptiness behind. That this is what brought you here, thousands of miles. You came to find the pure force of nature, to touch it and have it touch you, to have it flow through you. Now it overwhelms you, but soon you will learn how to master it, and you'll never be the same again. That other person you were is dead and gone. All your life has led you to this moment, and you know it's right."

I looked out the window at the park across the street. Queens Wood. I thought I could see through the trees and bushes. Down into the underworld there. I could see the bodies. I could see thousands of skeletons. All of them, locked in the earth.

"Yes," I said.

SEVEN

I said yes, but a couple of days later I was hundreds of miles away and in another country. It was impossible for me to sit still in my flat. I seemed to have only marginal control over my body. My nerves were agitated, my heart pounded frighteningly, and my hands wouldn't stop trembling. I felt light-headed and dizzy if I walked from one room to another. I kept going to the toilet, even when there was nothing left in me to get rid of. I tried to eat, knowing that hunger only made things worse, but it was all I could do to finish an apple, and that was no help.

My mind went from one extreme to another, and was filled with terrifying visions. I would go from depths of remorse and anguish to a cold, numb indifference. I was appalled at what had happened in Lina's house, at what I had done. But more than that, I knew fear, real fear, for the first time in my life.

Every moment I sat there, I told myself feverishly, brought me closer to the moment when the police would arrive, knocking down the door and dragging me away. I saw newspaper headlines and television reports around the world, all the way back to my dull little hometown in Ohio. Old neighbors and people I'd worked with in New Haven would be commenting about me in public: he was this, he was that, he always seemed . . . There were times when all I could think was that I wished the girl had killed me. To die like that would be horrible and pointless, but to survive with such a crime around my neck seemed even worse, somehow.

As soon as I had left Lina's house, the magic had begun to fade. The fantasy had paled into insignificance beside the terrible new fact that had taken over my life. I don't know if I was coming out of a dream or out of shock, but by the time I had reached my street I had felt utterly alone and ruined by the realization of what had taken place in Queens Wood.

No matter how hard I tried to explain it to myself, it was impossible to make sense of such an incident. Who was the Asian girl I'd killed? How had she come to be chained up in Lina's attic? It was all Lina's doing, obviously; it was her setup. But I still loved Lina, and my mind couldn't handle the thought that she might be psychopathic. I didn't want to believe that she had actually wanted a death to occur—though her reaction, the extraordinary fury of her lovemaking in all that blood, seemed to be pretty graphic evidence that it was exactly what she wanted. It was so unreal that at odd moments I could almost persuade myself it had never happened. But the wounds on my body were no hallucination, and the dreadful knowledge I carried in my brain was inescapably final.

I went out just long enough to buy a bottle of Scotch. I drank until I fell asleep, woke sometime during the night and drank some more, until I passed out again. It was the joyless drinking after nothing but unconsciousness, oblivion. I can't remember dreaming at all, which is the only good thing I can say about that long night.

The next day I felt worse, a hangover compounding the aches in my body. A hot bath helped somewhat, but I still couldn't eat anything more substantial than a bowl of oxtail soup and some toast. I couldn't shake growing claustrophobia. I began throwing clean clothes in the smaller of my two suitcases. I had to get away for at least a few days, perhaps forever. London was suddenly too uncomfortable to bear, and although I had nowhere I really wanted to go, I had to go somewhere.

There was an atlas in the living room, and I opened it to a map of Western Europe. In the yellow pages I found a long list of airlines operating out of London. I sat staring at the map and the list for quite a while, like a man who had the plan for his survival right in front of him, if only he could decipher it.

Paris, Rome, Madrid, Amsterdam, Berlin, Copenhagen—all the wonderful cities. But I couldn't think of them the way a tourist does. I wasn't going anywhere to see anything, I was going to hide out. To rediscover myself, if that was possible. And as I sat there thinking about it, I saw that most of all I would be going for the purpose of getting myself out of the reach of Lina Ravachol. I had no idea what, if any, relationship I still had with her, and I had to find out. But I wouldn't be able to do that so long as I remained in London, under her immediate influence.

I tried to picture myself in various cities—Zurich, Brussels, Venice—but somehow they made me feel vulnerable and exposed. Portugal was out of the question, because I remembered reading that James Earl Ray had gone to ground there for a while, and he didn't seem a good example to follow. Maybe a Mediterranean resort, one of the islands, or even the coast of North Africa. But every place seemed either boring or unappealing. I was beginning to think Malta might be a good choice when I found an even better one: Luxembourg. A tiny country, tucked in among France, Germany, and Belgium. Easier to over-look than to find, but close enough to several major cities. A person could get stuck on an island, but Luxembourg would be a snap to get out of, should the need arise. You could walk across three different borders. I knew nothing about the place, but I had an instinctive feeling that it was the right choice. I phoned Luxair and was able to reserve a seat on their afternoon flight that day.

I had to hurry now, but the sudden rush was both a blessing and a relief. I finished packing my suitcase, put my passport in my inside jacket pocket, and checked every room in the flat before leaving. I walked to the bank for some traveler's checks and extra cash. I had no idea how long I'd be away, but I also had a credit card. On the North End Road I waved down a taxi, and an hour later I had checked in at Heathrow. I bought a *Herald Tribune* and skimmed through it over a double Scotch in the bar. I was still edgy but the drink helped, and I had no trouble getting through passport control. I knew I could be arrested just as easily in Luxembourg as in London, but when my jet took off I felt a little safer.

It was a short hop, less than an hour. I took the airport bus into the city, and at once I had the feeling I'd come an enormous distance to an entirely different world. An illusion, no doubt, but a strong one. The usual modern steel-and-glass buildings were there, but Luxembourg-Ville was also a city of ancient fortifications, and it had that old-world, fairy-tale look that London lacked. It was built on high ground broken by deep ravines and gorges that enhanced the magic-kingdom appearance of the place. I knew I was in Europe now—the Continent, not an offshore island.

I had no trouble finding a room near the central train station. I got one at the first place I tried, the Hotel Eden, and they accepted my credit card. The room was small and the furnishings faded, but it had its own bath. It would do, I told myself as I kicked off my shoes. I poured a glass of duty-free Scotch and stretched out on the bed to finish the newspaper. I was safe, at least for the time being, and I think I finally began to relax a little.

It was after ten at night when I awoke, chilly and disoriented. I washed my face and teeth, went outside, and had a hamburger at the first fast-food place I came across. Then I strolled for a while up and back down what looked to be one of the city's main shopping streets. It was cold, and everything was closed, but I didn't care. I had come here to be lost for as long as it seemed necessary.

Things were livelier in the area around the train station, where my hotel was located. I discovered rue Joseph Junck, which was lined with the kind of sleazy bars that somehow draw the solitary traveler. Each one featured small-screen hard-core films, and each one had its own squad of lightly dressed bar girls. I went in and out of a few of these places, and finally settled for a drink in a slightly tonier establishment. It was small, but the furnishings were almost elegant compared with the others I'd seen on the street. There were no gynecology movies being shown, and a number of electric lanterns gave the bar a golden glow that contrasted favorably with the usual dark, gloomy interiors. The three girls on duty were already occupied, so I wasn't even hustled.

Another customer on his own finished playing a video game and returned to the bar with his glass of beer. He sat on the stool next to me, and within a few minutes we got to talking. His name was Colin Dean, he was from England, and he had been living and working in Luxembourg for the last five months. His hair, mustache, and goatee were coppery red and curly, but closely trimmed. He wore a rumpled tweed suit and he fussed a lot with a pipe that he never actually lit. He seemed to be a naturally morose person, but I found it easy enough to be in his company.

"I was at Leeds for three years," he explained. "I lectured in the English Department, and did part-time work at the university press. Editorial."

"Luxembourg must be more exciting than Leeds," I said, though I'd never been to Leeds.

Colin looked puzzled, as if he had never considered the possible advantages of one city over another. "I came here to get away from the wife," he said. "Someone told me about the opening here, I applied, was interviewed in London—and, to my surprise, I got the job. I didn't think twice. I was glad for the chance to get away from her, the bitch. We're separated, but still married, unfortunately."

"And what are you doing here? Work, I mean."

"I'm an editor in the Office of Official Publications of the Common Market."

"Very good."

"Actually, it's a monumental bore," Colin continued. "All their documents, official papers, reports, research studies—that kind of thing. Utterly unreadable, but of course that's beside the point."

"Well, it's the kind of thing that's bound to look good on your résumé," I pointed out. You only had to talk with this man for a few minutes before you wanted to cheer him up. "Are you going to stay in publishing, or go back to lecturing?"

"I think I've said all I have to say on the subject of J. Sheridan Le Fanu, so, yes, it would probably be publishing. If I can get in the door of a decent London house." Colin perked up marginally as he considered this. "I have a project now that's not without possibilities. A study on the nature of prosperity in the eighties. Has the makings of a good little monograph, if I can get rid of the statistics and transform the author's horrid Germanic style. Might be able to use it as an entrée. Sort of thing Routledge might be interested in."

He lapsed into silence, testing the draw on his pipe. I ordered two more beers for us. I had nowhere else to go, and Colin was having a peculiar tonic effect on me.

"Are you going to get a divorce?" I asked after we had raised our glasses to each other.

"She doesn't want one," he muttered unhappily. "That's the problem. Thing is, I'm due to come into a bit of money as soon as my old dad drops off, and she knows it."

"Meanwhile, you support her from here."

"I haven't sent her one penny," Colin snarled. "But even that doesn't bother her. She has a good secretarial job. Has it off with the boss in the back room, then comes home and has it off with the next-door neighbor in his kids' Wendy house. Though they've probably moved indoors now that I'm no longer on the scene."

"Sounds messy."

"Yes, well." Colin glanced up at me. "I can tell just by looking at you that you're not married, lucky bastard. What are you doing here, as a matter of interest? It's not the tourist season. If you're trying to escape instant cheeseburgers, chicken nuggets, and acid rain, you've come to the wrong continent, you know."

I smiled. "No. I came to get away from a woman too," I answered. "But just for a few days, I think."

"Oh? I've heard your American women are a pretty ruthless lot."

"This one's English. I've just come from your homeland."

"God help you."

"It was getting to be too tense, too . . . hairy," I went on. I didn't want to tell him much about Lina, not in any detail, but the urge to talk to this stranger was suddenly very strong, and he was probably the safest audience I would find. "I just decided I had to get away for a while, put some space between us and figure thing out."

"Take my advice and let her go," Colin volunteered "Women. They have us by the short and curlies, and they know it. Stay single, chum. Otherwise you don't have a chance."

"This one doesn't want to marry me," I said. "She'd be happy enough to keep the affair going the way it is I think. But she's kind of wild, and hard to keep up with."

"Christ, that's no good, is it?" Colin protested. "A constant drain on the old emotional batteries—am I right? I know the type. Whatever else you can say about marriage, at least it's emotionally relaxing. You can just sail along, playing the part. Unless it gets out of hand which it has in my particular case. No, you see, I've reached the stage in life where, by process of elimination, the good old find 'em, fuck 'em, and forget 'em philosophy is the only one that seems to work."

"I'm not that cynical—at least not yet."

"Ah, there you are," Colin said with a brief hint of a smile. "I think it was Oscar Wilde who said sentimentalists describe realists as cynics."

"Well . . ."

"She has you good and hooked, I can see."

"That's what I'm afraid of," I admitted.

Colin's prescription was a crash course in Luxembourg night life. That night and the following three, we hit every bar and joint on rue Joseph Junck and rue du Fort Neipert. We occasionally fondled the best-looking mercenaries, but for the most part we drank, watched the action, and discussed women and sex. There wasn't much more to Colin's so-called philosophy than what he had expressed in the first hour we met, but he was capable of elaborating it endlessly. He was a gloomy, bitter kind of person, but there was something I liked about Colin. Maybe he was just what I needed at the time, a disinterested stranger with his own problems.

The more we talked about women, the less Lina burdened my mind. Colin enabled me to deal with the matter at arm's length, by escaping it temporarily. I was no longer haunted by terrible images of that Asian girl. The terror of arrest and exposure diminished. I had other help in this regard; every day I bought an English newspaper, but found no mention of the crime. No word of a body being discovered. I had been absolutely certain we would be caught, but with each day showing nothing in the British press and each night boozy with diversion, that fear receded.

Once, on my third afternoon in Luxembourg, I had a very bad spell. I was suffering another hangover, soaking in a hot bath, when the thought that I had become a monster took hold of my mind. It wouldn't go away. It became so large, black, and engulfing that I found myself shaking violently, uncontrollably, on the verge of tears, maybe even hysteria. I knew that as a result of my own weakness I had traded in my life and become some other person, me but no longer me. I could never escape what I had done, even if I never saw Lina again. I could fly directly back to America and try to put together that old life—but I knew it would be a foolish, impossible gesture, not a realistic course of action. I wanted to seal off the killing as a mistake, an isolated incident, a fluke—to encyst it harmlessly in the past. But I understood, in that long moment of self-terror, that it couldn't be done. I'd taken a human life, thereby surrendering the last of innocence. There was a malignancy in me I could not explain away.

Finally I stopped trembling and gasping. The bath had gone cold. I dried myself off and dressed, hating that dead Asian girl more than ever. She had done this to me, by changing the game. She had tried to kill me first. I had never wanted anything like that to happen—no real harm to either person. I blamed her as much as myself, but I did blame myself. Without me, it wouldn't have happened. Being there ensured my complete guilt. I don't know why, but I still wasn't thinking about Lina's role in the incident.

On my fifth night in Luxembourg-Ville, Colin and I went to a discotheque. We danced and chatted over drinks with a number of young women. Colin was an even more improbable dancer than I, but he managed. His style with women was not at all ineffective. He remained typically morose and blunt. He quoted several times some line from Balzac about women having a fortune between their legs. His general argument was that all women should be whores; then men could deal with them honestly. The girls we talked to regarded this as charmingly outrageous, the kind of quaint attitude that was to be expected from an Englishman.

Eventually we left the disco, accompanied by a couple of typists who worked at the European Council of Ministers. Colin took us back to his cramped flat on rue Adolphe. He had the overly endowed brunette named Dani.

"Help yourself to the vino," he told me over his shoulder as he led her directly into the bedroom.

That left me with Violette, the petite, slightly tipsy one with the streaked blond hair. We had some distinctly imperfect red wine and then went to work on the rickety Scandinavian-style couch that looked as if it had been bought at a flea market. I'd had occasional one-night stands in New Haven, and this was the same—only the continent was different. It is not intense sex, just dogged and mechanical. Two bodies bumping each other to some kind of unexalted release in the darkness.

The girls left before dawn, tired but apparently cheerful. I could hear Colin snoring, not loudly but steadily, in the next room. I would have dozed off on the couch, but the flat was too chilly and I didn't know where to find a blanket. After a while I dressed and let myself out. A taxi took me back to the Hotel Eden. The desk-man smiled knowingly as I passed on the way to my room. I slept until the middle of the afternoon, when I was awakened by a phone call from Colin.

"How are you?"

"Pretty dead," I answered thickly.

"That was all right, wasn't it?"

"Yeah, well . . ."

"Better than waking to face the wife, I can tell you."

"I can't say much for your couch, I'm afraid."

"Sorry about that. The flat came furnished, but I think 'furnished flat' is an oxymoron. You know, like 'military intelligence.'"

"Uh-huh."

"So, what're you doing?"

"Sleeping. What day is it anyhow?"

"Sunday."

"I think I'm going back to London."

"Oh, dear, oh, dear. You really are determined to sacrifice yourself to that woman."

"Possibly . . ."

"Well, if your mind is made up, let's have a farewell drink. If you're going to go back to her, the least you can do is go back looking thoroughly shagged out."

"Uh, let me call you back when I'm conscious."

"Fine."

I scrawled his telephone number on a Luxembourg tourism brochure and hung up. I wasn't really sure I was ready to return to London, but I felt there was no longer any point in staying in Luxembourg. I was spending money but accomplishing nothing. I liked Colin, in a way, but his dubious charm was starting to wear thin. I knew that even a farewell drink would inevitably turn into another long night, and I didn't need that. I had to get myself in order.

I called the airport and learned it was too late to get a direct flight to London that day. I reserved a seat on the first departure the next morning. After a tepid shower, I dressed and went out for something to eat. Then I wandered a few blocks, until I found a quiet neighborhood bar, where I had two small, very slow beers. If there was no point in staying in Luxembourg, had I learned anything here?

I was beginning to conceive of my life as a series of bottomings-out, the illusion of gradual upswing giving way to the realization that I'd really been settling back, drifting down to some base point. I felt I was there again, but I didn't know what good it did for me to understand this. I had booked a seat to London. Why? Obviously I was going back because I had a flat to live in there, but also, ultimately, it meant I was going back to Lina.

I thought I'd come here to get away from her, to figure out how I could disentangle my life from hers. But now it seemed to me the simple truth was that I didn't want to leave Lina. I wanted to be with her, right now, held in her arms, lying between her legs, listening to her say things I'd never heard another person say. The upswing was no illusion with Lina. Besides, the killing had happened, and nothing could change that fact now. So why give up Lina?

Luxembourg was good for me. One way or another, it had brought me to some sense of myself, Lina, and our love. Colin had a hand in it too. I could see myself, if I left Lina, becoming somewhat like him: lonely, unhappy, bitter, and pursuing grim pleasures. That was the way my life had been going in New Haven, though I hadn't yet reached Colin's advanced state. The image of his drab, chilly little flat persisted in my mind like a warning. The sour red wine . . .

113

Most of all, there was Lina. It occurred to me again that I should despise her for what she had done. She had put my life on the line, and she had set up a situation that made a death inevitable. What kind of person was Lina, that she could do such a thing? But I couldn't hate her for it. I felt no anger at all. I couldn't explain it to myself, but now, a week after the event, she seemed more attractive than ever. That she could risk me, in every sense of the word, showed clearly how important I was to her. Somehow it reminded me of the story of Abraham, gambling his sanity and his son's life with a terrible god. What Lina had done was not so different, and she'd won. We'd both won. It may have been an act of blood and temporary madness, but I could see now that it bound Lina and me together in a way that could never be undone.

And, I told myself again, I really had known what I was getting into when I'd stood, naked, at the attic door in Lina's house. She had taken her time in getting me to that point. She had prepared me, tested me, and warned me many times. She had even tried to put me off altogether with those evasive telephone conversations and by not seeing me. Oh, yes, I had pursued her—and found her.

And so I knew that no matter how terrifying the reality might be, no matter what lay ahead, Lina was where I wanted to be. I was ready to accept that without reservation now, and I even thought I'd be able to exert my own influence and control over the relationship. The killing would not happen again. There was no need for it. All that mattered was that Lina and I be together.

I left the bar and walked back to my hotel. There were no messages for me. I was glad. I knew I should call Colin and say good-bye, but I was reluctant to do so. Better, I thought, to let it go. I didn't want him trying to look me up in London if he had a sudden urge to move back to England next week.

I went into the hotel lounge, off the entrance hallway,

and had one more beer. The place was empty, but it was cozier and more pleasant than I had expected. The Turkish bartender tried to sell me on the merits of a fine woman he knew and wanted me to meet. She was not like the other girls in this area, he explained with an arm-sweeping gesture that seemed to take in all of northern Europe. She was a lonely young widow who enjoyed good company. It would not be like throwing money at nasty bar girls, but, rather, the giving of a gift to a friendly acquaintance in need. All I had to do was talk with her over a drink, make friends, and so on. He was sure I would like her, and since I was a fine American, she would like me. I had to admire his slow, reasonable persistence, but I resisted the offer. I finished my beer, went upstairs, and fell asleep early.

The next morning, rested, recovered, sure of myself, I flew back to the only life I wanted.

II

THE POLITICS
OF CRUELTY

The central fact of our time is horror.
                    —ROY FULLER, *THE SECOND CURTAIN*

EIGHT

"The quality's pretty good, don't you think?" Lina asked. She and I were in the pit, watching a videotape of the killing game in which I had the lead role. She must have had some pretty sophisticated equipment, because the film picked up everything, even in moments of complete darkness.

It was strange, seeing myself play out that nightmare. Most of the time it was like watching some other person who had no connection with me at all. But there were a few moments when I felt anxious. The whole thing was perversely fascinating. I wanted to turn it off, but I couldn't.

The tape didn't stop with Lina's arrival onstage. It included our lovemaking scene in full. I sat back a little so I could see Lina out of the corner of my eye. Her gaze never left the flickering images on the television screen. She was rapt, and the look on her face was one of pride and wonder, almost transcendental.

If Lina knew I'd gone away, she gave no indication of it. I had telephoned as soon as I got back from Luxembourg. We arranged to meet the next day, and here we were. Watching Lina's very special home movie.

When it was over and the last images of the bloody tableau ran out, Lina turned the set off and took the tape cartridge out of the machine. She hefted it in her hand like a rock.

"We can never watch this again," she said.

That suited me, but I was curious.

"Why not?"

"Oh, I have something here I want to read to you," Lina said. She rummaged around among some papers in a drawer, then came up with a single page. "Here, this is why. 'I believe there comes a point in love, once and no more, which later on the soul seeks—yes, seeks in vain— to surpass; I believe that happiness wears out in the effort to recapture it; that nothing is more fatal to happiness than the remembrance of happiness.'" Lina paused, then asked me, "Isn't that exactly right?"

"Who said it?"

"Gide, in *The Immoralist*."

I didn't know the book, but I had to smile at the title.

"But you do understand what I'm telling you," Lina went on. "We can't ever let ourselves get to the point where we stop and try to go back. We can't repeat ourselves."

"Sure, I get it. We're not going to retire to a cottage at the seaside and dream about the good old days."

That got a brief laugh out of her, but then she was serious again. "Right, yes. There's no going back. Most of all, no going back *in our heads,* or we'll end up crippling ourselves. The point of love is that it's alive, growing, changing. It's not a fixed thing, and it never can be. It's a part of the force of nature, and so it serves nature's ends, not ours."

"Lesson over? Give me a drink," I said. "Give me some

Special. Give me some of that red-hot force-of-nature love. No, wait a minute. Don't move."

I put my head in Lina's lap and looked up at her. It seemed nothing less than a miracle that such a wondrous woman could exist, let alone be mine. Heavenly skin, perfect breasts, exquisite face, and those fiery blue eyes . . . Oh, yes, I could be content to pass my days in a magnetic field of such radiance.

A few days later I met Lina for lunch in a wine bar on Bruton Street. She was smiling, with news or a secret.

"Roger wants to see you," she said "He wants the three of us to have dinner tonight at the Feathers."

"Oh? What's it all about?"

"Nothing. I don't know. Just dinner, I expect."

"Really?"

"Mm-hmm."

"The three of us?" I asked. "I don't get it. The three of us haven't gone out together before."

"So?"

"Well, I don't know . . ."

"Is it all right?"

I shrugged. "Why not?" I couldn't object, but there was an air of inevitability about this I didn't much like. Nordhagen had introduced me to Lina; he had thrown us together, really, and I was grateful for that. But now I wished he would just quietly fade out of the picture.

"Does he know about your house?" I asked.

"Well, yes, of course he knows I have a house," Lina said, picking at her game pie.

"Does he know about the girl?"

Lina looked up sharply. "No." Her face was sure, but I thought I heard a note of hesitancy in her voice.

"Lina, tell me the truth."

"*I always do*," she responded quietly but fiercely.

"Then what is he to you?"

"I'm his personal assistant."

"What does that mean?" Her words had chilled me. "It means something more than answering his telephone and keeping track of his date book, doesn't it?"

Lina put down her fork and held my hand across the table.

"Don't run away with yourself," she told me. "Roger and I are friends. We work together, we're very close, and there's much we share. But we're friends, not lovers. If you haven't already noticed, let me tell you: you're my lover, my only lover."

"Then why does he have first call on your time?"

"Because that's the way it has to be, for now. And it's my choice. It has to be this way. Please believe me, Tom. No matter how it might seem to you, no matter what you might think, he is not my master. Roger doesn't own me."

Lina squeezed my hand, smiled, and went back to her lunch. I nibbled my potted shrimp, but I didn't have much appetite. I ordered another half-carafe of wine and thought about what she had just told me. After a few minutes I thought I saw something I hadn't considered previously. It might not clarify things, but it would certainly put them in a different light. If it were true.

"He can't do without you," I said. "He'd fall apart if you weren't there. That's it, isn't it? I know what Nordhagen is: he's a brilliant surgeon with wealth and social status and all that. But he's also a chronic loner, and he has problems—age, health, and demon alcohol. If he didn't have someone like you, if he didn't have *you*, he wouldn't be able to handle it anymore. You're his keeper."

"No, I'm not his keeper," Lina replied. "But there is something in what you say." Then she changed the subject smoothly. "We had a funny call this morning. An editor at some publishing company. He wants to meet Roger and talk about commissioning his life story. If Roger won't do it himself, this man will provide a ghost writer. But listen to this: he already has a title for the book. He wants to call it *Contoured Thighs: The Story of a Plastic Surgeon*."

"*Contoured Thighs*, I like that."

"I did point out to him that the profession is known as cosmetic surgery. Plastic! How fifties can you get?"

"Is Roger going to do it?"

Lina laughed hysterically.

I walked her back to Millington Lane and then had the rest of the afternoon to kill before our dinner with Nordhagen. I took a taxi to Leicester Square, walked around for a while, thought about seeing a movie but finally decided against it. I went into an amusement arcade and was surprised at the number of people playing video games in the middle of the day. I found an old pinball machine and used up my coins. Then I wandered around some more.

My mind was equally restless. I'd apparently come closer to understanding the Lina-Nordhagen equation, but there was still something about it that made me feel uneasy. If she wasn't his keeper, then what was she to him? She said she was his personal assistant, and now that I thought about it I recalled that on a previous occasion she had told me she was, simply, his assistant. Now, personal. Did the extra word—such a word!—mean anything or not?

Whether by accident or subconscious direction, I found myself outside a drinking club in Meard Street. I wasn't sure if it was Terry's or Toby's, but I knew it was one of Nordhagen's unpretentious watering holes. I'd been there a couple of times with him. I went in, sat at the bar as if I belonged, and asked for a pint of bitter. The only other drinkers were three hard cases at the back end of the room, playing cards. The barman asked me if I was a member, and his tone of voice told me he knew perfectly well that I wasn't. I told him I'd been in several times with someone who was a member, Roger Nordhagen. The name meant nothing to the barman, who pulled out a dusty, long-neglected notebook of names and studied the list of illegible scrawls. Once or twice he tapped the page, as if surprised to be reminded of someone's existence. But, sorry, no Nordhagen. I described him, but that only produced a helpless shrug, as if every club member was a short, elderly male. Maybe they were, at that. I wasn't eager; I'd only come in because I'd seen the place and I had nothing better to do for a while. But as I was getting up to leave, the barman had a change of heart. He'd probably decided I wasn't a detective for the licensing authority. Now it seemed that, yes, he did kind of recognize me. My friend, the member, was an elderly, short gentleman, yes? Well, he could propose me for membership and sign the form the next time he came in. Meanwhile, the barman would second me. We went through this ridiculous little ritual and, a £5 membership fee later, I got to buy my pint.

And so I sat in that dark, drab place, working my beer, thinking of Nordhagen and his secret life, of Lina and her secret life, and of myself and my own burgeoning secret life—and I wondered how they overlapped and fit together. Or if they did at all. The only conclusion I came to was that I truly hated afternoons. An afternoon is a desolate expanse of time if you have no way to get through it. There was something contemptible about being in a place like this, drinking alone. It was a kind of penance, since all you could do was confront yourself and accommodate the blemishes with alcohol. Daytime even diminished Lina slightly. She was as beautiful and challenging as ever, but . . . not fully the same person. We were night people.

By arrangement, I met Lina and Nordhagen in the small bar at the Feathers. I hadn't seen it before, but was directed to it by one of the men at the door. It was cozy, rather than small, and it was quite different from the piano bar. Here the decor was golden oak paneling, leather furniture, a massive fireplace, and sporting prints on the walls. The barmaids wore real clothes, and there were even people making use of the place. They looked as if they belonged—wealthy, tanned, silver-haired types with pretty, youthful companions. The Feathers crowd.

Lina and Nordhagen were waiting for me.

It had been a couple of weeks since I'd last seen Nordhagen. He looked more withered than I remembered. Frail and distracted.

We had a round of drinks and made small talk. By the time the second round was delivered, I thought the conversation was going nowhere and I wondered if the whole evening would do the same. It wasn't just the prospect of boredom that bothered me. I felt uncomfortable being with Lina and Nordhagen at the same time. If it were Nordhagen alone, that would be all right, not great but all right. I knew the boys-night-out routine by now. But if Lina was available, as she was, I wanted only to be with her. Roger was static interference, but apparently I would have to suffer through it. Now he was about to tell me a bawdy story.

"Lina won't mind, will you, dear?" he said. "This is a story about someone who has saved his money or come into a small inheritance, or made a killing on the ponies. It doesn't matter which; the point is that he suddenly has the means to indulge himself for the first time in his life. So he decides to give himself a real treat, and he goes along to the biggest, richest, most lavish bordello in the land. A real pleasure palace, you see. When he gets there he tells the madam he wants a unique experience in sexual delight. Something outrageously wonderful, damn the cost. All right, the madam says, she has just the thing for him. It's unheard of, it's the ultimate treat, and it's special to her house. What is it? Does he know what a Rhode Island Red is, the madam asks. Yes, he knows. Well, the madam has a Rhode Island Red that has been trained to give a man unbelievable sexual fulfillment.

"Of course this sounds crazy, but the madam insists. She guarantees ecstasy such as this fellow has never known, and she finally persuades him to give it a try. It was so utterly outrageous he just had to see what it was like. So the madam led him to a door, told him to go into the room, take his clothes off, and sit on the bed. Events would take their own course from that point on. Our hero did as he was told.

"It was a richly appointed Edwardian bedroom, with a huge bed—on which was perched the aforementioned Rhode Island Red. When our naked friend sat on the bed, nothing happened. The bird watched him and he watched the bird, and still nothing happened. Finally he moved a little closer, and the Red hopped away. Now this angered and excited the young man, and he went after the animal. It stayed out of his reach, and our hero began to get all worked up, trying to catch the Red. He chased the bird all around the room, across the bed, back and forth, and each time he thought he had it in his hands the squawking creature fluttered away from him. No matter how hard he tried, he couldn't catch the Rhode Island Red—and finally, in a state of furious exhaustion, our hero gave up. He felt foolish and cheated. He put his clothes on and stalked out of the room.

"The madam was shocked, horrified to hear that her prize pet had failed to do the job. She couldn't understand it. The Rhode Island Red had always performed brilliantly. This was a crushing development for the madam—as it had been for our hero. The reputation of her house was at stake. She told the young man to come back the next night, and she would make it up to him.

"Comes the next night, she greets him warmly, apologizing again for the unfortunate experience of the previous visit. Now her house is his, she tells him. He can stay as long as he likes, do anything he wants. But our hero is reluctant, because he is still unsettled by what happened with the Rhode Island Red, and he isn't quite sure what to do. So the madam fetches him a large, stiff drink and suggests he relax in the showroom for a while. When he's in a better state of mind, he can come out and take his pick of the girls.

"Fair enough, our hero thinks. He goes into the showroom, which is a kind of small, dark theater. Several other clients are seated in there, and our hero joins them, watching the action. It's a live sex show, of course, and they're all looking at it through a wall of one-way glass. On the other side, an orgy is taking place. The sound is piped in through a speaker. Boys and girls together, going at each other every which way. And before long, such a good show it is, our hero feels himself warming up. He is happier now, aroused, getting into the swing of things. Pretty soon he'll be ready to go out and get to work on some of the madam's girls. But he's enjoying the show so much he can't resist nudging the man in the next seat. What a show, huh? I've never seen an orgy like this, he says. The man in the next seat agrees. Yes, this is all right, he says to our hero. But if you think this is good, you should have been here last night. They had some guy trying to fuck a chicken!"

Nordhagen sat back and laughed boisterously, as if by telling the story he was also hearing it for the first time. Lina smiled, and I guessed it wasn't new to her. And I was laughing too. I'm not sure why. I felt as if I'd just strolled through a room full of people, only to discover that my dick was hanging out of my trousers. The story hurt, even as I laughed, and paranoid or not, I was pretty damn sure it was about me. But I didn't want even to begin thinking about what might be behind it. I still had to get through the rest of Nordhagen's evening, come what may.

We went to a private dining room somewhat larger and more traditional than the one I'd been in with Lina. We sat around a table and ate a full meal. Afterward, we had cognac, and Nordhagen talked me into trying a Cuban cigar. I don't smoke, but the cigar was so mild and fragrant I didn't mind. All through dinner I'd said little more than was necessary to hold my own. This was Nordhagen's party, let him lead. Eventually he sat up and cleared his throat, as if he was ready to deliver a speech. I could only hope it wasn't another pointed joke.

"Now, Tom," he began, fixing me with a steady gaze. "There are several things I want to tell you. I'm not sure I'll be able to trot them all out in the right order, so bear with me, hear me out. It hardly seems necessary to say this, since I know you to be an agreeable drinking companion who can listen as well as talk, but I want to be sure you understand that what I have to say is entirely serious. This isn't the vino talking. This is a matter of great importance to me."

"I understand," I said.

Lina was watching Nordhagen carefully.

"Good. Now I know about you and Lina. That is, in a general way I know about the two of you, and that you've hit it off rather well. What's between you is, of course, private to yourselves, but I am immensely pleased that you have taken so well to each other. The truth of the matter is, I had hoped something like this might come to pass. I thought I saw a certain quality in you the first time we met, Tom. I was glad when the opportunity came for Lina to meet you, and now it seems clear my first impression was not wrong.

"If all this sounds like I was engaged in matchmaking," Nordhagen went on, "that's not true. You aren't the latest in a long line of candidates I steer to Lina. You are actually the only person who has met her through me; work doesn't count, of course. But Lina leads her own life, as you should know by now.

"And Lina is very dear to me, very precious. I don't mind saying that I probably wouldn't even be alive now if she had not come into my life when she did. No, Lina, you know it's true. I've been a solitary person all my life. I have no family, no close friends. Oh, through my practice I've built up quite a network of friends, but they are, in the final analysis, strangers, acquaintances, contacts. Lina is the only person close to me, who knows me.

"Perhaps I should backtrack a bit here and tell you something about myself. I came to this country after the war. You might say I got in on the ground floor. My practice blossomed in the late fifties, and I've had a great run ever since. I'll spare you any false modesty, Tom. I know how good I am in my field. There's a man in Beverly Hills, another in Mexico City, one in Rio, an egregious twit in New York—and they're the lot. My peers. One other chap set up shop in Morocco, hoping to siphon off the Arab trade, but then he went away for a few days on special assignment and was never seen again. Some say Libya, others Uganda. Silly man.

"But, back to me. It's no secret I've done well in this profession. Very well indeed. The time is fast coming, however, when I must give it up. You have to know when to quit, and that time is near for me. So, I'm going to phase myself out—rather like a coal mine it sounds, but that's the way it is. I don't need the daily struggle at my age. I've lost the point of it all. Now, Lina, tomorrow is as good a time as any. Starting tomorrow, let's add no more names to our waiting list. No need for any announcement, as such; we'll just say we aren't scheduling any new appointments at this time. It'll taper off soon enough by itself.

"Well, there. I've said it, so it's definite. Doesn't feel too bad, either. What am I going to do with myself when the work runs out? I'm still alive, alert, and I'm not the sort of person who can move to Hastings or Eastbourne and stare at the sea until I keel over in the sand. No. I have one or two personal projects that will keep me busy. Quite busy, in fact. They're the result of years of slow, painstaking work, and I haven't been able to give them the attention they deserve. Demand. So I'll be all right with that. Lina has been involved with me on these projects, and she will continue as my assistant. Invaluable is a poor word to describe her help."

Nordhagen paused here to catch his breath, smile at Lina, and take another sip of cognac. His cigar had gone out.

"Now this brings us back to you, Tom," he resumed. "At the risk of seeming impolite, I must point out that the time will soon come for you to make a decision, dear boy. Your visit to London is of fixed duration, as you have several times insisted to me. At that time, you will face three possible courses of action. One, say good-bye to Lina and return to America. Two, persuade her to accompany you back to America. Three, stay on here in London.

"The first—if you think you can leave Lina, and want to—is your option. It's between the two of you, and there's nothing useful I can say about it. As for the second, I know, since Lina has already committed herself to her work here, that it's out of the question. So, now, that leaves the third possibility. If you want to stay on in London, Tom, I can help you. I have work for you. It's more than I can handle, even with Lina's help. If you want to join us, the opportunity is yours. You will be well compensated, and of course you will still be with Lina. Every day."

I liked that last bit, not least for its utter lack of subtlety. But there were problems, questions.

"I don't want to seem ungrateful," I said. "But I'm not sure I understand this. I am an M.D. but I'm not qualified to practice in this country. And I know next to nothing about your line of work. My surgical experience is extremely limited."

Nordhagen laughed indulgently. "My dear boy, I'm not about to suggest you take over my practice. No one can do that. No, the practice will die off, as it should. Nor will you have to qualify to work in this country. My projects are, of necessity, private and totally secret. As far as the immigration people are concerned, you will be a man of independent means who chooses to enjoy life in London. Your bank account will satisfy them, and I'm sure you'll have no trouble getting your visa extended."

I was about to interrupt, but he held up a hand.

"I do see your point," Nordhagen went on. "It's unusual to offer someone a job without telling them what the work will actually entail, and so on. However, that's the way it must be. For now, all I can tell you is that I have no doubt you are capable. Anything you might need to learn, I can teach.

"The details are trivial, but the basic question is not, and that is all you have to consider for now. It would be a big change in your life. I urge you to give it all the thought it deserves. I am merely opening one door for you. It's up to you whether you choose to step through it or not.

"But bear in mind one more thing, Tom. I have met you only a few times. We know certain things about each other, but overall we are still pretty much strangers. It says something about all of us, you, me, and most of all Lina, and my faith and trust in her, that I make this offer at all. But I think I'm right to do so, and the offer stands. Take as much time as you need, and when you're ready, come see me and we'll talk again."

Nordhagen sat back, stifled a belch, relit his cigar, and poured himself another large cognac.

"Can I ask you a question?"

"I may not answer it," Nordhagen said cheerfully, "but go ahead and ask."

"Is this place, the Feathers, one of the special projects you're talking about?"

Nordhagen and Lina both laughed at this. I found myself joining them. After all Nordhagen had said, my question seemed an almost antic diversion.

"I can tell you a little something about the Feathers," Nordhagen said. "I'm not an investor in it, I'm not a partner. I am a lifetime honorary member, so to speak. The Feathers, or the full use of it, was a gift to me from a grateful oilman. One of your countrymen, in fact, a proud Oklahoman. Without going into the details, which are messy beyond belief, I will tell you simply that I restored to him, with enhanced capabilities, the use of a rather important part of his anatomy. Several others had tried to help him, and failed, so there was almost no limit to his appreciation. I charged him one million dollars cash, and he thought that was not enough, so he threw in carte blanche here as a bonus. Of course, my privileges extend to my guests, as well."

Nordhagen was bragging like an old-time baseball player, and I could tell the drink was getting into his talk now. I pushed one step further.

"But you offered me a girl downstairs, you offered to give her to me, as a gift, like you could give someone away."

Nordhagen was nodding his head, smiling.

"Yes," he said. "I did do that, didn't I. Right here, in the heart of London. Imagine."

I had to let it go at that, sensing that Nordhagen would be happy to feed me ambiguities for the next hour or two. I had other things to think about. A few minutes later I thanked him for the meal and for the offer, and then Lina and I made our exit. Nordhagen saw us to the front door, then went back inside the Feathers.

Even later, when we were in the upstairs bedroom of Lina's house, my mind was distracted. I had what I wanted, but I still found it hard to believe. I didn't feel good about it, in fact.

Lina rubbed my back. "God, you're tense," she said. "Lie down." She took off her shoes and stockings, and gently walked on my back. It felt terrific, knots loosening from my neck to the base of my spine. She sat down next to me, and I raised myself on my elbows.

"He does know about the girl," I said.

"No. I told you. He knows only what he needs to know." I found it hard to accept. That chicken joke had been too eerie and close to home. Was I reading too much into what was nothing more than a bawdy story? The damn thing still bothered me.

"What about the girl?"

"What about her?"

"What did you do with her?"

"Forget it. I'm very efficient, Tom."

Lina moved slightly, and I rolled over, turning to watch her. She sat back against the pillows, her knees pulled up in front of her, eyes half closed.

"Where did you get her? The girl."

"All lives are cheap," Lina said. "Some lives are cheaper than others. It's just arithmetic on the frontier."

"Hmm?"

"Nothing." Her eyes were fully closed now, and she

began to unbutton her blouse, revealing some kind of undergarment that laced up to her cleavage. "You are going to stay, aren't you." It wasn't a question. "I mean, not just now, but—in London."

"I think I knew from the first day," I told her. "Or night. I knew without telling myself, because I didn't see *how* I could manage it."

"Now you know."

"Yes, now I know. But what did you tell Nordhagen?"

"Only what I had to tell him."

"Which was . . . ?"

"That I wanted you."

Her voice seemed to float out of a dreamy smile. Her legs were swaying gently, and she was unlacing the ribbons that held her breasts.

"Are you sure you do?"

"What?"

"Want me."

"Yes."

"Don't stop what you're doing," I said. "I want to watch you. I want you to make love to yourself. I want to see you take yourself as far as you can, and then beyond that. I want you to make love to yourself until there's nothing left."

"Mmmmm . . ."

And then, I was thinking, I would find out how much, if at all, she still wanted me. Love minus self-love equals—what?

But what I found was what I already believed. There was no end to her. Like her smile, Lina went on and on, into infinity. She was an endless horizon, and, yes, she did want me there, part of her. So I was there, enthralled.

NINE

I took my time, because I had the time. Maybe something would happen to alter the situation. Maybe something would occur to me. In the meantime, I had many practical matters to consider. I still had almost three months left of my term in Matheson Road, and it seemed to me that I should honor it.

What would I do about my condominium in Connecticut—sell it? All my belongings were back there, including a car. I should see my parents again, and explain to them in person that I was taking a job in London. But it all seemed too troublesome, and I didn't want to leave London. It wasn't that I didn't trust myself. After all, I had gone to Luxembourg and hid out there for a week. I'd fought my way out of my anguish, and I'd returned to Lina. I didn't doubt myself anymore. But now I didn't want to go anywhere without Lina. I wanted as much time with her as possible, and a solo trip home seemed a waste.

What sort of person was I becoming? I had taken a human life. Self-defense meant nothing; I had killed someone—as well as raped and abused her first. I was a doctor, I was in the business of helping people—and yet I had done these things. The strangest part of it was that I felt no remorse. I didn't think of it much anymore, and when I did, it was with a detached, almost academic curiosity, as if it were some scientific phenomenon. I couldn't force myself to feel guilt or anxiety, much less self-loathing. I wondered if I should, but it was becoming clear to me I wasn't that kind of person.

If, somehow, I decided to leave London after all when my time was up, would Lina let me go? Could she hold me if she wanted to, other than through the power of love? That videotape was pretty conclusive. But this line of speculation was most improbable. Where was the body? What about Lina's house? Could she edit herself out of the tape completely? It would be too tricky, too risky, and—to what end? If our love failed to sustain itself, I had no doubt Lina would lose all interest in me.

I saw Lina more and more frequently as the weeks went by, and if I had any vestigial doubts, she erased them. Each time I met her was like the first time—intense, inflaming, irresistible. I had had girlfriends, one or two, but I had never fallen in love. Nor had anyone become so attached to me. Until I came to London and met Lina, I'd had the basic, conventional ideas about love: If you were lucky, you met your ideal mate, married, settled down and raised a family. How different this was!

I do not hesitate to use the word *love* to describe what Lina and I shared, although it seems inadequate. I could hardly believe it possible for two people to exist at such an emotional and physical pitch, but we did. And it wasn't just that we were so good at enjoying the fantasies, the games, and the delicious sex together. They didn't let up, but if people have souls, ours interfaced. If that isn't love, I don't know what is.

London became a different place for me. I spent days walking, but I took little notice of what I passed. I can only say I must have wandered up and down every dull side street in Hammersmith and Shepherd's Bush, from Dawes Road to Westway. My mind may have been working, but I wasn't consciously thinking about anything in particular. The simple act of walking became an end in itself, and these unremarkable precincts were just right. People knew I was in London, people even knew where I lived in the city, but I was still the alien in an alien place. And it was a minute-to-minute pleasure, this walking, a selfish experience. Because, as long as I was out and moving through these streets, no one, not even Lina, could find me.

Eileen Fothergill gave up trying to cultivate my friendship. Eventually I could no longer avoid having sherry with her, and that was probably what did it. I was poor company, and it proved to be an awkward session. It was not just that Eileen was unattractive—she did her best to be pleasantly sociable—but the whole episode seemed insanely artificial and unreal to me, as if I were stuck in an amateur dramatic production. And all I wanted to do was get offstage. I don't know whether she got the message or simply wrote me off as a boring American, but I didn't care. The invitations and doorknocking stopped, and that was the result I wanted. Now, when we happened to encounter each other, we were polite, as neighbors should be.

I could never get Lina to come back to my flat again. Not that the place had any charm, but I sometimes wondered how she would look in those surroundings. Would they diminish her at all? Probably not, no more than a kitschy vase would detract from a rare orchid. Once, though, she picked me up in a cab and took me to a pub a few miles upriver. It was a chilly evening, but still light out, and we ordered hot whiskeys and stood out on the back patio, overlooking the Thames.

When I was alone I often wondered about Lina's background. Where was she from, what family did she have, where had she gone to school—the thousands of little things that made up one's past. But when I was with her I didn't ask. Lina might as well have been born the day I met her.

Finally came a morning when I went out and bought a pad of plain white paper, a felt-tipped pen, and a small pack of airmail envelopes. It took me the rest of the day to scribble out a long explanatory letter to my parents. I kept it general, vague, but I made it clear that I had been offered an excellent job at a good salary and that I had decided to take the opportunity to stay in London a while longer. It wouldn't occur to them to wonder at the ease with which a foreigner fell into such a position, and I larded the letter with disclaimers, saying that if I didn't like it or if the job didn't pan out, I'd be back in the States promptly. I gave no names, said only that I'd be working with other doctors.

I told them I was looking for a place to live and would let them know my new address as soon as I had one. I added that if it all developed as I hoped, they would of course be welcome to come and visit, that I would love to see them and show them London. There was no way I could not say that, although the prospect of their turning up at Lina's doorstep was rather alarming. I would make sure they never got her address.

A series of expensive telephone calls ensued, from them to me, me to them, and back and forth a few more times. It was mostly to assure them that, yes, I really did want to do this, that I was in no trouble and had no problems, and that I was thoroughly happy in my choice. My mother needed all this—she was unhappy about her son's moving so far away, and she also felt my action was an implied insult to American medicine. But my father made it easier for me, suggesting he take care of my condo and possessions. He would go to Connecticut, ship my things back to Ohio, and deal with the real estate people and the bank. He would either sell the condo outright and pay off the mortgage, or else rent it, whichever seemed the more profitable course. He would deduct his expenses from the resulting revenue. I didn't care, I was grateful to have someone take the whole messy business out of my hands.

I hadn't intended to tell them about Lina, but in one phone conversation they managed to get out of me the rough fact that I was sort of seeing a girl here. I should have included that in my letter, since it seemed to clear up everything for my parents. A job *and* a girlfriend—say no more! I could only hope they wouldn't start concocting fantasies of their own—a dream wedding in Westminster Abbey, for instance.

Now I had set things in motion. I had covered my bases back home, and I was open with Lina about what I was doing. All that remained was to talk with Nordhagen again and, soon, to tidy up things in Matheson Road with Owen Flaherty, the house-swapping agent.

But even at that late stage I wondered if I could, somehow, terminate the chain of events. It was a perverse fantasy. I could picture myself walking into Scotland Yard and confessing to a murder. A good old bloody ritual killing. Would the British love it? HUMAN SAVAGE CARVES UP CHINA DOLL, the headline might read. What would happen? There was still the problem of providing a body. I could see myself leading a squad of detectives to an ordinary house by Queens Wood. The woman there would say she'd dated me once or twice, then ended it, because I'd become a pest, chasing after her. She thought

I was weird. She would even let them look around. At the top of the house they'd find a bare, plank-floored attic. And then they would tell me to visit Bellevue when I got back to America (on the next jet, please). As comic nightmares go, this one was not without a certain black, Hitchcockian flavor. But why had it ever entered my mind? How could I imagine doing such things? Denouncing Lina. I think it was, oddly, a part of that process Lina described as closing my fingers around what I had in my hand. To imagine terrible things was also to eliminate them; even doubts and negative fantasies could be part of a larger affirmation.

During this period I thought a great deal about Roger Nordhagen. As he had pointed out, we were still really strangers to each other. But he was offering me a job, as yet unspecified, and I was accepting it. I was embarking on a significant change in my life. He seemed to be the least probable piece in the puzzle, but he was essential; without him I didn't see how I could possibly stay on in London. I was putting a lot of trust in Nordhagen, more than he was investing in me. But Lina was my support in this. Of all the things Nordhagen had told me, what I believed unreservedly was how important Lina was to him, how much she meant to him. She wanted me, and I thought that as long as she did, Nordhagen would keep me on, even if my employment with him should happen not to develop smoothly. Yes, the pieces were all there—Lina, Nordhagen, and myself. I couldn't see all of it yet, maybe not even the greater part, but the general shape was coming clear and it did seem to fit together somehow.

I got Nordhagen on the telephone and told him I wanted to see him. It must have been the right phase of the moon, because he said he was thinking of making the rounds and invited me to accompany him. It was the usual drinking-club circuit, with a few new ones added for variety (not much). We made a long, drunken night of it. Nordhagen pushed on with jolly determination, and some inner clock must have told him when dawn came, because he started ordering Bloody Marys. It was a grueling enough binge for me, and I could only guess what it did to someone of Nordhagen's years.

He reminded me of a man I'd once encountered at the hospital in New Haven, a patient in his mid-forties who looked as if he were approaching seventy. He was alcoholic, and glad to say so. He had no intention of stopping, and he told me, "Drink is suicide for Catholics, doc." He had a bright, chirpy laugh. He was delivered to the hospital more and more frequently; then I didn't see him again.

There could be no question that Nordhagen knew very well what he was doing to himself. If the alcohol was a greater problem than he made it look, which is what I suspected, then it was no surprise he was shutting down his medical practice. He had no choice.

We got our business over with early that evening, and I was happy with the way it went.

"I've decided to accept your offer," I told him. "I'm staying on in London."

"Of course you are, dear boy. Never any question."

He seemed genuinely pleased, and I felt better at once. My pay, I learned, would be £1,000 per week in advance. That was good enough for me, especially since I didn't figure to have any outlay on rent. Nordhagen said I would surely be moving my bank account to a branch in Mayfair, and he could arrange to have my pay transferred in from overseas each month, so that it would look like I was importing my own money into Britain.

"Saves all sorts of paperwork and forestalls the tax boys," he explained. "No point getting buggered about by that lot."

I asked him to tell me more about the special projects we would be working on, but he wasn't interested in discussing them at that time. Instead, he favored me with a long, roundabout man-to-man talk on the subject of Lina. I'd heard most of it the last time—how precious she was to him, and so on, but I listened dutifully. What he was getting at was that she was not to be let down, that he wouldn't tolerate her being hurt in any way. He was warning me. Nordhagen never came out and said all this in so many words, but he pursued his own windy course until the drift was quite clear.

I'm sure it did him good to get this across to me, but as far as I was concerned it missed the point entirely. I even had to suppress a smile. I was sure I didn't have the capability of hurting Lina. If we ever broke up, it would be because she wanted it to happen, not me. And beyond that, I truly doubted it was possible to hurt her. A capacity for being hurt may be regarded as an integral part of love, but in Lina's case it didn't seem to apply. She could give everything of herself, again and again, and then if it all went wrong, she could absorb that failure effortlessly. Because the failure wouldn't be hers. Other people might disappoint her momentarily—but hurt her? No. I didn't think so. Not even me.

The next time I saw Lina, another piece of the puzzle fell into place—and I didn't care for it at all. I told her when I planned to pack up my things and move them to Queens Wood.

"No," she said. "You can't do that."

I was stunned. We'd never talked about it, but I'd assumed all along I would be living with her. Being around her day and night was the point of all this for me.

"What?"

"We can't," she repeated.

"Why not?"

"Not yet. It's not the right time for it."

I stared at her blankly for a minute or so. "Why isn't it? I don't understand this."

"You have to trust me, Tom," she said. "You have to believe me. I'm right, and you'll see that soon enough. We can't live together now. Not yet. Please."

"Is it Nordhagen?" I could feel my cheeks burning. I felt misled and I was angry.

"Not at all, but there are reasons why we have to live apart. Don't worry—we'll be together as much as we want."

"Great, great." I gave a short laugh. "Now tell me where I'm supposed to live?"

"Oh. Roger has a place for you. I'm surprised he didn't tell you about it himself."

Move my bank account to Mayfair. Oh, yeah. Not Queens Wood, dear boy.

"No, he didn't get around to that," I said. "Not in so many words."

TEN

It was all right. Everything would be all right with Lina. If she said it was necessary, I believed it was necessary. What Lina promised came true, so I had no reason to doubt that when the time was right, as she said, we would live together. In the meantime, I would still see her every day, be with her nearly every night—and if we did not actually fall asleep and wake up together, that was a small point. I didn't like the way I'd learned I would be living apart from her, but it was primarily my own fault for having made the assumption.

Curiously, I didn't see Nordhagen again until I moved into my new lodgings. He had a room for me adjacent to his place in Millington Lane. It was a mini-suite, with access to the lane: a single bed-sitting room, a galley kitchen about the same as the one I'd hardly used on Matheson Road, and a bathroom with a toilet and a tub that was too short for me. It was central, it was next to my place of work, and it would do.

The furnishings, modern Danish teak, were adequate and looked new. The walls were rough plaster and had been freshly whitewashed. It was as cool and impersonal as a hotel room, but I had nothing to complain about.

"All right?" Lina asked.

I had expected Nordhagen to show me my quarters, but he wasn't around, which suited me fine. With Lina I didn't feel obliged to show any false enthusiasm.

"Yeah, it'll do," I said. "Where's the boss live—upstairs?"

"Roger's place is through the door on the other side of the offices."

"Oh, he owns everything here at the end of the lane?"

"That's right."

"It figures."

"Here's your key."

"Ah, thanks." I was my own keeper, more or less.

"And this," Lina added, handing me a fat envelope. "It's from Roger. He'll see you as soon as he can; it's just that he's been so busy. It isn't easy winding up a medical practice that's been operating for more than thirty years."

"I can imagine."

Inside the envelope were fifty £20 notes and a short letter explaining that the cash would tide me over and that Nordhagen wouldn't need me for a few days, so I could settle in, relax, and enjoy myself.

"Okay?"

"Yeah, fine."

But it was a strange transition. I was fully attuned to Lina and I had no reservations about staying on in London, but I did feel I should be doing something. Work, in fact. It had been a glorious six months of total freedom, and Lina was the focal point of my life now, but I still wanted to do something during the day, when she was working. However minor the job might prove to be, it was nonetheless essential. But it seemed I had a few more days on my hands, and no choice in the matter.

I took care of outstanding business, such as it was. I did move bank branches. I informed my parents of my new address and telephone number. I signed and returned various documents to my father. After all expenses, I'd made a little money on the sale of my condominium and car, and I had my father bank it for me in Ohio. I didn't need it in London, at least not yet, and it would be something to fall back on if things didn't work out here.

I bought a few things to improve my place of residence: a reasonable stock of liquor, a stereo system and scores of rock and jazz CDs, some plants, and a few books. I'd never read much outside of what had been required in twenty years of schooling, but I got some science fiction to help kill the time and, when I'd noticed it in the bookstore, Gide's *The Immoralist*. I also bought some new clothes to fill out my suitcase wardrobe. Lina put me in touch with a laundry service that picked up and delivered.

The walls were bare and the place was still pretty cold-looking, but I wanted to keep it that way. Characterless. I was settling in London but I didn't want it to look like I was happily making a permanent nest in this particular place. The more temporary and unappealing it seemed each time Lina came in, the better. I would keep my rooms in as stark a contrast as possible to her well-equipped house. If her place was a pleasure palace, mine was a monk's cell, and I hoped that would help hurry things along in the direction I wanted.

The first signs were excellent, in terms of our relationship. Lina came to me every lunchtime, and again every evening. Our inventiveness was not strained by the surroundings, and as usual there seemed no end to the delight we took in each other. I never noticed the room when she was there; it was only when she left and I was alone that the depressing sense of confinement hit me.

"Leave me a pop of Special," I said to her one day.

"Why?"

"It's a drag here when you're not around."

"No," she said. "We take it together, not alone."

"Why?"

"It's better that way. Moderation. I told you."

"It's heroin, isn't it?"

"I told you it's nonaddictive."

"Yeah? I figure it has to be an opiate. Right?"

"Opiates are addictive, aren't they?" Lina said. "Addictions make no sense. But it doesn't matter; I don't know what's in it. Secret formula, like Coca-Cola."

"You get them from Nordhagen?" She didn't answer this. "I hope you get the recipe before his liver conks out."

Lina smiled.

After a full week in that place I was downright edgy. I would hang around all morning, brooding on the fact that Lina was on the other side of the wall, just a few feet away from me. Lunchtimes were good, and never actually involved food, but they were too short. When she went back to work, I would push myself outdoors to walk or otherwise overcome the long afternoons. I could understand Nordhagen's being busy, but it didn't seem reasonable that I saw and heard nothing at all of him. I watched the expensive cars come and go, declining in number, but I never caught sight of Nordhagen. He probably went to the hospital to perform surgery in the afternoons, when I was out. It was the only explanation that made sense—if he still performed surgery at all. However, when I sat it out by my window one afternoon, nothing happened. The evening of the eighth day I was going to say something to Lina, but as it turned out, it wasn't necessary.

"Roger wants to see us later," she said.

"Good. When later?"

"Later later. We have some time to ourselves."

We took some THC, not for the first time. I liked it because it didn't filter Lina out, as Special did. With THC we were both still there, together. All the more so. Sex was long and slow, deliciously languorous. Even when I was in her, and Lina was caressing me with her silk panties, it seemed as if I could hold myself indefinitely at the very point of orgasm without letting go until it was impossible to tell where my skin ended and hers began, and we dissolved into each other like a rainbow in the sky.

We went out for a fast meal, and then, at Lina's insistence, we had a couple of drinks at a pub. I would be in great shape to see Nordhagen, I objected, mellowed out by sex and THC, slowed up by food, and now buzzed by drink.

"That's all right," Lina said. "It's better this way. In fact, I want you to take this too."

She discreetly handed me a pill.

"What now?"

"It'll make it easier, believe me."

"What am I being led to," I asked, half joking, still not taking the pill. "What are these special projects anyway?"

"Just one that counts."

"What is it?"

"Look, I'll take one too." Lina promptly slipped the pill into her mouth and swallowed it down with a sip of wine. "Now, here's one for you."

"Okay, okay." I took the pill. "Now tell me what it is, and what the special project is. I've only been waiting a week that's seemed like a month."

"All I can say is that at first sight it will seem a little— well, shocking. It *is* very disturbing, Tom, but you'll just have to face it. No going back."

"Nothing shocks me anymore," I bragged. "I just ride one wave to the next, and on and on."

"That's what you'll have to do tonight."

"So why the pill?"

"Just a little ballast to keep things steady and even."

148

"Is it necessary?"

"Maybe," Lina said. "But there's something else I want to tell you. I want you to remember that I *am* with *you* in this all the way, and no matter how it seems to you at first, you cannot lose sight of the fact that it is one more step for us."

She said this so quietly and seriously that I felt a shiver, and I knew she was talking about something bigger, more terrifying than what had taken place on the top floor of her house.

"Another step for the two of us," I said. "You and me."

"Yes."

That's what I wanted to hear. Two of us, Lina and me, not three—even if it was Nordhagen's project.

"I'm still here," I told her. "No going back."

Lina smiled and rested her head on my shoulder. "It'll be all right," she said. "You'll see."

I didn't doubt it. As long as she was with me all the way, I didn't care what it was. If Lina wanted me to join her in a double ritual suicide, I'm not sure I would have been able to back away. That is not cheap bravado, merely the realization that by now Lina was the only anchor in my life.

Nordhagen was waiting for us in the library of his house. The walls were crammed with books, but there was enough dust around to suggest the place wasn't much used. Aside from a small circle of chairs around a coffee table, the only other furniture consisted of a large bar in one corner, which did look as if it saw use, a desk at the back of the room, and a small table with a chessboard set up, a lamp, and an open chess book. On second glance, I saw that the chess pieces, apparently positioned in the middle of a game, were also dusty. Nordhagen must have read my thoughts, because he smiled at the table.

"One of Fischer's early games," he explained. "I found

a forced win ten moves before he finally hammered it out for himself. Ever since then, I haven't been able to change the position or tackle another game."

"Like retiring undefeated," I said, looking at the mass of undecipherable handwriting scribbled all over the page of the chess book.

"Something like that," Nordhagen agreed proudly.

He served drinks that measured up pretty well to the dosages administered at the Feathers. Once we were seated, I was surprised at the little doctor's appearance. The past few weeks had not been kind to him. His whole face seemed to have sagged, and he looked very tired. The lines were deeper, and there were brownish patches on his cheeks, giving him the look of a withered russet pear. I don't know if it was the pill Lina had given me, or Nordhagen's appearance, but for the first time I felt positively serene in his presence. More than that, I felt somehow superior, as if I were seeing his mortality take control of him, and that one coincidental by-product of it was a subtle strengthening of my position.

"This is an old, old site," Nordhagen told me. "From the outside it looks like any other converted mews, which it is. But it goes back a good deal further than that. It was used as stables in Victorian times, but before that, sometime in the eighteenth century, it gets lost. History does not relate. Now that might not surprise you, an American, but take my word for it, it is unusual. London is such an old city, Tom, that every square inch of it has been measured, observed, recorded, time and time again, throughout the centuries. Virtually all the way back to when it was largely swamp and various tribes fought one another for position."

"Hmm." I tried to sound interested. I knew Roger regarded it as bad taste to come quickly to the point.

"It's not unusual to be able to trace the history of any given piece of land in central London for several centuries. But this site seems to vanish a little over two hundred years ago. I've been unable to learn anything about what was here earlier."

"Maybe nothing," I suggested. "Maybe it was just open ground."

"No." Nordhagen smiled indulgently. "No. There was something here, as will become clear to you, dear boy, soon enough. But what it was remains, alas, a mystery. And I've made quite a study of it." He gestured idly toward the wall of books. "One of my special projects has been digging up the history of this part of London. This slightly less than half an acre is the only blank spot in the area."

"Hmm," again.

Nordhagen smiled ruefully, as if it amused him in some sad way that he could improve on Bobby Fischer but not do a thorough title search on his own property. He was sitting back comfortably, but I noticed that his eyes darted about nervously, evasively, and his fingers worried the arm of his chair. The more I watched him, the clearer it became to me that he was in a state of considerable anxiety and making an effort to contain it.

"My own theory," he went on, "is that something—let us say, rude—went on here a long time ago. Some sexually outrageous activity? Perhaps, but not likely, since many instances of that survive in the histories. Some murderous deed? I doubt it. Murder has its own charm, and again we find many examples of it in the area, dating far back. Something political, involving royalty? No, that's even less likely, as every dark royal secret has been duly noted through the centuries, no matter what the scandal, and by numerous sources. So, what it comes down to, in my theory, is something else. Something like cabbalism, some degenerate holdover from the Middle Ages."

"You mean witchcraft?"

"No, not really. Cabbalism: numbers, symbols, alchemical explorations—including nonsense like turning lead into gold, you know, the search for the philosopher's stone, and resurrecting the dead. That is cabbalism, not witchcraft."

I appreciated the use of the word *nonsense*. But I still wasn't very interested in ancient history.

"Cabbalism could explain it," Nordhagen continued. "Bad enough to come to a bad end, but secret enough to escape the histories. Perhaps what happened here left a nasty aftertaste, and those who knew about it simply let the memory die."

"Could be," I allowed. But I was finding it more interesting to watch Nordhagen. Maybe he was talking to distract me. I noticed a distinct tremor in his hand every time he lifted the wineglass to his lips. Oh, yes, I thought, this man has closed his surgery because his hands are gone. He really is finished.

"Well, let's go, shall we?" Nordhagen rose. "It's time to show you round—yes?" He looked hard at Lina, as if some sign from her could still abort things, but no such sign was given.

We left the library and walked along a narrow hallway toward the rear of the building. Nordhagen unlocked a low door tucked under the stairs.

"Cellar," he said. "The first clue. There were no cellars in stables. When I bought these buildings they were just a row of ramshackle garages for automobiles. I built up and back. And when we ripped out the old floor, we found this cellar. Let's go now."

Nordhagen was becoming so agitated I wondered if he wasn't about to suffer some kind of collapse or breakdown. I felt Lina's hand on my arm as we went down the winding stone stairs into the cellar. It seemed quite deep, and I was impressed. I had expected a small, cramped root-cellar kind of place, but this was large. We arrived in an anteroom that had been created out of cinder blocks. Nordhagen's work. He hesitated again before a massive oak door and looked at Lina.

"Are you all right, my dear?"

"Yes," she said.

Nordhagen gave a queer smile, and then he was fumbling with some keys. He had so much difficulty getting the key in the hole that I wished Lina would take it from his shaking hand and unlock the door. But finally the door swung open, and we went into a dark room. I knew at once it was huge, in spite of the darkness, because I saw flickering lights in the distance.

Then I saw Laurence Harvey.

"Oh, dear," Nordhagen muttered in irritation. "I forgot I put on *Expresso Bongo*."

I nearly laughed. He had a movie theater down here. The screen at the far end of the darkened chamber was showing a 16-mm print of some black-and-white movie starring Laurence Harvey.

I heard Nordhagen doing something, then the film went off and the room lights began to come on slowly. Very slowly. Lina's hand held mine more tightly now, and she pressed her body close to me. She had the same look on her face that I'd seen outside the door on the top floor of her house. Then she let go of me and moved back a step, and I turned and walked into the gradually brightening room.

It was very large. Beneath the movie screen on the back wall were an easy chair and a chesterfield, along with an executive swivel chair and some kind of table or console. But most of the rest of the floor space was taken up by a long, semicircular table. It was more than a table. The legs, every six feet or so, were solid blocks cut from thick wooden beams. The tabletop was made of oak planks nailed to a solid frame of doubled two-by-fours. Beneath this makeshift table was a maze of pipes and tubing that snaked up and down the full length of the structure. On top of the table were twelve (I counted them later) wooden cabinets, evenly spaced. They were an extraordinary sight. I walked toward them. I could sense Lina staying close behind me.

There was a narrow break in the middle of the table, and I slipped through it into the semicircle. It was darker there. I actually hurried toward the chairs on the raised platform at the back. I didn't stop to look around. I was positively terrified now. It was not fear for myself, although that might have been a footnote to the larger terror that engulfed me. But I knew I was standing in the middle of Roger Nordhagen's secret, and that it was the blackest, most impossible nightmare, something that blew to smithereens the most primitive notion of humanity.

I spun around sharply, and my eyes locked on Lina. It was a delay to focus on her, blotting out anything else. My peripheral vision shut down by itself. I wanted to find something in her face, an emotional touchstone, anything. But her look was one of a ferocious intensity that said nothing. Or everything. Now the lights came up here too, as I looked slowly around.

In each glass-doored cabinet was a living person. Lights came on over their heads, creating grotesque halos. They hung in special harnesses, and they swayed slightly, some of them, like giant Christmas-tree decorations in hell. They were naked, and they had black rubber cups that fit them like diapers.

They had no arms or legs. Forty-eight limbs expertly amputated. Gone. The work of a master craftsman.

Their faces. They were the faces of the damned in living hell, hideous with agony. Not physical pain, though they may have felt that too, but something worse. Some of them made weak moaning and whispering noises, muffled by the glass. Some twisted ineffectually in their harnesses, but most of them hung motionless in despair.

I don't know how long I stood there, gaping. I lost all track of my own body, as if I had been instantly disincarnated. I felt like a pair of eyes attached to a brain floating like a balloon in the deadened air. When it seemed I was about to fly away and vanish like a spray of vapor, I felt Lina touching me again, and I began to fall back into my body.

Nordhagen edged through the break in the table and joined us, nervous as a frazzled terrier. He was watching me, but in a rapid-fire series of short glances, not directly. I stared at him as if I were seeing him for the first time. All that I'd learned about the man meant nothing now, not in the face of this monstrous display. Here was the real Roger Nordhagen. My little puzzle. The mystery I'd hoped to solve. He was a self-made god—and obviously quite insane. Still, it was impossible for me not to confront him.

"Why?" I asked, startled by how deep and firm my voice sounded in that huge chamber.

"Why? Ha-ha!" Nordhagen yapped, then shook his head, smiling in disbelief. "Why? Why? What am I supposed to do, hire a fleet of mini-cabs and send them all home?"

"Why are they here at all, like this?"

"Why, why, why." Nordhagen's face brightened with interest. "You might as well ask why the Mayan civilization collapsed, why Kennedy rode in an open limousine in Dallas, why we came down out of the trees. What is why? There is no why; there is only *now*, and this—" waving at the array of boxed people—"*this* is *now*. This is the only fact that pertains. You don't start with why; you start with *now*. And *this* is a *fact* of *your life now*."

I was dizzy, but part of my brain was working abstractly on its own, noting that the group seemed about evenly divided between men and women. Most were middle-aged, one or two younger or older.

"Mad?" Nordhagen ranted on. "Does the word *madness* come to mind? That's all right. I don't mind. Read your Yeats, young man. Yeats said, 'Why should not old men be mad?' It all comes to this: there can be no other possible conclusion. But 'Young men know nothing of this . . .' and you have to learn 'why an old man should be mad.' Well, Thomas, think of it, if you will, as your apprenticeship."

Nordhagen waited, but there was nothing for me to say. Let him rave and rave. He was beyond me, beyond my help. He took my arm and started pointing things out to me.

"Look here," he said, "they're washed, flushed, cleaned, all taken care of. And there, see the IVs? Food, all the essential nutrients. No one can choke to death!" This last with a kind of hysterical pride. "Oh, yes, they're all taken care of and looked after. Protected. These are my people."

What I saw were people who wanted to die, longed to, but who were being kept alive in Nordhagen's cruel heaven. I saw the chafing sores, the slack, pallid skin, the crusted eyes and mucus-gummed mouths. I saw torsos and skulls covered with electrodes.

"Here is—well, you can't be expected to learn everyone's name right off, but we have some lovely people," Nordhagen chattered on, manic, proud.

We came to one man who was struggling to make himself heard. His eyes were bright with anger. Nordhagen opened the glass door.

"Yes, Reverend?"

"You're sick, morbid, twisted—" the wretched prisoner croaked, and the effort seemed to exhaust him.

"Yes, yes," Nordhagen agreed cheerfully. "I'm doing the best I can with the sick, morbid, twisted mind your God gave me."

"Don't dare blame God," the other protested feebly.

"No? Very well," Nordhagen said. "Te absolvo Domine."

He closed the glass door, and steered me on.

"Oh, here's someone," Nordhagen said, stopping me again. "You probably wouldn't know, being American and new to this part of the world, but he's famous in a minor way here. Did in the wife and nanny, and then came to me for a change of appearance to go with a proposed change of scene. I was happy to oblige on both counts. Confidentially, he is, in Dostoevsky's splendid phrase, a man who has almost returned his ticket to God. But then, so am I."

Nordhagen was almost back to his jolly old self now. He had that mischievous, twinkling smile, as if all this around us came to nothing more than an elaborate student's prank. But now that I knew what to look for, I could see how much effort it took for him to maintain the façade. Nordhagen did it, somehow. He was a thoroughly competent madman.

"Films? I show them films all the time," he said, lest I question their entertainment quota. "I've spent years compiling a decent film library. *Expresso Bongo* is a real favorite, and so is *Beat Girl*—the clash of generations is always stimulating, don't you think? What else? Oh, *The Brighton Strangler, Room at the Top*. Oh, I have hundreds. We can't neglect their minds, can we?"

How much time do you have to spend in the mad kingdom to belong there, I wondered. I turned to Lina.

"And what's your favorite film, little girl?" I asked, my voice sounding foreign to me.

"*River of No Return*," she answered immediately.

"More than any other moment in any other film, I love it when Marilyn Monroe says, 'The longer you last, the less you care.' "

Nordhagen smiled madly.

Lina smiled with love.

I looked from one to the other, then slowly around the deep stone chamber and its gallery of mutilated, force-fed bodies. Welcome to the floor of hell. Nordhagenville.

I grinned back at them, the way certain animals do in acute circumstances.

ELEVEN

The tour was far from over. Nordhagen took me around to each cabinet, telling me something about the various people, but I couldn't follow what he was saying, so powerful and numbing was the mere sight of this folly. I got the impression that most of his people, as he liked to call them, had been complete strangers to him. They were vagrants, drifters, street people. There were exceptions: the Reverend, the man who'd killed his wife and nanny—I think his name was Lucan—and a psychiatrist who had written several books and then, one day, disappeared mysteriously. He was one of Nordhagen's captive population, and apparently he never missed a chance to explain that Nordhagen suffered from acute narcissistic personality disorder. This delighted Nordhagen.

He took special pride in his control booth. Here he could change films, play music, control the food input, monitor the automatic functions, or plumbing, as he put it, and maintain a check on the physical health of each prisoner. I had seen the electrodes pasted to their bodies. It was his own comprehensive health system, Nordhagen explained proudly. The console beneath the movie screen was an alternate control system, simpler but located for convenience.

It was all undeniably impressive, a monumental tribute to the lengths unbridled obsession will go. Before we left the booth, Nordhagen put on some music to soothe his assembly. It might have been taped from a television broadcast, for the first thing that came out over the speaker system was the sound of a live audience and a voice introducing Max Bygraves, who sang "Underneath the Arches."

Next to the control booth was a tool storage room, then Nordhagen's changing room. It had a closet full of clean white lab jackets and aprons, a bath and shower, a toilet, a day bed, and a supply of linens. Next to that room was a small pharmacy. This was no larger than a walk-in closet, but it was lined with shelves, floor to ceiling, and they were full of bottled drugs and chemicals. The last room was an operating theater. Not the largest, best-equipped, by any means, but adequate for Nordhagen's purposes. I paid little attention to the familiar medical gear, because I saw at once the large drain in the stone floor and the garden hose coiled up on the wall, attached to a tap. Those two things said it all about this place.

Nordhagen had obviously devoted an enormous amount of time, work, and money to his black fantasy. Judgment seemed beside the point. Here was a scenario of enactment that beggared anyone's imagination. Almost anyone's, that is. I was in the company of the architect. No matter what finally happened, Nordhagen couldn't lose. Not by his own lights. He had already achieved so much, built his mad dream literally piece by piece. It seemed an almost trivial aside, albeit unfortunate, that other people had to be caught up in it. But then, they were also the entire point. All of this existed for them, and they for it.

"Well, I must leave you for a while," Nordhagen said when we came out of the operating room. "I'll just give them all a martini, and then I have to see to some paperwork upstairs. I'll leave you with Lina."

So he could even pump drinks into them. I was glad he was going. I needed to be away from him for a while. Nordhagen bowed out nervously, and I realized he was probably as glad to leave as I was to see him go. It had been as disturbing for him, maybe even more so. He had done something incredibly bold. He had revealed himself to me, a stranger. He had laid himself bare, his mad folly, his darkest nightmare fantasy. I was only the spectator; he had taken the risk. I could understand this, but it didn't make me feel any sympathy for the old fool.

Lina emerged from the shadows with a couple of large drinks. I downed mine quickly, eager for the alcohol to take hold. We sat on the cold stone floor, off to the side where I didn't have to confront the awful sight of those people. We didn't speak for a while. Lina was content to be there and see me through my silence. There was nothing she could say until I gave her a fix on what I was thinking.

"Well," I began at last, "where did he serve *his* apprenticeship? Somewhere like Auschwitz?"

"No. He isn't even German."

"That may be," I said. "But I couldn't help noticing the signs of Aryan overachievement."

"What does that mean?"

"I don't know. Maybe it means that I told you I'd be in *your* dream. Not his."

"The way to mine is through his."

That was pretty straightforward, and I took it as a positive note. Maybe Lina knew a way we could, together, pass through this fiendish domain without actually being touched by it. Wishful thinking, perhaps, but at that particular moment I was glad to embrace it.

"How did all this start? There has to be a beginning?"

"Does there, Tom?" Lina smiled sadly. "Of course you want to understand it, to explain it to yourself. But you can't, and you won't ever be able to, because it's beyond understanding, it's beyond any explanation. That should be the most obvious thing about it. The only logic and sense to it is Roger's logic and sense. You don't have to take it as yours, but you do have to recognize it, that it exists. All these people, this place—it all exists. It's here, it's the given, and that's all there is to it."

"Lunacy."

Lina shrugged. "That's an easy word. But it explains nothing. If you want to understand, you have to understand this: everything connects with everything else. It all flows together. *This* is not separate from anything else. What happens must be good; otherwise it wouldn't happen."

I wasn't ready to follow that. And I was distracted. I saw another door, which I hadn't noticed before, in the shadows of the back wall.

"What's in there?"

"Stairs to a crypt below."

"You're kidding."

"No. There's another room beneath this one. It's much smaller, and quite deep. As Roger said, something extraordinary must have existed on this site long ago."

And still did, I thought. "I want to see it."

"I don't think you do."

"Why not? What's down there?"

Lina looked as if she would continue to resist, but then she gave up. "Are you sure you want to see?"

"Yes, I want to see everything. Let's get it all over with now. Everything."

Lina unlocked the door and turned on the single dim lightbulb that hung over another narrow, winding stone stairway. As we went down the steps I noticed a drop in temperature. Lina stopped at the bottom and let me pass into a low, poorly lit crypt that looked as if it had been carved out of solid stone.

"It's a remarkable piece of work," Lina said. "The stones are set in such a way that a perfectly even temperature is maintained year round. It never varies. I believe there's a small church in Dublin with the same feature. Ideal for storage."

"More light," I requested.

The room seemed full of things, but I couldn't make out what. Lina pulled a string, and a couple of overhead fluorescent lights flickered on, casting the room and its horrible contents in a harsh whiteness. The crypt was full of human flesh, bodies stacked up like cordwood along the walls. There had to be a couple of dozen of them. Along with countless detached arms and legs. They were all in good condition, leathery and mummified, but well preserved in this special room. Experiments? Trial and error? Were these Nordhagen's pioneer people?

"My, my, work does pile up."

"Tom, are you all right?"

"Sure." What else? "I think it's a scream. A real scream."

I wasn't stunned anymore. I wasn't even shaken. I felt I had reached the peaceful bedrock of Nordhagen's kingdom. The point of absolute zero. It may be that my nerve ends had already sealed themselves off protectively, but I felt eerily settled, calm now. I turned away from the ghastly morgue—and I nearly fell through a hole in the stone floor.

"Watch it!" Lina said. "That's quicklime. Who knows how long it's been there. It may be part of an original plague pit. There were several in this area—Hyde Park is a big one."

"How convenient," I said, stepping around the opening. "Why doesn't Nordhagen make use of it?"

"I don't know. Maybe there's a problem with it."

"Maybe he just hates to say good-bye."

Back in the upper chamber, Lina led me to a small bar I hadn't previously noticed. All mod cons, as they say here. We took our new drinks and went to sit on the sofa, center stage. The lights were few and dim now, so that although we were facing the cabinets, it was impossible to see the inhabitants. I didn't like being there, but I tried not to think of them.

There was a major unspoken question hanging in the air between Lina and me. Would all this change our relationship, and if so, how? But I was in no mood to address it. I just wanted to get through the night and see where we were in a day or two. I put my head back on the sofa and sipped Scotch. Lina put her feet up and leaned back on me.

"Cruel," I said, as if I were playing a word game. "Cruel is what I'm thinking right now."

"Exactly," she said at once. I could see her pleased smile. "*Cruel* is the word, but you have to remember its full meaning, its roots and resonance."

"I know what cruel means."

"Do you, Tom? Do you know that it means a relentless thirst for life, an irreversible determination to live? Without life there is no pain; without pain, no life. To be cruel—that is a state of clarity and control. As long as you choose life, you also choose someone else's death."

I said nothing. I didn't want to hear any more words. I didn't want to think. I wanted to focus on this drink in my hand and let the rest of me shut down.

But Lina put her drink aside and snuggled lower on me. She began to stroke me, to pull my shirt out and unbuckle my belt. I was so remote it might have been happening to some other person, but she got through to me soon enough, and suddenly I felt dizzy with hatred. My body might, but *I* could not do this. I wanted to say no, but the word found no voice in me.

I grabbed Lina's hair and violently yanked her head up. I couldn't look at her, but I pushed her away and went to the farthest, darkest corner of the room and sat down on the stone floor. I faced the wall and hunched over, pressing my forehead against the cold rock. I was shaking with hatred. Not for Nordhagen, and certainly not for Lina. It was myself I hated, the horrible thing I had discovered I was. My body, my mind, all of me. Only now could I fully understand what Lina had meant when she told me I had come to this place to encounter myself. I couldn't even cry; I could only tremble uncontrollably, hating this dreadful new knowledge.

I don't understand madness. I should have taken more psychology courses, perhaps. Nordhagen had to be out of his mind, and yet he got along perfectly with the outside world. He not only coped with it, but he was a success in it. So what was he? If not a raving lunatic, then a vastly flawed, crippled man. It delighted him to trim a nose and make a pretty girl prettier, but at the same time he had no reasonable conception of the value of human life. It was whatever he, God's stand-in, made of it. From what I remembered, vaguely, I thought this would make Nordhagen not a psychotic, but a psychopath. Finely tuned, very much in control, but a psychopath all the same.

It explained nothing, as Lina had warned, but I knew I was trying to clarify it to myself—for myself. I needed desperately to differentiate myself from Nordhagen as much as possible. I too had killed, but my situation hadn't been remotely like this. What had he said to me that first night at the Carlisle? 'If I had not known you, I would not have found you.' Something like that. Words that haunted me now.

Sometime later, I got up and walked around the cabinets. I went through the open door into the anteroom and found Lina sitting on the stairs. We said nothing. She locked the door and followed me out of the cellar. We left Nordhagen's house and stood uncertainly in the lane for a few moments. It was still night, all night.

She came with me to my place, and in the chilly, dark room we shucked off our clothes and hurried under the covers, creating our own warmth. We made love like desperate, jangled teenagers, clumsily, anxiously. And that way, finally, I found release in Lina, and I began to cry. I couldn't stop. Lina held me, cradled my head on her breasts, and comforted me until there were no more tears.

In the grey predawn light we went out for a walk. The city was stirring, but not yet awake. We walked through Hyde Park until we came to the Serpentine, and there we sat on a bench by the water's edge. We watched a couple of swans, a flotilla of ducks and the free-lancing gulls. Lina rested her head on my shoulder. We fit together nicely. I thought we might look like a happy couple who had been out all night on the town, dining, seeing a show, then dancing at a disco until dawn. It was almost enough to make me laugh.

"How much of that nightmare is yours?" I asked.

"None of it."

"But you're a part of it."

"I walked into it," Lina said. "Like you."

"I mean, you're a participant now."

"So are you, if you think about it." I was trying to understand that when Lina continued. "Listen, Tom, I help Roger and I help those people as much as possible. I can't undo what Roger's done to them, but I help. That's all I do. It's all I *can* do."

It might not be the whole truth, but I could accept it, as far as it went.

"Didn't you want to get out?"

"Yes, of course, but I couldn't. Not by myself."

I had wanted to come out for the daylight, for the raw fresh air. I had wanted to see the green of grass and trees. The sky, the animals. I had wanted to hear the sound of cars and early buses. That jet on its flight path to Heathrow. I had wanted to see and feel and hear these things, to know again that, yes, they were all still there. Somehow, it had seemed important, something I had to do. But now that I was out here, I didn't care. I couldn't feel anything for them, one way or another. They meant nothing to me.

All that did matter was this terrifying miracle of creation huddled lovingly against me. Lina. I wasn't surrendering to her, I was finding myself with her. In her. More than ever, I knew all that had been my past life was dead skin. I'd come out of it, and I could never crawl back into it. Despite all the horror, there was—still—love.

"Lina."

"Mmm?"

"How long will it take Nordhagen to die?"

"I don't know," she said. "You're the doctor."

TWELVE

"Reverend Scott has introduced a motion," Nordhagen told his assembly with good cheer, "accusing me of murder and moral insanity. Is that the gist of it, Rev? Dear, dear, this is serious. But we don't go in for summary justice in our little society, so let's give this matter the consideration it deserves."

The little doctor was in his swivel chair, rocking easily back and forth. He sat at the console and spoke into a microphone that carried his words to speakers set in each cabinet. He had a large drink in his hand. The room and the cabinets were brightly lit. The assembly was in session. Attention was mandatory. The tape system played quietly in the background, an instrumental medley of old hits like "Sentimental Journey" and "Body and Soul." It was an ordinary night in the torture garden.

"Before we talk about murder as a crime," Nordhagen went on, "we must remember first of all that it is an experiment of nature. Into the biological order of this planet, nature introduced murder, through us human beings, of all God's creatures. And we in turn have made murder an experiment of society. Oh, yes. So it is an experiment twice over. Well, this raises the unavoidable question: Do we have the right, the jurisdiction, to pass judgment on an experiment in the works? I think not. I think our own maze of rules and regulations is preempted, co-opted by the broader scheme of things—the natural order, which must inevitably command our primary allegiance."

Nordhagen paused to catch his breath and take a sip of wine. The tape coincidentally launched into "Sweet Sue."

"So, the first item, murder, is dismissed as falling outside the purview of this assembly," Nordhagen resumed. "Now, are we all agreed? Good."

True, no one argued.

"Now, moral insanity. Well, my dear Rev, this is your special province, isn't it? A typical thrust, if I may say so without prejudicing the issue before we even consider it. Moral insanity. Very weighty indeed."

Now Nordhagen lapsed into silence, giving the matter some thought, preparing his defense. A pout formed on his ruined face, as if he were somehow offended by the subject.

I had moved the sofa off to the side of the room, away from Nordhagen's immediate view and away from the blind glare of those glass doors. I was wedged into the sofa, with my feet propped up in front of me. I could see what was going on, but I was removed from it as much as possible. Lina was lying next to me. We had drinks too, but alcohol was not enough. I felt like a piece of driftwood that had washed up on the shore of Roger Nordhagen's weird subtopia.

I had been going along with this for days, no, weeks, now. Time had become a blur, not fast but seamless. Once you enter a dream, a nightmare you can't get out of, throw away your watch and calendar.

I had work, I had duties. The infernal machinery required care and attention to keep it all running. It was an elaborate life support system. Food to be mixed. Drinks, drugs, medicines to be measured and administered. Entertainment, stimulation to be provided. And the sheer mechanical chores that had to be seen to every day: flushing out pipes and tubes, changing filters and dozens of i.v.s.

I even managed to improve things for the people in certain small ways. I treated sores Nordhagen never got around to; I lubricated the harnesses and skin at points of contact. One of the many perpetual problems was a war against infection—these people were almost constantly on one antibiotic or another.

At first I threw myself into the work. By dealing with small, individual problems one at a time, I avoided the larger picture, and I could feel I was doing some good in an otherwise impossible situation. But I soon found it harder and harder to care at all for these people. Their moaning and whimpering, initially piteous and understandable, became an aggravation. I was trying to help them; what more did they want?

I found myself saying "Shut up" each time I opened a cabinet door. I started telling them they were as much to blame for being where they were as Nordhagen was. I seemed to have no emotional response to these creatures anymore. I could hardly even think of them as human beings. Whenever I had to face them, part of my brain simply shut down and I went about my duties mechanically. Perhaps it was a way of protecting myself. Around these people you could quickly bleed to death inside. So I just hardened over, a human callus. And in a short time, I stopped helping. I went to them only when I had to, and I limited myself to those tasks that were necessary to maintain the system at its basic level, keeping it from the point of breakdown but doing nothing more. This wasn't my business, I reminded myself again and again. I had drifted, stumbled, walked into it, but it was not mine. However elaborate, however grotesque, Nordhagen's kingdom was nothing more than a way station for me. This train stops in hell en route to some other place. I had a through ticket.

I had various fantasies of action, and they all involved Lina and me: We would go to the police, bring the whole thing to a screeching halt. Excuse us, but there's something you should see in a cellar just off Mount Street, W1. Yes, well, it was a shock to us. We had no idea, etc. You can imagine how we felt when he first showed it to us. Blimey.

But then, what would the boxed prisoners say on the day of their liberation? She was in on it from way back. He too, although he was a newcomer. He helped run the show, he gave a hand. He didn't balk, he didn't run for the door. Shut up—that's what he said all the time. He didn't care. He liked it, he did.

He *didn't* like it. But neither did he care—that much would be true. What could I do? Going to the police was out of the question. One way or another it would destroy all of us, Lina and myself included. Even if, through some fluke or miracle, we escaped punishment, we would become human oddities, lepers for the rest of our lives, no matter where in the world we might go. My fantasies remained fantasies, with no scenario of enactment.

For a while I wondered if I really understood Lina's role in all this. She'd told me that all she did was help, but help can be an ambiguous word. I was sure she had never been involved in the meat-grinder aspects of the business, the mutilations and deaths. And more than anything, I wanted to believe that she hadn't actually been the bait for any of Nordhagen's prisoners—picking them up and luring them into the den of Doctor Death. I finally asked her one morning when we were alone in the pharmacy.

"Did you bring any of them here for Nordhagen?" I tried to make my voice light and casual, but anxiety made it sound strangled. "Did you find any of them?"

"What do you think?" she replied sharply.

"No."

"But you had to ask."

"I don't care," I said helplessly, afraid I was only making it worse. "But I want to know. We're both just hired help here, right?"

A look of bitterness flashed across her face, but then Lina gave a slight nod before turning and walking out of the room. A little more of the truth, I hoped. We were a part of it, but it remained Nordhagen's kingdom, Nordhagen's folly, his madness and his personal frenzy. Not mine, not Lina's—and that was all that mattered to me.

"Nobody can be innocent in this world, Doctor Habbash has noted," Nordhagen was advising his conclave. "The very notion of innocence is impossible."

He seemed to have moved on from moral insanity, but I wasn't following him closely. This kind of thing went on night after night. The sound system was giving us "Gentle on My Mind." I reached into the ice bucket for another bottle of Chablis and refilled my glass. I dipped a finger in the wine, then slipped my hand under Lina's blouse and bra. She gave a small jump at the cold, but smiled as her nipple responded.

"Now I am in a position where nothing can surprise me," Nordhagen rambled on. "I can see the future and recognize it as tragic, but that does not repel me or cast me into despondency. Far from it. I am driven by this tragic vision, seized by it, for this is the point: Those who see the future are destined to bring it about. And so nothing will surprise me. I resolved long ago to accept myself for what I am, an instrument of circumstance."

You maybe, but not me, I was thinking. Right now I was a doctor, custodian, caretaker, plumber, and all-around handyman in Nordhagen's kingdom, but I knew what was expected of me. In Roger's mind I was the successor. Lina couldn't keep it going by herself. She would need help. Nordhagen was grooming me to take over, to look after his people once he was gone. I was his apprentice, his crown prince. My love for Lina made it possible. She and I might reign down here for several decades. We had nothing better to do, right?

"The burden of history is on my shoulders," the old fool prattled on. "I do not carry it lightly."

Lina, dark angel, mystery embodied, meant more to me than ever. What there was left of life for me lived in her, and sometimes it seemed that she alone kept me alive. By myself, I would not have survived Nordhagen's kingdom.

"I don't ignore you," Roger said garrulously. "I listen, I see to you. Isn't that true? You have a say, your opinions are aired, your thoughts count."

He was getting louder. Pretty soon he'd be shouting belligerently into the microphone. Each night followed the same course. It would start off reasonably, if that word applied to anything here, with Nordhagen holding court, hearing complaints, pleas, conducting a mad dialogue with his people. Like a king receiving petitions. This would develop into an open-ended monologue by Nordhagen, a mix of lecture, sermon, argument, and pep talk. Finally, it would deteriorate into arrogance and recrimination. They were ungrateful—the one thing the little doctor found impossible to fathom.

So far I had avoided learning the intricacies of the console and the master control booth. The array of dials, switches, monitors, touch sensors, and electronic displays had no key or labels, so I didn't know how to use them. I didn't mind. Nordhagen told me, in another fit of boasting, that he could control a number of emotions and feelings in his people through the system, and I believed him. I had seen it. He could make them sleep, wake them, excite them, anger them, cool them off, tickle them, make them cry or laugh. He even seemed to have some way of registering their opinions; maybe one blink wired a yes through the system, two blinks a no. Thus, even here, they had a vote, for what it was worth. Sometimes, when Nordhagen really got into the swing of things, he would lean over the console, his hands moving rapidly, playing the board in a demented parody of Vincent Price at the organ in a B-grade horror movie.

I never found it difficult to square this Nordhagen with the jolly little boozer from Soho or the wealthy cosmetic surgeon who relaxed at the Feathers. Nothing contradicted. The riddle was solved, the mystery made clear. Nordhagen's secret was a wide and deep roaring river, an underground river that surged through his life. The only surprise was that he had been able to contain it for so long. And it was also clear now why he was drinking himself to death. There was no other easy way out. Like my Catholic patient back in New Haven, Nordhagen was incapable of admitting failure or defeat. He would ease himself out. He would go down, yes, but his kingdom would survive him, an insane vindication of itself and of him. Lina and I would see to that. Like Goering at Nuremberg, Nordhagen was capable of erecting statues of himself for posterity.

"You can't think of anything worse?" Nordhagen asked them rhetorically. "Your tiny little minds really can't conceive of worse alternatives?"

He was in the groove now, and the sound system backed him up with a sprightly version of "It's Only a Paper Moon."

"Would you really rather be a dust-covered Bangladeshi, landless, homeless, without work, subsisting on scraps of garbage on the side of a road? Or a child prostitute in those cages in Bombay? Or perhaps you'd prefer to be bloated with starvation, scouring the southern edge of the expanding Sahara for a few green shoots? You really mean *you don't like this* in comparison?"

This was a permanent loop in Nordhagen's brain, and it reminded me of the stereotypical mother telling her kids to eat every damn scrap on the plate because children were going hungry elsewhere. Even I could see the *non sequitur* in this tendril of logic.

I got up from the sofa and walked along the back wall until I stood with a clear view of Nordhagen and his assembly. He had come to his crescendo, and it held a kind of macabre fascination for me. He was ranting on hoarsely, working the console. His people twitched and swayed in their harnesses. They gave absurd bursts of laughter, followed at once by deep groans, lunging gasps, and unintelligible stammers. Their eyes rocketed up and down in their sockets, eyelids fluttering like spinning window shades. Tears trickled out of them, sweat slicked their skin, and then great shudders of ecstasy ravaged their diminished bodies as Nordhagen sent charge after charge into the pleasure centers of their brains. Pain and pleasure, pain and pleasure, and every gradation in between. When they screamed, it came as a rough chorus of muffled, attenuated agony. Cries and echoes in the heavenly city beneath the city.

I went back to the sofa and sat down next to Lina, who had not moved. I opened her blouse another button and unhooked her bra.

"He could hang on," I said. "He could live another year or two, maybe even longer."

Lina's body tensed slightly. I had exposed one of her breasts and was stroking it, caressing it, squeezing it, making it a sensual haven for us as Nordhagen rode out his hellish rhapsody at the console. Lina moved to my touch.

"I'm going to kill him," I said.

Lina's body continued to respond.

"I'm going to kill the son of a bitch." I liked the sound of it, and I felt good and hot, horny as hell.

The stereo was giving us "On the Sunny Side of the Street."

" 'With freedom such as gods may give, discover what it means to live,' " Nordhagen shouted manically into the microphone. " 'Man excels all the animals, even in his ability to be trained.' " And he raved on, laughing, screaming, lost in the depths of his dream.

I bent over Lina and opened my mouth to take her firm, rising breast. I sucked that glorious nipple.

Thirteen

If Nordhagen had any idea of what I was thinking, he showed no sign of it. Day after laborious day, night after insane night, the routine continued. I looked after the people in the cellar. Lina helped, but most of her time was spent on Nordhagen's paperwork, which was apparently voluminous. And the little doctor shuttled back and forth between us, keeping us both busy. My presence made it possible for him to assume the role of lordly overseer. He had more time to scribble and dictate his pseudo-philosophy, to drink and watch movies, and to orchestrate the nightly sessions with his captive audience.

This would not last long, I resolved. But I had to be careful. Any action I took would have to be thought out and prepared down to the smallest detail. There could not be the slightest possibility of error. The real problem, I believed, would not be Nordhagen but what happened after his death. He was known, a man of position if not actual prominence. His death would have to be done right; it would have to be neat, but not so neat it aroused suspicion.

The disposition of his estate would be complicated. He had money in Switzerland as well as Britain. He had bolt-hole properties abroad. There would be medical, police, legal, and tax authorities to deal with, and everything would have to be right because the entire burden would fall on Lina's shoulders. I had to stay out of it, as far as possible. Who, after all, would be more suspect than the recently arrived boyfriend of the dead man's personal assistant? Especially since the assistant probably figured in the will—always assuming Nordhagen had drawn up a will.

Getting some of Nordhagen's money had nothing to do with it. I couldn't care less, and it hardly occurred to me that Lina might come into a share of the estate. All I wanted was for the two of us to be free of Nordhagen. If we could simply have walked away from him, we would have done so. I never asked Lina about this, but I felt sure her loyalty to me was now greater than her loyalty to Nordhagen. We had to escape him, to get back on our own track, but there seemed to be no way out short of his death.

The cellar was another problem. I tried to think of a way to hide it. I wondered if someone would want to search the property when Nordhagen died. Would the courts or the tax men want to draw up an inventory of everything Nordhagen possessed? I didn't know the procedure. But the cellar had been closed, secret, when Nordhagen bought the place. Perhaps I could do a carpentry job and wall off the door, making it look as if there were no cellar at all. At least I knew there was no record of a cellar on the site. I was no carpenter, but walling up a narrow door was no big task. Yes, it might work.

I didn't discuss any of this with Lina. Not yet. It seemed enough that I had already said aloud in her presence that I would kill Nordhagen. She never mentioned it to me, which I took to mean she was not going to object.

It didn't seem likely she would ignore my words as idle talk, so I concluded that she was letting me work it out in my mind first. Then I would talk to her and find out if she was going to resist and defend Nordhagen, or if what I planned was what she had wanted all along.

Considering what I had been through, done, and seen, murder had no mystique for me. This was different from the scene in Lina's attic; it was cold, calculated, and premeditated, but as far as I was concerned it was just one more awkward chore to be taken care of and put behind me.

The need for action became clear one night when Nordhagen took me along for another of his binges on the town. I thought it would simply be the usual drunken spree, tedious and debilitating, but by now the worst drinking club was far preferable to sitting through another diabolical session in the cellar. And I was glad to help his liver on its one-way course to destruction. But the night was destined to become much more than that. Before it was over, Nordhagen's fertile madness would blossom forth with hideous new designs, extreme fantasies of the ultracruel. From anyone else they might have meant little, but Nordhagen had the means and every intention of making them real. So, as a matter of urgent, inescapable necessity, the working-out of the final solution to the problem of Roger Nordhagen began that night. It would be a long, hellish process, but I didn't know that as we prepared to leave the house. If I had, I might not have been able to go through with it.

"What about the East End?" I suggested. I was eager for any minor change of scene and I thought Nordhagen must know some interesting places.

"The East End is a myth nowadays," he answered. "There are clubs where low-grade villains socialize, of course, but they aren't much fun—neither the clubs nor the villains. London has changed, I'm afraid."

"Oh." I hadn't noticed that the joints we hit in Soho were such great fun.

"Half the people in the Soho clubs are villains anyway," he continued.

"I'd still like to go somewhere I haven't been."

"Fair enough. No problem there."

Nordhagen seemed to have a large part of London at his fingertips. We started out in Notting Hill and made our way through Bayswater to Paddington. The places we drank in were in no way dissimilar to the clubs of Soho—marginally less pretentious, perhaps, and with generally smaller crowds, but otherwise out of the same mold. The postal districts were different, but that was about it.

Nordhagen had insisted that I dress up for the evening, as he did, and later I found out why. When we had gone through a number of places and built up a reasonable alcoholic buzz, we took a taxi to Knightsbridge. He crammed a wad of notes into my pocket and winked merrily.

"Time to get rid of some money," he said.

We went into a gambling club. The place oozed wealth, privacy, and luxury, and it came as a sudden shock after the drinking dens we'd just left. I was seeing yet another side of Nordhagen.

The casino scene was like something out of a James Bond movie, but dull, as only real life can be. Accurate in every detail, it nonetheless added up to less than the sum of its parts. In spite of the surroundings and all the glamorous people, there was something forced and banal about gambling—at least there, that night. We got drinks, and then I watched Nordhagen lose money. He stuck to roulette and seemed to have no method but whimsy. I didn't do much better, though.

As if out of the pages of some comic script, two likely

looking females materialized at our elbows. I didn't mind. They helped share the load of Nordhagen's company. We drank, gambled, talked about nothing much, and otherwise treated these girls in the manner they seemed to appreciate. Nordhagen was obviously known in this place, and I got the feeling the girls recognized him. After a while it became too tiresome, and I started telling Nordhagen we had to go. He didn't argue.

"Where now?" one of the girls asked gamely.

I blinked and said, "We're going to a strip club in Soho."

"Marvelous," Nordhagen burbled.

But to the pair of dolly birds this was a stroke of lese majesty. Didn't we realize what we were on to, they hinted none too subtly. I guess we didn't. They weren't about to tag along to some sleazy dump and watch fat tarts going through dumb routines. I was glad, because I was hoping I'd be able to cut the long night short.

That didn't exactly work. Nordhagen took the strip-club gambit seriously, and when we were alone in the taxi he could not be dissuaded.

I wondered why he had waited so long to show me his casino-gambling side, and I wondered too what else might be revealed to me in due course if I served out my full apprenticeship.

The place he chose was sleazy, and the strippers were mostly fat, all of which seemed apt if unfortunate. We sat at a table near the bar, as far from the stage as possible. No one bothered us; it was a tired, sleepy kind of place.

"Things will have to change," Nordhagen muttered obscurely over his drink. "Change is necessary, however painful."

"Like what?"

This only seemed to heighten Nordhagen's dark turn

of mind. His face became gloomier, his finger moved in small, idle gestures. Slowly, he shook his head.

"I see terrible things ahead," he continued. "These are black times. Men are put in impossible positions."

And how! I thought. This was going on while a hefty woman pushing thirty lumbered about on the stage in a schoolgirl uniform. I wasn't an expert on the subject, but I would guess these schoolgirl uniforms were an essential component of British sexual fantasy. But Nordhagen's mumbled talk was about to drown out all distractions for me.

"I see terrible, terrible things ahead," he said again. "It's just . . . awful. Men made blind, their eyes cut out. Men made mute, their tongues cut out . . ."

"Are you talking about your people?" I asked anxiously. I couldn't believe this. I hoped he was doing a general Nostradamus number, and not dreaming up new work for me.

"It's so terrible," he went on, "but they're already so very unhappy. What can I do? They cannot bear this life. They need help to ease the strain. What they see, what they want to say—these things are too much for them."

I knew where this was going. Nordhagen could no longer manage the task of surgery himself. I was there now to handle nasty little jobs like this. Nothing fancy. Just remove a few eyes and tongues . . .

"Can't they be blindfolded and gagged?" I asked insanely.

"Oh, dear, no," Nordhagen replied immediately, with regret. "That would be worse, far worse. To have the ability but to have it blocked. Just think what that would do to them. No. The last chance must be eliminated. It will sadden them, of course, but they'll get used to it, and then, when they know beyond the tiniest doubt that it is impossible, the desire to see and to speak out will cease within them, and they'll find a new sense of peace. Now

GET UP TO
4 FREE BOOKS!

You can have the best fiction delivered to your door for less than what you'd pay in a bookstore or online—only $4.25 a book! Sign up for our book clubs today, and we'll send you **FREE* BOOKS** just for trying it out...**with no obligation to buy, ever!**

LEISURE HORROR BOOK CLUB

With more award-winning horror authors than any other publisher, it's easy to see why CNN.com says "Leisure Books has been leading the way in paperback horror novels." Your shipments will include authors such as RICHARD LAYMON, DOUGLAS CLEGG, JACK KETCHUM, MARY ANN MITCHELL, and many more.

LEISURE THRILLER BOOK CLUB

If you love fast-paced page-turners, you won't want to miss any of the books in Leisure's thriller line. Filled with gripping tension and edge-of-your-seat excitement, these titles feature everything from psychological suspense to legal thrillers to police procedurals and more!

As a book club member you also receive the following special benefits:

- **30% OFF all orders through our website & telecenter!**
- **Exclusive access to special discounts!**
- **Convenient home delivery and 10 days to return any books you don't want to keep.**

There is no minimum number of books to buy, and you may cancel membership at any time. See back to sign up!

*Please include $2.00 for shipping and handling.

YES! ☐

Sign me up for the Leisure Horror Book Club and send my TWO FREE BOOKS! If I choose to stay in the club, I will pay only $8.50* each month, a savings of $5.48!

YES! ☐

Sign me up for the Leisure Thriller Book Club and send my TWO FREE BOOKS! If I choose to stay in the club, I will pay only $8.50* each month, a savings of $5.48!

NAME: _____

ADDRESS: _____

_____

TELEPHONE: _____

E-MAIL: _____

☐ **I WANT TO PAY BY CREDIT CARD.**

☐ VISA ☐ MasterCard ☐ DISCOVER

ACCOUNT #: _____

EXPIRATION DATE: _____

SIGNATURE: _____

Send this card along with $2.00 shipping & handling for each club you wish to join, to:

Horror/Thriller Book Clubs
20 Academy Street
Norwalk, CT 06850-4032

Or fax (must include credit card information!) to: 610.995.9274. You can also sign up online at www.dorchesterpub.com.

*Plus $2.00 for shipping. Offer open to residents of the U.S. and Canada only. Canadian residents please call 1.800.481.9191 for pricing information.

If under 18, a parent or guardian must sign. Terms, prices and conditions subject to change. Subscription subject to acceptance. Dorchester Publishing reserves the right to reject any order or cancel any subscription.

JOIN NOW!

they are suffering torture through hope, and that must be ended. They will adjust, and they'll be better for it. But we must be decisive about removing the sources of their discomfort. We must be cruel to be kind."

If Nordhagen's mind was a grave, I could see the evil new flowers pushing up through the surface. They were shiny, black, lurid elaborations of evil, or terror. Madness, above all, the flowers of madness. Their roots ran deep into the heart of Nordhagen's being.

"I see what you mean," I said.

Only too well. This brief interlude in the course of a drunken evening on the town had sobered me quickly. Events were moving, and I would have to refine my ideas without delay. I couldn't hope Nordhagen would forget about this, lose it in the alcoholic haze. This was his baby, after all, his life's mad obsession. And I couldn't get involved, even if it was just—just!—the snipping of vocal cords and optic nerves. I had to stay out of it, because it wouldn't stop at that.

"I see terrible things," Nordhagen went on. "I try to avoid these things. I try to put them off. But the burden of history is crushing. The course of nature will not be denied. I see forced elective annihilations. New blood, always the demands of new blood. It's irresistible. The population is limited, of necessity, but there is always the force of new blood at the gates. Make way, make way. I see forced elective annihilations and sweet anarchy. I see such terrible things. . . ."

I was beginning to think I had misread Nordhagen by a wide margin. I thought he had wanted me to help him maintain the status quo, but now it seemed he had more in mind. Much more. He planned further mutilation, death (but only after getting their vote for it) and then—what? New blood. That could mean only another crop of candidates for dismemberment and installation in the chamber of horrors. I had thought the corpses in the crypt were the first run, his trial-and-error casualties, but maybe they were just the previous wave of a regular cycle.

"You try to hold back the bitterness," Nordhagen said. "You try to ignore it or explain it away, but it always comes back, like a night fog at the doors and windows. You think it must be some kind of unreasonable prejudice, some inherited class sense, but you can't avoid it; it won't go away, it's there, it's real, it's true. And so you face it, you accept it for what it is." Nordhagen's wild eyes locked on mine, and he continued: "A fact, a simple fact. *There are just too many goddamn people.*"

Oh. Okay, say no more. Please say no more, old man. Old spider king of London.

The end was at hand. It had to be, I couldn't take any more of this. I was the final piece, the element that made Nordhagen's equation work. My presence, my apprenticeship, my ultimate complicity enabled his sociopathic lunacy to achieve the full freedom it sought. Now he could do anything. Whatever residual inhibitions he might still have felt had crumbled and given way. The amiable little doctor was gone forever, and with him any measure of control, competence, and social charm. The monster had taken over, conclusively. I'd already made up my mind I was going to kill Nordhagen, but now for the first time I knew I had to do it immediately. I wanted to reach across the table and strangle him on the spot. He was no longer human, not even marginally so; he was some terrible deviant creation, requiring prompt extermination.

I had to come up with something fast. The problem was not killing Nordhagen, but how to do it without implicating Lina and myself. We were both caught in the incredible web of this man's bloody existence. He had us trapped there, and the more I thought about it the more I hated him, with a cold, passionless hatred. And I felt again anger at myself—for if Nordhagen was utterly mad, I had been his fool.

"'Animal life sometimes reaches its entelechy in a stream of intuitions . . . the presence of other bodies . . . the ferments of its own blood.' Isn't that wonderful? 'Ferments of its own blood.' What an extraordinary phrase. Do you know Santayana?"

"No."

"You're remarkably unread, dear boy." He smiled. "Even for a medical man, and an American one at that."

"I guess so." I didn't care. He could twit me all night and it would still be better than listening to more of his apocalyptic visions.

"Culture meant something to my generation. We read, we learned, we memorized—that's something that seems to have vanished from the face of the earth. Memorizing. But that's the old way, and one culture becomes the manure for the next."

Nordhagen went on quoting and name-dropping, the strippers went on stripping, and at some point a tiny door opened in my brain, a light came on, and I found the way out. It was in my hand all the time. Alcohol. Not only would Nordhagen drink himself to death, but he would do it soon. Any day now. Starting tonight, in fact. It would need a little time to set up, but it couldn't wait. I had to get started tonight, even before I had a chance to consult Lina.

Sometimes I wonder if Nordhagen wasn't secretly pushing me in that direction. Perhaps he wanted me to put him out of it. For all his dire forecasts of things to come, he seemed weary, lacking in enthusiasm. Maybe he had gone so far that the lunacy was finally running out of steam. I could hope that, but I no longer felt I could run the risk of waiting to see.

I had caught my second or third wind, and I felt fairly clearheaded. I upped the pace of our drinking. Usually I slowed Nordhagen down, but now I urged him on. By five in the morning he was jolly again, and pretty far gone. I helped him into his house and stretched him out on the couch in the library. I stood over him for a while, until he was breathing loudly but regularly, and I was sure he was lost in drunken sleep. Then I went to the telephone on the desk at the back of the room and called Lina.

"Does he have any appointments in the next few days?"

"No, nothing important," she said, quickly alert.

"Anything at all?"

"Not that I know of—why?"

"He won't be able to keep them anyway."

"What's wrong?"

"Nothing. Things are happening, that's all."

"I'll be there in a few minutes," Lina said. "As soon as I can get dressed and get a cab."

"It's all right; don't hurry."

"I'm on my way."

Nordhagen would sleep for hours, I knew. I needed to think. I had to have the plan worked out when Lina arrived. I was tired from the long night and the drinks, but I knew that if I didn't go ahead with this now I might never be able to do so. Then Lina and I would be stuck with Nordhagen until he finally got around to dying on his own, and that was out of the question.

"What is it?" Lina asked before she had the door closed behind her.

"Nordhagen's asleep on the couch in the library. He's drunk and he should be out for a few hours."

"So?"

"I want you to watch him, and when he shows signs of

waking up, I want you to get him to swallow two of these."

I handed Lina a bottle of capsules I'd taken from the pharmacy in the cellar.

"Sedatives," she said, recognizing them.

"Yes."

"Why?"

"Because I have to go downstairs and think. There's a lot of work to be done. It's going to take a few days, at least, and I want Nordhagen out of the way. I want him helpless, unconscious, for as long as it takes. He is unavailable, from now on. He sees no one, he talks to no one. We'll keep him heavily sedated. We'll give him vitamins and food supplements, and maybe a bit of soup if necessary. Whatever it takes, I want him kept immobile."

"Why?" Not resisting, just asking.

"It's all over, Lina," I said. "It's all going down the tubes. Whether we like it or not, it's happening, and the only question is whether we control the process or it controls us. I've made my choice. Nordhagen is on the way out; we're only helping him down the last few steps. The mad king has gone to sleep, and he's not going to wake up again. Ever."

Lina said nothing.

"Can you handle it all on your side?" I asked. "The papers, the authorities? Will you be able to deal with all that?"

"Yes." She nodded.

"Will there be any problems?"

"I don't think so. It's complicated and clever, but it's all very tidy. They'll want to see everything—" she gave me a sharp look as she said this—"and they'll go over it all with a fine-tooth comb. They'll take their shares, but, no, I don't think there will be a problem. Not for us."

"Good. Call me if he gives you any trouble?"

I went down into the cellar and walked around, as if taking it all in for the first time. We couldn't take a chance on people wanting to inspect the place, and now the idea of walling up the cellar door seemed foolish. There wasn't time, I doubted I could do a satisfactory job, and it would only postpone the ultimate problem anyway. My new plan was to convert the cellar into an innocent-looking storage area and recreation room.

The movie screen and projector could stay. So could the bar and the chairs. The drugs and medicines would be moved: the legitimate ones would go upstairs to Nordhagen's offices; the ones we wanted would go to Lina's house; the rest would be flushed down the drain in the operating theater. The medical equipment would also go up to the offices, and what was too big or unwieldy would be left here in storage. The point was to make the place look unused, or at least unfinished.

I busied myself working in the pharmacy, buying time. I had to think it all out. There were hundreds of bottles to sort through, but it was an easy task, requiring little attention. When I got them all into three distinct groups, I went upstairs to find some bags or boxes.

Lina and Nordhagen were not in the library. I felt a stab of panic. I ran through the rest of the ground floor, and found Lina upstairs, at the door of Nordhagen's bedroom.

"He got up, went to the toilet, and then came straight up here to bed," she explained with a nervous smile. "I don't think he even woke up; his body just moved on its own. He never saw me."

"Good old alcohol," I said with relief. "Is there any way into the offices from here?"

"Yes, in the little hallway behind the library there's a connecting door. The key's on a nail there."

"Good."

The less activity out in the lane, the better. Lina told me where to find a supply of shopping bags, and I moved all the legitimate drugs from the pharmacy up to Nordhagen's offices. Then all the easy gear from the operating room. I washed some unneeded and risky compounds down the drain and bagged all the drugs I wanted and took them upstairs.

By then I was exhausted. I'd been going for more than twenty-four hours, many of them spent boozing. I helped Lina get a dose of sedative into Nordhagen and went to my place and fell asleep on the bed without bothering to take off my clothes.

It was dark outside when I awoke. I was sweaty, groggy, and there was a pain in my stomach that was not due to hunger alone. I grabbed an apple, which didn't help, and went back to Nordhagen's house. The situation was unchanged. Lina sat, going through a stack of papers while Nordhagen snored roughly. I went downstairs. I found a liter of fruit juice in the refrigerator and dissolved some vitamins, minerals, and raw protein in it. I took the mixture up to Lina.

"Get some of this into him with the next dose of sedative," I told her. "You can powder the sedative—break the capsules and put them in the juice. That should make it easier for you. He swallows liquids by reflex."

It wasn't great for the old man's system, but it should be enough to keep him going as he slept. The worst thing that could happen would be for Nordhagen to jump the gun and die before we were ready.

Back in the cellar, I had to take time to feed the captive population. They had been neglected for a full day, and were probably in a state of great anxiety as well as physical discomfort. I put on a movie for them—*I'm All Right, Jack*, with Peter Sellers. They wouldn't complain.

I found a couple of push brooms, one in better condition than the other. I took them both, along with some surgical gloves and masks, and I went down into the crypt. This was a crucial test. This room had to be empty. I turned the lights on. The sight of all those mummified bodies and limbs seemed even worse than I remembered. I put on a mask and a pair of gloves, and, without hesitating, I dragged the nearest body and shoved it into the quicklime. I used a broom to push it down under the thick grey-white sludge. Then I waited. Five minutes. Nothing happened. He didn't pop back up and smile at me.

The rest followed. It was slow, nauseating work, but my mind blanked out and I went about the job mechanically. Even so, it was devastating. In medical school and in the hospital I'd seen plenty of dead bodies. I'd taken part in dissections and autopsies. But this was different, so different. They didn't look like human beings anymore, but rather like some kind of imperfect leather manikins. And yet, at the same time, their features were so terribly human still. Their hair was dull, but had color. Their eyes were shrunk and hardened in their sockets, but they still looked like human eyes. Their skin was puckered and pliable in places. Even their pubic hair stayed curly long into death.

By the time I shoved the twenty-seventh and last body into the quicklime, I was in a bad state. The only way to finish the job was in a spasm, a frenzy, and so I drove myself. I grabbed up arms and legs like logs, and I flung them toward the pit. Then I swept them in with the clean broom. They piled up like a knot of grotesque pretzels. I kept shoving, poking, pushing, terrified that they wouldn't all fit. But the last yellowed leg finally went under, and the surface of the lime remained unbroken.

That's an end to your hideous morgue, Nordhagen, I thought bitterly. The crypt floor was littered with dust and human debris, bits of desiccated flesh that had fallen off with the passage of time. I swept the room clean, then went upstairs. My mind was full of nothing but hatred for Nordhagen.

Lina was asleep in a chair, and Nordhagen was tossing fitfully. This shook me. I hadn't considered what a long day and night it had been for Lina. What if I had stayed in the cellar another hour or two, and the old man had regained consciousness?

It would be so much easier to inject sedatives, but I didn't want anyone to wonder about recent needle marks on Nordhagen's body. I didn't know when Lina had last given him a dose, and I didn't want to wake her. I broke two more capsules in his mouth and poured water after the powder. He gagged and dribbled some of it away, but most of it went down. The hell with it; I was doing him a favor keeping him asleep. The way I felt, if he woke up I'd punch his face in.

I carried Lina downstairs, put her on the sofa, and covered her with a blanket I'd taken from Nordhagen's bed. Then I poured myself a large strong drink of malt Scotch on ice with a splash of water and went back up to Nordhagen's bedroom to do my stint of baby-sitting. The old man's breathing continued noisy, but his pulse was all right.

I was calmer now, but still upset over what I thought had been a close call. The plan required constant care and scrutiny. I wasn't worried about Nordhagen going to the police if he happened to wake up and get away from us; that was no danger. But I didn't want a whole new problem. I didn't want to have to worry about Nordhagen's vengeance. No question, he had the money and the resources to find us and take care of us.

Even as I was thinking this, I realized that I was no longer engaged in the relatively simple business of murder. We were in a life-or-death struggle with Nordhagen, and if we didn't win, we'd die at his hands—or, worse, we'd end up in his cabinets in the cellar. That's what it came down to, Lina and me against Nordhagen. It gave me a better understanding of where I was and what I had to do. There could be no more slips, not even a near miss. Nordhagen was a far greater threat than the police.

Part of my original plan had been to move into a hotel or a convenience flat. I would make myself scarce and avoid attention when Nordhagen died. But now I thought that would be a mistake. People had seen me around the place, coming and going. It would be more suspicious to up and disappear at the crucial moment.

It would be better to stay where I was. If the police had any questions for me, I would just have to answer them. No, I didn't work here in Britain. I'm an American. I was renting this place from him. Met him in a bar, met his assistant. Moved into this spare flat he had. Sure she's my girlfriend; you're damn right I love her. That's the way, I thought. Stay as close to the truth as possible, and then hang tough. Oh, yeah, the old boy sure did drink. He could really put the sauce away. All over London there were bartenders and club proprietors who could testify to that. I'd be glad to draw up a list—I had an instant army of witnesses. I had to smile. It was all taking shape, and even Nordhagen was being a help.

I walked across the room and looked at him. He was such a pathetic figure, a short, slight man with a beach ball of a liver bulging under his shirt and a network of busted capillaries providing the only color on his pasty wreck of a face. And yet he was intelligent, a fine mind and an accomplished surgeon, extremely well read, cultured, and generous. It was hard to reconcile this man with the one who had brought death to dozens of people and mutilated many more, the man who slowly and with painstaking care had put together his very own kingdom, or concentration camp, in the elegant heart of London. I thought about Nordhagen, working by day to make pretty debutantes even prettier, adding the finishing touches God had forgotten; and then by night methodically going about his other business, his other surgery, in the cellar.

Lina was right: the word *lunacy* explained nothing. The more I thought about Nordhagen, the more I thought that word was irrelevant. I had come to the center of the mystery and found—nothing. Maybe it had been wrong to think there was an answer. Maybe Nordhagen was just another blind fact, a small part of the force of nature at work in the world. It didn't really matter now. Another, greater, force had taken Nordhagen's destiny in hand. Lina and I were that force.

I sat up into the next day. We'd passed the twenty-four-hour mark. Lina came upstairs and we talked. I had the worrying feeling that we were still too disorganized. I sent her back to her house to get clothes and whatever else we would need for the duration. She took the bag of drugs with her and returned two hours later. She made me something to eat, and then I went next door to my place. I showered, slept, woke up late in the afternoon, feeling much better.

Lina was sitting in the same chair in the bedroom, but Nordhagen was gone. I stood in the doorway, staring at the empty bed. Lina pointed to the bathroom. Nordhagen was in the tub, naked and snoring.

"He soiled his clothes," Lina said. "I got him out of them and washed him, but I couldn't get him out of the tub."

"Well, it's convenient, I guess. And neat. He didn't wake through all of that?"

"Not really. He muttered a bit, but nothing intelligible. He just needed wrestling."

"It's a good sedative."

"Oh, about that," Lina said. "I think I gave him three last time. I had a job getting him to take them, and I think I counted wrong in the fuss."

"It won't kill him. I hope."

Lina went downstairs and made sandwiches for us.

"Do you need a rest?" I asked while we ate.

"I'm all right."

"Why don't you take a nap for a couple of hours. Then you can sit again while I do some more work in the cellar. It may turn out to be a long night."

She nodded. I hadn't told her what I was doing down there, and she hadn't asked.

When Lina woke later, refreshed, we forced more of the enriched fruit juice down Nordhagen's throat, along with more sedative.

As I went down to the cellar, I was thinking about Nordhagen's people. They were undoubtedly hungry again, and in acute terror. What, they must be wondering, was going on? A routine is a routine, even in hell, and theirs had been disrupted. They hadn't seen Nordhagen in two days. They'd seen me go into the crypt once and come back later. I wanted to put them at ease. I let them see me walking casually about. I turned on the music. It was all business as usual, more or less. I could tell by the way they watched me that they were all thinking the same thing: Where is Nordhagen? Spot of bother, folks, he's got himself in a spot of bother. How I would have liked to tell them that the little doctor had been rendered every bit as immobile as they were; he was anatomically intact, true, but there still seemed a certain justice to his present condition.

I didn't bother with the food. Instead, I gave them all a monumental serving of gin and tonic, laced with something colorless, odorless, tasteless, and conclusive. While I was going about this I was perfectly calm, but then, when I sat down on the stool in the control booth to wait, I looked at my hands—and they were shaking. Badly.

The irony did not escape me. To save these people from Nordhagen I had to kill them. It was the only way, I kept telling myself. But my mind, perversely, conjured up images of Cambodia, and I couldn't help wondering if I was some new Pol Pot, come with a solution far more disastrous than the original problem. But if it had to be, let it be. If these people had been given a vote on it, would they really choose to hang on, literally, to be muted and blinded and continually tortured until the same end came to pass, as it inevitably would with Nordhagen's wonderful "forced elective annihilations"? And I remembered something else Nordhagen had told me: Sometimes it's necessary to be cruel to be kind. These deaths could not be avoided, but I, at least, was making them painless. I was sending these people on their way with a colossal gin-and-tonic!

I sat in the control booth, in the soft green-and-orange glow of the electronic displays, and stared at my trembling hands until the last vital signs disappeared from the monitors. Then I put on a fresh mask, a new pair of surgical gloves, and went to work.

I took them, one by one, out of their harnesses, out of the cabinets, and down into the crypt. There, at the lip of the pit, I vented their torsos to keep them from puffing up like balloons on their own gases. I pushed them into the quicklime. The pit took all of them, and I thought of it now as some infinitely elastic bubble of death growing beneath the skin of London. When I was done, I sat for a minute. My body ached, and I toyed with the idle notion of jumping into the pit after all those bodies, swimming into their number. But whatever it was that I craved, it wasn't painful death.

I had intended to carry on with the job of dismantling the cabinets and the rest of Nordhagen's infernal machinery, but this act of miniature genocide had done me in for the night. I dragged my body upstairs, found Lina, and collapsed in her arms. I could hear Nordhagen breathing stertoriously in the bathroom.

"It's done," I said weakly. "It's done with."

Lina brushed my hair from my forehead, and she caressed my face. She helped me into a spare bedroom and took off my clothes. She pulled the covers back and put me on the sheet, face down. She left the room, came back a minute later, and I heard her shoes hit the floor. She sat on my butt and rubbed me with alcohol, cool and soothing. She exorcised the demons massed in my neck, throughout my back, arms, and shoulders. And at some point, while she worked my body expertly, I floated off into a deep and dreamless sleep.

The first thing I saw when I opened my eyes was the ugly naked body of Roger Nordhagen. He was standing, tottering, in the doorway, a look of total bewilderment on his face. I jumped out of bed in terror and panic, but he was going nowhere. He swayed sickly, his eyes fluttered up, and he slumped to the floor. Cursing under my breath, I dragged him back into the bathroom, slid him into the tub, and forced more sedative down his throat. I didn't care if it killed him; I just didn't want to see the bastard on his feet again.

Lina was asleep in the chair. She had set an alarm clock on the table next to her, and I saw that it would have gone off in another fifteen minutes. I was furious, sick with fear. I wanted to slam the clock against the wall and scream at Lina. But then I saw that it was very bright outside. The clock showed three-fifteen, and that meant I had been out for nearly twelve hours. No wonder she hadn't been able to make it. She should have awakened me, but at least she had set the alarm. My anger was gone now, but there was still a lot of fear in me. This second close call had been closer yet. I didn't want to warn Lina and risk upsetting her, but our schedules would need more careful structuring.

Then the telephone rang shrilly, and I shouted incoherently in surprise. A few seconds later the doorbell bonged in a dreadful imitation of Big Ben.

"I'll take care of the door," Lina said, instantly awake. "Leave the phone." She hurried from the room.

I couldn't stand the sound of the telephone, so I got out of the bedroom fast, shutting the door to muffle the ringing. I went into the bathroom and stood over the tub. Wake up, I was thinking, come on, wake up right now. My fists were clenched rock-hard, and it was a good thing Nordhagen was drugged into the twilight zone, because I might well have pounded his brains out on the bathtub faucet if he had so much as opened an eyelid.

"It was only the postman," Lina said with a sleepy smile when she returned. "A couple of parcels. Medical samples. Roger gets them all the time."

"Do you think we should have answered the phone?"

"No, that's all right. But if it rings again I'll take it. They know me, they don't know you."

"They who?"

"Probably no one important," Lina said. "Social acquaintances. Roger knows a lot of people through his practice, and they're always trying to get him to go out to dinner, or to some function or other. I can handle it; don't worry."

"I thought he didn't socialize."

"He didn't; not much at least. Once in a blue moon. That way he managed to maintain his network of contacts while cultivating his image of an elusive, mysterious person."

"Clever man," I said.

"He was very clever. It was accepted that he appeared only rarely. It fed the image, and so it was good for business. Some people came to him not just because he was good, but because he had that mysterious quality."

"And it helps us."

Just then the alarm clock went off with a clatter. Lina silenced it before I could destroy the damn thing. We looked at each other, smiled, and began to laugh like two children who had gotten away with something. Lina came to me and we hugged. I knew we hadn't gotten away with anything, but we still had the game in control.

"Are you sure there's no one else who might be calling him up on the phone? He had no close friend?"

"No, not as long as I've known him," Lina said.

"How long is that?"

"Long enough to know if there were someone."

"Okay. I gave him more sedative a few minutes ago. He won't move for some time now."

We went into the spare bedroom. I was still undressed. Lina took off her clothes, and we huddled under the covers. We kissed and held each other. No sex—there was no need for it just now—only the giving and taking of comfort in each other's arms. We didn't sleep, but we held ourselves in a dreamy, restful state for an hour or so.

The worst was over, I kept telling myself. Nothing the future held could ever compare with what I had already gone through in disposing of the people and corpses in the cellar. When it came time to take care of Nordhagen, it would be as easy as clapping a mosquito.

"Keep an eye on him," I told Lina when I started downstairs later. "Not just to see that he stays put. The thing that worries me, giving him all these pills, is that he might vomit and suffocate himself without waking. Make sure he's breathing."

This idea bothered me so much that when I reached the cellar I cut a piece of plastic tubing and brought it back up to Lina. I told her how to use it if there was an emergency. I didn't want her to have to waste time running for me.

The next stage of the plan involved sheer physical labor, and little else. I had to dismantle Nordhagen's elaborate construction: the table, the cabinets, the console, and the entire support system. I began by hammering the cabinets apart. It was slow, tiring work, and I was not in the best of shape after months of drinking and late nights. I had to stop frequently and catch my breath. I was soon drenched with sweat.

There was a ventilation shaft that went from the cellar up through the roof of the building, and I gave a lot of thought to the idea of torching the whole wooden structure. It would burn, and since the cellar was all stone, the fire would be safely contained. I finally decided against it, though. Day or night, there were too many people on the streets of Mayfair, and someone would surely notice smoke in smokeless central London.

So I hammered, sawed, and hammered some more. It was tricky with those joints that had been put together with screws, but fortunately there weren't too many of them. I tried unscrewing them, but my hand soon lost its grip in cramps, and I had to saw around them. It made for some odd cuts, but I could only hope no one would bother examining the woodpile carefully.

The wood did pile up. For a long time it seemed I was making no headway, but then it reached a point of critical mass, where I could believe I really would finish it, and I found it easier from that point on. The circular saw that had helped Nordhagen put together this monstrosity now helped me take it apart. It's not as bad as tearing down one of the pyramids of Egypt stone by stone, I told myself, although it seemed much the same kind of job. If anyone did ask about the huge load of lumber stacked up in the cellar, Lina could say she knew nothing about it. Perhaps Roger intended to build something, or perhaps it was left over from when he had converted the mews. Who cares? It was losing its sinister character and going back to being plain wood.

The electronics and plumbing were another matter. Every piece of metal that fit went into the quicklime, disappearing nicely. This included some expensive medical equipment, monitors and the like, which had no reasonable excuse for being in the consulting rooms of a cosmetic surgeon. The rest—pipes, tubes, pumps, i.v.s—I disconnected, cleaned, and stored in the now empty pharmacy. The last items were the glass doors from the cabinets. I thought of leaving them by the lumber, but they would look kind of peculiar, a dozen of them begging to be explained. I ended up smashing them to bits with a hammer in the crypt and sweeping the shards into the all-accommodating hole. The last of the glass stayed stubbornly on the surface of the lime, and it took some doing to tamp it all under.

I swept the cellar a couple of times. I stacked and restacked the lumber, trying to make it look less conspicuous—but there was a hell of a lot of it, and finally I had to leave it. Now the horror chamber looked as innocent as it ever would. A movie screen, a bar, an impressive stereo sound system, the wood, the tools, miscellaneous medical gear in storage—yes, it all added up to nothing special. An unfinished recreation room? Yes, that was a reasonable possibility, one might conclude.

I sat for a full hour or more, and I told myself it looked fine. But I knew the room so well, and its horrible past was so fresh and vivid in my mind, that it seemed to cry out its abominable story. I had to bring Lina down, see her smile, and hear her say, "I don't believe you," before I could believe it really was all right. She hugged me, and I felt a strange sense of pride. I felt somehow cleaner, as if in dismantling Nordhagen's nightmare I had also atoned for myself.

"What about the quicklime pit?" Lina asked.

"I'm not sure what to do."

It was the only problem left in the cellar. I could use some of the plywood to make a rough cap that would wedge into the opening, and I could pour cement over that level with the floor. But new cement would stand out brightly in the middle of all that ancient stone, no matter how I might try to disguise it with dust and dirt. Which would look more intriguing to a potential snoop, a new cement cap or an open lime pit? New cement, we decided—that always makes a person think of buried bodies. We put a couple of two-by-fours across the pit and laid a sheet of plywood on top of them. That made the opening "safe" without appearing to hide anything.

Before covering the pit, I used the brooms to probe as far as possible in all directions. I felt no contact and pushed the brooms in too. By now I had developed a fondness for this pocket of the past. Without it, Lina and I would have had far less room in which to maneuver.

All of this work took five long sessions, with time in between for eating and sleeping. I had lost all track of day and night. I was working my way through some dark tunnel, hoping it would come out somewhere. Nordhagen drifted on his way in an artificial coma, and he caused no further trouble. But I knew we were running out of time. The old man was alive but deteriorating. His skin had taken on an awful pallor, his breathing became slowly weaker, and it was obvious that the way we fed and drugged him did no good to an already ravaged system.

When I finished with the cellar, a new uncertainty took hold of me, one I hadn't expected. I had thought it would be easy to kill Nordhagen, but now I wondered about it. Was it really so necessary? Couldn't we revive him and explain the new situation in such a way that he would come to accept it? It would all depend on Lina. I was the new boy, and a traitor to boot. But Nordhagen felt so strongly about Lina—could she persuade him? Or would he go berserk, regarding her betrayal as far worse than mine?

I didn't like to think of Nordhagen as a living, active enemy. With his kingdom gone, he would have only the two of us, and he would focus what was left of his impossible mind on us all the more intensely. There was no sensible way to prolong this man. He had to go. It was time for him to return his ticket.

We held on an extra day and a half to get to Friday. Then, through the morning, we let Nordhagen revive to the point of semiconsciousness. He was groggy and pliable, and the pain showing on his face was undoubtedly due to a blockbuster headache. At noon we put on surgical gloves and began to feed him whiskey. High-quality malt. It must have been pretty rough on his stomach, and he constantly gagged and retched, but we kept on pouring the stuff into him. He whined through his teeth between swallows. When he tried to keep his mouth shut, I went and found a funnel in the kitchen. I got it between his teeth by smacking the side of his head a couple of times. Then I filled the funnel with whiskey and held his nose. Some oozed out of his lips, but most of it went down. It was a very effective method. When the alcohol took hold of him, he stopped resisting. I took the funnel away, and he drank peaceably. All we had to do was refill the glass and make sure he didn't waste time. We had to get a lot of it in him in a short period of time.

One bottle should have been sufficient, but I was in a hurry and I opened a second. Nordhagen had momentary flashes of lucidity. His face formed a silly smile that stayed to the end. He looked at Lina and me with something like affection as he drank, as if we were doing him a favor. But then, maybe we were. I couldn't say if I was doing something I had decided myself to do, or if Lina had secretly engineered this, or even if it was what Nordhagen had intended me to do all along. It came down to the same thing in the end.

"Go smiling . . . the sweet, sweet darkness," Nordhagen mumbled.

Yes, he was conscious enough to know what was going on now, and he was smiling about it. Good, I thought, and pushed the glass to his lips again. His eyelids grew heavy, and his eyes were unseeing. As I watched him slipping, the thought came to me that we wouldn't be able to use the Feathers anymore. Too bad.

While I kept getting the Scotch into him, Lina pressed his hand around the two bottles several times. Later I did the same thing with the glass.

He lasted longer than I had expected, which seemed only to confirm my fears about his ability to live a few more years. I was glad we were doing this; it seemed more and more correct with each passing minute. Nordhagen sensed he was going under, and he struggled to raise himself slightly.

"Death is . . . funny. . . ."

I wanted to push him down and shut him up, but I couldn't.

"Like trying to . . . midwife a void . . . The way is . . . take a deep breath and . . . make it your last. . . ."

He tried—I'll give him that—he tried. His chest swelled and his face flickered from grey to blotchy red to blotchy purple, then to ash-white. But he exhaled in frustration.

"Damn," he griped.

I'd had enough. I pushed him, and he seemed to cave in on the bed. His eyes closed. A tiny ghost of a whistle came from his mouth. He didn't seem to be breathing, but I knew he was. He still had a very faint pulse.

"It'll be a while yet," I told Lina. "His autonomous functions are forgetting to do what they do. It'll be a while yet, but he's as good as gone."

I got up and walked around the room, always keeping an eye on Lina. I had hardly looked at her during the whole procedure, but now I wanted to see how she reacted to his death. She sat there for a while, gazing at Nordhagen. Her face seemed to be without expression. When she was ready, she rose and turned away from the bed, her hand touching his lightly as she left.

We had things to do. Lina went out through the offices and walked to Mount Street to find a taxi. She was going to Queens Wood. The day before, she had taken a shopping bag containing a few items of my clothing to her house. We had tidied up Nordhagen's place, and I spent the next hour going over it all again, erasing our fingerprints everywhere except in the library, where they would not seem inappropriate. Twice I returned to the cellar and looked around. Even then I wouldn't have been completely surprised to find an army of corpses, it was so hard to believe the nightmare was really over.

I sat by a window and watched the lane for a while. Both sides were, for the most part, just the backs of buildings, but there were a couple of other converted mews houses like Nordhagen's. We counted on those people being out during the day. Anyhow, they presumably paid little attention to our comings and goings. It seemed a reasonable risk. If someone did place Lina or me here close to the determined time of Nordhagen's death—well, we had it worked out as best we could. Sure, he had been drinking. More and more, lately. He seemed all right, buzzed but not blitzed. And then we had to go. . . .

I checked him every ten minutes until I was sure he was dead. Then I checked him again every five minutes for half an hour. I had to be sure nothing but divine intervention would bring him back. Finally I had no doubt that the life was well and truly gone from him. Everything was in place. I deliberately left from his house, not the offices. The front door locked automatically behind me.

I had a jacket on, no hat, no overcoat. I carried nothing. I strolled to Green Park and took the tube two stops to Leicester Square. I walked the rest of the way, crossing the river on the footbridge. Walking was once again a great pleasure for me. I had timed it well. Lina was waiting near the platform. She had two small suitcases, one for each of us. Our train pulled out of Waterloo Station ten minutes later.

We had reserved a room for two in my name at Wheeler's hotel on the sea front in Brighton. We went out once or twice, but spent most of the weekend in our room. It was a very mellow, relaxed time. We looked out the window at the sea front. We held each other. We slept.

III

CULTE DE MOI

Everything is a dangerous drug except reality, which
is unendurable. Happiness is in the imagination.
—CYRIL CONNOLLY, *THE UNQUIET GRAVE*

FOURTEEN

Everything went to Lina. Everything, that is, except a solid gold card engraved with the word *Thanks*, which was sent to that oilman in Oklahoma. The only surprise was that Nordhagen hadn't been able to come up with one other thing to do with some of his money. Lina got it all, or most of it. The tax people took a good bite of what was in the four U.K. bank accounts and safe-deposit boxes, but there was still plenty left over, along with the property in Millington Lane. Lina knew that a lot more money waited for her overseas.

The will, which neither of us had ever been sure actually existed, made things simple. It took time, of course, and Lina had to deal at length with solicitors, accountants, bankers, and a variety of other interested parties. We lost time together. For a while we saw each other only at night and on weekends. It even began to annoy me, as if we were still in Nordhagen's grip. His wealth felt like an invisible net that had fallen on us, and I wasn't always sure we would be able to find our way out from under it.

But there were no problems arising from Nordhagen's death. Lina "found" him Monday afternoon. ("Since he closed the practice, I've only been working part-time, helping him with his papers.") Alcohol was the obvious cause, and it was noted that Nordhagen's liver was heavily scarred and in an advanced state of fibrosis. No problems, no questions. Lina had him cremated, and there was a memorial service, which I didn't attend.

I was just the friendly neighbor-tenant. There was nothing on paper between Nordhagen and me, so my rent had to be formalized. No trouble with this, since the solicitors understood that Lina would be getting the property, and she was agreeable. We made an arrangement for me to pay the estate in the interim. But Nordhagen continued to pay it, actually, because my secret wages continued to arrive in my bank account each month—a nice touch, and one I appreciated.

I was sure the police would come around once they learned that Lina was the sole heiress and that she had a boyfriend living on the property. But they never came to see me, and if they spoke with Lina, she never mentioned it. There really was nothing suspicious about Nordhagen's boozy death, you see.

I continued to live in the flat in Mayfair. Moving out to Queens Wood didn't seem like a good idea, for a number of reasons—not least of which being that Lina was hardly ever home. There was a better chance of seeing her at Millington Lane, a few minutes snatched here and there during the day. And she often stayed with me at night. The plain, cold room didn't inhibit us at all. In fact, some of our wildest, best moments were spent there—which seemed to be yet another confirmation that what was strong between us was strong in and of itself, and depended in no way on anything outside of us.

I made a couple of telephone calls to my parents,

which served to mollify them for the lack of letters. One or the other of them wrote to me regularly, a growing pile of letters read once and mostly forgotten on the floor under my bed. It was not uncomfortable, hearing them, talking with them, but there was something strange about it. They were still the same people, solid, utterly familiar, the people I had grown up with and whom I'd left back in America last October. But I was different, far different, and I felt distant. I was in some new orbit, in relation not only to them, but also to their whole world.

"What are you going to do with this place?" I asked Lina one evening. We were sitting in Nordhagen's library, reducing the stock of liquor in leisurely fashion.

"Why? Do you want to live here?"

"No. Not particularly."

The place had too many ghosts for me, and the aura of recent terror. Real or imaginary, who needed it?

"Amen. So sell."

"I think I will."

"And the pit?"

"Let the buyer beware he doesn't fall in it. As far as I'm concerned, it was always there. Roger never used the room, to my knowledge. The pit is ancient history, nothing to do with any of us. The buyer would probably choose to cap it with cement, or maybe I can get the solicitors to suggest that. Either way, they'd be unlikely to go poking around in it."

"Still, if some historian or archaeologist got wind of it . . ."

"No." Lina shook her head. "It doesn't make any sense. People didn't hide treasure in quicklime. Nothing of any value or interest would be in it. A lime pit is just a nuisance, that's all. Why, if we tried, I bet we couldn't even persuade anyone to bother probing it."

"Maybe."

"And suppose they did haul out a corpse," she went on. "That would be the worst thing, right? But what would it have to do with us? They couldn't tie us in to it."

"They could date the bodies," I pointed out. "Roughly, but they could tell the person died and was put there during Nordhagen's ownership."

"Nordhagen. Exactly. Not us."

"Well . . . I guess so." I began to think she was right. What evidence was there to link us with any of those deaths? None. Was there? "It's your decision," I told her.

"I think I will sell it. And the house in Queens Wood."

"What?" I jumped a little at that, causing Lina to smile. "I thought you said you'd never leave that place?"

"Let's take a walk. I want to show you something."

We went through Hyde Park in the last of the evening light. It was very pleasant, and I had come to like the gentler London spring, the way it eased into summer. By contrast, the change of seasons back in New Haven seemed sharp and violent, forcing you into sudden adjustments. We came out on Bayswater Road and walked in a leisurely fashion toward Notting Hill.

"What do you think?"

Lina had stopped me in front of a large, square brick building. Three floors. Completely detached, with walls separating it from the commercial properties on either side. There were curtains in the windows, but the lawn needed mowing and the place looked as if it were not in use.

"Where's the For Sale sign?"

"It's not on the market yet, not officially. But I heard about it, and I like it. There's a private-entrance garage in the rear, a fine deep cellar, and no neighbors at night."

"Sounds good," I said evenly.

"It's Georgian."

She added that as an afterthought, but it meant nothing to me. I was still pondering the private-entrance garage, the fine deep cellar, and the lack of neighbors at night.

Time began to swing more in our favor as Lina cleared up the business of Nordhagen's estate. We had more hours of the day together, and I became involved in speeding the process of disencumbrance.

We sold Nordhagen's possessions in assorted lots—the books, the medical equipment, the furniture. We packed his clothes in bags and delivered them to a charity for homeless indigents. It was pleasing to think that vagrants, who were some of Nordhagen's victims and potential targets, might end up wearing his clothes. Nordhagen had little else of value—some unremarkable art and a few modest antiques. We sold them too. And we threw out several trash bags full of his papers—rambling, obscure stuff that didn't seem worth deciphering.

The solicitors needed little prompting. Yes, they thought the pit should be covered. They saw to it for Lina. They hired builders, who did, I hear, a first-class job. There was a bonus in this, because the builders were also glad to do a woman a favor and take that lumber. What did she want with a bunch of old wood anyway? So they paid a small sum, no doubt a bargain price, and hauled it all away.

We kept a few things: the liquor, the stereo system, the screen, projector, and film library (not that I ever wanted to see *Expresso Bongo* again). The rest of Nordhagen's miscellaneous possessions, those that were saleable but not worth the bother, went to Oxfam.

Lina went ahead with her pre-emptive bid for the house on Bayswater Road. She got the place. While that was in the works, she put the Millington Lane property on the market, and it was gobbled up quickly by a left-wing trade union "as an investment." This amused Lina greatly.

The first time I saw the inside of the house on Bayswater Road, I was taken aback by its size. The look of it from the street was deceptive. What were we going to do with all that space?

Lina had ideas. Plenty of them. The sale of Nordhagen's property paid for Bayswater Road, and the sale of the Queens Wood house paid for the extensive renovation. She never had to touch the main inheritance. She and I lived in one room and the kitchen while an architect and a team of builders went to work.

One large room was given over to the aquarium, which was enlarged, and the stellar planetarium. Another room was transformed into a more elaborate version of the sunken pit in Queens Wood. This took up some of the cellar, but, as Lina had said, it was spacious and deep. I wasn't unhappy when the cellar was made into a gymnasium, with adjoining steam bath, showers, and hot tub. A smaller room required little to turn it into a screening room. At my suggestion, another corner of the house was redone as a bar. The roof over what would become our bedroom was opened and skylights were installed. Lina had plans for a kind of patio-garden on the roof.

It was pretty late in the day when I realized that the house in Bayswater Road was becoming a variation of the Feathers. Not quite as elaborate or rich, but the same basic idea. The only thing missing was the service staff. When I mentioned this to Lina, she laughed.

"No," she said. "You're confusing the framework with the fantasy. Actually, I was thinking that this would make a fine commune for prostitutes. You could have any number of self-employed girls freelancing here, making use of the facilities. Run it as a nonprofit enterprise; keep the money moving around in circles. But the laws are too tricky, so it'll just have to be our fun house."

"That's okay with me."

Days, weeks, months—there were times when I thought all the busy-ness would never end. But there finally came an afternoon when the last of the carpenters packed up and left, and I realized they wouldn't be coming back. I shut the front door and went to find Lina. We went into the bar and had a drink.

"You don't have to see anyone," I said.

"No."

"Not tomorrow, not the next day or the day after that. You don't have to see anyone."

"No." She laughed.

"And there are no more workmen coming here."

"Not unless something breaks down."

"Yeah, but otherwise . . ."

"Otherwise, no one."

"Cheers."

"Cheers."

We sat for a long time, smiling, drinking, looking at each other. It was nice. Home at last, I was thinking, we're home at last.

It was very quiet.

FIFTEEN

I thought it was unnecessary business, but it was business all the same that set us off on our grand tour. It seemed that the only way to exorcise Nordhagen completely would be to settle once and for all the matter of his overseas property. Until we did, it would hang over us like some cloud of uncertainty.

Boredom may have had a small part in it too. Although we never discussed it in so many words, Lina and I both needed a break; we needed to get away from London for a while. And so, not long after the house on Bayswater Road was refurbished and we were settled in, Lina and I packed and left the country.

We spent a week in Geneva. The lake was probably beautiful at some other time of the year, and I soon tired of walking around what struck me as a rather dull Protestant city. I could get no feel for the place, but admittedly I didn't make much effort.

Lina saw to her business. She went armed with only a single scrap of paper, on which were typed the names of three banks and three long account numbers. Even with the sanctity of the Swiss banking system, Nordhagen felt compelled to spread his money around. Lina consolidated the accounts into one, and at the same time learned that she was richer than she had thought.

"Where did he get so much?" I asked. "I don't care how good his practice was, that can't all have come from cosmetic surgery."

"No, I don't think it did," Lina admitted. "But some of the people who ended up in the cellar—before they were permanently imprisoned, I think Nordhagen let them 'buy' their freedom."

"They had money? I thought most of them were street people."

"Most, but not all. Some had money."

And there had been more than the twelve in the cabinets, I reminded myself. There were the .others, in the crypt.

"And then he didn't go through with his part of the deal."

"You can't deal with the devil," Lina said. "But if you're up against it, you'll try anything—even signing away whatever you have."

"I don't know how he got away with it for so long."

"He was very clever, and in his own way cautious. Someone went missing, and then their money disappeared into Switzerland. If you were a friend or a relative or a business associate of that person, what would you think?"

"That they'd run away to start a new life under a new identity."

"Exactly," Lina said.

"He was an extraordinary little monster."

"I think some of it is old money," Lina went on. "I don't know much about his past, but I got the impression he came from a wealthy family. He had no living relatives, so it's reasonable to assume that whatever there was in the family made its way to him as they died off over the years."

"The last of the line," I said. That was a comforting thought. "You handled his paperwork . . ."

"The smallest part of it. The British part. He depended on me, but he kept a lot from me. Most of what I know was put together from odd remarks and hints dropped over a period of time."

"Tell me," I said, "how you and Nordhagen came together in the first place."

"I answered an ad," she replied with a smile. "And of course I got the job. It was that simple."

"What happened to your predecessor?" I wondered if she had ended up in the crypt.

"Oh, Roger went through receptionists at a regular clip. Either they didn't take to him or he didn't feel comfortable with them."

"But he did with you."

"Yes."

"And was that horror show already in the cellar when you came on the scene?"

"Yes."

"How long did it take him to show you?"

Lina shrugged. "A while. He was much more terrified of me than he was of you."

"Because you were there to act as a buffer." Lina nodded, and I went on, "Why didn't you turn him in then, when you had the chance?"

"I used to wonder about that all the time," she said, swirling the ice cubes in her drink. "I could give you a lot of reasons. Fear, to start with. I was afraid he'd add me to his collection if I didn't convince him he could trust me. And then, I didn't want to see Roger and those mutilated people turned into media freaks. And I didn't want to cast myself in the role of the good girl who did the right thing. Good citizen Ravachol. My namesake would spin in his grave.

"But I think the real reason, if there is one, was that I realized at the time, subconsciously, that my life could go one of two ways from that point. I chose the way that was right for me. You see, Tom, I went through pretty much the same thing you did. You've just followed my trail. And maybe the reason behind the reason, why I chose this way instead of the other, is that I'm greedy, selfish, hungry, ambitious. But I don't regard those as vices. I'm not a hypocrite. They're just part of the basic will to live. The world doesn't care, Tom; the world just goes on. That's all. That's everything. And I've chosen to go with it, to be out in front rather than ground down slowly over the course of an ordinary life."

Lina looked as if she were about to continue, but she stopped herself with a laugh—at herself, it seemed—and then looked away. I wanted her to keep talking because her words were hypnotic, and because I knew she was telling me about myself. But already she was drifting out of this rare mood.

"What did you feel, watching him die?"

Was this a cruel question? I had been waiting for the right time to put it to her. She was looking out the window at Lake Geneva, and she didn't move for a long moment. Then she turned and met my stare.

"Very little," she said. "Relief, for myself, for us. And maybe even for him. But otherwise, nothing."

I'm not sure I fully believed her, although her face was a picture of cool certainty. Was it really possible that she could mean so much to him and not feel anything in the hours that led to his extinction? But then, she had assisted ably at the time. I finished my drink in silence.

* * *

From Geneva we flew to Rome and changed planes. Later that night we had a two-hour stopover in Bahrain. The following morning we landed in the deadening heat and humidity of Bangkok. We had intended to stay a few days, but the atmosphere was so oppressive we left after only twenty-four hours. We took a domestic Thai flight to Phuket Island, in the Andaman Sea, far to the south-west of Bangkok. There we located a Thai businessman with an unpronounceable name, who studied Lina's documentation with great care before smiling and producing a set of keys. He gave directions to our driver. Years ago, it seemed, Nordhagen had chanced on Phuket. He liked what he saw, bought a piece of land for a pittance, and had a simple bungalow built on the site.

"He came here every year for two or three weeks alone," Lina said as we bounced over the rough road. "He called it his bolt hole, and he sometimes talked of retiring here."

I laughed and shook my head. Phuket might be a wonderful place, but Nordhagen was a man with a cellarful of bodies, some of them still living, so it must have been weirdly comic to hear him talk of serene retirement.

Nordhagen's bungalow was monastic in its simplicity, spartan in its furnishings, and it overlooked a pristine beach that showed no signs of ever being used.

"I don't want to stay here," Lina said abruptly. We were literally in the doorway, and the driver stood behind me with one of our suitcases. "I don't want to stay here even one night."

I didn't care that much one way or the other. I saw traces of mildew. It would probably take a day of work and errands to make the place fit for living, so I was happy enough to turn around and head for a hotel. The driver was glad too; we were making his day. He helped us get a decent hotel room. I hit the bed and fell directly into air-conditioned sleep, while Lina went back to see the local agent.

"He's going to sell it for me," she said later that evening. "I just want to get rid of it."

"Think you'll ever see the money?"

"Oh, yes," Lina smiled. "He'll make a killing on it. And good for him. That property is going to be valuable. I'll have to take whatever he says I'm getting, but some money will get back to me, and I don't really care how much or little it is. I just want to get rid of the place."

"I thought it was gorgeous. What bothered you?"

"I don't know," Lina said. "Roger's presence, maybe. It seemed more vivid there than in his London house. *Something* got to me the minute I opened the door. The bungalow is so small and bare, there's hardly anything to it . . . but an echo of Roger."

"I'm sure it's for the best," I told her. "Closing out another part of the Nordhagen story."

"Mmm."

The next day we caught a flight to Pattaya, a resort less than ninety miles south of Bangkok. This, I thought when I saw the place, could be the future of Phuket. Beautiful beaches with luxury hotels, a long list of recreational activities from golf to parasailing, nightclubs, bars, discos, and an invasion force of oversexed Germans, Scandinavians, and Japanese. But Lina and I found it easy enough to rest and relax in Pattaya, and that was what we needed.

Lina was a shocker on the beach. She looked beautiful and sexy, but it was more than that—it was her skin. Almost everyone in Pattaya was burned or brown, deeply tanned or Asian-hued. I was pink flesh, rapidly turning red. Lina stepped out, not just white, but shocking, brilliant alabaster. She was the most striking, exotic sight in this exotic place.

Those were incredibly happy days for the two of us. Lina was ravishing, and it seemed that we had found the furthest extension yet of our freedom. The past, which might be summed up in the word *Nordhagen*, was a diminishing speck on the horizon. We had come thousands of miles physically, light-years in other ways. That was the best part of Pattaya, I thought, the feeling that you were as far away from the rest of the world as you would ever get.

We would lie on the beach by day, letting the surf wash up around us, playing games with each other, or just dozing. Always in touch. At night we ate, drank, and danced in one place after another. We were alone and soaring together. We thought we would stay a few days, a week at most, but three weeks passed dreamily in Pattaya before we finally departed.

We made brief stops in Hong Kong, Tokyo, Honolulu, and Los Angeles en route to Panama City, where Nordhagen owned an apartment. It was sublet year-round, the net income remitted quarterly to Switzerland. I spent the entire time in Panama City in our hotel room, while Lina saw the local agent and arranged to have the apartment sold. It was, as far as we knew, the last of the Nordhagen encumbrances.

I considered visiting my parents in Ohio, a quick stopover to let them see me and meet Lina, but I finally decided against it. I had no good reason; I just shied away from it at the last moment. I couldn't bring myself to go through with the necessary charade. Instead, we stayed in Miami one night before flying back to London.

It was a cold, grey, wet morning when we arrived at our house on Bayswater Road. Lina turned on the heat. I brewed a pot of tea. The house was chilly, and so were the sheets. But we took off our clothes, crawled under the covers, sipped the hot beverage, and rubbed our bodies together. For three days and nights we hardly left the bedroom. We were lazy and relaxed, letting the jet lag ease out of us. The skylight over our massive bed was terrific. We spent hours staring at the sky.

* * *

FINISHING TOUCHES

The good wave we rode flattened out slowly in the succeeding weeks. For a while Lina and I went out almost every night. We ate our way through the best restaurants in London, devoured new films and live music like popcorn, and danced and drank in the trendiest, most glittering clubs in the city. Whatever gets one through the night. And as the nights rolled by we found ourselves watching other people with greater attention: how they moved, how they acted, how they talked and made plays for one another. It became as richly mysterious and engrossing to us as the culture of a newly discovered Stone Age tribe would be to anthropologists. Lina and I were anthropologists of the night. The city and its people became our primary source of entertainment and study. It was as if two night dwellers were trying to learn something about themselves by observing others who prowled the same darkness.

Beneath all this nocturnal activity, some kind of hunger or restlessness worked away at us. Lina and I didn't have to talk about it—our relationship carried a substantial unspoken freight—but we knew it was happening. I had no idea whether it would build and lead to something, or whether it would simply carry us along on an underlying stream of boredom. I had no idea at all.

For a while, we amused ourselves with a couple we met at a discotheque. Tony and Sally were quite attractive, but in the third year of an apparently troubled marriage. He was in advertising, and she was exploring what it was to be a woman. Her brand of feminism struck me as shallow, little more than good old male-blessed permissiveness, but maybe that was what the exploration was meant to reveal. Like many who reach some form of impasse, they sought escape in spurious freedom, as if by proving they were attractive to others they would rediscover what was attractive in themselves. We went out with Tony and Sally four or five times.

Clearly they were building up to some soap-opera entanglement that had an air of suburban inevitability about it.

"Ménage à quatre?" Lina asked me.

"Do you think it'll wreck them?"

"We can but try."

"I don't know. It doesn't seem worth the bother. All those horrid little scenes. The two of them chasing us like idiotic puppies."

But we encouraged it, and Tony and Sally, thinking they actually controlled events, responded energetically. Each time we danced was a new adventure. Sally clutched my hand, pressed it, molded it to her admittedly worthwhile breasts. Her thigh worked between mine. Her hand slid cautiously south of the small of my back. While we danced in this way, she would whisper a line of comprehensive endearments to me: "I love everything American. . . . You really know how to enjoy life. . . . I could do this all night, every night. . . . Mmm, it scares me how much you turn me on. . . ." This last was a favorite, and it was usually accompanied by the enforced tightening of my grip on her right tit, along with the insertion of her tongue in my ear.

Tony was different. Tony was cool. Tony was a man of the world, a rising ad exec in the big city of London. Tony mined a vein of flimsy charm for all it was worth. Lina handled him effortlessly.

"I just have to look at him right in the eyes," she told me, laughing, "and he's halfway to coming in his pants."

I believed it. Lina could have that effect, and although Tony was no groper on the dance floor, he obviously yearned for Lina. Maybe he thought he had married slighty below himself. Lina fostered the illusion of availability while holding him off. Thus, Tony was kept in a state of lathered but unrewarded anticipation. He made me think of a Yorkshire terrier trying to mount an Irish wolfhound. Try as he might, he would never reach the glorious heights.

Lina and I began to lose interest, and I genuinely thought I would hasten the end when, on the dance floor one night, I told Sally, "You've got a great pair of jugs, honey, and I bet you give good head too." I thought she would be turned off by such blunt crudeness, that it would offend her basic English sensibility. But no, alas. She grooved on dirty talk, and now that I'd given her a sample, she wasn't shy about asking for more.

This led to a bizarre finale. Sally rang one afternoon, and I answered the phone. She wanted to talk to me, she said. She was alone and she was thinking about what I had said. Did I really think she had a good body? She wasn't too big, too horsy? Sometimes she hated her breasts and thought she was top-heavy. She was insecure, she told me; she needed to hear a man say she had a great body and was very attractive. Then she started telling me what she was wearing, which wasn't much but was lacy and magazine-sexy. She wished I could see it, but since I couldn't, she would describe it to me. In great detail. Then she wanted me to tell her what I honestly thought—my most secret male thoughts about her. I made it up, intensifying it steadily as I knew she wanted.

"She's getting off," I told Lina, my hand clamped over the mouthpiece. "Right now. It's a phone job."

Lina stifled her laughter and made a variety of gestures to fuel my inventiveness. And so it was that Sally and I consummated our nonaffair by way of the London telephone exchange. The next day, Lina and I requested a new, unlisted number. We avoided the club where we'd met and gone dancing with Tony and Sally, and we never saw them again.

When I thought about them, I was reminded of something Lina or Nordhagen had told me: Without pain there is no life. It seemed to me that even as they pursued what they regarded as vital new pleasures, Tony and Sally were actually engaged in the self-infliction of necessary pain; if they could hurt themselves they would demonstrate that something worthwhile still lived within them. At the end of the script, they would be back together, characters enhanced, wiser and more appreciative of what they had in each other. Or, alternatively, modernly, the pain would lead to a final break and the start of their new, separate lives. Whichever, pain was the essential. Pain was the gateway.

Another summer was on us. Wimbledon was in full swing, and the city was full of visitors. We still went out most nights, but we were less compulsive about it by now. Many evenings we never bothered to leave our roof garden. We would sit and drink, watching the darkness accumulate over London. We would talk, or not, as it suited us. It was on such a night, with the sky unusually clear and the stars brighter than the city glow, that Lina began speaking about boredom.

"Do you think we have it too easy because we have too much?" she asked.

"No. Why?"

"Sometimes I feel I'm going stale," she said. "It was a constant challenge, a constant *terror*, to hold Roger and his little world together. But now I feel I'm not being tested."

"How do you want to be tested?"

"I don't know yet. Perhaps if we got rid of all the money. Then we could start making it all back again. There are so many different and daring ways."

"Sure. We probably could," I allowed. "Pete Townshend once said the thought of losing all his money didn't scare him because he knew he could pick up his guitar and earn it all over again. So what's the point?"

"Maybe not money, then. Maybe something to do with other people . . ."

"You mean, a-humping we will go, with Tony and Sally in Surbiton? What's the point of that? It's a drag playing out the whole deck when you already know every card in it. I can wash my own ears. Besides, the only test there is whether or not it's possible to keep a straight face."

"No, not that. You're right, of course."

"What, then?"

"I don't know, Tom." It was a rare moment of true uncertainty in Lina, and I didn't know how to handle it. I waited until she spoke again. "I just keep thinking, we have it in our hands but we haven't figured out how to close our grasp around it. We haven't really learned how to pick it up and use it. Instead, we're letting it melt and trickle away through our fingers."

I didn't have to ask what she meant. Lina was talking about power once again. Our elusive old friend.

"What do you want to do with it?"

"I don't know. Something."

"Why?"

"Because it can't just sit still. It wants to move. It wants *to do*."

I had never heard Lina so circuitous about anything. It could mean only that she wanted me to start suggesting things. I decided to cut right through all the underbrush.

"We could kill people," I said. "But it's been done."

Lina smiled. "Killing is not an end in itself."

This was neither yes nor no. "What's your fantasy?" I asked. The reliable fallback.

Lina gazed into the distance. From our vantage, the lights of London glittered away to the south and east of Hyde Park.

"Sometimes," Lina said, "I think I'd like to see it all fall down. The city deranged."

"I've become rather fond of London," I said lightly. "It would be a shame to mess it up too much."

"Not the physical city, not all the beautiful buildings. But the psychological city. The order."

"You mean all that IRA-style bullshit?" I laughed. "The British love nothing more than to toughen up in the face of the latest outrage. Making the British feel good about themselves is the role of the Irish, isn't it?"

"Oh, I wasn't thinking of making people feel good about themselves," Lina said. She had a distant smile on her face. "I wasn't thinking about making them feel good at all."

For a long time we said nothing. The night around us seemed to be a palpable presence. I wouldn't have been surprised to extend an arm and find I could touch it— amorphous, tactile night. Eventually, I started talking.

"I'm still here," I said. "A lot of things are coming into my head. I'm incapable of looking back now. You made it impossible for me to do so, and I'm glad of that. Nordhagen did the same thing for me, but in a different way. No going back. I'm not that person anymore. *Love* is a word we haven't used much at all with each other. Maybe because it seems small and inadequate, or maybe because we've never needed a vocabulary of even one word. But right now it keeps coming into my head, and I want to say it: *I love you, Lina, I love you.* The first weekend I spent with you I had the feeling I had come to the end of my life. I didn't understand it right away. It took time, but I figured it out, and then it was simple. Living with you is everything to me. More, it's more than I had ever hoped or expected in my life. And I don't want it to end. I don't want to lose you. If I did, I'd step off the roof or beat my brains out against a prison wall. I'd have no choice. I'd self-destruct. I don't feel bored. I think that's something people talk themselves into for reasons that don't often bear up under closer examination. I guess what I'm trying to tell you is that I'm with you all the way, whatever happens, whichever way our love grows. But I don't want us to take a wrong turn and lose our way. We might never get out again, and that would be the worst thing that could happen to us. It'd be the end of us, and no other fantasy, not even power, is worth that. The real test, the real challenge, is not to throw away what we have between us, what we are. But to keep it, and fly it to the maximum. That's all I want."

I should have felt good, getting all this out, but as soon as I stopped talking, a clamorous apprehension seized me. It was like a premonition or a vision, in which my mind showed me Lina saying: *Yes, I'm your fantasy, but the point you're missing, Tom, is that I am also my own ultimate fantasy, I am power, and so power is also your ultimate fantasy, and the reason you cannot resist me is because I am the irresistible force of nature, and our love will fly to the maximum because there is no wrong way, there is no other way at all. We are the only way.*

This vision or flash of insight disturbed me profoundly, and the aftershock continued in spite of the fact that Lina actually said nothing. She was looking out into the night, holding my hand like a life line. Then she turned to me, and I saw that her eyes were full of tears.

Sixteen

Think of it as a hobby. A man needs a hobby. Tonight my pleasure is to watch. I am in a closet that has been turned into a small theater. It's cramped and stuffy, but the play tonight is real life. Drama, comedy, and tragedy all rolled into one—you can't beat that. The window is made of one-way glass; on the other side, in the guest playroom, it looks like a mirror. London is my peep-show . . . and tonight I'm going to watch a man try to fuck a chicken.

I don't know where she picks them up, but it doesn't matter. It isn't difficult, either. The city is full of people out on the streets looking for something. Do they know what? Will they recognize it when they get it? Will it be as good as they had hoped? But wait. The lights come up to a soft glow and the stage is lit. The door opens. Enter dramatis personae, a man and a woman. The play begins.

He likes the room. He's knocked out by it, and says so. They throw their coats aside. She goes to a liquor cabinet to get some drinks. He is still checking the place out. Nice decor, he says. Kinky, but he likes it. His eyes widen as he notices the implements on the wall—the whip, the handcuffs, the ropes and chains, the hoods and assorted masks. His eyebrows dance when he comes to the standing rack and the leather horse. There's an old school desk too. It's a romance.

He asks her if she collects antiques. No, she says, she uses these things. Just for fun and games, you understand. He does, of course. He hasn't encountered this scene before, but he likes it. He's game.

She's worth it, isn't she? What a looker, what a face, what a body. Some dress too—all those diagonal slits crisscrossing her thighs and cleavage, a web of them in back. Every way she turns and moves exposes a new fantasy of glimpsed flesh. He is so busy watching her he has trouble getting his glass to his lips without bumping his chin. He's not much good at small talk, either, but we can excuse that. This is an action play.

Who is our hero? Late thirties, early forties maybe. First signs of grey in his hair. A businessman, at a guess. Probably not a very energetic or successful one, or maybe it's just a dull business. Any ambition left in that face is strictly residual. His life may change, though. He still can't believe his luck.

She gets up to put on some music. He tags along and takes advantage of the opportunity to come up close behind her and peer over her shoulder like they do in the movies. He kisses her ear (another ear washer!). She smiles back at him, leans against him for a brief moment, then glides away. The music comes on, and now he joins her on the couch. Enough of watching her; let's get down to it. But he is smooth. He won't rush it like some callow youth. Her smile is encouraging. He strokes her hair, fingers it gently, and he tells her sweet things. There seems to be something continental about this manner, and it occurs to me that he might be a Euro-businessman.

She wants to change into something else. Fine. And she tells him to get out of those clothes. Mmm, kiss, kiss.

She goes behind an Oriental screen, and he crosses the room to strip by the bed. There is both more and less of him with his clothes off: more flesh, running to slack and flab, less presence. He keeps his underpants on, and now he looks like a protodumpling.

She comes out from behind the screen and—hey, what is this? Wow! That's what it is. She's all done up in silver suede: high boots, tight microshorts, and, above, only a ribbon around her throat. Her long dark hair tumbles down to her waist. His Europoise is slipping badly. This is the call of the wild, and he is ready to answer it.

She gets the whip and shows it to him. Smooth animal skin. Doesn't it feel . . . good? So thick at one end, so . . . delicate at the other. What's the matter, any problem? You can't win the prize, she tells him, if you don't play the game. He reaches for a peekaboo nipple, but she moves away. Oh, yes, he'll play, for man excels all the animals even in his ability to be trained.

Down, get down. He does. No, not just on your knees. All the way down. Crawl to me, she says, and he crawls. He reaches her boot. Kiss it. Good. Now crawl up this leg. That's it. Now around behind. Very good. He's trying so hard to please I hope he doesn't falter. What a wonderful thing is man! Now kiss the back of the thigh. Now up. It's tight, but, come on, get your tongue in there all the way. Yes, there.

Now she turns around, puts her boot on his chest, and pushes him over on his back. She stands over him and dangles the whip in his face. Lick the end of it. Suck it in. You can do that, can't you? Sure he can. She's taunting him, but he loves it. This is new to him, this is fun.

Now she tells him to get up and sit at the school desk. It isn't easy, but he fits. He's wedged into it. She stands close to him, one breast inches away. She holds his hair to keep his head still. Isn't it a fine breast? Yes, he agrees. No, it's more than that; it's the most perfect breast you've ever seen, she tells him. Yes, he says hungrily, it sure is. Now she tells him to put his tongue out as far as he can without touching the nipple. Very good. Now hold it there as long as you can. He tries hard, but finally he gives up and lunges for it, ignoring the pain in his scalp. She lets him have a taste, but then she pushes his head away and steps back from him.

He extricates himself from the school desk. Can we go to bed now? his face asks silently. Please, teacher. The game was just fine, I liked it, it worked. I'm ready, oh, so ready. Can we go to bed now? Please, teacher, let me fuck you blind.

Stop, she commands. Hold your hand out, palm down. That's right. One more trick. He's a naughty boy, isn't he? Admit it. A little piggy with naughty thoughts in his piggy head. Tell the truth. Yes, yes, he confesses. He has dirty thoughts about her. She should rap his knuckles. Make your piggy noises. Oink oink, he says shamefully. Oink oink oink oink oink.

The whip flies out to him before he realizes it has happened. He feels a warm, pleasant sensation in the soft fleshy area between his thumb and forefinger. Yes, it's turning a dull red. He is shocked, but thrilled. She'd laid the whip end on him like a hot kiss. It didn't even hurt. He didn't know the whip could feel so—good. He has been chastised. The teacher smiles. He will be rewarded. Oink oink. She unbuttons her shorts and slides them down her legs.

But the truth is, the game is already out of hand. The next time the whip comes, it rips a fingernail away. Before he can react to this, the whip cracks again, taking out an eye. He crashes to his knees, hands covering his bloodied face. He is wailing, paralyzed in unthinking agony. Only she can deliver him from this, and she comes to him at once. She grabs his hair and yanks his head back from his hands. She has a shiny smile of a knife in her other hand, and with a swift stroke she draws the blade deeply through his throat.

The rest of him is science, but I can't think about that now. It's time for me to intervene. London is my peep-show and *I am in it*. Only I can deliver her from this. She is on her knees in his hot spill of blood, and she is crying for me.

"Tom!" she screams. "Tom! Where are you?"

I'm with her in an instant. I have her in my arms; I'm kissing her, hugging her, comforting her, but it's as if she doesn't know it yet.

"Tom! Where are you? Tom!"

She is crying in terror, like a child lost in the dark, a creature in unfocused pain. My body takes charge of hers. We lock and roll on the floor. I am taking her, working her, fucking her clear.

"Tom, get in me, get in me, fillmefillmefillme, oh, please get in me, *get inside me!*"

The way home.

He drove an Escort. So do we. There must be a million of them on the road. Ours changes color regularly. I've gotten good at it. Call it a hobby. A man needs a hobby. We put him in the trunk of his car, next to the spare tire. I drive until I find a good parking space. It's a big city, and there are plenty of places to park, in spite of what people say. Then I walk along and get into the Escort Lina is driving. Someone may have seen me? But that wasn't my hair color, my beard or my mustache. I have a much thinner build too. The key is, get them in and out fast, before they're reported missing. They're found soon enough.

These things do happen. We give it a good run, but we don't push any pattern too far too long. We're not in a game with the police. Headlines might help foster the desired state of public mind, but they can become a net negative. We take care.

For instance:

FINISHING TOUCHES

Lina and I are in Hyde Park. It's a beautiful day, hot and sunny. There aren't many such days in London's short summer, and you have to take advantage of them. People are sprawled everywhere, sunning themselves. Lina and I are like any other loving couple out to enjoy the day. We find a good spot and stretch out on the grass. We say things to each other and maybe smooch a little. We are far enough away from anyone else to have a bit of privacy.

After a while, we notice someone. A man alone in a deck chair. He is about eighty yards away. He already has a tan and is burnishing it now. He has a floppy white sun hat pulled down over his eyes. A newspaper under his seat.

We're on the high ground and we have our own newspaper. It's folded like a small tent, sheltering the gun. Lina has a clear view and can pick her spot through the telescopic sight. The gun resembles a .45 automatic and fits neatly in her purse. But it's something else. It's powered by a battery in the grip. It is smokeless and virtually silent. It makes less noise than snapping your fingers. Click.

The man gives a small start. Does he have time to think he's been stung by a bee? His hand moves instinctively toward the pinprick in his side but never reaches it. The fléchette carries saxitoxin, which I've learned to extract from shellfish. Call it a hobby. Once in the bloodstream, saxitoxin is instantly fatal. The man never gets to say ouch, and he will stay in the deck chair until someone gets around to wondering about him.

The fléchettes are even easier to use at night. Whether in crowded streets, like Picadilly or Charing Cross Road, or in darker places. Lina and I may be walking arm in arm, or one of us may be out alone. People are always falling down dead in this city. More than ever, lately.

I have come to understand and accept that I am no less

a sociopath than Lina is—if that is the right word for us. But then, I think all people are sociopathic, or most of them, if only by omission and indifference. And what has happened to me—it's as if there were another part of me that had been waiting all those years for this. Call it conspiracy, serial murder, revolutionary justice, madness, ego anarchy. We're secret anarchists. Call it history. It is all of these and more. And less: because the point is not to take it too seriously. It just happens, like the rain.

Lina and I have taken in one of the world's homeless children. She is thirteen, slim, barely five feet tall. She comes from Chiangmai, or somewhere in that northern Thailand territory. It cost all of £100 to rescue her from hunger, whoredom, heroin, and early death. And it wasn't hard to get her into this country. Money is the great enabler.

She had another name, but we call her Asia. She doesn't speak a word of English, which is fine. She has long black hair, a face that is pretty in the best, truest sense of the word, and bud breasts that are just beginning to round her.

Our house is a palace to her, and she hardly ever wants to go out. Asia is with us all the time. She doesn't like clothes, and we don't make her wear them. She moves through the house like a cat. She takes possession of a chair, rather than just sitting on it. She uses her whole body in everything she does. Asia's language is physical contact, and she rubs against us, sits on our laps and at our feet. Sometimes she even purrs and lick-kisses us. Asia is endlessly affectionate. Lina and I have only to glance at her to raise a sweet, girlish smile. We're definitely better for having taken this child into our lives. Asia sleeps with us, light and playful as a kitten, a silky miracle of warmth and life.

We found Asia, and she found us, at the right time. Summer had passed, and autumn, two seasons of blood ritual. The manipulation of a city and its people. We pushed our inventiveness, and we took death as far as we could. We hung up some numbers, we had an effect. But in the end, it was only an effect. Even terror turns to numbness after a certain point.

We needed a rest. We had atomized ourselves, and we needed time to fall back together. Then we went and bought Asia, as if we knew she was looking for us, and we brought her back to London. It took only a few days, but Asia proved to be a new dimension in our lives. She enhanced us in ways we might not fully have understood but which we definitely felt. It isn't humanly possible to sustain love at a constant fever pitch. Sometimes, not often, Lina or I would drift off into our own moods and thoughts and could not snap out of them. Then, responding intuitively, Asia would bridge us back to each other.

Asia stepped into our house, our life, and she became a part of it at once. She fitted in as if she had always belonged. I liked to think of her as the materialization of the love between Lina and me. Our child? Yes, perhaps, but something more than that. We shared the same bed as equals. Lina and I were two people, two bodies, but one life, one love. With Asia we were now three, but still one. Not a triangle, but a trinity.

I wonder whether it would have worked as well as it did if Asia spoke English. Would language, as it so often does, create strains and tensions? Maybe, but it didn't happen, even though Asia inevitably picked up some English words from us. She used them only occasionally, and at a practical level. Otherwise, she avoided speech, as if she understood that we communicated best in a more natural way—with smiles, frowns, laughter, gestures, and touch.

We stayed in through most of the winter and spring. The three of us hibernating together, pleasing one another sleepily. Rest and recreation, in roughly equal measures. It was a kind of recovery too, for during those months we were also building up our strength for whatever lay ahead.

My father suffered a stroke that winter. With typical parental consideration, they didn't tell me until he was back home. They didn't want me to disrupt my work and fly home unnecessarily—there was no immediate threat to his life, although you never can tell in matters of the heart. It was a disabling stroke, however, and it ended any chance that they might travel to London to visit me. In a series of telephone calls, I told them, almost as often as I told myself, that I would soon get home to see them.

But at the same time, I wondered if I would ever see Ohio again. It was so far away, the land of the past. Sometimes it seemed like an alternative universe, beyond reach altogether. I didn't really want to go back to it, but I did think of it now and then, as a mental puzzle to be toyed with idly. The past. When you are twenty, what do you remember of being ten? How little I now recalled of being twenty, which was recent, part of my adult life—and yet light-years away. The past is impossible. Personally, I think psychiatry is overrated. It's all about the past. It's a form of intellectual magic, and, like all magic, it works only if you're willing to accept what you think you see.

Take Nordhagen and his chamber of horrors, for instance. That was even more recent, a black hole that had sucked me in—but already it was receding into history, sealed off in the past. The episode was becoming no more than a strange curiosity, a miniature seen through a telescope backward. I did all that? How strange!

And what of last year? The summer and autumn of London terror. All those dead. It wasn't a mistake. I don't even think it was a wrong turn. It was just something we had to go through. A Nordhagenesque Moebius strip, maybe. We were right to escape it when we did, just as we were about to find Asia.

We'd been hoping to create, then build on, some kind of momentum, and that was our false goal. Now, as England warmed into a new summer, I could see that trying to orchestrate death and terror was beside the point. They are part of the force of nature, which will flow and flow ever on. Instead of trying to steer it ourselves, we would have to learn to let it go its own way. Death and terror will follow, like leaves falling out of trees. We had been trying to gild the lily.

"You've got to think of people as raw materials," Lina tells me. She says: "They are the ore of life, but all ends are irrelevant, so what you make of them doesn't count as much as the process itself. Only the process matters, since it is the course of nature, and we can help it only in small ways. We are the cutting edge, that's all. But it's enough. It's everything. We are the bacteria on the floor of the boundless jungle."

I agree. The possibilities are infinite. The way ahead is the only way. We're young, we're ready. The winter was good, but now we're downright itchy. It's stepping-out time.

See you there.

EPILOGUE

ZOMBIES

I have this fantasy. I'm sitting here with a gun in my hand. It's a beauty, but I'm not sure why we have it, because we don't use guns. Not since the days of the fléchettes, and even then, nothing like this. Guns are messy. Anyway, this one is a 180 laser submachine gun and it weighs only ten pounds. It fires .22-caliber bullets at the astonishing rate of thirty per second from a drum magazine. The barrel is only nine inches long, and the whole thing fits easily in a small briefcase. It comes equipped with a helium-neon gas laser, which emits a pencil-thin beam of scarlet light that appears as a red circle on the target, a three-inch dot at two hundred yards. If it hits the eye, it is blinding but harmless. The range is one mile, or, with a silencer, four hundred yards. On automatic it can chop down telephone poles, rip through sheets of steel or cinder-block walls, and perforate a Rolls-Royce. A gun that will give you your money's worth. And I'm sitting here, admiring this thing.

The door opens.

Lina and Asia come into the room.

They look at me and I look at them.

"Ready," Lina says.

Brrrp-brrpbrrp, two seconds, three at most.

Then what do I do? Turn the gun around and look down the barrel into its good, good darkness? Hello, friend I have been waiting for.

Such a gun. Lina picked up a Middle Easterner one day, and he had this thing in his briefcase. We sent him back out into the world a somewhat different zombie from the one he'd been, but a zombie still. We kept the gun as a souvenir. In a crowd, pivoting smoothly, he could have taken out two hundred people, no sweat. Never mind a mile, imagine what it would be like at ten feet. I hate to think of such a gun in London.

London is still our home, and our number one garden; there's always someone to meet here. But we also explore other fields now. All of Europe is just across the Channel. So many cities. So many people. The only countries we exclude are those in the eastern bloc, where our work would be spiritually redundant, and Luxembourg, which was good to me at a time when I needed help and which I still think of as a possible future home, should we ever need to leave London.

We take Asia with us, of course. She has made our life hers. The trinity is indissoluble. What can hurt us? How can we be stopped? Hubris? You hope!

Lina gets by just being the woman she is, with her looks. She plays along with the men, and that's how they end up playing along with her. Even Asia got somebody once. She went out for a walk one afternoon. Lina kept her in sight to make sure nothing went wrong. It took less than an hour, and some guy followed her home. All the way. Asia hadn't said a word; she didn't even have to nod her head. She just smiled, and he followed, and she smiled some more. Hello, friend. You don't have to find us; we'll find you.

We let them go. We don't keep them. Unlike Nordhagen, we're not into collecting. If we have a collection, it's out there on the streets. You can get too wrapped up in possessions, and then you lose sight of the larger picture. We are not in a process of accumulation, but, rather, one of constant reduction and refinement. If you look carefully, you'll see my people out there. They are my special projects. My works of art.

What we are doing came about in this way. One evening the three of us were watching an old film from Nordhagen's library. It was *White Zombie*, a fine old horror story, with Bela Lugosi lurking about in his jungle stronghold. It was fun, and we all loved it, although Asia found it so scary she kept burrowing closer to Lina and me.

That got me to thinking about zombies, and I haven't been able to stop since. It comes down to this: they're all over the place. Zombies to God, zombies to the void. Zombies on the right and zombies on the left. And the great army of zombies in the middle. Once you begin to see things this way it's impossible to see them any other way. This was not a revelation, still less an explanation of things to me. But I did take it as a clue, a sign along the way.

Death is the final thrill. The last, best confection. The only question about it is whether to savor its rich mystery in delicious, protracted anticipation, or grab the sweet and eat it in a rush.

Now the door opens.

Lina and Asia come into the room. They're smiling.

"He's ready," Lina says.

I smile. Every time I look at them they seem more beautiful, these two women who are my life and love. I put the gun away.

Someone is waiting downstairs in the guest playroom. Ah, business. Always someone new to meet and help along the way. Nice, I think as soon as I see him. His eyes are wide open, glassy, and well lubricated. Sorry I can't do anything about the redness, friend. You'll just have to go easy on the juice.

"When Asia came in, you should have seen the look on his face," Lina tells me. "He was sure he was going to have the two of us."

I laugh at this. "I don't know of any religion in which the mere mortal gets to fuck the goddesses. But I guess you have to have hope to have faith."

I check his pulse, and it's fine. He has been given the usual mix: some Special to occupy his mind and make him feel good, and a muscle relaxant so he won't do any moving around.

Now I take my whisk out of the sterile wrapper. That's what I call it, a whisk, but it's actually pure platinum wire forming a small loop at one end. Platinum is expensive, but it's the best thing for the job. It's very fine, hairthin, but as tough as you'd expect platinum to be. It took me a while to work out the optimum design, and then a lot of practice to perfect the operation.

"Okay," I tell Lina and Asia.

They each take hold of an arm, to make sure our friend doesn't move reflexively. It's a delicate business. His eyes are open, and now I raise one eyelid a little farther. I ease the loop up and in, oh, so slowly and carefully. The one tricky bit is making sure the loop curls back to the front as it clears the ridge of the skull socket. Then you're up in the forehead, home free. The rest is a gentle twirling motion. That's why I call it a whisk. You have to do a lot of stirring to make a good pudding. Leave no lumps. It's better to be thorough, and not to rush it. When done, extricate carefully, so as not to swing the loop and damage the optic nerve. Then, the same procedure through the other eye. *Voilà!* Another zombie. Outpatient brain surgery. Trepanation without trepidation.

I've done this so many times now I can get right outside myself and watch it all happen. Just like a movie.

Later, we take him back outside and ease his passage into the flow of humanity. Crowded places are best. They just fade into the throng.

When we come home, we need to get the tension out. We need rest. We may eat, or drink, or take some THC. Or we may not do anything but lie in bed and float on the dream for hours and hours. We're all that gets us through the night. I sometimes think we're all that keeps us alive. But that's love, isn't it?

I try not to think of numbers. There are only so many days and nights in a year. Only so many people. We're just working on the fringe, but numbers don't matter. The thing is not to become obsessive about it. I try to do what I do well, and the rest takes care of itself.

Call it—whatever you want to call it. Whatever gets you through the night is fine. I don't call it anything.

We all have fantasies. Even now, as I lie in bed with one arm around Lina and the other holding Asia, and we float on the dream, the sweet dream that we are—even now I can see so many things. I think we must have the future in us all the time. It's only a matter of getting it out, drawing it out the right way. And you can do that, as long as there's love.

The door opens.

Lina and Asia come into the room.

"Ready," Lina says.

Our eyes meet. Such love! I can see it now. I keep thinking that death is too much of a good thing.

On the other hand, you never can tell. Next time may be different. Or the time after that.

FATHER PANIC'S
OPERA MACABRE

THE HOUSE OF TILES

It was late in the afternoon when the Fiat overheated. Neil had watched with a growing sense of annoyance and anxiety as the temperature gauge edged slowly upward. He still had plenty of gas in the tank, but no coolant or even plain water for the radiator. It was the time of day when, in any event, he would be looking for a town with a small hotel or a guesthouse to stay at for the night, but the last village he'd passed through was nearly an hour behind him. Surely it would be better to continue on in this direction now. He was bound to find help somewhere soon, a town, a farmhouse at least—if his car would just hold up a little while longer.

Neil wasn't sure exactly where he was anymore, but he knew that he was probably still in the Marches, most likely in the Monti Sibillini, a range of mountains once thought to be the home of the sibyls of classical myth. The dominant peak in the near distance had to be Monte Vettore. Somewhere in this area was the Lago di Pilato, where according to legend Pontius Pilate was buried, perhaps even in the lake itself. Now and then Neil glimpsed another range farther off, which he assumed to be the Gran Sasso, part of the Apennines. Tomorrow, or as soon as the car was checked out and ready to run, Neil's route would take him in that direction, and eventually back to his apartment in Rome. A breakdown would be a minor nuisance, but he knew approximately where he was, and he wasn't lost.

This was Neil's second excursion since he had arrived in Italy, and he now felt quite comfortable driving around the country by himself. A couple of months ago he'd made the same kind of rambling tour of Tuscany. It was predictably beautiful and delightful, but perhaps a bit too familiar. Tuscany has been hosting visitors for centuries, its hill towns and byways have been endlessly written about, painted and photographed. Some of that must have seeped into Neil's mind over the years, via books, magazines, television and Italian films, because there had been moments when he felt the strange sensation of having already been in a certain town or village, though it was in fact his first visit to the region.

This time out he wanted to see some part of the country that was less well-traveled and not as heavily visited by outsiders, to avoid the obvious routes and hopefully to find here and there a little of the old Italy—assuming that it was still there to be found. A friend at the Academy had suggested that Neil try Abruzzo and the Marches, which proved to be a good idea.

He had driven east from Rome to Pescara, stopping only twice along the way. It was the shortest route to the Adriatic coast. From there he turned north and drove the A14 as far as Ancona, an uninteresting run that took him through one beach resort town after another. But when Neil finally left the *autostrada* behind and began to circle slowly inland, he soon found himself in exactly the kind of countryside he had been looking for. The land rose up steadily, wrinkling itself into steep hills and mountains.

The roads were all narrow, frequently little more than country lanes that snaked along the rims of deep canyons and gorges, plunging, rising, curling unpredictably. The towns and small villages Neil passed through were perched on high cliffs, terraced along rippling hillsides, or nestled in tiny vales.

It would be inaccurate to describe the Marches as isolated or out of touch with the rest of the country and the world, but it was somewhat out of the way, and it was definitely a little rougher and wilder than any other part of Italy Neil had experienced so far. It was old, and in some villages almost the only people he saw were elderly, the young having moved elsewhere for college or jobs.

In some places there was nothing to see other than a few ramshackle old stone houses clustered around a small central square where old men sat outdoors, drinking wine, playing cards, chatting idly among themselves or dozing in the sun. Neil spoke Italian fairly well but he found it difficult to get a conversation going with these people. They were polite, but their reticence and open but distant stares reminded him—lest he forget for a moment—that he was an outsider among them.

The needle was just touching the red band at the far right side of the gauge now. Perhaps the car needed oil, not coolant. It didn't make much difference though, since he didn't have an extra quart of oil with him either. But he had checked both fluid levels before leaving Rome, so there had to be a leak somewhere in the system.

Neil had spent nearly a week meandering around the Marches now, from Loreto to San Leo, Gradara, Macerata, Camerino, Visso. He'd taken in some of the obvious sights like the Frasassi Caves and the Infernaccio Gorge, but for the most part what he liked best was simply wandering around the old towns, taking in forts and palazzos that dated back hundreds of years but were still quite impressive, gazing at art and architecture that survived from a time when the world was completely different, but still human, still ours. At such moments Neil could almost taste the past in his mouth and feel it on his skin. The phantom sensations of half-forgotten or lost history—it still amazed him that he was actually making a fairly successful career for himself out of these unlikely and insubstantial impressions.

Now he was in the emptier upper reaches of the province, a place of black stony tarns and ragged windswept grasslands, the whole laced through with sharp ridges, rocky outcroppings and narrow dark glens. The asphalt gave way more often to longer stretches of loose and rutted gravel. It was easy to suspect that you had strayed off the road and onto a rural path that had fallen into disuse and now led nowhere, but Neil had already learned that it wasn't necessarily so—it was just the way the roads were in this area.

Still, it happened to him now. The road dipped down and swung in a long arc around a high stone shelf. When he came out on the far side of it, he saw a large house and several low outbuildings on the hillside a few hundred yards ahead, and he could see that this was not a through road after all, that it ended at the house. No matter. Neil still felt a sense of relief. He would at least be able to get water for his car and directions back to the main road and the nearest town.

As Neil drove slowly closer, the road wound down through clumps of trees and stands of tall thick brush before rising again. His angle of view had changed so that when he finally came out into a clearing he was looking up at the house, and it suddenly exploded in dazzling light. It was catching the sun on its descent in the west, Neil realized. The house had looked a kind of dull buff color at first, but now it shimmered like burning gold.

The effect was so striking that Neil shifted into neutral

and just stared at the house for a few moments. He noticed that the façade was covered with painted yellow tiles, scores of them, each about two feet square. The house was old, many of the tiles were chipped or cracked, but the clever light trick still worked. The person who conceived and built it had probably been dead for decades, but Neil silently said thanks—his pleasure disturbed only when he noticed steam billowing out from beneath the hood of the car.

STICKS AND STRINGS

Neil turned the key and got out. He put the hood up to help the engine cool off faster. Now that he looked carefully at the radiator, he could see that it was in poor shape. The fins were corroded, and in places had completely rotted away. No real surprise there. He'd known it was an old car when he bought it from the art historian Lydia Margulies, who was just finishing her stay at the Academy when Neil arrived. But the car was a bargain, and it had not given him any trouble until now. Still, this was something he should have anticipated and taken care of before he left Rome.

He started walking toward the house. For a moment Neil wondered if it was one of the many abandoned farms that could be found across the Italian countryside. There were no signs of life and the only sound was the loud hiss of the strong breeze in the trees. Three large brick chimneys protruded from the red pantile roof, each containing four separate clay pipes, but no smoke came from any of them. He noticed that several of the individual roof tiles were cracked or had slipped.

But it occurred to Neil that if the house had been left derelict, most of the windows would surely be broken by now, and none of them were. It was a large boxy building, three stories high. The windows on the first two floors were tall, wide rectangles, but those at the top level were small and circular, almost like portholes, suggesting an attic with a low ceiling.

Neil found traces of a footpath as he approached the house—he could feel and see a bed of tiny white chipped stones beneath the thick coarse grass that had claimed most of the ground. There was a long balustrade marking off a terrace immediately in front of the house. It was made from a purplish-grey stone that Neil had seen elsewhere in the region. The same material had also been used for the weedlined paving stones on the terrace and the broad steps that led up to the front door. A few stone urns graced the balustrade, but they held no ornamental shrubs or flowers.

As he passed along in front of the house, Neil hoped to see something through the windows, but the rooms inside were blocked from view by heavy drapes. The glass panes were coated with a thin layer of grime. Up close, he noticed that the impressive tiles covering the house looked merely faded and dull when the sun's rays didn't hit them at the right angle, their gloss muted with dust. Most of them were blank, simply colored yellow, but a few, seemingly placed at random, also contained rust-brown markings or motifs. They were unfamiliar to Neil but made him think of indecipherable runes, clotted Gothic lettering and dead Teutonic languages. He knew that there was still a strong Germanic presence farther north, particularly in the Italian alps, and that in Friulia there were people who spoke something that was neither modern German nor Italian, but a vestigial hybrid of old Low German and Roman Latin. So this house seemed out of place in the Marches, but that only pleased Neil. It was just the kind of unusual thing he'd hoped to find in his meandering explorations.

A somewhat larger yellow tile was centered directly above the front door. It contained a dark red sketch of a human head, seen in profile, drawn in a few bold strokes. It was crudely heroic but striking, and it suggested a prince or a warrior. He had a flowing moustache and wore a conical helmet from the Middle Ages. Then Neil noticed the man's eye. It should have been only partly visible on the left side of the head, as seen naturally in profile, but the entire eye had been sketched in. It was not turned forward with the rest of his face, but out, directly at anyone coming to the house. It was an anatomical impossibility that made Neil smile.

There was no bell or knocker, so he rapped his fist on the wooden door. After a minute or so, he tried again, longer this time, forcefully enough to hurt his knuckles. Still, no sound came from within. He pounded the door with the fleshy side of his fist, and then with the fat part of the palm of his hand, but again to no result. Finally, he decided he would have to go around to the back of the house and try to find someone there.

As Neil turned to walk down the steps, he was startled to see a child sitting on the balustrade, at the farthest end. A little girl, maybe eight or nine years old. Surely he hadn't failed to notice her as he approached the house. She must have come out and hopped up there while he was knocking on the door. Somebody is home, Neil thought gratefully.

The girl's short legs stuck out slightly in the air. She appeared to be playing with a puppet in the shape of man, made from sticks and string. She held her hand out and walked the puppet back and forth and in tight circles on the grey stone balustrade. Her head bobbed rhythmically and her lips moved as if she were talking or singing quietly to herself as she played.

Neil didn't want to frighten her so he smiled broadly to convey his friendliness. As he got closer he could hear her voice—it was surprisingly harsh, and she spoke in a language he didn't recognize. It sounded tangled, vaguely Slavic. With each step he took toward her, the tempo and volume of her speaking ratcheted up, as if she were narrating his harmless movements into an event of absurd tension and melodrama. It was the kind of silly thing that a dreamy child would do.

She wore a black skirt that came down to her ankles and heavy black shoes that looked too large for her feet. A man's plaid outdoors shirt hung loosely like a light jacket over her grimy sweatshirt. In the declining sun her hair appeared reddish-blonde, but it was matted in a thick frizzy clump. The sun was just above and behind her, almost directly in his line of vision, so it wasn't until Neil came within fifteen feet of her that he realized she was not a child at all. Far from it, she had to be at least forty—probably older. Several of her teeth were missing, the others stained or chipped. She had blotchy red cheeks, the skin around her mouth was lined and the flesh beneath her hooded eyes was purplish and sunken. But it was the crazed look of gleeful malice in those eyes that most disturbed Neil. His smile quickly faded away.

The woman's plump stubby fingers worked the sticks faster, making the puppet dance and jump wildly. She bounced up and down on her perch, and her voice was a loud mad rant. Neil said something in Italian but it had no effect on her. The poor woman probably suffered from some mental illness or defect, perhaps genetic in origin. He felt very uncomfortable in her presence and didn't know what to do next.

The puppet distracted him. In spite of his own reluctance, Neil found himself moving closer to peer at it. The stick figure was a little over a foot in height and had been fashioned as a human skeleton. But the bones and details were so well done that Neil realized it couldn't be made out of carved sticks, it had to be manufactured. Then he noticed the naturally misshapen skull, the toothless jaw, the tiny leathery pieces that might be tendons or gristle, and the dull brownish stains in certain parts of the bones.

The woman was laughing raucously, but then she suddenly froze in silence, as if a switch had been turned. Her eyes were staring blankly past Neil. Before he had time to react, she hopped off the balustrade and scurried away from him, around the side of the house and out of sight, the gruesome puppet dangling from her hand.

MECHANICAL FIX

From the way the dwarf suddenly halted her strange act and stared past him, Neil knew that someone else had appeared. He turned back toward the house and was relieved to see a young woman standing alone at the top of the stone steps by the front door. Neil turned on the friendly smile again. In a relatively isolated spot like this he expected to be met with some caution or even unfriendliness. The dwarf had already unsettled him a bit, so he wanted to appear as harmless and unthreatening as he actually was. He held his arms out and opened his hands in a gesture of helplessness.

The woman came down to the bottom of the steps, and Neil stopped a few yards from her. She looked refreshingly normal in black designer jeans, a long-sleeved white blouse, stylish sunglasses and sandals. She didn't seem at all concerned, but merely perplexed by his presence.

Neil quickly explained the situation, pointing to his car. She nodded her head slowly while he spoke, as if she could not quite grasp his point. But then she stifled a big yawn and smiled sheepishly at him, and Neil realized that he had probably awakened her from an afternoon nap. He apologized for disturbing her, repeating that unfortunately his car could go no farther without water. He added that he would also be grateful for directions to the nearest town where he could find a room for the night. Now the woman seemed to be more awake and she gave a brief nod of comprehension.

"Si, si. Acqua."

"Si, grazie."

"I can tell from your pronunciation that you're an American," she then said in smooth, lightly accented English. "Am I right?"

"Ah, you speak English. Yes, you're right, I am American. I'm living in Rome for a year, as part of my work. I took some time off to drive around and explore the countryside. My name is Neil O'Netty, by the way."

"I'm Marisa Panic," she replied, pronouncing her last name *Pahn*-ik. "I'm pleased to meet you."

"And you." Neil gently shook her offered hand, which felt pleasantly cool and dry. "When I first came around the bend and saw the house, I was afraid there might not be anyone at home."

"Oh, we're always here. Onetti? That's Italian."

"O'Netty with a *y*," Neil explained. "It's Irish, but I am Italian on my mother's side, which is how I got a head-start on the language."

"I see. You do speak it well. And I think you're from Massachusetts. Somewhere in the Boston area?"

"Right again." Neil laughed. "Southie, then Medford."

"It's not that you have a very strong accent," Marisa told him. "But I spent a year at B.U. on a student exchange program."

"Aha." Neil was delighted. It had been a while now since he'd had a chance to converse in his own language.

It felt comfortable and relaxing, like getting into his favorite old clothes. "Well, I think your English sounds better than my Italian."

"Thank you." She smiled. "I don't get to use it much here."

Neil found her very attractive. Marisa's skin was milky white, with a faint rosy glow, and she had long cascading waves of very fine black hair that was not glossy but had a rich, subdued luster, like polished natural jet. She was about 5'6" tall and her body was sleek but gloriously voluptuous. Neil wondered what color her eyes were—even through the sunglasses, he could see flashes of light in them.

"Are you still studying?" he asked.

"No, I finished last year. The University of Parma."

"Really? Parma is one of the cities I plan to visit while I'm here." It was true. He loved *The Charterhouse of Parma*, and Stendhal had, in a way, been an inspiration and a small factor in Neil's recent success.

"I can tell you a couple of good places to stay, clean, not expensive," Marisa said. "And some excellent family restaurants."

"Great. Thank you."

"Are you traveling alone or with—?"

"Yes, I'm on my own."

"Let's see to your car. Then we can have some refreshments."

As they walked briskly toward the Fiat, Marisa clapped her hands sharply three or four times and called out a couple of words that Neil could not recognize. He saw a man emerge from one of the low worksheds on the nearest rise. Marisa shouted something else to him, and the man went back into the shed, reappearing a few moments later with a large plastic container and a funnel in his hands.

"What language were you speaking to him?"

"I'm not sure what you would call it," Marisa replied with a laugh. "These people have been with my family for a long time. It's some kind of local dialect from Dalmatia, I believe."

"Is your family Italian?"

"On my mother's side, like you. My father's family, well, they say if you go back far enough, they were the original Illyrians. I don't know any of that ancient history, but my grandfather and his family came here at the end of World War II, fleeing the Communists on the other side of the Adriatic. They bought this old farm, which had gone to ruin during the war."

They had arrived at Neil's car. The man came hurrying along a few seconds later. He had the rough, ruddy features and large leathery hands of somebody who had worked outdoors for decades, and he might have have been anywhere from forty to sixty years of age. His clothes were stained and torn, he had the same gnarly, raggedy appearance of the dwarf, but he was of average height and build. He ignored Neil and glanced subserviently toward Marisa as he set the plastic container and funnel down on the ground. He used a rag to remove the radiator cap, which was still hot to touch. Neil stepped closer to take a look. No liquid visible, as he feared.

Neil sat inside and turned the engine over, then got out again to hold the funnel while the man angled the bulky jug and carefully poured a small but steady stream of water into the radiator. Neil watched it swirl down through the funnel. A minute later, he could see it accumulating and moving inside as the pump circulated the liquid. The system took a lot of water, but finally the radiator was full.

"All right, now let's see," Neil said.

As soon as he put the cap on and snugged it tight, the pressure inside increased and tiny jets of water appeared in several places on the body of the radiator. Soon it was hissing audibly and the rising steam was visible in the air. The man pointed theatrically. Neil frowned.

"How far is it to the nearest town?"

"Four miles back to the road," Marisa said, "and about another eight miles from there. Your car wouldn't make that, would it?"

"I doubt it. Can I use your phone to call for a tow?"

"I'm afraid there's no telephone here," she answered with a look of apology. "My brother has a cell phone, but he's away on business until the end of the week."

"Could I trouble you to drive me to the town, and then I could make arrangements to have my car picked up?"

"My brother has the car too," Marisa replied with another look of sincere regret. "It's the only workable vehicle we have."

Neil's car was boiling out clouds of steam now. As he went to switch it off, Marisa started speaking quickly to the workman. It sounded like she was asking him something. He nodded and answered her at some length. She turned to Neil and smiled.

"He thinks the radiator is ruined."

Neil gave a short laugh. "I think he's right."

"But he thinks they can patch it up enough tomorrow so that you'll at least be able to get to town and replace it."

"Oh, that'd be great," Neil exclaimed, his spirits lifting. "Thank him for me, I'm really very grateful."

"Of course you'll stay here tonight."

"That's very kind of you. I'm sorry to impose on you like this. I hope it won't be too much of an inconvenience."

"Not at all," Marisa said, smiling brightly. "We have plenty of room, and I'm so glad to have some company for a change. Come on, get your bag, whatever you need, and we'll go inside."

THE BOX ROOM

"You mentioned something about working in Rome. What business are you in—banking, finance, technology?"

"No, nothing like that," Neil said with a smile. "I have a one-year fellowship at the American Academy. I'm doing some research for a book I'm working on. And also writing it, of course."

Marisa had slipped her arm through his as they walked. It was a common practice in many European countries, so Neil knew better than to read too much into her simple gesture. But he enjoyed the closeness and the physical contact with her.

"Ah, you're a writer."

"An author, yes."

"That's marvelous." Marisa gave his arm a little squeeze. "What kind of books do you write?"

"Historical fiction, sort of." Neil always felt a little awkward trying to explain his work. "Anyhow, I've only written three so far."

"But that's wonderful. They must be very good for you to be chosen for the Academy. It's very prestigious."

"The first two disappeared almost without a trace," Neil told her with a rueful smile. "But the last one did much better."

"What is it about, what period of history?"

"The 1590s, in Italy. It's called *La Petrella* and it's a retelling of the story of Beatrice Cenci and her family."

"Oh, of course. I remember that," Marisa said excitedly. "Beatrice conspired with her mother to murder her father, and she was then tortured and beheaded in public for it, even though her father had raped her. She was only about, what—fifteen years old?"

"That's right."

"It's a famous story."

"Yes, but not in America. I discovered that there hadn't been a full-length fictional treatment of it in many years, so I decided to try it. I found Beatrice by way of Nathaniel Hawthorne, who saw Guido's portrait of her in the Barberini Gallery and fell in love with her. I read Stendhal's account of the case, and many others. But my version is quite different."

"You changed the story?" Marisa asked.

"Not the facts or the incidents," Neil said. He felt that he was talking too much about something that could not really interest her. "But the feelings and motivations of the people. Beatrice is usually idealized, portrayed as an innocent, still virtually a child."

"Wasn't she?"

"I tried to make her both innocent and knowing," Neil said. "When I did more research and read some passages from the actual court documents of the case, I found it all much more uncertain and open to interpretation in different ways. There's a moral ambiguity to Beatrice, which is probably why she fascinates me."

"I see. But her father—he really was an evil man?"

"Oh yes, he was a monster."

That seemed to please Marisa, who smiled broadly. "I'd love to read your book."

"I'm sorry I don't have a copy with me, but I'll be happy to send you one when I get back to Rome."

"Thank you. Signed, please?"

"Of course."

Marisa squeezed his arm again and Neil smiled at her. She was so attractive, pleasant to talk to and be with, and his encounters with women had been disappointingly few since he'd come to Italy.

They reached the front door, but before she opened it Marisa turned and looked around as if she were checking the weather. Then she led him into a dimly lit entrance hall. As soon as the door clicked shut, Neil noticed how quiet the house was. There were two large armoires and a couple of free-standing coat racks, along with a pair of heavy upholstered chairs made of very dark wood, and a long ornate wooden bench. All of this furniture was old, chipped and dusty. A gloomy corridor led straight into the house from the entrance area. Off to the right was a wide flight of stairs that led to a landing and then angled up toward the center again.

"I hope you won't mind waiting for a moment while I go and make arrangements for your room and bed? We so seldom have visitors, I want to make sure they open the window and change the linens."

"Don't go to any trouble for me," Neil insisted politely. "I'd be fine on a couch with a blanket."

"Oh no, we can certainly do better than that." Marisa led him into a small sitting room and turned on a floor lamp that had a battered shade with a fringe. "You can sit here. I'll be right back."

"Thank you."

As soon as he was alone, Neil noticed that it was an interior room. It had no windows, no other doors. There were two plain wooden chairs, both so dusty that he decided not to sit down. Boxes of old books were stacked up against the back wall of the narrow room. He went closer and looked at them but the titles were in a language he didn't recognize.

Neil began to feel uncomfortable in his breathing. He was asthmatic, though he had such a mild case of it that he rarely experienced difficulties. A single Benadryl capsule was usually enough to quell a reaction. But now he could taste powdery alkaline fungus in his mouth—even before he spotted the patches of it on the lower side walls of the room. Neil's lungs tightened, he could feel himself losing the ability to breathe in and out.

He turned toward the door, forcing himself to move slowly and carefully, as he had learned long ago—sudden exertions only made matters worse. Now he felt a little dizzy, lightheaded, as if he'd just been hit by a very powerful nicotine jag. This was something Neil didn't associate with asthma. His thoughts were foggy and vague, but he wondered if it was an effect of the particular fungus in that room—not mildew, it was something else, something new and deeply unpleasant to him—and he could imagine invisible toxic clouds of it being sucked in as he breathed, quickly absorbed into his blood, and then sluicing chaos into his brain.

Neil reached for the doorknob but his hand seemed to wave and flap listlessly in the air. Wow—the word formed in his mind with absurd calm and detachment—he couldn't remember the last time he had a reaction this strong and swift. He might even fall down.

But then Marisa opened the door and smiled at him.

Il Morbo

"You look pale," she said, taking his arm in hers again.

"I think I'm just a little tired, that's all," Neil said. "I did a lot of walking and driving today before I got here."

"Dinner is later, but we'll have some wine and snacks now."

"That sounds very good."

She led him down the long corridor toward the rear of the house. There were any number of doors on either side, but all of them were closed. They passed three more staircases, one that went down on the left side, then farther on another that went down to the right, and at the back, one more that led to the upper floors.

"Too many rooms," Marisa said, almost to herself. "It's impossible to take care of all these rooms anymore. Most of them are closed and never used. There's no need for them."

Neil nodded sympathetically. "Do you have any brothers or sisters? I mean, aside from the brother you mentioned."

"No, only Hugo. That's part of the problem. He's

away on business often and has no interest in running things here. Neither do I," she added in a lower, almost conspiratorial tone.

A familiar story, Neil thought. He couldn't imagine someone like her remaining here for very long, even if it was her family home. A bright young woman who had recently finished her university degree—work and life and love were all to be found elsewhere now, out in the world.

He felt better as they stepped outside, his breathing was almost back to normal. They walked to a stone patio with a weathered wooden table and several chairs. It was located a short distance from the house, at an angle that allowed them a very attractive view of the sharp ridges and deep vales that unfolded in the distance.

He also saw, directly beyond the yard around the house, a gradually rising series of terraces and still more outbuildings. Men were working the plots, kids were playing, and Neil occasionally caught a glimpse of a woman in a woolly jacket and long skirt peering out of one hut or another.

He and Marisa sat at the table. A bottle of red wine and two crystal goblets had already been placed there, and two older women soon appeared to set down platters of food. Neil knew immediately from their features that they were not related to Marisa.

There were slices of cold sausage, black olives, cuts of three or four different kinds of cheese, something that looked like *pâte* or a meat pudding, a couple of loaves of bread, butter, a bowl of dark olive oil and a few jars and dishes that contained unknown sauces and spreads. The wine, which Marisa said they made from their own grapes, was a dark ruby-maroon in color and had a little too much of a tannic edge, but it was drinkable.

"*Robusto*," Neil managed to say.

Marisa was no longer wearing sunglasses. Her eyes were deep blue, frank, open, curious—perhaps he was reading too much into them this soon, but they were so easy to gaze at. The breeze played in her silky black hair. She had such striking features—strong cheekbones, a wide mouth, rosy full lips, a proud nose, clear smooth skin with a pearly luster—altogether, they grabbed your attention and held it.

Neil and Marisa nibbled at the food, drank the wine and talked for an hour or more about books, history, Italy, America, and their lives. He felt very comfortable and relaxed with her. He was usually not one to volunteer much information about himself, but he soon found that he wanted to tell her things, that he enjoyed her questions and interest.

When *La Petrella* was published and Neil had to give quite a few interviews, he quickly developed a brief biographical sketch that satisfied most questioners. How he had stayed on in Worcester after graduating from Assumption College. The six years of substitute teaching by day, bartending nights and weekends at the Templewood Golf Course or at Olivia's. All of the reading and writing he had done in odd hours, slowly accumulating the first novel, and then the second. How both of those books were indifferently reviewed in only a few places, and barely sold. How Neil had decided to give fiction one more chance, and—bingo. The glowing reviews of *La Petrella*, the solid sales, the trade paperback that sold even better, and the film option. It was a happy American story, neat and edifying.

But with Marisa, Neil wanted to say more. He told her about the death of his mother, which was followed only a few months later by the breakup with his longtime girlfriend, Jamie, and how those two events had forever changed him, diminishing his expectations of life and instilling in him a certain resignation to melancholy that even now, almost four years later, showed no sign of going away.

"Ha, it serves her right," Marisa said of Jamie. "She left you just before your book came out and did so well. I'm sure she has kicked herself many times since then. Better you found out sooner than later. You should be glad she left when she did."

He wasn't, but Neil laughed at Marisa's words and part of him hoped that she was right about Jamie kicking herself. Still, even after the book was published, she had never called or written, never made any attempt to revive the relationship, and he'd long ago accepted the fact that it was dead.

Marisa spoke softly but quickly, her voice fluid and pleasing to the ear. She had a way of filling any brief moments of silence that arose. Neil gradually learned more about her, and it was pretty much as he had already guessed. She had returned home after college, intending to stay for a month or two, the summer at most. Her degree was in history, which meant that she could only teach or go back to college for a postgraduate degree, neither of which appealed to her. She had been thinking of moving to Florence. She could always find a job like waitressing to earn money while she looked for an opening in a more interesting line of work—perhaps fashion, magazines, the arts. Florence was a lively creative city, there were always opportunities for bright young people who looked for them.

But she soon was caught up in "keeping things going" at home. Her parents and two surviving grandparents were all in varying stages of illness or frailty. It was impossible just to walk away. Her family and the tenants needed her. Marisa's brother Hugo was often away on business—he was a rep for a medical supply company—and his financial contributions were very helpful to the household.

Marisa seemed to understand that the whole enterprise was by now hopelessly outmoded, a relic of the

275

past, and doomed to collapse, though she didn't say so. But she apparently regarded it as her family duty to do her part and see it through as long as her parents and grandparents were alive. As she spoke of these things, Neil could see that she was forcing herself to smile and affect a light tone, but there was loneliness and sadness in her eyes. It wasn't hard to understand why she was so grateful for a visitor.

Neil noticed a group of six or seven men standing together on one of the terraces. They appeared to be watching him, and Marisa. Neil wondered what those people would do when the farm finally went under. Perhaps they thought he was from the bank, and wondered the same thing. Even at some distance, they seemed alien, slightly wild, lost people.

A heavy mist was drifting across the hills and settling around them, a low grey cloud of moisture. It came with surprising swiftness, obscuring the sunset and the views. Marisa frowned.

"*Il morbo*," she said.

"What?"

"This fog. It's a regular feature of the region, especiallly up here at these altitudes. The local people call it *il morbo*."

Neil shivered, feeling a sudden chill. "That means sickness, illness, the plague," he said.

"Yes, exactly." Marisa laughed. "Sometimes it blows through and is gone in an hour, but it can linger for a couple of days—and when it does, you do start to think of it as a plague."

On the terrace above, the men were losing their individual definition in the mist, becoming a cluster of dark shadow figures. The air was grey and full of floating globules of wetness.

"Let's go inside," Marisa said.

PASSEGIATA

She led him up a flight of stairs and along a short corridor. They took a sharply angled turn, so that they appeared to be heading back the way they had just come, though by a different passage. They went through a doorway, across a raised gallery that was open above an empty room, and then into yet another corridor. Their footsteps made an echoing hollow clatter on the bare floorboards. The floor itself seemed to tilt slightly one way and then another, or to sag in the middle—it was never quite solid and level.

Marisa held his arm snugly against her as they walked, and Neil could feel the movements of her hip. The way their bodies touched, the way Marisa smiled at him—he wanted to believe she was seriously flirting with him, but he decided it wasn't serious. Not yet, anyway. Now that they were indoors, he noticed a sweet woodsy fragrance about her. Juniper? Whatever it was, he found it deliciously attractive.

"The layout is a bit crazy," she said apologetically. "At

one time we had many relatives living with us here—cousins, aunts, uncles, in-laws. The rooms were divided and altered many times over the years to accommodate everybody and their belongings."

"I see."

"There was a story that a couple of hundred years ago this was not a farmhouse, that it was originally a monastic retreat or home for some obscure religious order that eventually dwindled away."

"Is that right?"

"You can still see religious carvings and symbols in certain places on the old woodwork, so maybe it's true."

"I like places with a mysterious history," Neil said.

"Yes, so do I, but now it's just a big nuisance."

They turned a corner and were in a wider area, a cul-de-sac. There were two doors, one on either side of the dead-end wall. Marisa opened one of them and went into the room. Neil followed.

"I hope this will be all right," she said.

The room was large, almost square in shape, and sparsely furnished, but it looked comfortable enough. The tall narrow window was swung open and the air in the room was clear, with no trace of mustiness—that was the most important thing as far as Neil was concerned.

"Oh, this is fine," he said. "Very nice."

"There's a bathroom just outside, through the other door. Perhaps you'd like a little time now to unpack your things, to rest and wash up before dinner," she suggested.

"Yes, I would."

"I'll come back for you in, say, an hour and a quarter? I don't want you to get lost wandering around this place alone."

Neil laughed. "Again, I'm sorry to impose on you like this. I'm very grateful for your kind hospitality."

"It's no trouble at all." Marisa hesitated, or lingered, for a moment in the open doorway, smiling warmly at him before she turned to leave. "Make yourself at home here. I'll see you again in a little while."

He smiled back at her. "I look forward to it."

Neil stood and listened as the sound of her footsteps faded away, and then he surveyed the room again. There was a queen-size bed with ornate dark woodwork, an armoire, a chaise and one other chair, a clothes rack and a couple of small énd tables. A bedside lamp and a standing floor lamp provided the only light, but they would do. A threadbare rug covered much of the plank floor. The walls were bare, and had been whitewashed so long ago that they had turned grey. He noticed an unlabeled brown bottle and two drinking glasses on one of the tables. He removed the glass stopper from the bottle, took a sniff, poured a few drops and tasted it—grappa. He splashed a little more in the glass. A nice touch.

Neil went to the window, rested his arms on the stone casement and leaned forward to look outside. He suddenly realized that his room was in a wing that had been added on to the main body of the house at some point. It was toward the rear of the house and on the far side, which explained why he hadn't noticed it either when he first approached the place or later, when he was sitting on the patio. Directly below him now, a drop of almost thirty feet, there was only a narrow curling path of ground between the house and the rim of a deep rocky gorge.

Neil finished the grappa and set his small travel alarm for forty-five minutes. He took off his shoes and stretched out on the bed. The mattress was soft and comfortable, and the large down pillows were lightly scented with cedar. Neil shut his eyes and dozed off almost immediately. When the alarm beeped he got up, gathered a few things and went into the bathroom. There was a huge old tub, a toilet with a water tank above it, a sink and mirror. The stone tile floor felt cold through his socks. Neil washed his face, shaved quickly, brushed his teeth and changed shirts. He felt better, clean and awake again, refreshed by the nap.

As Neil stepped back into his room, he heard a noise. It struck him, because until now he hadn't heard any sounds in the house other the ones he and Marisa made walking. This sound was raspy and grating, repeated in a steady rhythm, as if one piece of metal was being scraped against another. It sounded quite close by, so Neil walked the short distance into the corridor to see if he could find where and what it was. He still had a few minutes before Marisa was due to come and fetch him. Neil vowed not to embarrass himself by getting lost.

It was almost completely dark outside and very little light penetrated this inner corridor. He saw a few widely spaced electric candles mounted in sconces on the wall, but they were not turned on and there was no switch to be found in the immediate area. To make matters worse, once he was in the corridor Neil could not get a true sense of direction on the metallic noise. It was still there, somewhere around him, but elusive.

As his eyes slowly adjusted to the gloom, he began to discern a very faint shaft of light not too far down the passage to his right. Good enough, he thought. He would check it out and then return to his room.

Neil was still wearing only socks on his feet. The floorboards felt weak in places, almost spongy, and they groaned softly beneath his weight. It would be a real surprise if dry rot and woodworms hadn't already taken over large portions of the interior of the house, particularly in the rooms that were closed and unused, dark and damp.

The light came from a recess in the wall. Four steps led in and up to a landing with a wooden ceiling so low that Neil had to bow his head slightly when he got to it. There was a very small open area on the right, an alcove with a narrow built-in bunk. The pale light came from several votive candles in blue glass jars that stood in a line along a single wall shelf.

There was a young man lying in the bunk. He looked to be a teenager still, certainly no older than twenty. His skin was clear, his features boyish, his hair cut short and neatly arranged. A red sheet covered him from his feet to his chin. A stark iron crucifix was mounted on the wall directly above the boy's head. The skeletal Christ figure looked like it might have been carved out of ivory that had turned brownish-yellow.

Neil stood there for a moment, taking all this in, trying to imagine an explanation. He stepped closer and studied the youth. There was no sign of breathing—in fact, the boy's skin looked icy blue, though that was probably an illusion caused by the glass candleholders. Neil took one candle and held it below the boy's cheek, illuminating his face with a clear light. Oddly, all that did was make the blueness more apparent.

Unlikely possibilities flashed through Neil's mind. The boy had just died and was laid out here as at a wake. But why wouldn't Marisa tell Neil about it? Even more to the point, why would they put the body up here in this absurd little raised alcove instead of a proper sitting room downstairs, or the nearest funeral home? That made no sense. Perhaps the young man had died some time ago, and the family knew a way to preserve his body more or less perfectly, as it now appeared. But that seemed no less implausible.

Neil leaned forward and lightly pressed the back of his hand against the young man's gleaming forehead. It felt very cold and hard. When Neil took his hand away he saw a clear rosy-whitish impression of his fingers on the boy's skin. It disappeared in a second or two, heat vanishing.

Then Neil thought he heard a faint exhalation, and he became aware of the metal noise again, rasping some-where nearby. He stumbled back, his socks slipped and he had to grab the wall to keep from falling on the stairs. Neil returned quickly to his room.

POCKETS

Neil had no time to think about what he had just seen before he heard Marisa's heels clicking loudly down the corridor. She appeared in his open doorway, a sudden irresistible vision. She looked gorgeous. She was wearing a fashionable short, tight, sleeveless black dress with a scooped neckline. It was a dress perfectly designed to emphasize the generous curves and elegant lines of her splendid body.

It was impossible not to stare at her—Neil realized he was probably gaping like a teenage boy. But it also occurred to him that she had obviously chosen to dress like this for him and no one else in this place. Marisa's body filled his vision—it seemed to fill the entire barren room with the explosive richness of life.

She knocked needlessly on the door frame. That was when he finally noticed the smile on her face—playful, expectant.

"You look lovely," he told her.

"Did *signore* try his bed?"

"Yes, he did."

"And was it satisfactory?"

"Yes, it was very . . . comfortable."

"You're quite sure?" Mock-doubtful.

"Well, I think so."

"Nothing else you need?"

"Now that you're here, I'm fine."

She laughed. "That little rest did you some good, I'm thinking. You don't look so tired now."

"I do feel much better. Refreshed."

"Good, I'm glad. Are you ready to go downstairs?"

"Sure."

Neil put on his sports jacket and Marisa took his hand in hers as they left the room. She startled him by turning to the right in the corridor, so they were bound to walk right past the steps leading up into the alcove. He was even more surprised when she stopped at the entrance and turned as if to go up the steps—but there were no steps, only an open doorway into another room, this one quite small, with a circular staircase down to the ground floor. He must have misjudged the distance, he told himself. The stairs and alcove must be a little farther along that corridor. Neil almost asked Marisa about the dead boy, but decided not to for the time being.

Now they were in a large warmly lit room that featured a regulation size English billiards table. There were several overstuffed armchairs off on either side of the room. At the far end, a sofa and a couple more chairs were arranged around a portable television set. The billiards table was in quite good condition, complete with string pockets, but the rest of the furniture was the same kind of battered old junk he'd seen elsewhere in the house.

"Do you play?" Marisa asked.

"I have played pool, but not proper billiards."

"I'll teach you later, if you want. It's not hard to learn. The rules, I mean. The game itself is another matter."

"I'd like to learn." As long as she was teaching.

"This is the room where Hugo and I kind of hang out," she explained as she went to a small bar near the television set. "He likes to play billiards, so I learned just to give him some competition. Not that I'm very good. One of my uncles was crazy about the game and had this table shipped here from Paris. He died several years ago. The television gets two or three channels on a good night."

Neil nodded sympathetically, but he didn't know quite what to say. It all seemed so dreary and depressing. Even this large room, with its clutter of furniture and its warm lamps, where at least two people spent some time and relaxed, somehow still felt dark, empty and lonely, bereft of life. Only family love and loyalty could keep somebody in a place like this, but even allowing that Marisa had an abundance of those qualities, Neil thought she was bound to go batty sooner or later if she stayed here for very long.

"The table is beautiful," Neil said lamely.

Marisa poured two glasses of wine and gave one to him—the same house red, he discovered when he took a sip. Either he was getting used to it or this was a better bottle, because he found it more agreeable now. Marisa perched herself on the fat arm of a heavy armchair, her legs open to the extent that her dress would allow. Neil's throat tightened and his heart felt like it was booming in his chest.

Jamie had a somewhat fulsome figure too, at first, though in time she had become obsessive about taking off weight. Perhaps that was part of the big fuzzy why— why it all went wrong for them.

"There are a couple of things I should warn you about."

"Oh?"

"Nothing serious." Marisa smiled. "It's just that my relatives are all still pretty much old world people. By old world I mean, you know—before the War. That was the world they grew up in and they still have a lot of those ways and attitudes. They might seem rather—"

She hesitated, unable to find the word she wanted. "Different?" Neil offered. He was the writer.

"Yes." Marisa smiled gratefully. "Different."

"Thanks for telling me," he said. "But I'm sure it won't be a problem as far as I'm concerned. I'm always glad to have the chance to meet and talk with people who lived through that period."

"Good." Marisa was still hesitating about something. "Oh, and if you don't like the food, please, you don't have to eat it. Just have some bread and salad, and I'll fix you something else later. I can tell them we had a lot to eat on the patio earlier."

"We did, and I'm not that hungry now." Neil resisted the urge to smile at her warning about the food. "But I'm sure it'll be fine."

"Thank you."

"Not at all. I'm the guest here."

"One more thing."

"Yes?"

Marisa stood up and stepped close to him. The thin gold bracelets on her wrist gleamed in the light as she put her glass down on the bar. A vibrant blue opal the size of a quarter dangled from a black ribbon that hung tightly at the base of her slender throat. How he wanted to kiss that throat.

All of that lovely black hair, the fire in her eyes, the silky texture of her skin, the way her perfume seemed to settle around him and draw him still closer to her, the movement of her tongue moistening her lips just as she was about to speak—Neil was completely captivated by her physical presence, dazed by its power. Dazed, but still aware.

"I hope you don't mind, but I told them that you are a

friend of mine from the university. Well, you're a little older, so I said you were a visiting lecturer there and we became acquaintances. That was rather naughty of me, I know. I should have spoken with you about it first."

"Oh," Neil said. "But, why?"

"Like I said, they're kind of funny that way. If they thought you were a stranger, they'd sit up awake all night, worrying, wondering—who is this man, who sent him, what does he really want? Where they came from and what they went through, a stranger at the door—you have no idea how much it could disturb them. It's crazy, I know, but I thought it best not to risk upsetting them, at their age." Her eyes peered up at Neil, her expression submissive and childlike. "I'm sorry."

"That's all right." Now Neil allowed himself to touch her, putting his arm around her shoulder, stroking her back soothingly. "I understand and I'm sure you're right that it's better for them this way."

"Oh, thank you so much."

"Besides, I really was a teacher for a while."

Marisa smiled brightly, her body resting against his, her head on his chest. God, her hair felt so good on his cheek. He felt her hand on the small of his back. She looked up at him again and opened her mouth as he leaned forward to kiss her. Marisa's tongue met his aggressively, her arm tightened across his back and pulled him closer. Neil could feel the same anxious desire and tension in her body that simmered within him. Their kiss was long and deep, lingering. Finally, Marisa pulled her head back a couple of inches. Now her smile was intimate, complicitous. She slowly ran the tip of her finger along her wet lips.

"Well, hello."

"Hi . . ."

"We'd better go in now," she said.

"Mmm?" Neil kissed her neck and throat. Marisa

sighed with pleasure, but then gently put her hands on his chest.

"Really. My uncle is a priest. If he were to walk in and find us like this, I'd never hear the end of it."

Neil must have frowned or pouted. Marisa kissed him consolingly, her tongue teasing him.

"Be patient," she said. "We must."

"Okay," he said, smiling. "Let's go."

Marisa took his hand and led him through a doorway into an empty enclosed passage that led to another door. When she opened it, the first thing Neil heard was the familiar sound of metal scraping on metal.

GASTRONOMICO

There were six people already in the dining room when Marisa and Neil entered. They were seated at one end of a table that could hold twelve or fourteen. They were all elderly and they looked half-asleep, propped up in their chairs, barely moving until Marisa approached and spoke to them or touched them on the shoulder. Neil held back a few steps. He couldn't understand what Marisa was saying but the gentle affection in her voice was clear enough. There were three men and three women—Marisa's parents and grandparents, he learned. Neil stepped forward and smiled and nodded to each of them when Marisa gestured toward him. They glanced briefly and vacantly at him, but none of them nodded or said anything. Handshakes were obviously not on.

One of the grandmothers had several small spoons on the table beside her plate, and she was sharpening them with a metal file. Neil stared at this curious spectacle for a few seconds before the old woman suddenly grinned at him and made a crisp scooping motion with the spoon she held.

"Fruit spoons," Marisa explained with a laugh. "You know, like for eating grapefruit with?"

"Oh, yes." Neil still couldn't imagine how he had been able to hear this persistent but not loud sound all the way upstairs. Yet he had no doubt that it was indeed the very same sound.

"Grandmother sharpens them every evening," Marisa explained, as if it were a perfectly normal activity. "It's one of the few things she can still do around the house, so I suppose it makes her feel a little bit useful."

"That's good for her, then." And perhaps it was, but Neil had never heard of anyone sharpening fruit spoons before. He took it to be an unusual but harmless display of eccentricity.

"Yes, it is." Marisa smiled gratefully.

The room was large, but aside from the table and chairs the only other furniture was a sideboard adjacent to the other door, which apparently led to the kitchen. The two long walls were hung with tapestries so faded and dusty that it was impossible for Neil to make out the scenes depicted on them. The room was lit only by candles, which didn't help. The wooden floor was bare and it sagged or tilted in places, just as it did elsewhere in the house.

The same two women who had served them on the patio now came into the room with bowls and platters of food. Marisa asked Neil to help her pour the wine, and he was grateful to have something to do. The men, who wore stiff, old-fashioned suits that almost resembled uniforms, exchanged a few quiet words with each other and then laughed briefly. Neil sensed that it was at his expense—perhaps they thought it absurd or humiliating that he let himself do a servant's work. And at a woman's bidding, no less. Not that he cared in the least about such a silly, antiquated attitude. He also noticed the women casting gnomic glances at him, but they remained silent.

A place had been set at the head of the table, though

no one occupied that chair. Neil hesitated, uncertain whether he should pour wine in the glass there too, but then Marisa nodded yes.

"My uncle—ah, here he is."

The priest came in through the doorway from the billiards room—Neil noted—and walked briskly to the table. He had wiry grey hair that was cut short. Although he looked nearly seventy he stood tall and straight and he had a sturdy, muscular build that conveyed strength and energy. The standard collar and black jacket made him look like just another diocesan priest, but he also wore a purple sash across his tunic, a medallion of the Virgin Mary, and there were several small pins and medals affixed to his lapels and breast pocket. He smiled and kissed Marisa lightly on the cheek.

"Father Anton, this is my friend Neil O'Netty from America," Marisa said, introducing them. "Neil, this is my uncle, Anton Panic."

"I'm very pleased to meet you," Neil said.

"Thank you, thank you. So nice." The priest's head bobbed several times and he clasped Neil's hand tightly. "So nice. Thank you."

Father Anton's eyes danced behind thick lenses, and Neil wondered if the frames could actually be genuine bakelite.

"Thank you, and your family, for your hospitality," Neil said to the priest, sensing that Father Anton was the decisive figure in the household. "I'm very grateful."

"No, please. Our pleasure to have a guest."

Neil and Marisa sat opposite each other, in the eighth and ninth places at the table. One of the servant women carefully set down a large covered porcelain tureen on the table between Neil and Marisa, and then left. Neil bowed his head slightly when he saw everyone else do that, and Father Anton said Grace in Latin, adding a few more words at the end in the family's other language. The old men chorused "Amen" loudly, and then laughed again, as if at a private joke.

Food was passed around. Neil loaded up on bread and salad, as Marisa had suggested. The bread was coarse and crusty, with a fresh yeasty smell. The salad contained various greens, mushrooms, peppers, tomatoes and chunks of cold meat sausage. Neil drizzled dark olive oil and balsamic vinegar on it. He also took a helping of a soupy rice dish.

The old man beside Neil nudged him in the arm. Neil assumed this was Marisa's father, though in fact he looked only marginally younger than the two grandfathers. He must have been in his early fifties when Marisa was born, but late births were probably not unusual on remote farms. It was clear that the man wanted Neil to help himself from the tureen now. He glanced at Marisa, who nodded reluctantly.

"But we can skip it," she said quickly.

"Oh. Well, let's see."

"You can just pass it along to them."

"That's all right."

Neil didn't want to appear rude. Even as Marisa was speaking to the others, apparently explaining how much she and Neil had eaten just a little while ago on the patio, he lifted the lid of the tureen. It appeared to be some kind of stew, brownish in color. Neil took the iron ladle and swirled it once through the liquid, stirring up small bits of meat, potatoes and—skulls. Tiny skulls that must have been very young birds, probably baby chickens. There were scores of them in the stew, each one roughly the size of a misshapen marble. O-kay. Neil smiled wanly at Marisa.

"I think you were right."

As soon as Neil lifted the heavy tureen and passed it along the table, the others broke into jolly laughter, and it felt as if some tension went out of the air. They were all fully awake now.

"I'm sorry, I warned you," Marisa said. "I wasn't sure, but I thought it might be something like that. Old tastes. It's an old recipe."

"That's okay," Neil assured her. "It's probably quite good, but I think I'd have to get myself in the right state of mind to try it."

"Mr. O'Netty," the priest spoke up. "Zuzu informed me that you have written a book about the case of Beatrice Cenci. Yes?"

"Zuzu is a family nickname for me," Marisa told him. "Don't ask me what it means, but it goes back to when I was a baby."

"I like it." Then he turned toward Father Anton. "Yes, that's right, my last novel was about the Cencis."

"Aha."

The priest spoke English slowly and with difficulty, but he was eager to hear about Neil's version of the story. He seemed particularly concerned that Neil might have been critical of Pope Clement VIII, for refusing to spare young Beatrice's life. Neil babbled on about what a thorny moral problem that was, even in today's world, and how he tried not to take one side or the other. A novel was not a debate, et cetera—the usual points he had made in numerous interviews. It was strange, speaking past six people who couldn't understand a word he was saying and ignored him. But Father Anton nodded every few seconds and appeared to be listening carefully.

Neil thought he was probably speaking for too long, but he couldn't focus his mind. His words seemed to vanish immediately in the air, and the only thing he could hear—on and on—was the muffled crunching sound of all those little bird skulls being eaten.

293

BILLIARDS AT HALF-PAST TEN

To Neil's relief, dinner in that house was a functional matter, not a social event. Marisa's parents and grand-parents ate energetically and loudly, but surprisingly quickly. They drank one large glass of wine each, and when they were finished they shuffled off out of the room, scarcely even glancing at him as they left. It was probably his fault, Neil thought. If he weren't there, they would chat and linger at the table as families do—or did.

Though somehow he doubted that. The priest, Marisa and Hugo were the practical, capable ones who kept things going here. Without their efforts, the farm would be sold and the old folks packed off to a nursing home. Not that they seemed to appreciate it. Neil thought they acted as if they took all this for granted, which amounted to a terrible ingratitude. But—old people, old ways. They weren't going to change now.

When the others left, Father Anton came and sat beside Neil. He had a few more questions to raise and points to make about history and literature, which was apparently a matter of some real interest to him. Neil did his best to speak sensibly and not get carried away. He had no special theories or insights. History was interesting, it provided useful plots and frameworks as well as a magical sense of distance, of stepping into another world, another time and place. He felt very comfortable with it.

But all Neil really wanted to do was write tales that were like operas—gaudy, full of intensity, screaming emotion, high drama, sudden action, and troubled characters driven by primal human desires. That was the big stuff, as he thought of it. History itself wasn't the point. The critics had seen much more in *La Petrella* than Neil thought was there, including a few mysterious literary techniques he didn't even understand. Which made him feel kind of like a secret phony at times, but that was their business.

Father Anton was polite and intelligent, and after ten minutes he got up, clasped Neil's hand again, and said good night. He went around the table to kiss "Zuzu" on the forehead, and then left the room.

"He likes you," Marisa said. "I can tell."

"He seems very nice. But why is he living here? I mean, priests are usually assigned to parishes or schools," Neil added.

"He could be retired if he wanted, at his age. But he is on a kind of sabbatical instead. He is working on a paper for the Pope."

"Really?"

"Oh yes. Father Anton has known every pope, going back to Pius. He found a place at the Vatican early in his priesthood, and ever since then he has been very, you know what I mean, well-connected."

"Wow. What is his paper about?"

Marisa shrugged. "I'm not sure. Something to do with the history of conversions in Christianity. That's why he was so keen to hear what you had to say about how you make use of history in your books."

"Ah, I see."

The two servant women entered the room then and began to gather up the dishes and utensils. Neil thought he saw a sudden darkening of Marisa's expression. Then she turned to him, and smiled again. She pushed her chair away from the table and stood up.

"Shall we get out of the way?"

"Absolutely."

They went back into the billiards room. Marisa asked Neil to pour some more wine for both of them. She turned on the television and fiddled with the rabbit ears until she got a reasonably stable picture. It looked like some awful game show, but she turned the volume off. Then Marisa went to a shelf and picked up a pocket transistor radio that looked about forty years old. She rolled the little tuning wheel until she found a station playing some Abba-like Europop. The relentlessly cheerful tinny sound hung in the air like a bouquet of desiccated flowers.

"They aren't necessary for me," Neil said, nodding toward the radio and the television as he handed Marisa a glass of wine.

"I know, but it looks good. In case."

"In case?"

"You know. If someone comes in on us."

"You really think they would?"

"It's possible." Marisa shrugged, her eyes sad. "Better to give them a little while to get to bed."

"You're a grown woman."

"Don't make fun." Marisa turned away, pouting. "You can see that they don't think that way. They never will."

Neil put his drink down on the bar and stepped close behind her. He put his arms around her and kissed her hair and neck. "I'm sorry. I wasn't making fun. It's hard for you here, isn't it?"

She seemed to sigh and relax a little in his embrace. She gave a slow nod and her free hand reached around to rest on his hip. Neil's hands spread across her belly. When they brushed up against her breasts he felt her quick intake of breath, then the long slow exhalation, a vibration within her body, a silent cry of pleasure and deep need.

Marisa slipped out of his arms, turned around and leaned close to kiss him. Her tongue danced and teased, licking across his lips. She pressed her hand to his chest, as if to hold him back at a certain distance, but two fingers slipped between the buttons and touched his skin. She was smiling brightly again. Then her fingers tightened on his shirt and pulled him closer for one more kiss before she moved to the sofa.

"Let's sit," Marisa said. "Just for a little while."

"Okay."

They sat just a couple of feet apart on the sofa, their bodies turned to face each other. Neil caught a glimpse of Marisa's pearl grey panties and he realized that her legs were bare. It occurred to him that all of this might be a colossal tease and nothing more, but he doubted it, and in any event he didn't care if it was. Would he rather be alone in his room upstairs, trying to finish Rose Tremain's *Restoration*? Uh, no.

"So, tell me, why haven't you found someone else?" she asked. "It has been some time since this other woman left. A handsome young author like you, and very successful. I think the women would be knocking on your door day and night."

Neil laughed. He knew he was quite ordinary looking. But it was true that after the publication of *La Petrella* some women he'd known only on a casual social basis suddenly seemed to find him much more fascinating and worthy of their attention. Not to mention the strangers.

"I haven't been a monk."

"Aha."

"But no one serious." It was time to turn the tables. "And what about you? I can't believe you didn't have plenty of boyfriends when you were at college, in Parma."

"*Boys*, yes," Marisa said dismissively. "Anyhow . . ."

Neil watched the way her lips moved as she took another sip of wine, the slight tightening of the muscles in her throat as she swallowed. It was not unlike a fairy tale, he thought, or a romantic opera. Marisa was the beautiful young princess imprisoned in a remote castle by the evil queen or king, in this case by a whole van-load of elderly relatives and a bunch of tenant farmers. And that made Neil the prince who comes to rescue her, et cetera. It was the kind of old-fashioned story he liked—but it only took another momentary flash of sadness in Marisa's eyes to remind him that it was a very different matter for her, with no easy alternatives or solutions.

Still, there was nothing he could do. Invite her to Rome? Offer to take her with him when his car was fixed and he left? Sure, he could do that without any commitment on his part, but he sensed that Marisa would simply decline the offer. She had intelligence, spark, wit, and a desire to escape, but she also seemed resigned to play out the role that had been assigned to her for now by family and circumstance.

Her free hand rested across the inside of her thigh and her hair curled around her face, tumbling down over her shoulders like a gauzy wimple. She glanced at the door to the dining room and then back the other way toward the circular staircase. She leaned closer to Neil—who let his gaze linger on her cleavage. By now he was convinced that Marisa liked him looking at her this way, with voyeuristic intensity and undisguised desire.

They continued chatting for a few minutes but Neil was hardly aware of what they actually said. It was nothing important, just talk intended to pass whatever amount of time it took for Marisa to feel comfortable.

At one point she went to get the wine bottle from the bar. When she came back to the sofa, she sat right next to him. Their knees touched and she let her hand rest lightly on his leg. It was all Neil had been waiting for, the final signal. He ran the back of his fingers over her cheek, then trailed them down to stroke the inner curves of her breasts, her skin so silky and lovely to touch. Her hand moved between his legs, just brushing his cock.

Before they kissed again, he saw Marisa quickly scan the room once more. Apparently reassured, she let her eyes close and her kiss was hard and wet, full of aggressive passion. When their mouths parted, she smiled at him with her eyes—it was a look of recognition.

Marisa suddenly turned and stretched out her body, lying down on the sofa so that her head rested on Neil's lap. She nestled her cheek against his erection. She pushed her feet into the cushion and raised her legs, so that her dress slipped back and exposed even more of her thighs. Her knees swaying in the air, together, then apart.

"Ah, you want me so much," she said softly. "Don't you?"

"Yes, I do."

"Do you think that's a good idea?" Playful, teasing again.

"It's the only idea."

"But we can't rush. Desire is all anticipation, isn't it?"

"Not *all* anticipation."

Marisa laughed. "And fantasy, imagination."

"Not *all* fantasy and imagination," Neil insisted, grinning at her. "It involves action too, and fulfillment."

"But the right action."

"And what's the right action?"

"Oh, but that's where imagination and fantasy come in," Marisa said, as she continued to move the side of her face against the bulge in his pants. "I'm sorry, you're so sweet to me, but I don't want to rush. You'll be gone, you know, and I'll still be here. Remembering this."

"That's all right," Neil said, moved by her words.

"So many nights I spent in this room, on this couch,

299

the television and the radio turned on. But I was alone and all I could do was imagine moments like this. What we would say, what we would do."

"Well, I'm here now."

"Better than any dream."

"I doubt that."

"No, really," Marisa protested. "I don't like boys. I imagined a man a little older, though not too much! A man considerate, intelligent, experienced, understanding. You're even more, you're a gift."

"So are you," Neil told her. His right hand was between her legs and he slid his finger beneath her wet panties, stroking her, gently pushing on and entering her. Marisa's body heaved and squirmed, her desire storming, barely contained. With his other hand he caressed her cheek again and rolled his fingertip along her upper lips—she took it, sucking hard. "And what did you imagine yourself saying?"

Marisa tugged on his finger, then opened her mouth as she looked up at Neil. "Two." He was confused for a second, but then understood, and he slipped his middle finger into her mouth too. Her eyes were fierce with need and desire. "Three." Three. "Four . . ." Four, her face taut, her teeth biting hard on his flesh. Eyes wide, staring up at him.

He continued stroking her swollen clitoris. She was so wet and hot, and he was enthralled by the way her body responded. Then she pushed his fingers away from her mouth and grabbed his head with both of her hands, her fingers clutching his hair, pulling his face down as she lifted herself to kiss him again, her tongue thrusting, her lips squeezing and pressing and pulling on his mouth and tongue, their chins now dripping with saliva. Marisa tasted so sweet and felt so wonderful. And how utterly glorious it was to break free of thought at last and plunge into the tornado.

Sound Chooses to Echo

They made love with gasping urgency and quickness on the scarred leather sofa. After only a few minutes of resting, Marisa slipped out of Neil's arms, sat up and straightened her dress. Her panties hung from one of her ankles. Neil reached down to remove them. He held them to his face for a second, smiling at her, and then put them in his pants pocket.

"Oh? What's that, your trophy?" Lightly mocking, playful.

"No. I just don't want you to put them back on."

"Ah, good. I'm not through with you, either."

"I'm glad to hear it."

Neil zipped his pants and buckled his belt. Marisa slid closer and leaned against him as he put his arm around her. Reckless, reckless—he knew that, but he didn't care. What really bothered him about their quick fuck was that it had been just that, a quick fuck.

"We both needed and wanted each other so much," Marisa said. "The first time had to be like that. Thunder and lightning."

"Yes." Neil gave a soft laugh. "The first time."

"And how do you know it won't be the same way the second time?" Marisa asked with a naughty grin. "And the third? We might make a lot of thunder and lightning, you know."

"That's great, if we do," he told her. "But I also want you in a bed, yours or mine, where we can take our time and really make love."

Marisa wriggled closer in his embrace, sighed happily and kissed his chin, running her hand along his leg. "So do I, and we will. But first we had to wait until they were in their rooms. And then—we couldn't wait a minute longer! But that's okay. Every time is good in its own way."

They sat together like that for a while longer, kissing, touching each other, all tenderness, affection and dreamy smiles. Neil loved the way she felt in his arms, the softness of her skin, the fragrance in her hair, the sweet spicy taste of her mouth.

Reckless, yes—but what the hell, if she got pregnant, he would marry Marisa and they would have a child. He would still write his books, it might even turn out to be a happy marriage and—Neil almost laughed aloud, it was such a startling and improbable thought. But what surprised him most was that it didn't scare him at all. His personal life had been drifting nowhere the last few years. Before that too, probably. Perhaps he had reached the point where he secretly hoped that some outside event would force a dramatic change that sent his life in a completely new and unexpected direction, and he would have no choice but to go along with it.

Things like that happened in opera all the time. Part of Neil's brain knew that in the cold light of day he would see it differently, rationally, and that he would probably want to drive away from Marisa and this house with no complications or lingering ties. But for now that part of his brain had no voice. He only wanted this wonderful erotic interlude to continue. Let the two of them see how much pleasure and deep comfort they could give to each other in a short period of time.

Marisa took his hand and they rose from the sofa. They ascended the narrow circular staircase. She smiled back over her shoulder at him when he put his hand on her hip. How he enjoyed the way her body felt as she moved, the smooth, elegant working of her perfect flesh and taut muscles. He slid his hands under Marisa's dress, caressing her thighs. She stopped near the top of the stairs, enjoying his touch, murmuring softly to herself. She turned and sat down on the top step, and opened her legs wide to him. She pulled the front of her dress back with one hand, while the other one partly covered her lush triangle of fine black hair.

Neil leaned forward, gripping the iron stair with his hands to brace himself. He ran his cheek down along the inside of her thigh—ah, it was so silky, warm and soft. Neil imagined he could feel an electric charge building as his skin moved over hers. His tongue probed between her fingers, but she wouldn't help him. Finally he touched and had a fleeting taste of her hot wet inner flesh, so tantalizing. He felt the little jump her body gave, and heard the brief but sharp intake of her breath. Marisa gently took his face in her hands and raised it. She was smiling so warmly and happily. Her hair fell over him as she pulled his face to her breasts and held him there for a moment. Then she slid her body back a little on the floor and stood up.

"My lover. Come on. Not here."

Neil took her hand again and followed her back into the corridor. It was very dark, except for a glimmer of light farther down on the right, where his room was. Marisa started to walk in that direction, but Neil looked to the left and saw the same faint blue glow he had seen earlier. He decided it was the perfect opportunity. He tightened his grip on her hand, and wouldn't move, so she turned around.

"Your room is this way," she told him. Her voice was low, almost a whisper. She tugged his hand.

"What's that blue light?"

He started walking toward the alcove. For some reason he expected Marisa to resist, but she didn't.

"Oh, that. You want to see? It's interesting."

They carefully went up the short flight of steps. There was barely room enough for both of them on the tiny landing. The alcove was virtually the same as before, with the shelf of votive candles still lit and the crude iron crucifix on the wall, but the bunk was empty—bare wood.

"What's this all about?"

"Remember, I told you that they think this house was once a religious retreat, something like that?"

"Oh, yes."

"Okay, so. My uncle thinks that this was a special place they used, where one priest or monk could shut himself in for a while to meditate or to pray." Marisa pointed to a couple of spots on the side walls. "You can see where there might have been hinges for a door. If you were inside, it would almost be like lying in a coffin, so it would help you to think about death, and God, and the life to come. Your movements would be completely restricted. You couldn't stand up or walk around, the way you could in your room. You have no window, no view. No distractions at all. There is nothing to do but lie there and think and pray. You see? Unusual, isn't it?"

Aside from the way she kept her voice down, she reminded Neil of so many bright young guides who explained things at the many historical sites he had visited.

"But why the candles now?"

"Oh." Marisa waved her hand dismissively. "The old women keep them lit all the time. They believe this story so strongly, they want to have it ready in case the soul of some holy man ever returns. Or to honor them all, like devotion candles in a church. Something like that."

"I see."

It made reasonable sense—except for the young man Neil had seen lying there in the bunk. The red sheet on him. His cold blue skin, the way it had appeared to react to his touch. But now Neil was wondering if perhaps he had imagined all of that. He couldn't mention it now.

"I used to think the candles were dangerous," Marisa went on. "But we depend on them in this house. We only have one generator, no connection to the national grid. But there's never been a fire so far. After a while, you get used to things and don't even think about them."

"Yes."

They backed out of the alcove, made their way down the dark steps and a few moments later were in Neil's room. There was no lock in the door but he felt a little better in some vague way when he pulled it shut and the old latch clicked loudly in place. He switched on the small lamp that was on the bedside table. It created a pocket of golden light around the bed but left the rest of the room in shadows.

Neil had his back half-turned to Marisa for a moment but he felt her presence close to him, like electricity in the air, a growing force of barely contained energy. She reached around him from behind and started tugging his shirt out, unbuttoning it, quickly unbuckling his belt, unzipping his pants again. Her hand slipped into his pocket for a second. Neil pulled his shirt and undershirt off, and immediately felt Marisa kissing his back, rubbing her face on his skin. Her mouth so wet and hot. His pants fell to the floor and he stepped out of them. He yanked his socks off, and was naked. He could feel her body give a slight shrug, he heard the rustle of her dress falling, and then he felt her bare breasts pressing against his back.

Marisa had removed her silk panties from his pocket and now she had them wrapped loosely around her hand as she took his cock and began to stroke it, sending waves of exquisite sensation through him. He reached behind with both hands, caressing her fanny, pulling her even more tightly to his body. She continued stroking him and he was very hard again. "Mmm," she murmured happily.

Neil turned and kissed her, his hands on her breasts and between her legs. He sat down on the bed, pulling her with him, but she stayed on her feet and straddled his legs. Marisa gently pushed him flat on his back, without breaking their long wet kiss, her body poised over his. She felt so wonderful and he loved the way her hair trailed across his skin. He moved farther onto the bed. She moved with him, letting her breasts hang so that her nipples just grazed along over his belly and chest. Then she swung one leg over him and lowered her hips, her body suddenly drawing him into her, seizing him in one swift, sure movement that made him gasp with pleasure.

She leaned forward, letting him kiss her breasts and suck her nipples as their lower bodies heaved violently together. Neil reached down to stroke her wet hard clitoris at the same time as their bodies were thrusting furiously, making the large bed rock and groan. Marisa's cries grew much louder, she no longer cared who might hear anything.

It was longer the second time, but not slower, and the pleasure they experienced was far more intense, ravishing both of them. Their bodies were drenched with sweat when they finally lay still together. Marisa kissed his neck, her lips moving weakly, the lightest of touches. Neil could only hold her in his arms.

He must have dozed off for a little while. Marisa was

kissing him and telling him that she couldn't stay in his room all night, but that she would be back in the morning. Neil gave a little groan of unhappiness, but he smiled sleepily when he opened his eyes and saw her.

"Your face is red, all around your mouth," he said.

She grinned. "So is yours. And your lips are swollen up."

He smiled. "So are yours."

"Not just my lips!"

They laughed, kissed and hugged again, but then she left and the light went out and Neil immediately fell back into a deep happy sleep.

He was naked and cold, and he groped blindly for something to cover himself with. Then the voices entered his brain and stubbornly dragged him back to near-consciousness. Neil sat up slowly and opened his eyes. There was a little grey in the light that came through his open window. The voices were coming from somewhere outside. They were unintelligible, foreign, but surprisingly clear and sharp in the predawn silence.

Neil stood up and listened. He could still hear the voices, though they were a bit fainter now. He crossed the cold floor to the window. The air was very cool, but the cloudy fog—*il morbo*—had disappeared. It was still fairly dark outside but he could see things clearly enough.

In the distance, on one of the ridges about a hundred yards away, two men were walking. But no, there were three of them. They were moving in a direction away from the house. Their voices carried so well that it seemed to Neil almost like a ventriloquist's trick, as if they were standing on the ground just below his window. But he still couldn't understand anything they said. Their voices were gruff, angry, or so it sounded to Neil.

Then he realized dimly that two of the men were dragging and yanking the third one along. They appeared to hit and kick him, as necessary, to keep him moving. A struggle of some sort was in progress, but at such a distance it seemed merely curious to Neil, almost abstract. It went on like that for a little while longer, and then the three men disappeared beyond the downward curl of the winding ridge.

Neil stood there a moment longer, until he realized that he couldn't keep his eyes open and that he was nearly asleep on his feet. He was still so tired. He turned around and went back to bed, pulling the sheet and blankets up over him, clutching them tightly just beneath his chin.

Then he heard—somewhere in the distance, outside—a gunshot. But it was there and gone in an instant, and sleep had him.

THE SECOND DAY

A sound, a metal click too small and distant to stir him, nothing more than a transient pinprick on the otherwise blank expanse of Neil's sleep. But then something else, different and closer, a whisper of cloth, accompanied by a feeling of movement—his own. Marisa was in bed with him, he realized, suddenly aware of her warmth enveloping him, her radiant skin on his and her hair fanning across his belly as she took him in her mouth.

"It's all right," she told him when she wriggled up and settled into his arms beneath the sheets. "My uncle is in the grotto. He says Mass there for the farmers every morning and then he visits with them afterward. He won't be back for a while."

"The grotto?"

"The *grotta rossa*, they call it. It's a cave in the mountain, it's on the other side of the hill out back. Over many years, they made it into a shrine to Our Lady. I'll show it to you later."

"What about your parents and grandparents?"

309

"Oh, they don't climb the stairs anymore. The only one who might walk in on us here is my uncle. He would be upset and hurt."

"And angry?"

"Well, maybe a little."

"What about the—the servants?"

Marisa sighed—unhappily, it seemed to Neil. "They will stay away until I instruct them to clean your room and make up your bed. When we go downstairs."

"Do they bother you?" He had spoken without thinking, so he quickly added, "Or am I just imagining that?"

She hesitated before admitting, "It is difficult."

Neil could tell that she didn't want to talk about it. They lay still for a few more moments, but then Marisa sat up in a sudden quick movement and smiled irrepressibly again. She was so beautiful, her black hair mussed, her magnificent breasts swaying slightly as she turned her body to face him, her eyes sparkling with life. She kissed his lips, his cheeks, his neck, his ears, a quick flurry of affectionate butterfly kisses. Neil felt a fresh wave of emotion surge through him, not merely lust or desire, but something more complicated and harder to define.

Suddenly he remembered that the men there were going to patch his radiator today, and then he would drive away to find the nearest town and a repair shop. An inn for the night. At least, that was the plan. But now Neil felt no urgency about leaving. He wondered if Marisa would ask him to stay for another night. Instead of letting him take a room in town. He could hire a taxi to drive him back here and pick him up again when his car was ready—which might take two or three days, if they had to order out to get the correct replacement radiator.

"Come on, now," she said, interrupting his thoughts. "We don't have *that* much time. I want to watch you shave."

* * *

They ate breakfast on the patio. It was a mild sunny morning and the air was sweet. Neil had deliberately chosen to wait until mid-September for this trip, knowing that the hordes of the summer visitors would pretty much be gone by then. He and Marisa had fresh fruit, omelets and strong coffee. Neil felt awake again, though still a little tired.

They saw Father Anton returning to the house. He had a long brisk stride for a man of his apparent years. When he noticed Marisa and Neil on the patio, he veered off the path and stopped to say hello and exchange a few pleasantries with them, nodding and smiling. But it seemed as if his thoughts were on other matters, and he soon left them to go inside.

"It's much different today," Marisa said. "Better, easier, you know? Yesterday they didn't know you and they were kind of uncertain. But today, it's like you are part of the household."

Neil laughed. "Good. I was afraid that I was causing you problems with them. Not to mention the inconvenience."

"No," she scoffed. Neil loved the way emotion showed in even the smallest of her facial expressions. "It's good now, it's okay."

"Well, I'm glad."

"So, I was thinking. Since it's such a lovely morning, perhaps you would like to go for a walk. There are plenty of old paths and trails, and the countryside is quite nice around here."

He smiled at her. "I'd love to go for a walk with you."

"Ah. I was hoping you would say that." Marisa moistened her lips. "I want to touch you again, right now." Then she laughed happily at her own impatience. "Damn!"

A few minutes later, equipped with a small picnic bas-

ket and a large beach towel, they set off. When they had
walked a little more than a hundred yards, Neil stopped
for a moment and glanced back. Now he could see the
side of the house where his room was, though he wasn't
sure exactly which window was his. So they had to be on
the same ridge where he had seen the three men early
that morning.

"Is something wrong?" Marisa asked.

"No, not at all. I just realized that the way we're going
is in the view I have from the window in my room."

"Yes."

"I woke up early this morning. Just for a moment."

"You did?"

"I heard voices out here and I saw some men on this
path."

"I should have warned you," Marisa said. "Those people make noise day and night. The old ones stay up late,
drinking. Then the younger ones get up early to go about
their work. They have no consideration. I'm very sorry, I
hope they didn't disturb you."

"No, I fell right back to sleep."

"I'm glad."

"I thought I heard a gunshot."

"Yes, they hunt early in the morning," Marisa explained. "Sometimes they bring back a deer, or ducks
and geese from the lake. They need the food. It's such a
shame, you know."

"What is?"

"The land looks so beautiful—and it truly is. But it is *so*
difficult to live on, almost impossible. All of the work
that has to be done, it never ends, and it never seems like
enough."

They walked for nearly an hour. It was easy going, as the
path never rose or descended too sharply. They stopped
a few times to enjoy the views and to kiss. Marisa told

him how she and her brother had explored all of the countryside for miles around as children, and she got Neil to tell her a little bit about the book he was working on. It was another Italian chronicle from Stendhal, he admitted. Marisa thought that was wonderful, but Neil knew the critics would probably tear into him for repeating himself. Oh well. For one thing, he didn't have a better idea.

The sun was almost directly overhead when Marisa led him off the faint path and through a brief stretch of high brush and small trees. A few minutes later they came out into a mossy clearing at the base of a rocky wall, an area not much larger than a good-sized living room. A clump of spindly birch trees provided some shade. A narrow stream of water flowed down the rocks and disappeared into the thick brush at the perimeter.

"We're here," Marisa announced. She spread the beach towel on the grass beneath the birches.

"Perfect," Neil said. He set the picnic basket down and went to the stream. He had worked up a light sweat, so he splashed his face with water. It was very cold and it felt great. A perfect place for a picnic.

Marisa was kneeling on the towel, sitting back on her heels. She had already removed her canvas shoes and tossed them onto the grass. She was wearing a peasant-style blouse and a loose skirt that came to mid-calf, but which was now bunched up just over her knees. Neil sat beside her, resting his back against the trunk of one of the birches.

"There's a bottle of wine in the basket," she said. "Some fresh bread, mortadella and cheese."

"Mmm."

She leaned forward on her hands, and she was like a big beautiful cat pressing against him. Still on her hands and knees, she positioned herself over his lap, and smiled up at him.

"Or would you like to play with me first?"

"*Mmmm . . .*"

Neil reached under, slipping his hand inside her blouse, caressing her breasts, teasing her nipples. His other hand moved beneath her skirt and up the back of her thigh—the sudden thrill of finding that she had no panties on, that her flesh was so hot and moist already. His finger moved into her easily and stroked and rubbed her. Marisa's eyes were closed, her mouth open, and she sighed and groaned with something more than pleasure, some longing and need so great that it seemed almost heartbreaking to Neil. Then she whipped her head back, hair flying, and her mouth tightened, her breath sharp and fast, grunting with ferocity. Neil stroked and caressed her until she sagged down on her forearms and rolled her face in his crotch. Feeling how hard he was, she lithely swung her body around so that her backside faced him. She pulled her skirt up over her hips.

"Please, now . . ."

Neil quickly pulled his pants down, knelt behind her, took hold of her and then thrust into her. Such dizzying pleasure, laced with a passing spasm of sharp pain. Marisa cried out urgently.

"Harder, harder . . ."

She swung her head back and forth in the air again. Neil grabbed her long hair in one hand, carefully pulling it taut. She tilted her head back, and then he could see the wild smile, the roaring look on her face—her eyes open and fiery, urging him, challenging him.

"*Harder harder . . . make me feel you . . . more . . . MORE!*"

Her cries were so loud now. Sweat stung Neil's eyes as he slammed into her again and again, and Marisa went down, her face pressed against the towel, her arms splayed out, hands clutching the cotton, her eyes closed again now, and he forced her hips down to the ground too, his body pressed on hers as he came, his face buried in her hair.

"My lover . . ."

"*My* lover," Neil said, stroking her face.

"Ah." Marisa put on an impish smile. "I think maybe you better not say anything more right now."

"Will you come to Rome? At least to visit?"

Her eyes widened in mock-suprise. "See what I mean?" She pressed her finger to his lips. "*Sssh*. Who knows?" She kissed him again.

It was the middle of the afternoon by the time Neil and Marisa arrived back at the house. They found two men pondering Neil's radiator, which was on a large sheet of plastic on the ground. They were daubing it with a tar-like substance. Much of the front end of the car had been dismantled, with loose parts scattered all around. One of the men launched into a long and detailed explanation— to Marisa—that involved hand-waving and pointing to various tricky places on the radiator. Neil didn't understand a word they spoke but it was quite obvious that he wasn't going anywhere that day. He didn't mind, in fact he felt a distinct sense of relief.

"It's difficult," Marisa explained. "There's so much corrosion, so many spots for them to patch up."

Neil nodded. "I can see how bad it is."

"Maybe by tomorrow?"

"Okay."

"Anyhow, if they can't get it working again, my brother will be home by the end of the week."

"Even better."

Marisa tried not to smile. "It's a good thing they don't speak English. You're very naughty!"

Neil smiled at her. "I'm trying."

THE LAST NIGHT

Neil was exhausted by the long walk and their intense lovemaking, so he was glad when Marisa suggested another late afternoon siesta. She led him back to his room, promising to return for him later. He was also grateful to hear that they were excused from dinner with the family that night. He had no desire to find out what might be on the menu this time. Though in all fairness to them, it was their house and he was the intruder, and Marisa's family probably felt just as uncomfortable as Neil had.

But what a bizarre, sad household it was. What would he make of all this without Marisa? As Neil stretched out on the bed and nestled his head in the soft pillow, he realized that since he had arrived there yesterday he'd had almost no time to think about anything. The one instance when he had a few moments alone, Neil had heard the unusual metal scraping sound and he had discovered that peculiar alcove, which may or may not have had the body of a young man in it. Otherwise, Marisa was with him, occupying his thoughts and attention, or else he was too tired and sleepy to think.

Marisa was wonderful. He loved the way she made him respond naturally, instinctively—without the need for thought or analysis. She had such a gift and an appetite for living, it seemed to him. It was a terrible thing that she was stuck here, so unfair and unnatural. Her own personal life was indefinitely on hold.

Neil had to find the right way to speak to Marisa about it, to make her see that she had to do something—for her own sake. She could at least try to get away for a few days every month, to Rome, anywhere. Just to be among other people, to stroll about a city, eat in a restaurant, see a movie . . .

He was about ten years older than Marisa was, but that didn't seem to matter to her and it certainly didn't to him. Maybe a real relationship would never work out, but Neil had a strong sense that he could not just drive away and let go without even trying.

He had to leave . . . but he had to see her again . . .

. . . wanted her . . .

His eyes closed.

"Do we have to wait for everybody to go to bed again tonight?" Neil asked, smiling at her.

"You're so naughty, I love it," Marisa said, laughing. "No, we don't. I have a special place I want to show you."

They were finishing a light meal in the billards room. Some vacuous Euro-techno music droned on the radio in the background. Marisa looked very pretty, very girlish in a dark blue-green plaid skirt that almost reached her knees and a white short-sleeved blouse that was somehow even sexier to Neil because it was buttoned all the way to the top. She wore several thin silver bracelets on her wrists. She had braided some of the hair on the sides of her head and tied it with beaded blue bands.

"I had to tidy it up while you were sleeping," Marisa continued. "I had not been down there for years."

"*Down* there?"

"Yes." She pointed to the floor. "There's a huge cellar beneath this house. It's full of things my family brought with them after the war and have never used since. I don't know what we'll do with it."

"But they were lucky they could take anything at all with them," Neil said. "By the end of the war tens, probably hundreds of thousands of people had nothing more than the clothes on their backs."

"Yes, I suppose. Anyhow, when we were children, Hugo and I had our own little clubhouse down there. It's buried in the middle of everything. It was a good place to hang out on rainy days. Later, I used to like to go there alone, to read or just to think. You know?"

"Sure." Neil nodded. "The childhood retreat, the adolescent haven. We all had private hideouts like that."

Marisa laughed. "Hideouts—yes, that's the word."

She took his hand. Neil thought that they were heading toward the front of the house, but as usual there were so many turns and passages that it was impossible for him to keep a sense of direction. They finally arrived at the door that led to the cellar. As soon as Marisa opened it, Neil heard the sound of an electric generator. She flicked a switch and some lights went on below. The narrow stone stairs descended along an interior wall that was made of rock and mortar, and were open on the other side.

"Watch your step," she warned him.

Neil nodded. The air was cool and damp, but he could tell from his first few breaths that it probably wouldn't bother him. The unbroken flight of stairs was steep and long—it was more like two normal floor levels down to the bottom, Neil estimated.

They had not quite gone halfway when Marisa stopped and turned to him. She pointed out across the expanse of the cellar now visible on the one side. Single lightbulbs dangled from cables here and there, providing some illumination, though much of the place was cast in shadows.

"Look at it," she said, sounding exasperated.

"I see what you mean."

The place was a vast warren of storage areas, shelves and platforms, all of them full of boxes, cartons and trunks. One area contained metal racks jammed with clothing on hangers—coats, dresses, suits, shirts. Another part was given over to larger items that were covered with tarp, unusual shapes, some kind of equipment or tools.

"This is only half of it," Marisa told him. "It's the same on the other side of this wall."

"Wow, it looks like they brought everything with them."

"Oh, no, not at all. You'll never guess."

"Guess what?"

"What my families did, before they came here. Both of the families, my mother's and my father's. They worked together."

"Weren't they farmers, like here?"

Marisa laughed. "No!"

"Then I have no idea."

"Don't worry, I'll show you."

At the bottom of the stairs she led him around the wall into the other half of the cellar. At first it looked like more of the same, a maze of aisles and clogged passages through a sea of accumulated possessions. It was hard to see much because the lightbulbs were widely scattered and dim, but Neil noticed a few unusual items—large rolls of canvas, for instance, a collection of grotesque puppets, some faded banners mounted on poles.

"Yes?" Marisa prompted.

"Still no idea," Neil said. "Unless they ran a circus."

"Ah, you're getting warm."

"Really?"

"Yes, they had a travelling show, not really a circus. In good weather they would go from town to town, the larger villages, throughout the entire region. They had a puppet show, they staged little plays, usually stories from the New Testament, things like that."

"Are you part gypsy?" Neil asked jokingly.

"No way," Marisa exclaimed. Neil found her sudden use of such an American expression endearing. "Those people, they call themselves Roma now, but they were trouble wherever they went. They made it very hard for families like mine. Nobody liked or trusted them. Gypsies, I mean."

"Nobody likes the gypsies," Neil echoed, trying to keep the sarcasm out of his voice. "Even today, even in America."

"Of course. But never mind them. I want to show you something that my great-grandfather did. I'm not sure if he started it. Probably not. But he was a master craftsman. Now forgotten, unknown."

The sadness in her voice struck Neil. They had come to a long table that was covered with wooden boxes, each one about the size of a medicine cabinet. Marisa went to one directly beneath a lightbulb and lifted the lid. Neil stood close beside her. She carefully peeled back a sheet of something that looked like parchment or vellum, revealing a mask of a human face. The detail was remarkable.

"It's wax," Marisa said. "Look how fine the work is."

She slipped her fingers under the mask and lifted it—and Neil could see that it was almost paper-thin and translucent.

"Go ahead, it's okay," she told him. "You can touch it."

Neil took one edge of the mask between his fingers, rolling them over the filmy wax. It felt strong enough not

320

to tear easily, but also very soft and supple. It had a slight oily slickness.

"What did they do with them?" he asked.

"They wore them in the plays they put on. And I think maybe they showed them, like an art exhibition—you know? One of the banners they used translates as 'The House of Masks.' You see, the trick is, he cast them from real people, and then he used the casts to make these masks. He had some formula he developed to make the wax like this."

"It's beautiful," Neil said. "But doesn't your grandfather know how it's done? You could do something with this, you know."

"Yes, he must know, but he won't say. He won't talk about it at all anymore." Marisa shook her head sadly. "I'm so afraid it will all be lost, because Hugo and I just don't know what to do about it."

"Your father?"

"Same thing. He probably knows, but if I try to bring up the subject, he switches off. Like *that*," she said snapping her fingers.

Neil looked down the length of the table—tables, as he realized there were three of them lined up end to end. "All of these boxes—"

"Yes, each one contains several masks."

"Do you take care of them?"

"Ah, good question, my lover." Marisa was still holding the mask in her hands. "Hugo and I are the only ones who have ever even looked at them in the last fifty years, yet this is how they are. The temperature and moisture in the air here must be just right. And wax is a remarkable substance in the right conditions. It doesn't change."

"Fifty years. God. It does feel a little oily."

"Yes," she agreed quickly. "I think they were conditioned or rubbed with some kind of plant oil to help preserve them this way."

Marisa laid the mask back in the wooden box and arranged the cover sheet over it. She closed the lid and fastened the hasp, and then looked up at Neil with a quizzical expression on her face.

"I was a history student at university," she said. "You write about history. But do you have any idea how much history is here, in this cellar? I mean real history? What they saw, what they lived through?"

"Look at them," Neil said, his voice suddenly loud. "Your parents and grandparents, all still alive. All that history. You should get them to tell you about it, everything they can remember. Write it down, or better yet, get it on tape. Marisa, you can still do this."

"Ah, they won't talk," she said with a shrug of resignation. Then she smiled again. "Come on, we're not there yet."

BETWEEN SLEEP AND DEATH

They only had to go a short distance farther. Neil noticed that they were nearing one of the outer walls of the cellar. The dark expanse of rock loomed above them, and it was laced with alkaline encrustations, which in certain places appeared to glow with a faint greenish phosphorescence. Neil could only wonder at the age of the house and the labor that must have been involved in the construction of the cellar walls alone.

They stepped out of the shadows and stood beneath a lightbulb in a small clear area in front of what looked exactly like a miniature house. There were two wooden steps up to the narrow door, on either side of which was a tiny square window. The house was only about eight feet wide and not quite twice that in length. The back end stood flush against the cellar wall.

"This was one of the wagons they used a hundred years ago," Marisa told him. "Probably long before that too. Who knows."

"A wagon?" Neil was surprised, but then he could see that it made perfect sense. He saw where the wheels had been, and that the front steps, as he first thought of them, were in fact where the driver would sit when they were travelling. The house was painted in blue and gold and the curved roof was red—at one time it must have been very bright and eye-catching, Neil thought. There *was* even a small but ornate overhang above the door. It was a relic of history, as Marisa had said. Neil could easily imagine a train of these wagons making their way over the unpaved roads of a Europe that had long since vanished.

Marisa seemed to sense what he was thinking, and said nothing for a moment. Neil was still taking in details, like the small wooden box fastened beneath each window, to hold a flower pot.

"It's astonishing how much they brought over," he remarked. "I don't know how they ever managed it."

"They were lucky to get out," Marisa replied. "They told me it was the end of the war, but I believe they must have started long before that. They probably began sending the wagons overland at least a year before. And how they managed it, that's simple. They bribed their way."

"Oh, of course."

"Gold, jewels."

"You must try to get them to tell you more," Neil said. "The details, what it was like every day and night for them. Real history is not just in the big events, but in what ordinary people lived through. You should do it, not necessarily because you want to do anything with it, like turn it into a book, but for yourself. For you to know."

"Yes, I should." Marisa turned to a small table nearby. She took a wooden match and lit a candle. No electricity inside.

Neil followed her up the two steps. She opened the door and went in. She put the candle on a shelf and then lit a couple of others that were already placed around the room. Neil had to duck his head to get inside. One of the candles must have been scented because he immediately noticed the fragrance of lavender in the air.

"Close the door," she said, smiling broadly. "Take your shoes and socks off, make yourself at home."

Neil slid the bolt in place—this door actually locked. Marisa pulled the tiny curtains across the windows.

The floor inside the wagon was covered with an old oriental carpet. There was almost no furniture, just a small low table surrounded by cushions and pillows— dozens of them, in various sizes and colors. On the table was a bottle of wine, already opened, with the cork sitting loosely in place, two glasses and a platter of antipasto covered with a glass lid. There was even a shallow bowl of water filled with floating purple flowers.

It all reminded Neil of the way that some guys he had known would prepare their apartment when they were having a girl in for the evening. But here—in this dismal pit of a cellar beneath an old house out in the middle of nowhere. His poor Marisa. It was touching, but ultimately so sad. And yet, Neil was happy to be there with her.

"It's great," he said. "You must have done a lot of work."

Marisa gestured as if she were wiping her brow, and then stifling a big yawn. "You had a nap today. I didn't!"

"Ah, baby. Let me pour you some wine."

"That sounds very good."

They stretched out together on the pillows, half-sitting, resting back, their bodies touching, Neil's arm around her shoulder. He unbuttoned her blouse enough so that he could slip his hand inside and hold her breast.

"Mmmm."

They relaxed like that in silence for a few moments. Neil was still thinking of how to phrase what he wanted to say to her when Marisa began to speak, her voice quiet, reflective.

"Do you believe in life after death?"

"What?"

"I mean, my family does. They're devout Catholics—more Catholic than the Pope, my uncle always says—and they believe in life eternal through Christ. I was just wondering, do you?"

"I was raised a Catholic too."

"And?"

Neil smiled, admiring the way she wouldn't let him dodge that one. "No, I stopped believing that a long time ago."

"Are you sure?"

"Well, yes. But you never really know. Until."

"Ah."

"Do you?"

"Do I what? Believe that?"

"Yes."

"Not the same way," Marisa said. "But I think maybe we do live on in another form. You know what I think it is like? Have you ever been just a little bit awake, but still almost totally asleep? You have an awareness, but you feel like you have no body. You feel like you're floating in a vast ocean, but it's not water, it's not air. There's no color, nothing to see. You are just *being* there, and *there* is nowhere. You're alone. All alone. You don't see anything, you can't smell or hear anything. Nothing touches you, because you have no body. There is nothing you need, nothing you want. You don't even have any thoughts. No memories to please or hurt you. And yet you do have some kind of awareness. I don't know what other word to use. Awareness. Like, you know you exist. And you understand. Yourself. Everything. Your awareness encompasses all your memories and experiences, and more, but it isn't limited just to them, it never calls them up as scenes or words. Do you know what I mean? Your awareness is complete. In this—nothing. And the amazing part of it is, all you have is this awareness, but you are *content*. You can be this way forever, regardless of whether you're lying in a grave or your ashes were scattered to the wind. You still *are*, and you're content."

"What would be the point?" Neil asked after a moment.

Marisa laughed, dispelling the solemn mood. "We used to talk like this at the university, late at night. Student talk."

"That's all right. But I have no answers."

"Of course, nobody does. I was just talking, imagining out loud," she said apologetically. "I've gone so long without anyone to talk to."

"You have to get away from here."

Marisa propped herself up on one elbow. "Impossible."

"No, it's very possible."

"Never mind that now. Let's be bad. Let's fuck."

Neil smiled. He started to pull her to him to kiss her, but she slipped out of his arms, giggling. She crawled across his body and reached behind a large pillow for something on the floor. Neil ran his hand up her leg, stroking her thigh, his fingers teasing. She murmured happily and wiggled her feet in the air, but rolled off his lap and sat up.

"Here."

She was holding a wooden box. It was just like the ones on the tables outside that contained the masks.

FIGURES IN WAX

"I want to try something with you," she said, her eyes shining with promise and anticipation. "If you don't like it, that's okay."

"What is it?"

"You'll see!"

Marisa put the box down on a pillow beside them. She pulled her skirt up and swung her body so that her legs straddled his and she was facing him, half-sitting on his lap. She loved this position and so did he. Neil put his hands on her bare thighs for a moment, and then finished unbuttoning her blouse while she did the same with his shirt. She was wearing a half-bra that unhooked in front. She looked wildly sexy with her clothes hanging open like that. She kissed him teasingly, her mouth wet, her tongue dancing and licking lightly, but she pulled back every few seconds. She had his slacks open now. Her touch was tantalizing—again and again Marisa's fingers brushed slowly along his cock, and then moved away. Neil cupped her breasts in his hands, bending forward to suck and tug her hard nipples between his lips, teasing them with his tongue. Although they were still only playing—their eyes were open, smiling, widening, urging each other on—he was already completely caught up again in the long beautiful whirl of desire and arousal. But then she put her hands on his face, holding him for a moment.

"These are the most remarkable masks my great-grandfather ever made," Marisa said as she reached to open the box—Neil had almost forgotten about that box. "I put one of them on once. It was incredible. Now I want to do it again, with you. I want you to see what it's like."

It sounded kind of silly, but Neil shrugged. "Okay."

"Ah, my lover, I love your romantic soul."

"And I love yours."

Marisa carefully lifted a mask from the box. It was clearly unlike the one Neil had seen before, on the table outside the wagon. This mask hung in the air almost like some clingy, nearly transparent fabric. Marisa spread her fingers and the facial features in the mask became apparent. The eyes, nose and mouth were open, though little more than slits.

"Me first," she said.

Neil gave a short laugh. "Fine."

She tilted her head back slightly, closed her eyes and shook her hair away from her face. Then she raised the mask and let it fall gently into place on her skin. She blinked her eyes a couple of times and moved her lips open and shut, twisting them once or twice. She smiled at him. She looked almost the same, but different in some subtle way Neil couldn't immediately define. Younger? Her strong features even stronger, more dramatic? They wore these masks in Bible stories, he reminded himself. Like masks or makeup for opera singers, they were probably intended to heighten and emphasize certain basic character features or flaws for the benefit of an audience. With Marisa, he thought, the mask made her look even younger than she was, like a fierce, precocious teenager. Her expression seemed to convey even more forcefully the great depths of her powerful sensual nature.

Neil touched her cheek, and was astonished. It still felt like her skin, warm, soft and silky smooth, and yet he thought he could also feel some added vibrancy, like a wild hidden current that suddenly finds its outlet. The mask fit the contours of her face amazingly well.

Marisa picked up another mask and held it open for him. But before Neil would put it on he had to test it and make sure that it wouldn't trigger an asthmatic reaction. He thought of wax as essentially odorless, but there was no way of knowing what chemicals might have been used in the preparation of the mask. He put his face close to it, and inhaled. Again, closer and more deeply the second time. Yes, there was something, but it was not the kind of chemicals Neil had feared. Mint? Anyhow, it was all right.

"It's hard to believe this is actually wax," he said. "It's so fine and supple. It's almost as thin as plastic wrap, but it has body."

"I know, but there are dozens of different kinds of wax in nature and they are very adaptable. Are you ready?"

"Sure."

Marisa helped him position the mask over his face. It seemed to float in the air for a second before settling down on his skin. Neil blinked his eyes a couple of times—he could feel the mask close around them, but there was no impairment or discomfort. He touched his eyebrows—he could feel the mask over them, yet at the same time Neil had the illusion of touching the hair itself. It was remarkable, just as Marisa had said.

Now he caught the essence of the mask in his nostrils and mouth. He thought he detected a sweetness, like honey. As in honey, bees and beeswax? That made sense.

Something else, stronger than any of the mints. It had to be wintergreen, Neil thought. He could almost feel it shooting light into dormant and dark corners of his brain, it was so invigorating and stimulating.

Marisa ran her fingertips over his face, smoothing down a few loose parts of the mask. Her touch was exquisite, setting off tiny flares of pleasure in his skin. She smiled when she saw him react.

"Are you all right?"

"Fine," he replied.

"Are you sure?"

"Oh yes," he said emphatically.

Her face was very close to his. She touched his lips, licking along them slowly—Neil trembled with sudden delight. Her breath seemed to enter his pores. It was soft and sweet, as delicious as the air on a beautiful summer night.

"You don't want to take it off?"

"No . . . not yet . . . and don't stop what you're doing . . ."

"I haven't even started." Marisa took his lower lip between her teeth and bit until it began to hurt him, and then she pressed it tenderly between her wet lips for just a moment before releasing him. Anticipation . . .

She kissed him hard and pushed him back on the pillows, her tongue thrusting into his mouth, and it felt like their faces were merging, possessed of each other in brilliant consuming flames of desire. Energy and hunger for her roared through him, every nerve in his body seemed to pulse and buzz anxiously. He rolled Marisa over onto her back and then broke their kiss as he pulled her blouse wide open to get at her breasts, rubbing them with his face—it felt like a wonderful shower of sensation in their skin, a cascading rain of pleasure. She wrapped her legs around him and dug her heels into his backside, pulling him into her as she cried out, urging him on, her voice loud, becoming a long staccato shriek that filled the little room.

Their bodies glowed like hot coals. Everything seemed so vivid to Neil, the infinite beauty of the way their bodies fit together and how they felt in the perfect peace and silence afterward. But Marisa could not wait more than a couple of minutes. He was still in her, his face on her shoulder. She gently turned his head a little so that he could see her eyes.

"My lover."

"Mmm . . ."

"Now, tell me."

"Tell you what?"

"Wasn't that the best fuck you ever had?"

She put her hand over her mouth, as if she'd said something naughty, but it didn't hide her impish smile.

Neil laughed. "By far," he answered truthfully.

"But, no." Marisa shook her head contrarily. "I don't think so. The *next* one is."

She slid out from under him and sat up. He saw her hand reach back to the wooden box. Too soon, he was thinking in a haze. I'm thirty-five, not nineteen. She had another mask in her hand. She reached between his legs and began to stroke him with it.

She was right.

Neil had no idea what time it was when he awoke, but it was so quiet that he could hear one of the candles guttering. He felt cold. Then he looked around and discovered that he was alone in the wagon. His face felt tight and somehow unnatural—the mask, he remembered. He pulled at it and he could feel it with his fingertips, but he couldn't get ahold of it.

"Marisa?"

Perhaps there was a back room—but no, as soon as he

looked he saw that there was a rear door, but no other compartment in the wagon. He was alone. Neil stood up, still plucking at the mask. He thought he could feel the edge of it, but his attempts to push or roll it back failed.

"Marisa!"

It was a trick, just the kind of thing she would do. To tease him. He could imagine her laughing, then acting sheepish, the naughty girl. He would undoubtedly forgive her, but right now he felt angry. It seemed impossible to get the mask off his face. She would know how to do it, some simple method, or perhaps you had to use a liquid solution of some sort.

He tried the door, but the bolt wouldn't move—it was rusted in place and didn't budge. Neil kicked at it repeatedly, until he was out of breath. He stood in the little room, gasping, trying to think.

The mask felt hot and very tight on his face—it seemed almost to be alive in itself. On him. He tore at it in a rage, trying to dig his nails into it and rip it away. Neil felt the sudden raking pain in his cheek. It was as if he were scratching deeply into his own skin, but his fingers slid uselessly along the smooth, unyielding surface of the mask.

By the River Sava

The wagon rocked. The rear door splintered, tore loose and crashed to the floor. Neil was stunned. He had no idea at all what was happening. He could only stand there and gape at the sudden terrifying eruption of noise and violence. Three men in dark uniforms rushed through the open doorway. Two of them carried pistols, while the third had a short, wide-blade sword. Their boots thudded heavily. The men shouted angrily at him in a language he didn't understand, though it did sound familiar to him, probably the language of Marisa's parents.

Neil had no doubt that they meant to kill him. Fear paralyzed him, but he opened his mouth to protest. The first man hit him hard across the side of the head with the butt of his gun. Neil was dazed and fell against one of the side walls. Before he could recover his balance, two of the men set on him. They pummeled him about the head and face with their weapons. Neil held his arms up in an attempt to ward off the flurry of blows. The men kicked at him, yanked him across the room, and flung him out the door.

Neil flew through the air and landed painfully on hard rough ground. He was outdoors. He moaned and couldn't move for a minute. His head was pounding and he could taste his own blood in his mouth, but—absurdly—his mind still tried to calculate: the rear of the wagon had been backed up against the cellar wall, so there had to be an entrance to the outside there that he had not been able to see, one large enough to admit wagons, and—

But the immediate reality overwhelmed attempts at thought. Someone kicked him again. Neil jumped to his feet. The night air was full of shouting voices, loud cries and sporadic gunfire. He saw that he was in a group of a dozen or so men. They were in an open area, a kind of courtyard bordered by wooden barn-like buildings—none of which resembled Marisa's house. The area was illuminated by a few street lamps mounted on wooden poles and by some rooftop spotlights that slowly swept through the darkness. The armed men in uniform—were they the police, or soldiers?—quickly herded Neil's group across the square. He saw a similar group of men ahead of them—but then it vanished into an alley between two buildings.

One of the men near Neil suddenly stumbled and lunged a couple of paces out of the group, trying to regain his balance. A guard stepped toward him and almost casually stuck his knife out, into the man's throat. The man fell, gagging, spurting blood and clutching uselessly at his throat. The guard stood over him and shot him once in the back of the neck. The man's thick hair fanned like wheat in a sudden gust of wind. He fell flat on his face and didn't move again.

Neil's eyes frantically scanned the area as he ran with the others. He saw numerous bodies on the ground. Off to one side a man struggled with a guard, but two other guards hastened to converge on him, and he fell beneath a torrent of knife thrusts. Then the first guard stomped on the man's throat several times with his boot.

The narrow alley was directly in front of them. The guards smoothly funneled Neil's group into the dark passage with more angry shouts and kicks, and by jabbing at them with their knives. At the other end, twenty or thirty yards ahead, another cluster of guards took control of the group and marched them across a much larger piece of open ground—though it was not actually open, Neil realized, when he saw the barbed wire fencing. The area was lit by more spotlights and several scattered bonfires. A three-quarters moon emerged from behind some clouds and added to the garish lighting. He saw a wide ribbon of water in the distance. For an instant he could even see that it was moving—a river.

But nearer, all around, were the bodies of dead men.

Neil and the others were made to lie face down on the ground. Here every guard—and there were many more of them—carried both a pistol and either a sword or a club. One man raised his head to look around and a guard swiftly stepped in and kicked the man in the face. Neil was careful, moving his head only fractions of an inch at a time to see as much as he could of what was happening. A kind of low-level pandemonium reigned. No one seemed to be in charge, but it was obviously a killing ground.

Suddenly Neil had to restrain himself to keep from shouting because he recognized someone. He had a clear view as two guards were leading a man past Neil's group—it was the same man who had brought the water for the radiator of Neil's car the other day. Perhaps he ought to shout to the man, even if it brought some punishment. The man would recognize him, perhaps he would say something, tell someone—but then the man and the two guards disappeared from sight.

Now someone from Neil's group was hauled to his feet

and brought a few yards ahead, where he was engaged in an apparently heated conversation with three of the guards. He was a young man, in his twenties. He repeatedly shook his head at whatever the guards were saying. Then a priest arrived on the scene. Neil again wanted to shout—an instinct learned in childhood, that you can always turn to a priest for help. But it was so startling to see one in all of this madness—what was he doing there? The priest spoke briefly with him, and then walked briskly away.

The guards immediately began to stab and hack at the young man with their swords, slicing off pieces of his shirt and chunks of flesh from his back and arms. One of them pushed a knife into the man's midsection and slashed downward, spilling organs in a huge gush of blood. His scream was cut off when another guard swung a club and smashed it into his mouth, sending teeth and more blood through the air. The helpless man was still twitching wildly and gasping raggedly as they dragged him out of sight. Neil turned his face downward and away.

What lunacy was this? He knew from the sharp grit pressing against his face on the ground that it was no dream, no hallucination, and yet his mind did not seem to be functioning clearly. He'd been in the wagon with Marisa, they had put on the masks and made love—twice, three times? But then Neil realized he still had the mask on his face, he could feel it there again, tight on his skin, the taste of honey and wintergreen. He reached to touch it, to pull at it—a club blow on the side of the head rocked him.

A few moments later, when he opened his eyes, he saw a priest again, but a different kind of priest. Eastern or Greek Orthodox, perhaps. He was fifty or sixty feet away, he had an unusual hat or vestment on his head, and his beard was full and squarish. The guards were talking to him in an animated fashion but the priest simply ignored them. He looked about forty years old. He didn't move or acknowledge the guards in any way. His eyes remained locked onto an invisible point no one else could see—the priest appeared to be focused entirely on his own thoughts.

One of the guards suddenly grabbed the priest's beard and hacked at it with a knife. Patches of wet redness opened on his face, but he sat still and had the same distant, stoic look in his eyes. The others were laughing along with this or else silently watching with smirks of mild amusement. After the guard had slashed off several chunks of hair and skin, he stepped behind the priest, knocked the headpiece off, pulled the man's head back by the hair and slowly dug a knife through his throat. The priest's eyelids fluttered open and closed a few times, then remained half open. After a few moments, when the eruption of blood slowed, the guard dug in harder with the knife. He couldn't manage it and became increasingly angry. Then one of the other guards came up with a hatchet and attacked the back of the neck, where the spinal cord and the brain meet, and after a few swings—flesh in the air like chips of wood—the priest's head was finally cut loose. The guard shouted happily and held it in the air, while the body sagged and toppled to the ground.

Think. Try to think. If I could only think—

He was aware of others in the group being moved, lifted up and taken somewhere beyond his line of vision, one at a time. Neil thought again of the man who was supposed to fix his car. Was he a prisoner too, like the rest of them? Or was he with—

A shout and a painful kick in the ribs told Neil it was his turn. He got up, feeling certain that he was about to experience his own death. He had no idea why, and there was apparently nothing he could do about it but go along with it. As two guards pushed and steered him roughly, Neil wondered if he could somehow break free, run and dodge their bullets. Run toward the river and escape? But he had already seen others try that and he knew that it would be a pointless gesture.

They passed a small group of guards tormenting a man who staggered blindly in circles. His hands were tied behind his back. The guards had put a strange wooden box with bolts and leather straps over the man's head. It seemed to fit tightly and was probably smothering him. They cut his belt and tugged his pants down, and then jabbed their knives at his genitals. The man jumped and twisted, trying vainly to avoid each cutting thrust, but he couldn't see anything. His cries were muffled by the wooden box. The last glimpse Neil had—one guard was furiously slashing off a thick strip of flesh from the doomed man's pale buttocks.

A short distance farther, they came to a large cluster of guards. The circle parted to admit them and Neil was held tightly by two guards. He was allowed to watch a teenage boy, who seemed to be begging for his life. Neil couldn't see the people the youth was addressing, but he saw the desperation in his face. The boy made the sign of the cross, bowed his head, looked up hopefully and invoked the name of Jesus Christ, and then repeated the same sequence of gestures and words. One of the guards nudged Neil and nodded, as if to say that this was what he would be expected to do. Neil assumed that it meant he was to make his peace with God before he died.

The crowd tightened and necks craned, and Neil couldn't see what was happening. Everyone was quiet, but one voiced intoned softly. Then the guards began to laugh and clap, and suddenly Neil saw the boy's face again. He stood up, smiling cautiously. For just a moment, an air of bizarre gaiety seemed to prevail. But then two guards seized the boy. A third one held him tightly by the hair, pulling his head back. A fourth stepped forward to hit the boy's face with a metal tool—pliers. As soon as the boy's mouth opened, the guard clamped the pliers on his tongue. The boy struggled and tried to close his mouth, but couldn't do anything. With his other hand, the guard carefully slipped the blade of a knife between the boy's teeth. One of the other guards kicked the boy in the groin to make things easier. The boy's mouth opened wider involuntarily and he gave a strangled cry. The guard quickly flicked his wrist and came away with the boy's tongue in the pliers. This brought an enthusiastic burst of applause and more cheers. The boy was dragged off, his mouth foaming red, and a few seconds later Neil heard a gunshot.

Then he was hauled around to the center of the circle and flung to the ground. In front of him, torn and muddied, covered with gobs of spit, was a book in some unrecognizable language. Neil tried to think. The script was Cyrillic, he knew that much. When he looked up, Neil saw Marisa's uncle, Father Anton, smiling down at him.

The priest showed no sign of recognition. He was speaking softly and calmly, his hands making small gestures in the air, as if explaining things. When he finished, he pointed down to the book on the ground. Father Anton gazed at him with implacable indifference. Neil sensed that he had just a few seconds to reach some decision, and he understood. Marisa told him that her uncle was doing a study on conversions. That's what this was, a conversion. He was expected to renounce the book on the ground, whatever it was, and to proclaim his faith and allegiance to the one true Church.

The teenage boy—so that was what he had done. He had given in, he had renounced his faith, spit on the book and sworn himself to Christ. That's why they had cheered. But then they had cut out his tongue. Why? Probably so that he would not be able to recant—in the brief moment when he saw the pistol being aimed at him.

"*Padre Anton,*" Neil said anxiously. "*Padre Panic. Sono gia un cattolico.*"

The priest registered mild surprise, perhaps at both the words and the use of the Italian language. Neil could sense a flutter of curiosity among the guards around him, who fell silent and edged closer.

"*Sono gia un cattolico,*" he repeated firmly. "*Dove e Marisa?* She will tell you. I'm a friend of hers." That involuntary lapse into English only seemed to confuse the priest. "*Devo vedere Marisa! Dove e Marisa, il mio amico, il mio caro?*"

Father Anton laughed as if he had just heard something ridiculous. A young man elbowed his way through the circle of guards and stood over Neil, who recognized him immediately—here was the person he had seen lying in the alcove bunk, in the house. Now this handsome young man glared at Neil. He wore a black leather coat over a grey suit. He swung his arm back. Neil saw the blackjack coming all the way.

Wow, a genuine leather blackjack—he thought, before it hit his head and sent his brain reeling into darkness— imagine that.

STARA GRADISKA

The moon danced wildly in the sky above him. He was still there. He could hear the shouts, the screams, the random gunshots. His head rolled painfully on bare boards. A dark building floated by, then a tower. He was moving—he was being taken somewhere. When Neil finally got his eyes to focus he saw that he was lying in the back of a small open truck. It was kind of like an old army jeep. The driver and an armed guard sat a couple of feet away, in front of him. They passed a bottle back and forth between them and were talking loudly. Neil closed his eyes when he saw the guard start to turn his head to look back and check on him.

His head throbbed and his body ached, and every bounce on the dirt road only added to his pains. But they were nothing compared to what he had already seen there. He felt charged with fear and impatience—his body was shrieking at him. He had to act fast and somehow get away.

The vehicle slowed and turned a corner. The buildings on either side were dark or dimly lit. They seemed to be in a part of the place where there were few people about at present. As the jeep gathered speed again, Neil pushed himself up with his feet and slipped over the side. He rolled on the ground, got some balance and rushed toward the shadows. A few seconds later he heard the squeal of brakes and a shout, just as he ducked around the corner. The unhappy sound of reverse gear.

Neil looked around. He was in another patch of open ground that was surrounded by ramshackle two-story wooden buildings. Spotlights swept the area methodically. He could see more guards stationed or walking patrol, no matter which direction he turned. There was nowhere to go, they would grab him in a minute if he tried to flee.

The building beside him was dark—and the door opened when Neil tried it. He slipped inside. There was no lock, but he was out of sight for the moment. He knew it was only a temporary refuge. Sooner or later he would be found if he stayed there. Then he heard a loud noise and felt the building shake briefly. The driver and guard were cursing unintelligibly, and then they began to laugh. In trying to take the corner they had backed into the building itself. From the window, he saw them glancing around. Then they drove off, apparently deciding that someone else would catch Neil.

He was safe, for now. He sank to the floor and sat in the darkness. It felt good to rest his back against the wall, to be alone. But his mind was still swarming with unbearable images and raging confusion.

And then he became aware of the mask again. It was still on his face. As soon as he thought about it, he could feel it seem to tighten, choking his pores as if it were trying to enter his body through his skin. Suppressing panic for a moment, Neil tried again to remove it. Be calm, he told himself, find an edge and work it back. But he got nowhere with it. He could feel his fingertips on it, he could even make a small portion of it move slightly—but then it always slipped away from his hand and back in place. It was impossibly filmy to his touch, but on his face it felt heavy and oppressive.

He finally gave up, sobbing once out loud and banging his head back against the wall in frustration.

Someone laughed.

Neil froze. The shocking human sound had come from only a few feet away. He could hardly think at all now, let alone know what to do. He heard the soft pat of childlike footsteps on the floor, followed by a very loud click, and then an overhead light went on. There were piles of clothes everywhere, the floor dotted with random heaps of them. Nothing but clothes. The woman grinning hideously at Neil was the same dwarf he had seen on the balustrade when he arrived at Marisa's house.

She was one of them, she would alert the guards—

The woman read his panic and immediately made calming gestures to stop him from doing anything foolish. Neil was thinking that he ought to kill her and turn the light off. Her voice sounded like that of a toy doll, but there was something soothing in her tone. She held her finger to her lips. Neil sat where he was. It occurred to him that he was dead anyway, so what was the point of resisting, much less killing someone else? He felt tired. All of the energy he had somehow summoned up in escaping from the guards and then hiding in this barnlike building was now gone. His head ached and the mask felt like a huge clamp on his face. Let it be. Roll into it.

Noise, the sound of activity outside. The woman went to the window to take a look, then quickly turned away. She gestured with her hand for Neil to follow her. They went up a large, open flight of stairs to the second floor, which was covered with more mounds of clothing. There was no sorting, no order, just random tilting piles of ordinary clothes, as if they had simply been thrown down where they were.

The woman kept gesturing and Neil followed her to the front side of the building. There were two windows overlooking the open ground outside. She went to one and pointed Neil to the other. He no longer thought of her as a threat to him, and yet he didn't feel that she was a friend or ally. This place was like a concentration camp, but without the Nazis. The dwarf woman was perhaps a prisoner, but one allowed to live because of the work she did with these clothes, or because someone liked her—some insane reason. He didn't know, he had no idea, just fleeting guesses.

Why was he there?

Dozens of guards had assembled in the yard outside. The spotlights were fixed, illuminating the whole area in a harsh light. Everyone seemed to be standing around expectantly. Neil could feel the sense of something about to happen, and yet it was such an utterly barren scene—his novelist's instinct found it completely unworthy. Of anything.

A moment later, three large trucks arrived, each one full of women. They ranged from teenagers to the elderly. The guards immediately swung into action, pulling or flinging the women off the trucks. The older women were dealt with summarily, either shot in the head, stabbed or clubbed to the ground. Within moments, there were bodies everywhere and the spurious air of order had given way to chaos and mayhem.

It was worse for middle-aged women. Guards hacked at their skulls with axes, chopping off clumps of hair and flesh. They were pulled out of their clothes, beaten, slashed and kicked. Long knives or wide swords were inserted into them, then twisted, and yanked. Pistols were roughly forced into their mouths, vaginas or

345

anuses, and then fired. Ears and noses were slashed off before their deliverance.

Neil sagged against the window frame. He gazed at the guards who were doing all of this. They didn't look angry, so much as determined. Like homeowners who had a job to do, because they could not bear to live with a certain pest. Whether you sprayed them in groups or crushed them beneath your heel one at a time, they had to go.

Two guards held a woman face down on the ground. Another guard pulled her hair so that her head was raised up a few inches. A fourth guard came and stood over her. He had some tool in his hand. A saw. He began to saw the back of her neck, like a log. The woman's body quivered like wire strung too tight, electric, and then collapsed. The guard swung her loose head and rolled it away like a bowling ball.

The youngest fared worst of all, their breasts hacked off, knives thrust into them, their loins doused with gasoline and set afire. Or they were fucked first, repeatedly, until someone decided they were no longer worthy. He saw one girl held bent over at the waist and entered from behind. When the guard in her was about to climax, he waved his fingers excitedly in the air. Another guard stepped up, swung a hatchet and decapitated the girl. It wasn't clean, it took three blows, but that only seemed to enhance the pleasure of the one who was coming in her. Then the guard with the bloody hatchet held up the girl's head and pushed her lips back to expose her teeth—evoking loud cheers and laughter. She had long straight hair, parted in the middle. A style that would fit in easily in Rome, Paris, London, New York or San Francisco.

Neil turned to the dwarf woman perched on a pile of clothes at the other window. It was as if he wasn't there. Her expression was blank, but she was totally caught up in what she was seeing. She gazed outward, like some-one watching the crucial scene in a gripping movie. Un-derstandable, and yet—how could *anyone* watch *that?*

Neil had felt such fear, but now he saw fear as some-thing shallow, a surface ripple. In his blood and in his bones, in his whole body, he felt his own death now, and he knew it didn't matter. Not even to him.

He looked outside once more. It was like a Bosch painting, except that Bosch lacked the imagination or nerve for this horror. In some forlorn part of his brain Neil heard Abba singing "Fernando" in a tinny voice. And there, almost directly below him—he saw Marisa. She was watching the scene, close up. She was in a group of six or eight people, all of whom wore civilian garb. She had on a long black dress and leather coat. Her hair was done up in braids that were coiled tightly to her head.

Marisa . . .

The dwarf woman gagged and giggled.

Marisa turned and rested her head on the shoulder of the young man standing beside her. His arm went around her, then rubbed her shoulders and back com-fortingly. She looked up and he kissed her. No doubt about it, Neil was certain that it was the young man he had seen in the alcove, the same one who had knocked him out with a blackjack.

A little implosion, that's all.

Opera.

Neil turned and ran.

MISERERE

As if he should be surprised! Neil felt angry at himself. He had seen Father Anton at work. If her uncle, a priest, could be implicated in this, how could Marisa not be? Still, it was crushing to see her out there, calmly taking everything in. Kissing her lover. Was that Hugo?

The dwarf woman called out to him. Neil's foot snagged and he fell onto a large pile of clothing. He rolled over and came to rest, lying on his back. For a moment he thought he might never move again. He wanted only to remain there, burrowing in, hiding in the drifts of old clothes. He inhaled deeply. He could detect the whole range of human smells that lingered in the dresses, skirts and blouses, even terror and death.

He closed his eyes, allowing himself to imagine for just a second that when he opened them again he would be somewhere else. In the Italy that he knew. In his car, which worked. On a road, to somewhere.

But where was the house, where was his car?

What had happened to him?

He opened his eyes and saw the dwarf woman smiling

down at him. But she wagged her finger and shook her head. Neil understood. She was right. If he just ran impulsively like that, he would inevitably give himself away and soon be captured. That wasn't the way to do it. Neil nodded in agreement and almost managed a faint smile.

She had seemed positively deranged the first time he had encountered her, but now he understood the mad, antic gleam in her eyes, the grinning and harsh laughter. He was where she lived.

The woman took his thumb in her pudgy little hand and tugged. Neil pushed himself to his feet. Outside, the screams and gunshots continued. He followed the woman through the mounds of clothing, toward the back of the upper room. It was much darker there, no windows, no electric light. They came to a door in the side wall. She opened it. Neil saw stairs disappearing down into complete darkness. No, he didn't like that.

The woman made a series of gestures, and Neil realized that she was trying to give him directions, to tell him which way to go. To escape? What else could it be? She would have called the guards and turned him in by now if that was her intention. She pointed to the front of the room and held her hand to her ear—Neil noticed that the sounds of the bloody rampage outside were slowly diminishing. The woman was telling him to hurry now, while so many of the guards were still preoccupied. This was his best opportunity. Okay, he understood. The directions were simple, which probably meant that his chances were almost nil. But he would try.

He stepped through the doorway and turned to nod appreciatively to the woman. Her head bobbed, she waved, urging him to go, and she closed the door. Neil put his hand on the wall and made his way slowly down the stairs in complete darkness. He had no trouble and he found the door at the bottom. He listened carefully for a few seconds, and heard nothing but the muffled sounds from outside.

The door opened directly into the adjacent building. The room was dark, but enough light penetrated from the front windows. Neil saw that this building was almost identical to the one he had just left. A large room and piles of clothing—though they were smaller and fewer in number. He moved quickly to the far side of the room, at the back. He found the next door that he was looking for, but it wasn't where it was supposed to be. He expected to find a door that would let him out at the rear of the building, but this door was in the side wall again and it clearly led into the next building. Neil wondered if he had misunderstood the woman. He must have. Well, he had no choice but to go on.

The ground floor room in the next building contained dozens of bunks, cots and bed mats on the floor. They looked too mean and wretched to be for the guards. But there were no inmates, the beds were all empty. The room was bathed in the same eerie grey-white light from outside. Neil hurried to the other rear corner. He groaned aloud when he discovered that once again the door was in the side wall. Then he noticed the quiet—there was no more gunfire. He had to keep going, and hurry.

He opened the door a crack and saw that there were lights on in the next room. His view was blocked by a wood partition. He opened the door a little more and eased himself quietly inside. There was a strong smell of alcohol in the air. Then he heard the sound of someone moving about. Neil had never fought with anybody in his life, not even in grammar school in Southie—a remarkable but, he sometimes felt, dubious achievement. One person he could deal with—*maybe*. Two or more? Ha ha.

Then he saw it, on the other side of the room—the door in the back wall, the door he needed, to get outside. It was about thirty feet away. Neil stared at it. The floor was bare, aside from a few small wood crates and boxes lying about. There was nothing at all between him and the door that he could crawl behind or use to hide himself if he had to.

Neil moved carefully and slowly, testing each step, edging along the partition. The sounds he heard were slight, impossible to figure. He inched his face along the wood. Then a sigh, and a woman's voice, just a few words that were answered briefly by another woman. Neil was puzzled by this, but also vaguely encouraged. If these women were prisoners too, like the dwarf, they might be willing to help him.

Neil crouched and slowly expanded his angle of vision into the room. He saw some worktables that were cluttered with jars, boxes, hand tools and clumps of packing straw. Then the back of a woman's head came into view, grey hair tied up in a bun. She was seated on the other side of the tables, her back to Neil.

He leaned a little farther beyond the partition and saw the other woman, also grey-haired. She was bent over, apparently engaged in some chore. She was about ten feet away from the woman seated by the tables. Two older women. It occurred to Neil that they could be sorting out and packing up any valuables taken from the victims, like coins and rings. If that was the case, there might well be a guard in the room, watching them, still out of Neil's sight.

But then the woman straightened up and he recognized her as one of Marisa's relatives, her mother or one of her grandmothers. So the other one, with her back to Neil, was probably also a relative. Of course, they were all in on this madness. That seemed to make it a little less likely that there was a guard with them.

Neil took a deep breath and stepped around the partition—it was the back wall of some wooden shelves. He scanned the room quickly, saw that there was no guard, just the two women. He moved around the worktables. There were no front windows—an unexpected help. The women looked at him, then at each other, and they began to laugh. Neil stopped as if he had run into a brick wall. The open floor of the large room was strewn with the dead bodies of small children. There were dozens of them, boys and girls, infants and toddlers, some dressed, some naked, their skin color ranging from bone white to a pale grey-blue.

The old woman who was seated on a long bench was the grandmother who had been sharpening fruit spoons. In fact, she had one of those spoons in her hand now. On the bench beside her was the body of a small girl, her head resting on the woman's lap. They were laughing louder now. The woman pushed the girl's eyelid back and deftly used the spoon to scoop out the eye, which she then held out for Neil to see. He couldn't move. Then she reached toward the table, turned the spoon and dropped the eye into a large glass jar of clear liquid—the alcohol. There were already dozens of eyes in the jar, like shiny blue and brown pearls. Neil saw two other jars on the table, full and capped. He looked at the bodies on the floor and saw those that had been done—their empty eye sockets dark, thin strands of fleshy membrane trailing across their faces. And the rest, all around him, waiting.

He felt like a piece of ice, or stone, but he walked carefully toward the woman on the bench. She was still laughing, but her eyes were watchful. As he drew closer, she stood up and quickly scooted a few yards away. The child's head thumped on the bench, and then the body slid off. Neil went to the worktable. And there was grandma's favorite set of spoons, a dozen or fifteen of them, in different sizes. He took one in his hand and ran his finger along the edge. Sharp enough for the grisly work at hand, but was it sharp enough for him?

Neil put the spoon in his pocket and, without even glancing at the two women, went quickly to the back of the room. He opened the door, slipped outside and looked around. Arcs of light, moving zones of exposed ground. But there were also wide, shifting pockets of darkness, and Neil ran into the darkness. He expected to feel a bullet in his back at any moment. He kept running, veering off, swerving back, always hugging the darkness.

No alarms went off, no shots were fired, but Neil had a sense that he wasn't going to make it. His breath was ragged now, his chest and legs were tightening in pain, and a cramp was stitching through his abdomen. He kept on, gasping loudly but driving himself forward. Don't stop.

Then he hit the fence. Barbed wire raked across his scalp and dug into his throat, belly and thighs. He bounced back, hit the ground, and now he couldn't move. He couldn't even breathe. Flat on his back—there was the moon again. It wasn't his asthma, he realized. He'd had the wind knocked out of him, but that was all. Slowly his chest began to move again—oh, the sweet, sweet taste of air.

But he knew that the light would find him soon, he had to move. Neil dragged himself under the fence. Another twenty tortuous yards of dangerous open ground, and then he was in the woods, safe for the moment. He tried to follow the general direction the dwarf woman had indicated. Before long, however, he could sense the river nearby, and that was all he needed. For a few minutes he stumbled around, struggling in the darkness with thick brush, saplings and swampy ground underfoot. Finally, Neil found a clear patch of solid land at the water's edge. He sat down to let his body rest.

The idea was to swim to the other side and thereby escape. But what was on the other side? *Where* was the other side? The river looked so wide that he doubted he could make it across. What if he gave up and surrendered? If he begged to see Marisa, would she come?

Would she recognize him, and save his life? But Neil immediately felt a sense of shame and anger. How could he even consider that possibility? He had seen her world, and the only alternatives were to flee or to die.

He took the spoon out of his pocket and began to scrape his face with the edge of it. He dug in hard, not caring when he felt pain and his own fresh blood. Then the pain blossomed across his face and into his head, and he had a sense that he was breaking the mask in places. Hope electrified him and he gouged at his cheeks and chin and forehead even more energetically. It was like fire breaking out in his skin and then penetrating his brain. He bent over in agony. The spoon fell from his hand.

He saw the water in front of him and it looked so sweet and soothing. That was where he was supposed to go. The other side. He waded in and began to swim. Cold, too cold. But he didn't care. Neil swept his arms and kicked feebly. Then the body of a dead man bumped into him. He pushed it away, but another one bobbed against him, and another, and suddenly he saw that he was surrounded by countless bodies floating in the river. They moved slowly, drifting along at the edge of the current.

Go with them.

No . . .

You're one of them.

No . . .

You are. This is where pain ends.

No. Let someone else kill me. I want to see it happen. Neil turned and splashed his way back to land. He dragged himself under a clump of thick bushes and nestled close to the ground, curled up protectively. His face felt as if it had long jagged strips of raw exposed flesh. Had Neil broken the mask, ripped parts of it away? He couldn't tell. His brain wouldn't focus on anything, and that didn't even bother him. He didn't care anymore. He was so cold and wet, and he had nothing left.

REVIVAL

Neil shivered so violently it seemed as if his whole body was trying to shake itself to pieces. His clothes were wet, clinging to him. He felt the dank cold deep in his bones. His limbs were stiff and had no strength. He was on the ground, lying in tall grass.

Daylight. So much easier for someone to see him. At first he thought it was morning, but when he cautiously raised his head and looked around, Neil saw the big house—Marisa's house—shimmering with golden light. It must be late afternoon. He felt a tremendous sense of relief, but it was soon followed by a wave of confusion. How had he come to be there, outside the front of the house, and at this hour of the day? What had happened to him last night? Why had Marisa left him? Where was she?

The mask—fear and panic boiled up in Neil again as he realized that the mask was still on his face. For a brief moment, he had begun to consider the possibility that everything he'd experienced there had been nothing more than a long bizarre hallucination, or dream. That he had arrived there, fallen into a mysterious trance or had a brain seizure that somehow unleashed him on a journey into deep corners of his own subconscious mind. That seemed unlikely, and the presence of the mask disproved it.

Unless the mask was merely another imaginary sign of his continuing mental breakdown. Is this dementia?

Neil stood up and looked back, away from the house. He saw his car, still where he had left it. The hood was raised and the front end was partly dismantled. He moved a few steps to get a better angle and then he could see the radiator lying on the ground. That appeared to clinch it. There was no way Neil would have tried to take the radiator out by himself. He wasn't mechanically adept, he had no tools with him, and there was no point to it, especially in this remote spot. Someone else had done it, Marisa's workman, just as Neil remembered.

But he also noticed that the cluster of shacks and huts visible on the nearest ridge were half-collapsed, with doors gone or hanging loose, roofs caved in, all of them utterly dilapidated. No one lived or worked in them. And the grounds immediately around the house looked even more overgrown with weeds and brush than he seemed to remember—thick coils of brambles and briars sprawled about, slowly spreading, creating impenetrable thickets around the building.

The windows were gone—another small shock. The sun still caught the tiles and lit them brilliantly, but all of the windows were vacant, dark and empty rectangles in the face of the house. In some of the frames he could see jagged shards of glass that hadn't yet fallen away, but most of the glass was gone. So was the front door—not just open, but gone. The house stood open to the elements, and to anyone who happened to come there.

Like him. Neil walked along the crumbling balustrade, gazing at the old house and its surroundings. There was no sign of human life anywhere, nor any indication that there had been for many years. Again he wondered if he had somehow imagined everything—Marisa, her family, the workmen, the passion and fantastic sex, the billiards room, the cellar, the wagon, the horror and savagery he had seen. If only he had imagined all that. It was just a big crazy dream. Ha ha.

But how could he have conjured up all those peculiar details, like the bird skulls in the stew? And the sensory memories that were still so vivid to him—how it felt to be inside Marisa, the touch of her wet mouth on his skin? No, it wasn't possible. Besides, his car and the awful weight on his face told him it was something else, something unfinished.

Neil hesitated. He glanced back toward his car again. He could just walk away. Follow the gravel road until it brought him to another road, take that one and keep going until he either flagged down a passing car or reached the next town.

Then find a doctor—please take this thing off my face.

No. Not yet. He walked into the house. It was gloomy, but enough sunlight reached the interior for Neil to find his way around. Instead of going upstairs and trying to get to the bedroom where his things were, he began to check the ground floor rooms. The house was silent, except for the rush and swirl of the mountain wind as it blew through the corridors and passageways, which only added to the feeling of emptiness.

He went through several rooms that were almost bare, containing a few pieces of rotting furniture. The floors were littered with broken glass, grey grit, and mats of damp dust. Paper wasp nests clung to the upper walls, the empty ceiling fixtures and dangling sconces. Wide bands of wallpaper had peeled off and crumpled to the floors.

So far, everything he saw argued that the house had

been abandoned years before. But he couldn't be sure yet. These might be some of the rooms that had been left unused by the family, as Marisa had explained to Neil. He was beginning to think that he would find nobody, but he also believed that he would find *something*—something that made sense of all this to him.

Then Neil opened a door and recognized the dining room. The long table and the sideboards were gone, but some of the chairs remained, dusty and scattered, lying on their sides. The wall tapestries were shredded and black with mildew. It was impossible to imagine that anyone had eaten there in years.

Neil walked quickly to the far end of the room, opened the door and made his way along the short, unlit passage. The windows in the billiards room were shuttered on the inside, but thin lines of fading daylight allowed him to make out various objects in the prevailing gloom. The billiards table was still there, and apparently in good condition. It startled Neil to see the sofa where he and Marisa had spent time. And the little television, the radio. Even their wineglasses—he stood frozen, staring at them. Finally, he went closer and lifted one. A small pool of red wine swirled at the bottom. Neil immediately recognized the strong tannic bouquet.

It was no dream or hallucination—none of what he had seen—unless he was experiencing it all again. Or it had never ended. The mask was still on his face, after all. But the mask didn't explain anything. He'd encountered the dwarf woman, Marisa, the workers and servants, Marisa's family—all of that—well before they got to the masks. Neil felt like a dog chasing his own tail. It was a waste of time. It wasn't possible to make sense of experiences that seemed to arise from some lost pocket of reality, a place that had its own logic and reason—all of which escaped him. He had the irrational feeling of being caught in someone else's dream world. But that would mean he had no chance of escape, which he knew was absurd.

He turned the television on, but the screen stayed dark and there was no sound. The generator was off. He tried the radio, and the sexy, breathless voice of a woman singing in French squiggled out of nowhere. Neil laughed. There were batteries in the radio, and they still worked. He almost switched it off, but didn't. The radio station and the song reminded him that there was still an outside world. *His* world. He increased the volume, and it sounded good, it was like bright light and fresh air.

Neil picked up the box of matches Marisa had used and lit a candle. He carried it with him as he crossed the room and ascended the circular iron staircase to the second floor. In the corridor, he turned and made his way to the bedroom he had used. The door was closed. Before he tried to open it, he went into the bathroom. His toiletries were missing.

Neil looked in the mirror and saw himself—bruises and lumps on the side of the head, scratches, crusted spots of blood, all the signs and marks of what he had experienced. And his features were subtly different, younger and smoother, but also more drawn, tightened, as if with pain and deep inner hurt. He scared himself. The mask. He turned quickly away.

The bedroom was different. The furniture was still there, each item exactly where he remembered it. But there were no sheets on the bed and no blanket. Neil's things were gone—his overnight bag, the shirt and jeans he'd left out, the Rose Tremain novel he was reading—all gone.

Movement—he heard a sound outside. More than one—there were sounds in the house, both above and below him. Neil cupped his hand around the candle and walked quickly back into the main corridor. He saw the faint blue glow down the corridor at once.

As he approached the alcove, one of the servant women came down the steps into the corridor and walked right past him without a glance, as if he didn't exist. Now he even heard the sound of people outside, carried through the open window at the end of the corridor. Nothing unusual, just the distant, ordinary sounds of people at work, talking among themselves.

The young man was in the bunk. The same young man he had seen the first time there, and who had struck him with a blackjack, and who had kissed Marisa at the scene of that unspeakable atrocity. But now he wore the black uniform Neil recognized. It was not the uniform of any police force or army, at least none that he could recognize, but it only seemed the more frightening for its lack of definition.

The young man's skin was bone white, puckering at the corners of his mouth and eyes. His body didn't move at all, there was no sign of breathing. Neil grasped one hand and felt for a pulse. Nothing. He let it drop back onto the blackclad shirt. The blue votive candle flames danced in a brief flick of the wind.

Neil was about to turn away, but he saw the young man's face seem to turn ruddier, flushed with sudden color. The slack skin on the face tightened, the chest rose slightly, and a soft sigh of breath broke the silence. Neil could not move. The eyes opened, and turned.

The handsome young man smiled as he reached for Neil.

ZUZU

Neil backed away instinctively, but then he noticed the expression on the face of Marisa's lover: his smile was warm and loving, his eyes were filled with—gratitude? His hands grasped feebly at Neil's arm and then his cold fingers brushed Neil's skin and rubbed his palm tenderly.

Neil yanked his hand away. The candle slipped out of his grip and was extinguished when it hit the floor. Now the tiny space was lit only by the votive candles, the air suddenly colored a chilly blue. He was fascinated and horrifed by the look of pain and sorrow on the young man's face. It was as if he could not bear to be parted from Neil's touch.

Fear and hatred welled up within him. Neil lunged forward, grabbed the young man's throat and began to squeeze as hard as he could. But now Marisa's lover smiled gratefully up at him again. His eyes blazed with light, his smooth cheeks glowed with a rush of life and color. Neil felt a terrifying sensation, as if his own strength and energy were flowing through his hands, into the body of Marisa's lover, who was gaining vitality and starting to push himself up from the bunk.

Neil forced him back down, and moved away. A hand gripped his shoulder. He shook it off and spun around. Father Panic. The old priest grinned at him. Then he spread his arms wide and stepped closer, as if to take Neil in a comforting paternal embrace. The alcove seemed impossibly small, a death-box in which he was trapped. He could feel Marisa's lover behind him, clutching and tugging at his shirt.

He shoved the priest back against the wall in the landing and rushed past him, down the short flight of stairs, into the dark corridor. Neil's brain teemed with confused thoughts. It seemed as if his presence alone brought these people back. Were they real in themselves or was his deranged mind creating them before his very eyes? He had to get out of the house as fast as possible, and then far away from there.

"Ustashas!" Somewhere outside but close by, men shouted gleefully and triumphantly. "Ustashas! Ustashas!" Then he heard gunfire. Had war somehow broken out in Italy and fighting engulfed even this unlikely corner of the Marches? But that was an absurd idea. The madness was *here,* either a part of this house or a part of himself.

Neil felt trapped on the second floor. He heard the sounds of Father Panic and Marisa's lover in the alcove. The only sure quick way he knew to get out was back down the circular staircase into the billiards room. He shut the door tight and then descended the stairs as fast as he could. It wasn't until he reached the bottom step that he noticed that the lamps were all on and dozens of candles were lit, filling the room with a warm soft glow. As Neil walked slowly toward the bar he realized that all the shouts and sounds of movement about the house had vanished. The only thing he heard now was music, a dreamy mindless techno burble from the radio.

The television was on, but silent. A handsome young man wearing only pajama bottoms and a sexy young woman in a revealing nightie were talking, their faces and gestures overly expressive. The stage set was meant to suggest an expensively decorated ultra-modern bedroom, but everything was so polished and tidy that it resembled a display in a furniture store. An episode from an Italian soap opera, Neil thought absently. Then the pretty couple on the screen hurled themselves into each other's arms, pressed their bodies tightly in a feverish embrace, mashed their open mouths together and tumbled backward onto a huge bed.

Marisa was stretched out on the sofa. She was wearing only a black bra and a half-slip, and the large blue opal that hung from a ribbon at the base of her throat. Her hair was wild, her eyes shiny, her mouth wet. She raised one leg, bent at the knee, and held her hand out to him. Turn around now and leave, or stay forever. Neil sat down beside her.

"My lover . . ."

"Take it off me."

"What?"

"The mask. Take it off my face."

"What mask? There is no mask."

"Please."

"Silly."

"Marisa, *please*."

"Zuzu."

"Zuzu . . ."

She smiled, caressing his cheek. "Kiss me."

"Let me go."

"No one is keeping you." She looked hurt, pouting, and she turned her face slightly to the side. "Go, if you want."

The sense of urgency and fear within him disappeared. He couldn't leave. She understood things he didn't, things he had to know. She was the only one who could show him the way—to anywhere, or nowhere. He felt as if he knew nothing, and she knew everything.

But even more than that, he wanted her again, he wanted to kiss her and touch her and enter her, be one with her. The room was golden, the air was sweet with her fragrance. He wanted to taste her again. He felt the heat from her body, like a deeply soothing radiance that reached into him, giving him comfort and peace. He put his hand on her thigh, his fingertips moving lightly over her beautiful skin.

She turned her head and smiled at him again. Neil kissed her and he felt her arms come around his shoulders. Their eyes closed as their tongues touched, their faces pressing together, skin to skin—mask to mask—and he felt once again as if they were a part of each other, sensation fusing them in a fire of infinite wholeness and pleasure.

He saw a child, a boy about seven or eight years old, dressed in rags, looking thin and frightened. Then a hand grabbed the boy's hair and jerked his head to one side.

Neil tried to open his eyes, but couldn't.

Marisa was dressed in black. She was the person holding the boy by the hair. Her face alive, wild. She swung a ball peen hammer into the back of the boy's skull, the crack of bone creating a million screaming fractures in Neil's nerves and brain.

Zuzu's mouth sucked at his—and he had the distant, almost abstract sensation of flying slowly into her.

The boy's blinking and vacant eyes were replaced by those of a girl about the same age. Her round face was gaunt and hollow. Her eyes closed and she turned her face away slightly, and then Marisa drove the axe blade into the back of the girl's neck, at the top of the spine.

He still couldn't open his eyes, nor could he pull his face away from hers. His body churned and he kicked violently. He pushed against her and rolled away, peeling her arms off him. His face felt as if it were being eaten and burned with acid as he broke away from her and fell off the sofa. Neil quickly got to his feet. She looked like a big cat, holding herself up half off the sofa, her arms straight, her hands flat on the floor. Zuzu grinned at him through the long black hair that hung across her face.

"My lover," she said. "Without me, you're lost."

Neil turned and ran, bouncing off the walls of the dark passage into the dining room, and then into the next room. Broken glass cracked beneath his shoes. Open windows. Neil grabbed a sill, swung his body out and then let himself drop to the ground.

He didn't know which side of the house he was on. The air was grey and full of moisture. He was in a thick wet fog—*il morbo*. He could barely see five feet in front of him. Still he ran—staggered—as fast as he could in the circumstances, his eyes fixed on the ground just ahead. He hit saplings and tripped on rocks, pushed through thickets and crawled over rocky ridges that suddenly loomed before him, blocking his flight.

Finally he had to stop. He bent over, gasping for breath.

When he looked up, two men wearing black uniforms stood in front of him. They laughed as they took him in hand, and they didn't even bother to draw their pistols.

GROTTA ROSSA

They walked for some distance. Neil couldn't make out anything in the fog that swirled and blew around them, but the two guards knew where they were going. He tried to speak to them, a few words in Italian, and then German, but they merely laughed at him. Their hands were like iron clamps on his arms.

Neil's face was raw and the cold air grated painfully across his skin. He couldn't tell whether the mask still clung to him or not. In certain places it seemed to be gone, but he felt a lingering tightness and weight around the eyes and mouth. Nonetheless, it hardly seemed to matter anymore. Real or not, there or gone, the mask was almost irrelevant to his situation now. The guards had him and could do whatever they wanted with him. He thought about resisting, struggling, perhaps breaking free and fleeing, but he sensed that it was useless to try. He would simply wander around in *il morbo* until he fell off a cliff or they caught him again.

Then they were on a smooth wide path, and a high stone outcropping in the side of a hill appeared before them. The guards force-walked Neil to a cleft in the rock, and then inside. Within a few yards the path turned, and they emerged in a large, roughly circular open area. A limestone massif ran through the Marches, Neil knew, and limestone lent itself particularly well to the formation of caverns.

They were in the grotto Marisa had mentioned to him. It was lit by mounted torches and banks of candles. There was a simple wooden altar on raised ground. Behind it stood a rusty iron cross that was taller than a man. A few plain benches served as pews. A narrow stream of water bubbled out of the rock and flowed in a cut channel through the makeshift chapel. There were several plaster statues of the Virgin Mary around the place, the largest of which stood beside the source of the stream. Mary's robes were blue and white, and her face was painted with unnaturally bright enamel colors—red lips, blue eyes, shiny white skin.

Several people sat on the benches and another group stood in a tight huddle behind the altar. Neil recognized Father Panic and other members of Marisa's family. Then he noticed a third group of people, in a side area that was not as well lit. They were the workers and farmhands, dressed in rough clothes or rags, kneeling submissively on the damp bare rock. There were a couple of dozen of them. Their heads were bowed, their hands clasped as if in prayer. He saw the dwarf woman. She was the only person in that group who knelt with her head up, looking around calmly. When she saw Neil she grinned maniacally at him, and then shook her head.

Guards were posted all around, but they looked relaxed and they had their pistols holstered. They stood, watching, waiting.

Neil was brought to the area between the benches and the altar, and forced to kneel beside the fast-moving stream of water. His hands were tied behind his back, and then his ankles as well.

The same lunacy again, Neil thought. A conversion and baptism, but then what? His only fear was that they might cut his tongue out, as he'd seen them do with others. Could he pre-empt it—if he recited the Apostles' Creed, for instance, demonstrating that he was already a Catholic? Neil was not even sure that he remembered all of the Apostles' Creed anymore, and he knew it only in English. But if they would listen to him again, if he had a few seconds to explain, appeal . . .

The circle of people behind the altar fanned out a little and gazed at him. Father Panic in his vestments, Marisa in a black blouse and black skirt that reached just below her knees. Her lover, also in uniform. A few guards and older people stood with them. She looked so young and beautiful—but the sinister black uniform made her look like a girl scout from hell.

Neil watched her hopefully. When Marisa finally looked directly at him, her expression showed no flicker of recognition, or even of interest in who he was or what was happening. She turned her head and spoke quietly with the young man, who smiled, nodded and replied to her. Neil opened his mouth to address her by name, but a guard immediately shoved a thick rag between his teeth, rammed it halfway down his throat. A bitter alkaline taste filled Neil's nostrils and lungs—it was the same hideous fungus that he had experienced in the box room. He began to gag, trying desperately to spit, push and force the cloth out of his mouth. His body jumped wildly but the guards held him in place.

The handsome young man turned slightly and reached down to pick up something from the floor behind him. It was a wooden box with leather straps and metal bolts. He came forward and shoved the strange device over Neil's head. The straps were cinched tight under his throat. The bolts were turned—and Neil felt flat metals plates tighten against the sides and back of his skull. He could hardly breathe, his lungs were in extreme distress. His brain reeled. Then men were grunting close around him as they turned the bolts forcefully, relentlessly.

The last thing Neil heard—before he felt the bones in his head begin to crunch and splinter—was the sound of men and women laughing.

NOTES

1. In an apparent attempt to ape the Germans, the [Croatian] Ustashas set up a number of concentration camps. Being far less organized than their mentors, or lacking the technology, they often resorted in these camps to knives with which to murder Serbs, Jews, Gypsies and undesirable Croats. The most infamous camp was at Jasenovac on the Sava river, on the border of Bosnia. Tim Judah, *The Serbs: History, Myth & the Destruction of Yugoslavia* (Yale University Press, 1997).

2. Seven hundred thousand men, women and children were killed there alone in ways that made even the hair of the Reich's experts stand on end, as some of them are said to have admitted when they were amongst themselves. The preferred instruments of execution were saws and sabres, axes and hammers, and leather cuff-bands with fixed blades that were fastened on the lower arm and made especially in Solingen for the purpose of cutting throats, as well as

a kind of rudimentary crossbar gallows on which the Serbs, Jews and Bosnians, once rounded up, were hanged in rows like crows or magpies. Not far from Jasenovac, in a radius of no more than ten miles, there were also the camps of Prijedor, Stara Gradiska and Banja Luka, where the Croatian militia, its hand strengthened by the Wehrmacht and its spirit by the Catholic church, performed one day's work after another in similar manner. The history of this massacre, which went on for years, is recorded in fifty thousand documents abandoned by the Germans and Croats in 1945 . . . W.G. Sebald, *The Rings of Saturn,* translated by Michael Hulse (New Directions, 1998).

3. In *Kaputt*, his memoir of World War II, the Italian journalist Curzio Malaparte recounts the following incident, when he and Raffaele Casertano, then the Italian minister in Zagreb, met Ante Pavelic, the Poglavnik (*fuhrer,* or leader) of the Croatian forces:

"While he spoke, I gazed at a wicker basket on the Poglavnik's desk. The lid was raised and the basket seemed to be filled with mussels, or shelled oysters—as they are occasionally displayed in the windows of Fortnum and Mason in Piccadilly in London. Casertano looked at me and winked.

" 'Would you like a nice oyster stew?'

" 'Are they Dalmatian oysters?' I asked the Poglavnik.

"Ante Pavelic removed the lid from the basket and revealed the mussels, that slimy and jelly-like mass, and he said, smiling, with that tired good-natured smile of his, 'It is a present from my loyal *ustashis*. Forty pounds of human eyes.' " Curzio Malaparte, *Kaputt,* translated by Cesare Foligno (E. P. Dutton, 1946).